The waves were singing.

Clara stopped, jaw slightly unhinged, and stared. Of all she had seen, this caught her, shook her, insisted that the world she was moving through was not anything she had seen before, was nothing she understood. The waves were singing, and though the sound was not quite human, it belied an intelligent musicality. She edged away from the bank of the river, wondering what other secrets it might hide.

For the first time, it struck Clara that not only might this place not be entirely safe, but there might be something human—or not quite human—watching her, marking her movements. Was she alone? She couldn't see anyone else, but someone had made the wonders lining the streets and bordering the Seine. The thought was unnerving.

And then she realized she had no idea how to get back.

By Rowenna Miller

The Palace of Illusions

The Fairy Bargains of Prospect Hill

THE UNRAVELED KINGDOM

Torn

Fray

Rule

The PALACE OF ILLUSIONS

ROWENNA MILLER

REDHOOK

Cover design by Lisa Marie Pompilio
Cover images by Shutterstock
Cover copyright © 2025 by Hachette Book Group, Inc.
Author photograph by Emily R. Allison

Redhook
Hachette Book Group
1290 Avenue of the Americas
New York, NY 10104
hachettebookgroup.com

First Edition: June 2025

Redhook is an imprint of Orbit, a division of Hachette Book Group.
The Redhook name and logo are registered trademarks of Hachette Book Group, Inc.

The publisher is not responsible for websites (or their content) that are not owned by the publisher.

The Hachette Speakers Bureau provides a wide range of authors for speaking events. To find out more, go to hachettespeakersbureau.com or email HachetteSpeakers@hbgusa.com.

Redhook books may be purchased in bulk for business, educational, or promotional use. For information, please contact your local bookseller or the Hachette Book Group Special Markets Department at special.markets@hbgusa.com.

Quote on p. ix excerpted from E. T. A. Hoffmann, *Nutcracker*, illus. Maurice Sendak, trans. Ralph Manheim. New York: Crown Publishers, Inc., 1984. Originally published as *Nussknacker und Mausekönig*.

Library of Congress Cataloging-in-Publication Data
Names: Miller, Rowenna, author.
Title: The palace of illusions / Rowenna Miller.
Description: First edition. | New York, NY : Redhook, 2025.
Identifiers: LCCN 2024044926 | ISBN 9780316571944 (trade paperback) | ISBN 9780316571951 (ebook)
Subjects: LCGFT: Fantasy fiction. | Novels.
Classification: LCC PS3613.I55275 P35 2025 | DDC 813/.6—dc23/eng/20241001
LC record available at https://lccn.loc.gov/2024044926

ISBNs: 9780316571944 (trade paperback), 9780316571951 (ebook)

Printed in the United States of America

LSC-C

Printing 1, 2025

For the former Snowflakes and future Sugarplums,
all of the veterans of the Mouse and Tin Soldier battles,
and every inhabitant of the Land of Sweets,
especially Nora and Mae

And Marie is believed to be still the queen of a country where sparkling Christmas woods, transparent marzipan castles, in short, the most wonderful things, can be seen if you have the right sort of eyes for it.

—E. T. A. Hoffmann, *The Nutcracker and the Mouse King.*

Translated by Ralph Manheim.

Chapter One

PARIS WAS BEAUTIFUL. Even in winter, with its long evenings that stretched pale and gray into a swift nightfall, even with the cold rain driving into the Seine and spattering the broad avenues. The lights only shone more brightly through the gloom, and Paris remained, always, beautiful.

At least, that was what Clara Ironwood had been told. Many times. Usually while she was squinting at her notebook through smudged spectacles or wrestling with a particularly finicky bit of clockwork, adjusting some wheel or cog with her minute silver-and-walnut tools. Always in the vaguely sympathetic, slightly chiding tone that told her that other people simply didn't understand.

Work was beautiful. And Clara liked work. She loved it. Work was, in fact, as necessary as breathing, as water. If she had a problem to solve, she was happy. If she had diagrams to draw or grease on her fingers, she was in heaven. Paris—what could sudden rain showers and crowded sidewalks have over creating something beautiful?

She had been in Paris for months, through a cold autumn and into a gray winter, and she was already behind. Not behind on the

1

official timetables given to her by the Exposition Universelle, of course, but on her own exacting schedule. The Exposition was set to open in less than six months, and she had every week of those months carefully chiseled into precise blocks of time.

This week's strictly ordered calendar was devoted to finalizing the placement of the mirrors, mechanics, and electrical wiring for the ambitious masterwork she had been invited to help design: the Palace of Illusions. She needed to have her plans drawn within the fortnight, ready to begin manufacture in the dedicated workshop. The architecture of the palace was complex, and the mirrors that created the illusions, already in production, revealed every corner and left few places to hide the gears and pulleys and, most novel of all, electric lights that produced, on demand, a particular kind of effect not entirely unlike magic. It was a challenge greater than any she had ever encountered.

And she would not, no matter what happened, ask Fritz for help.

She sketched out another few lines in her notebook. All the guts and gears of the palace had to be invisible despite all those mirrors. She considered another angle, then imagined the placement—no, that didn't work, either. Nothing had ever taken her so long, and she was beginning to question her skills. The numbers were larger, the scale greater, and the inclusion of electricity made the project more complex than her usual fare of clocks and music boxes, but it should not have been as difficult as it was.

"Still fiddling with it?"

Fritz Krieger. Damn it.

"Good afternoon, Herr Krieger." She set down her glasses. By Jove, they were dirty.

"It is now more accurately good evening, Miss Ironwood. I

thought someone ought to inform you that the staff is leaving. If you insist on staying late again, you will need to lock up on your own." As if to spite Fritz's impeccable manners and perfect diction, he had rakish dark curls and a single dimple set deep in his clean-shaven cheek, so that he always looked like he was about to pull some prank at Clara's expense. He hadn't, of course—that would have been horribly unprofessional for a well-respected architect like Fritz Krieger. His firm didn't win the bid for one of the buildings for the Exposition Universelle by keeping a delinquent on staff. But she couldn't shake the feeling that he wanted to put ink in her tea or drop crickets down her back.

"That's no trouble," Clara replied. She shifted so that Fritz couldn't see the sketches, but it was too late.

"Still trying to mask the machinery completely? You are asking too much of your own exceptional work, Miss Ironwood." Fritz shook his head. There it was—the constant suggestion, never stated yet always implied, that he was her superior in the fine art of clockwork. Whether that was on account of his being German and she American, or the difference in their sexes, she was never quite sure, but it grated on her. "Now, I will ask again, given the polite nature of our working rapport. Would you care to have dinner with my sister and me on Sunday?"

"And I will decline again, with my regrets."

"I do hope it is because you have some dashing Parisian beau taking you on a long stroll down the Champs-Élysées, not because you are planning to work all afternoon." Fritz smirked.

Clara's teeth set themselves on edge. "Tell your sister I give her my thanks for the kind invitation." Fräulein Alma Krieger was a perfectly lovely woman, all downy blond hair and broad smiles, the faint scent of gingerbread trailing her everywhere. But Herr

Krieger's insouciant smirks and patronizing suggestions over Sunday ham—that would be too much to bear. Clara had already, to her chagrin, agreed to attend their Christmas Eve party, and had yet to concoct an excuse plausible enough to extricate herself from that particular hell. At least she had several weeks before she had to subject herself to rounds of charades and pass-the-button and forced conversation.

"Do not waste all your hours here, Miss Ironwood. Paris in the first snowfall—ah, it is very beautiful."

Clara inhaled slowly, and exhaled before replying. "Good evening, Herr Krieger."

She began again on her calculations, fighting a headache that crept into her temples as she ran the numbers again and again. It simply wouldn't work. She sighed. It was almost as though her thoughts were blocked, bottlenecking at some narrow point in her brain and never making it onto the page.

The headache, she decided, was to blame, even though she wasn't entirely convinced it hadn't been caused by trying to wrangle those calculations. The lights blazed over her worktable, but long shadows had overtaken the windows, and she decided it was time to lock up for the night.

Fritz was right—it had started to snow, a light swirl of flakes settling on bare branches and melting on the streets. Winter here would be nothing like home. Milwaukee, she was sure, would be blanketed in white from Thanksgiving onward. The streetlamps came on as she walked home, passing the new Pont Alexandre III, the gilt shimmering in the last of the sunset. At least, she thought as she skirted a pair of children catching snowflakes on their mittens, no one would chide her for working through that holiday here, as Parisians and Fritz Krieger alike were blissfully unaware of the customs of turkeys, oysters in stuffing, giblets in gravy, and dining room tables overflowing with relatives.

She felt a brief pang of something she could have mistaken for homesickness as the children laughed together, comparing the intricate snowflakes outlined in brief intensity on their dark mittens before they melted. She and Louise had done the same thing as children, until Godfather showed them the trick of catching snowflakes on dark cardstock instead. The flakes lasted longer, and he let them borrow his magnifying glass so they could examine them more closely. She wished she could tell the two girls that particular trick, but her French was abysmal and, of course, she was a stranger to them.

Godfather—she shook her head. She hadn't written to him since arriving in Paris, and they hadn't parted on good terms. He had been agitated, angry even, at the thought of her taking the job with the Exposition. He clearly didn't think she was good enough yet. But then, of course, she was never good enough for Christian Elias Thrushman, master clockmaker, and she never would be.

"Clara! Miss Ironwood!"

Madame Boule, her landlady, waved enthusiastically from the door of her first-floor apartment. No, not *premier étage*—Clara corrected herself. Ground floor. There was a French term for it, she knew—but couldn't recall it and gave up, frustrated. *"Bonjour, Madame Boule, et comment—"*

"Thank you as always for your kind attempts in French, Miss Ironwood, but I do appreciate practicing my English!" Madame Boule was too polite to say what she meant—it was Clara who needed practice, but months of trying hadn't produced much improvement in her accent. "You had a package arrive today. I kept it in my apartment instead of leaving it at your door—thieves and busybodies multiply at Christmas, *n'est pas?*" She beckoned, and Clara followed her.

Madame Boule had been a widow for thirty years, her husband lost during "the 1870" as Madame Boule put it. She kept a framed photograph of him on the mantelpiece, draped in black crepe, and had assiduously run the building she had inherited from him ever since. It was tempting to cast Madame Boule as a tragic character, a modern-day Miss Havisham ever mourning her lost youth, but in reality, she was a merry, red-cheeked woman who, for all accounts from the longtime neighbors, was a shrewd businesswoman. She had turned the management of a middling-rate building into a real estate career spanning fine properties in several arrondissements.

"And here it is—from America, *non?*"

Clara took the box, brown paper smudged and stained after a transatlantic trip. It took both hands and some support from a hip to manhandle the package. "Yes—that's my parents' address," she confirmed.

"A little Christmas good cheer, no doubt. You are coming for Christmas dinner after Mass, yes? I will not hear of you eating alone on blessed Christmas Day!"

"Of course, yes, thank you." Clara backed awkwardly toward the door, wrangling the box through the doorway.

"If you wish to come to Mass, you are most welcome then, too!"

"Thank you, but no, Madame Boule, I—" The box corner caught on the door and Clara wrested it free. "I am not Catholic."

"Oh, yes, but still. You are always welcome nonetheless. There are always many—how does one say?—eligible young men at Mass on Christmas. Their mothers make them attend." She winked, and though Clara would typically have grimaced at such a suggestion, when it came from Madame Boule, she couldn't help but laugh.

"Thank you, but dinner is more than enough festivity for me." She managed to get the box up two flights of stairs and into her own apartment, a feat that nearly involved several complex equations, and finally heaved it onto her rickety tea table.

She caught her breath. Her mother's delicate handwriting on the paper, their family's address in Milwaukee inscribed in familiar script. She could almost see the house between the loops of the letters, its turrets and porches of brick near the lake, her mother's joy and her father's pride. It would be decorated for Christmas now. Every year Mother directed the long-suffering maids Georgie and Beatrice in hanging holly and evergreen and red velvet bows while her sister, Louise, quietly followed behind, straightening bows and taking down excessive greenery and arranging artful bouquets of white roses and red berries. Soon they would be baking gingerbread and mince pies and a grand snowy white cake for the Christmas Eve party.

She clamped her eyes shut on a pair of unexpected tears.

There was a keen letter opener in her desk, and with a few deft swipes Clara had the paper off and the box open. On the top was a letter from Mother, several pages in perfect handwriting, and another from Louise, full of charming observations and funny stories about people Clara would never have thought to ask about. And underneath—Mother had outdone herself. Tins of shortbread and ginger cookies, hardy enough to survive the trip, and homemade pralines and divinity, and marzipan and sugarplums from their favorite candy shop. To add some cheer to her admittedly spartan apartment, paper poinsettias and impossibly detailed paper snowflakes. At the very bottom, several brightly wrapped packages were marked in bold print, *Do Not Open Until Christmas.*

She set them on the table one by one, the cheerful pink and blue paper tied with gold ribbon. Two were marked from Mother, one from Father, another from Louise and—

She stopped.

A misshapen little bundle at the bottom, wrapped in wrinkled gold paper, with her name written in a thick handwriting different from her mother's. Godfather Thrushman.

She held it warily. Whatever it was, Godfather hadn't bothered with a box, instead padding it with tissue before mangling a bit of gaudy paper around it. Perhaps it was a peace offering. He had always given them the most wonderful Christmas presents when they were children; sending her one now could be a sign that he wanted to go back to how things had once been between them, doting godfather and precocious godchild. She traced the familiar handwriting, bold and almost jarring, the script of a man who wrote too quickly for niceties.

Then again, it could be another jab taunting her imperfections, shipped thousands of miles in the guise of a gift. She pulled her hand away from the familiar script. "Do not open until Christmas," she whispered to herself, and set the package next to the others. Then she noticed the leather book that had been tucked underneath the gift.

Her breath catching a little, she recognized the book of foolish children's stories Godfather had written for her. For Louise, too, ostensibly, but they were always really for her. He made them up, off the cuff, she was sure, and then wrote them down later in his book, in his best handwriting, not the scrawls and scribbles he used to take his personal notes. When she had been laid up with measles, Godfather had relayed the story of a conniving mouse queen living under their kitchen stove; she remembered the story and the malaise of fever mingling together and flipped through the slim volume, finding "The Queen of Mice" between "The Glass Palace" and "The Ugly Mr. Sandmann."

She laughed at the discovery of that story. Mr. Sandmann had been an acquaintance of Godfather, or perhaps of Father—she had never been quite sure. He came sometimes in the evenings, sitting with Father and Godfather in the study and smoking cigars, talking over, as Godfather put it, "gears and clocks and sealing wax, cabbages and kings." Clara had always hated Mr. Sandmann.

She didn't know why—he was, it was true, a very ugly man, with a bulbous nose and almost bulging eyes, but Godfather was not very handsome, either, and that never upset her. There was something that roved, greedy and slippery, in Sandmann's eyes, something that put her in mind of a grasping crow in the fingernails that he didn't keep clipped.

"Silly Miss Clara." Godfather had laughed when she had burst out that Mr. Sandmann scared her awfully. "Let us write him into a story or two and then he shan't be any bother ever again."

Never any bother again—she traced the old ink steeped in Godfather's voice, the stories dragging poor Mr. Sandmann from one misadventure to another.

The Sad Tale of the Nutcracker
by Christian Elias Thrushman,
dated 24 December 1880

Once, there was a king who kept no army. His people were happy with this situation, as they did not want to send their sons to war, even if the sons occasionally complained that there was no honor in harvesting barley and digging ditches and all the other tasks they were set to. This was all due to the fact that there were no enemies or foes to fear in that part of the world, save one, whom only the king knew of and only the king knew how to fortify against. The king had only one rule, lest he be forced to instigate conscriptions like the neighboring kingdoms did: that no one be allowed to question who this foe was or why the king employed his particular methods of defense.

This arrangement suited most of the subjects well, and for many years they lived happily in prosperity, and nothing threatened the little kingdom. The proclamation, however, extended even to the royal family, and though the queen let the business of the state alone and busied herself perfecting her recipe for sausages, the king's only child, a daughter, grew to appreciate that something was rather strange about her kingdom compared to the histories and geographies her tutors made her read.

For one, the guards on the ramparts of the castle were not men, as you have assuredly already guessed, astute reader Louise, as you know all the farmers' sons were busy digging ditches instead of serving in the army. Instead, the guards were all clockwork owls with eyes as wide as dinner plates. For another, the king's personal bodyguards were not soldiers, as you must know without my telling you, esteemed listener Clara, but clockwork foxes with tails as full as bottle brushes. The reason for this, the princess ascertained, was that the major general of the Forces of Defense was a clockmaker.

Despite the internal consistency of this logic, the princess was quite certain that it did not square with the lessons she had learned at the insistence of her tutor, nor with the descriptions of other lands that her correspondents, princesses all, sent to her. In fact, she was forced to describe the entire situation as "quite peculiar," with no uncertainty.

Still, she was well aware of the prohibition on questions, and knowing her father the king to be a disagreeable man when crossed, she instead sought out the clockmaker, who served as, you will recall, intelligent reader, major general of the Forces of Defense. It was a strange title, she thought to herself, as there were no subordinates to salute the major general aside from clockwork animals, but she found it less strange to call him simply "sir," and he seemed quite content to be addressed thus.

"Sir," she said, upon entering the offices he kept on the top floor of an underused tower in the east portion of the castle, which was quite stuffed full of his inventions. They would be too many to number here, but the most dazzling were a golden bird who could recite the longitude and latitude of all of the major cities in the northern hemisphere, a little dog who danced a mazurka, and his prized creation, a nutcracker of surpassing beauty that could crack any nut that had ever been found in the shell. "Sir, may I inquire as to how you are able to keep so many clockwork owls in good working order on the ramparts?"

"You may indeed," he said, and he took the girl all over the castle on his rounds, demonstrating his particular methods of oiling and calibrating the owls. They peered over the land with their dinner-plate eyes, and scrutinized the princess as she mimicked the clockmaker's movements.

"Sir," she said when they had finished their ministration, "may I inquire as to how you are able to keep the foxes in such good working order?"

"You may indeed," he said, and he took the girl to their particular barracks, which consisted of a hutch made of silver and glass, lined with silk cushions. The foxes preened their bottle-brush tails and stood to attention when the clock-maker commanded, and they marched proudly before the princess as she mimicked the clockmaker's orders.

The princess, emboldened by her success, then asked, "Sir, may I inquire as to how the owls and the foxes, as keen and bright of toys as they may be, are able to protect our fair castle and country?"

The clockmaker pursed his lips and scowled. "You know very well that you may not make such inquiries. You must learn to ask fitting questions."

The princess considered this all the next day, and as evening fell, she found the clockmaker making his rounds to the owls. "Sir," she said, "may I inquire as to how we are so fortunate as to never be attacked or even put at ill-ease by any aggressive forces as I have so often seen in my histories?"

The clockmaker pursed his lips and scowled. "You know very well that you may not make such inquiries. You must learn to ask fitting questions."

The princess considered this all the next day, and as evening fell, she found the clockmaker amid the foxes and their silken cushions. "Sir, may I inquire what our walls are made of, to be so strong?"

"You may indeed," the clockmaker said. "Our walls are made of the hardest nuts, mortared with marzipan, so that no force may breach them. And when the castle is locked up quite tight, by my own good clockwork, there is no way in or out." This was quite true—to the clockmaker's exacting specifications, the castle had been built much like a music box.

"What could breach such walls?"

The clockmaker pursed his lips and scowled. "You know very well that you may not make such inquiries. You must learn to ask fitting questions."

Fascinated by the clockmaker's revelation (though not entirely surprised, as she had long held that the walls bore an uncanny resemblance to almond paste), the girl turned instead to her tutor. A wily and untrusting sort of man, he set the girl to work canvassing her books for the answers to such questions as "what can break thick marzipan?" and "what can surpass nuts for sturdiness?" but the books yielded very little.

Undeterred, the tutor set to work in a small laboratory he

had made for himself on the top floor of an underused tower in the west portion of the castle, and devised a projectile made of one-half saltpeter, one-half nightshade, and one-half good tea. He tested it upon a secret passage deep in the recesses of the castle where he thought no one might notice. Alas for him, the clockwork mice in the walls took note in an instant, and within the half hour, the foxes had put him under arrest and he was summarily shut up in a casket made of gingerbread and banished to sea.

The clockmaker was beside himself, tearing his hair and weeping openly, much to the embarrassment of the king and of the queen, who had brought out a platter of her best sausages for the occasion of the banishment.

"Most unhappy clockmaker am I!" he said between sobs. "I, who have done all my most esteemed sovereign has asked, have left this castle open to attack!"

The princess, who had her fill of being told her questions were not fitting, implored her father that, as his heir, she must be informed as to the nature of their defenses. The king, having quite forgotten that his daughter was far past old enough to be trained in her future office of monarchy, confided that their only neighboring enemy was a horrid pastrycook named Sandmann who had so utterly rotted his teeth that he was turned back by the very sight of marzipan.

The princess at once grasped the gravity of their situation, knowing that there was now a gap where the wicked pastrycook could breach their walls.

"What are we to do?" she asked of the clockmaker, which, though it was quite necessary, also produced an unfortunate deluge of fresh wails from the beleaguered man.

"Most unhappy clockmaker am I!" he cried again. "There is one who was my best and most crowning achievement, and I must now send him to guard the passage that was ruined by that fool of a tutor." There was more gnashing of teeth and incomprehensible wails, but eventually they coaxed from him that, with the proper almonds no longer available to make the marzipan, only a stout and hearty guard could serve in place, and only one such guard in the entire palace would serve.

And so the nutcracker, a sturdy and handsome fellow of nearly three feet tall, had to be installed alone in the lower parts of the castle, away from all his friends and relations (that is, the other inventions of the clockmaker), to serve as guardian until such time as the castle fell to ruins or disuse. To give him the honor due his position, he was named chief chatelain of the castle and given the key to the gates to guard as well. It may be said, to the princess's credit, that she learned her lesson well, and never again asked a tutor the sorts of questions best left to a clockmaker.

Chapter Two

"I'VE QUITE NEARLY figured it out," Clara announced as Fritz wandered into the workshop at a little after ten o'clock, buffering the pride in her voice. It had taken an infuriating week, dozens of sheets of scratched-out calculations in the bin, and several more late nights ending in headaches before she had finally dragged the correct dimensions onto formal plans. But she refused to be foiled in the perfection of the Palace of Illusions.

"You have worked out how to lay out the lights? That is—"

"No, I've figured out how to set up the underlayment without it reflecting in the mirrors." She gathered the sketches and equations she'd been working on through the dim predawn hours and handed them to Fritz before he'd had a chance to take off his overcoat and hat. "See? It just means adjusting the placement of the back rows of mirrors slightly, and building lower-profile casings, which will mean raising the platform in the back slightly."

Fritz's brow tightened and then released as he scanned the pages. "You are right, fräulein. I would never have admitted it could be done." He seemed genuinely pleased, which surprised Clara—she had expected antagonism.

"But I still need to work out how to incorporate the lights. Lights! Of all the novelties we could have to deal with, electric lights must be the most difficult to manage." All the wires, the lines, the difficult calculations, the potential for setting something on fire. "I'll work on those refinements so we can get plans to the construction foreman."

"You needn't bother, you know—they won't start working on it until after the New Year. You have holidays in Milwaukee, yes? Or does everyone work through the Christmas season in America?"

"No, it's just me," Clara replied blithely. Fritz's teasing couldn't dampen her spirits—she had solved a puzzle, and that was her favorite feeling in the world. Now on to drawing up the formal plans, even if they wouldn't be needed until January. That gave her plenty of time to perfect the designs, and perhaps begin to work out the timing of the lighting clockwork.

"Do you ever take a rest? Upon finishing a project or"—Fritz waved the sheets of paper covered with her sketches—"working out a particularly difficult problem?"

"Solving one problem just makes me want to solve another." Clara permitted herself a small smile. "Perhaps I can help with some other project, if it's necessary."

"We are quite on schedule in this office, so I don't believe that will be required." Herr Krieger leaned closer with a conspiratorial smile. "As I hear it, several other firms have projects that are quite behind. At the main entrance gate, I've heard, the turnstiles have hit a snag that has descended into a quagmire, and I am given to understand that the marble to finish the finials in the Petit Palais is delayed, and there's some sort of stall on the Quai des Nations—well, that is always the way of these things."

"I can only imagine all the ways an endeavor of this magnitude can go wrong," Clara said, trying very hard not to imagine any such thing.

"Yes—and of course, having snapped up the privilege of hosting in the auspicious year 1900, the board is quite determined this shall be the most impressive world's fair ever known. Monsieur Lavallé on the board, now—do you know, he was haranguing me just yesterday that we cannot produce a reasonably realistic clockwork automaton for one of his displays?"

"Perhaps we could," Clara said. "It would be quite an experiment, though." Godfather had made mechanical dolls and animals, but their peculiar and repetitive movements left quite a bit to be desired when it came to realism. A humanlike automaton would be something worthy of the new century's first Exposition Universelle.

"Even you do not have the time, I am quite sure, Miss Ironwood! Once they start outfitting your Palace of Illusions, they will have many questions and find plenty of things to ask you to change."

"I haven't been in the building itself since—oh, it's been over a month. Do you think I could ask someone to let me in?"

"Ask someone! Why, I have never had any trouble just telling the workers and whatnot I am there with the—oh, I see." Fritz paused as Clara raised an eyebrow, chagrined for a rare moment. Of course the workers assumed confident, competent, and *male* Fritz Krieger had business being in the under-construction buildings for the Exposition. Clara, on the other hand—a nondescript woman asking to be allowed in? Hardly the same. "I say, I can take you over this afternoon."

"But you're busy, and I don't have to go today—it's only that I wanted to get a sense of those ceilings again, just in case—"

"No, nonsense! The fresh air will do me good. At any rate, I haven't seen le Palais des Illusions since they started the interior work. It would do well to get a better idea before they go installing those mirrors and lights."

Clara acquiesced. Sometimes, she allowed, Herr Krieger was not unpleasant company, even if it often seemed he was forcing words into silences that were quite happy being left alone. Still, he did seem to know everyone and everything about the Exposition, and that was helpful.

Fritz insisted on buying a ham-and-butter sandwich the size of a baseball bat from a street cart and sharing it with Clara as they walked. The Palace of Illusions was part of the Exposition grounds on the Champ-de-Mars, adjacent to the Palace of Optics. Clara had thought, upon receiving the initial invitation to work for the Exposition, that the use of "palace" was a fanciful European affectation for what must be, in truth, something more like the exhibition halls at the state fair. She had been thoroughly disabused of this idea when she had been given the initial tour of the Palace of Illusions and its neighbors.

"Take more, I cannot possibly eat this entire sandwich," Fritz pressed between mouthfuls that suggested he could, in fact, eat the entire sandwich. "How do they make ham and butter on bread so delicious?"

"It's ham, and butter, and bread," Clara replied, accepting a large chunk of baguette. "It's impossible for that combination to be bad."

"This is true. Now—what do you think, Miss Ironwood? The Pont Alexandre, is that too much gold?"

"I haven't the faintest idea," Clara answered, busy looking at the new electric lamps installed along its walkways. "It's more gold than I would use if I were gilding a bridge, but I don't have any bridges to gild, so I suppose Paris knows better than I do."

Fritz laughed. "There may be a time and place for restraint, and I suppose France has decided that the Exposition isn't the time or place. Paris will be an electric fairyland by the time the fair opens, I believe. But for now—what a mess!" Fritz grinned as they approached the Champ-de-Mars. Even from the other side of the Seine, the noise and dust rose in a haze from the grounds as construction reached a fever pace. "Welcome to the new century."

Clara couldn't help but laugh. The Exposition was a celebration of progress, industry, and modernity, but underpinning it all was the same old dust and noise of so many centuries before.

A few words from Fritz, and the palace was open to them. Clara's project focused specifically on the lights and mirrors that would provide the spark of enchantment within the Palace of Illusions—the sense of gazing into eternity, as she envisioned it, but ever-changing. Not quite like the enormous kaleidoscope in the neighboring Palace of Optics, but rather a gentle undulation of light and color, timed and executed with invisible clockwork precision.

She had no hand, of course, in the actual architecture. For the better—Clara would never have dared to design the dramatically arched ceilings, like something out of the illustrated *One Thousand and One Nights* she had read with Louise as a child. The ornate curves and points of the space reflected much of the rest of the Exposition's architecture, the blending of organic and geometric, rounded yet sharp.

It made the process of designing the mirror and light display an absolute nightmare.

Corners everywhere, odd angles—and for the effect to work, Clara had to hide all of *her* work. She took a few notes in the black notebook she kept in her pocket, spots that might prove problematic if the mirrors weren't adjusted perfectly. She had to be confident she had accounted for every detail.

Fritz returned from a stroll around the Palace of Optics. "You ought to see the trench they've got over there for the giant telescope—are you finished here?"

"Herr Krieger," Clara said after a brief hesitation, "I imagine I'll need to be here quite a bit in the coming months. I wonder if it might be possible to have some sort of pass written up."

Clara waited patiently. She was used to navigating the world that ran just beside Fritz's, the one with the same sort of work and the same offices and the same burnt tea in a battered carafe on the cart down the hall, but entirely different all the same. No one asked Fritz what his business was in the office, or asked him to type up a letter, or assumed he was someone's spouse loitering about the drafting tables.

Herr Krieger paused, running, she imagined, the calculus that brought his view on how things ought to be done in line with how the world actually operated. Clara needed no such recalibration. She knew full well that the doors that opened to Fritz Kriegers were often closed to Clara Ironwoods. To his credit, he didn't linger uncomfortably on the discrepancy. "That's a brilliant idea! You know, we probably ought to all have passes or some such," he said. "I'll bring it up right away."

"Thank you." Fritz Krieger wasn't a bad sort, she acknowledged. He had, to her surprise, taken to working with a woman with little comment. That was far better than her usual experience—even Godfather's clients tended to evade direct communication with her and assume any technical work was in fact Thrushman's.

"I've another couple of measurements to take at the back," Clara said.

"Then I shall take a look around outside to see how the pavilions for the colonies are coming along," Fritz confirmed. "I suppose you can find your way to Siam and meet me there when you've finished?"

Clara nodded and retreated to the back of the hall, which would be hidden by mirrors and unseen by visitors. This was her sole space to hide the inner workings of the illusion itself. She fished her tape measure from her pocket, double-checking the moldings and a few corners. She was scribbling in her notebook when she heard footfalls.

"I'll just be another moment!" she called, assuming Fritz had returned, impatient, from Siam.

"I do hope I am not intruding." Clara started as a second figure entered the hall. The man was young, her own age or only a bit older, with light brown hair a bit unkempt and pale green eyes. "I was told I might find you here as you were not in your office."

Clara eyed him warily. She had expected the foreman she had worked with before, a stocky man with a dark bristle of beard. "Are you with the Exposition?"

"No, I am afraid I am not." He took a step forward; she retreated two steps. His accent was similar to Fritz's, but softer, lighter. "I am here to check on you, Miss Ironwood, not the building, if I may be so bold."

Every flight instinct within Clara flared instantly. She had, of course, thought through what she, a woman alone in a strange city, would do if cornered by a man. She had considered the possibilities of having her handbag nabbed on a dark street or of indecent things happening on the streetcar. She had not considered the possibility that a stranger would seek her out, by name, in a deserted palace still under construction. She took a shaky breath and stayed where she stood. "I don't need any help, then, thank you."

"Perhaps you do not understand. I am a—well, you would say a relative, I believe, of your godfather. From Nuremberg."

If that was supposed to reassure Clara, it had the opposite effect. "How do you know who my godfather is? How do you know who I am, or how to find me?"

"Your godfather, he wrote to me. I am a nephew—or, perhaps cousin, second cousin?"

"Well, which is it?" Clara crossed her arms.

"I am not sure of the term in English, we always used 'nephew' and 'uncle.' That is our custom, in my family." He smiled, but Clara did not return the gesture.

"He didn't tell me about you."

"No? I am not surprised. He was quiet about his past, yes?" Clara didn't reply. "I am Nathanael Nussbaum. I am related to him through my mother, so our names will not be the same, you see."

"Sure." A likely story, thought Clara. "You don't even seem to know my godfather's name from all your talk about him."

"He calls himself Thrushman now," Nussbaum replied. "Christian Elias Thrushman, but back home, he was—"

"All right, you know who he is. But frankly, I still do not know who you are, not really. And given that we have no chaperone, I will kindly ask you to leave."

"I should have expected that you would be cautious. It is wise, I suppose, to be cautious. I ought to have brought Uncle's letters, to prove to you that I am who I say."

Clara wasn't sure if even that would have reassured her—letters could be faked and, even if they were legitimate, would prove only that Godfather wrote to a relative named Nussbaum, not that this man was who he claimed to be. The young man looked innocent enough; in fact, his green eyes had a wise depth to them and his smile was downright disarming. Still, she reminded herself, pickpockets and streetcar scoundrels might have nice dimples, too. She scanned the hall, immense and filled with alcoves and corners. The main entrance and exit were choke points by design, created to funnel fairgoers in and out. In cramped mazes behind the walls, there were service hallways, branching to nondescript exits and connections to other exhibits.

She could make a run for it. But Nussbaum, though he wasn't an imposing figure, looked wiry and athletic. She was sure he could keep up with her in the twists and turns through the corridors and outrun her in the open, if it came down to that. And if she was overreacting, seeing a threat where there was only a distant relative of Godfather's, she would look a fool dashing like a child through the palace. That could be a tragic blow to the fragile credibility of a female clockmaker.

"I should have considered that making your acquaintance in a more…traditional manner would have been less disrupting." The white flag he offered was embossed cardstock—the card of a local hotel. "This is where I am staying. Please, call for tea some afternoon."

She gingerly accepted the card, extending only her arm and keeping her distance. "Thank you."

"I do not wish to alarm you," he continued, "but it is of some importance that we speak. Sooner, I think, rather than later."

She waited, anticipating some hint or explanation, but none

came. She tucked the card in her pocket. "Thank you," she repeated. "I'll look you up some other time," she added, unwilling to commit to anything.

Before Nussbaum could reply, Fritz reappeared. "I thought you had abandoned me in Siam, Miss Ironwood, and here you are having a chat!"

"So sorry, Herr Krieger, we were finished here." She hastily joined Fritz, who raised a quizzical eye but didn't question her.

Nussbaum remained in the palace, watching them as they left.

Chapter Three

EVEN AFTER A walk home in a cold drizzle and a supper of cold ham, Clara's mind was running at full speed. Was it plausible that Godfather had an associate, a relative, even, in Paris whom he'd asked to—to do what, exactly? She bit her lip to keep from scowling. To check up on her? To report if her work was satisfactory, if she'd cracked under pressure, if she'd given up on the Exposition and taken a job as a shopgirl selling stationery or hosiery?

Well, he could report back that she was quite well, thank you, despite Godfather's insistence she couldn't manage the level of skill the Palace of Illusions would demand. That was the last conversation she'd had with Godfather, when she'd told him that she had been offered a job with the Exposition and she would be taking at least a year abroad. She hadn't expected him to be pleased, exactly; after all, she managed quite a bit of their workload in his little Milwaukee clock shop. Still, she had not anticipated the eruption of bitter derision that had corroded their relationship beyond repair. Gears and wheels can be reshaped if bent and refitted if they fall loose, but if they're eaten through with rust or acid, they can't be salvaged. Godfather had deemed her adventure sure to fail, claimed her work was amateurish and unskilled, and all but told her he would never have let her stay on with him if it wasn't for a sense of near-familial responsibility.

So much for what he knew. And that was the trouble: He *did* know. He knew the caliber of work she produced every day, and yet—no sense dredging through it again, Clara chided herself. She turned her mind instead to her work, mapping out the lines of electric lights she would add to the Palace of Illusions, considering their variances, the reflected worlds upon worlds of the mirrors. Like a full-size version of the music boxes Godfather used to make with layers of mirrors and enameled figurines. She sketched out a few more plans but found her gaze drifting to the lumpy gold-wrapped package sitting on her table.

It wasn't labeled with *Do Not Open Until Christmas* the way the gifts from Mother were. Perhaps that was intentional—Godfather might have liked for her to open it whenever she pleased. And the appearance of someone claiming to know him, claiming to need to talk to her—what if the package was intended to be opened as soon as it arrived? "Oh, hang it all," Clara muttered, and picked up the package. Who cared what Godfather intended? He didn't mark it one way or the other, and she was tired of guessing. He always kept her guessing, and she didn't have to put up with it, not thousands of miles away from him.

She peeled away the gold paper and then the layers of tissue. As the last bit of tattered paper fell away, she knew what Godfather had sent.

His ugly old nutcracker.

Carved in the shape of a grotesque little man, protruding eyes set in an unnaturally round head and skimpy cape jutting from slumped shoulders, the wooden nutcracker had been polished to a dark sheen over years of use. She didn't know if Godfather had made it or not; she guessed that it was older. Perhaps much older, she considered, as she turned the little man over in her hands and appreciated the craftsmanship. German provenance, likely— Godfather came from Nuremberg originally. Clara remembered evenings in front of the fireplace, passing the nutcracker and a bowl of walnuts between them, trading jokes and stories. She'd thought the nutcracker's disproportionate body and ghoulish features vulgar and strange as a child, even feeling a bit afraid of its unyielding stare. She'd never expressed much fondness for it and couldn't imagine why Godfather had sent it to her. He hadn't bothered to include a note.

Still, it was a gift. A gift with, it appeared, no criticisms or jibes, but instead a shared memory of a gentler time between them.

She took out her stationery and wrote a kind if perfunctory note. *Thank you ever so much for the gift. I have many happy memories…* She sighed. That was true enough. No need to say anything more.

She sent the letter by the next morning's post, set the nutcracker on a high shelf, and didn't think of it again as busy weeks passed and winter deepened over Paris.

As she came home from work late one evening, one week before Christmas, Madame Boule flagged her from her door off the courtyard. "Miss Ironwood! A telegram for you!"

Clara's heart skipped a beat. Mother never sent telegrams— she thought the expense foolish when a letter got there within a month. There was no reason anyone would need to contact her urgently, unless—Father's health wasn't what it once had been. Or perhaps something had happened to Louise, or—

"It just arrived this afternoon," Madame Boule said, handing her the flimsy paper. Clara's hands shook. As much as she wanted to read it in private, she couldn't wait to see what news she held in her hands.

It is clear you do not understand the gift. Look softer. Godfather.

Clara's anxiety melted into anger. She stuffed the telegram into her pocket.

"Is everything all right?" Madame Boule asked.

"It's fine. Everything is fine. My godfather's idea of a joke, I suppose—thank you." She turned on her heel and retreated to her apartment.

Once unwrapped from her trustworthy wool coat, Clara calmed down a little. Godfather Thrushman certainly hadn't intended to give her a start, and he must have had something important to say if he had decided to respond to her thank-you note with a telegram—and he had done so immediately, she wagered as she worked the math on when she'd sent the note and when he'd likely received it. As to what that important message was, Clara hadn't the slightest idea. Why did Godfather have to speak in riddles and questions instead of simply telling her what he wanted? All those long hours at the workbench together, he never once came out and told her what was wrong with her designs or how to fix them. Instead, he was always questioning, riddling, making her guess and second-guess herself until she was ready to tear her hair out.

She picked up the telegram again. *Look softer.* She paused, remembering the first time he had told her that, coining an expression only they understood. She still remembered how it felt, years ago, to stand next to Godfather in the Ironwood foyer as he examined the inner workings of their beautiful old grandfather clock. It had stopped, and Mother, missing its cheerful proclamations of the hour, had called upon Godfather to fix it. But he'd had other ideas.

"Tell me, Clara," he had said, the two of them peering into the hollows of the clock, "what do you see?"

To Clara, the inside of the clock had been a dizzying labyrinth of gears and wheels, chains and weights. Godfather had taught her what most of them did, how the weights balanced the pendulum, how the gears were supposed to fit together. She squinted, determined to discover what was wrong with the clock and impress Godfather, but couldn't find even a hint. "Nothing, Godfather," she answered glumly.

"Ah, but you see many things, don't you?"

"Yes, but I don't know what's wrong!" She sighed, scanning each part of the clockwork. "I'm looking hard, but I can't find anything."

"Don't look harder," Godfather had replied, more gently than usual. "Look softer. Look lighter. Look to understand. Pretend you don't know anything about this old clock, and ask it to show you."

She had closed her eyes, taken a slow breath, and opened them, seeing the clock as though for the first time. The brass fittings and dark wood, the shining plates on the face where a ship sailed through the hours. She looked carefully at the ship—something she hadn't noticed before, a bit of lint captured by the gears.

She peered deeper into the clock, finding more lint festooning the back of the face and, eventually, a mouse's nest trapped in the housing.

"Very good," Godfather had said, producing his tools and carefully extracting the mess of dried grass, cotton batting, and shredded paper. She wondered afterward if he had seen the mouse nest from the beginning, or if he had truly let her make the diagnosis. In either case, once the clock was clean, Godfather showed her how he calibrated the weights and set the gears to whirring again. As the pendulum resumed its steady arc, Clara felt the deep satisfaction both of solving a problem and of earning Godfather's approval, unsure if those two things could be extricated from each other.

Now, the nutcracker. She pulled it down from the shelf and gave it another look, carefully, slowly this time. Softly. She avoided its blunt, questioning gaze as she examined its face, and deliberately turned its bulging eyes to the wall as she traced its carved epaulets and hussar's boots. She slid a fingernail under its cap, an oddly informal hat given his uniform. As a child, it always reminded her of the nightcap Ebenezer Scrooge wore in their *Illustrated Dickens*.

There was a latch.

She started and pulled her hand away. "Silly fool," she chided herself out loud, her voice thin in the empty apartment. Why did she feel, suddenly, frightened? Fear over a nutcracker wasn't practical, or scientific. Godfather would have scolded her, that was for certain. Determined to approach the problem methodically, she set the nutcracker under a lamp and turned the flame all the way up. She pulled out her tools and found her magnifying glass, then scrutinized the join. It was minute, a silver mechanism entirely hidden by the brim of the cap. She gently probed with the tip of a thin file, and with a sudden whir and pop, the cap flipped open, exposing a hole the size of a walnut in the poor nutcracker's head.

Heart beating faster, she turned the nutcracker upright again. He stared at her with those ghastly eyes, and she swallowed the macabre fantasy that his grin had grown wider, his eyes more lurid when the cap had opened. She tipped him away, letting him stare at the floor instead, and peered into the hidden compartment.

Inside, there was a slim piece of what might have been glass, and might have been crystal, and might, if she wanted to indulge in daydreams, have been carved starlight, as it seemed to glow. But no—of course it was only reflecting the light of the gas lamp. She turned it away from the lamp, but the glow didn't diminish.

Fascinated, she fished the trinket from inside the nutcracker's head, finally appreciating what it was. A magnifying glass, but smaller, more delicate even than the one she kept in her tool kit. The purest lens, and not only was it carved like a gem set into a circlet of gold, it seemed to be etched with whorls or swirls or—she could have pretended it was a language, even, foreign cursive rendered in miniature.

She admired it in the light of the gas lamp, and then confirmed that, to her amazement, it seemed to emanate a faint light even in the dark. Enamored with the craftsmanship of the glass, she silently thanked Godfather for sending her a pleasant puzzle for once. This was as it had been, when she was young—his tricks and riddles employed for fun, for wonder, rather than to demean or exasperate her. She ensured that the latch would work again if she closed it up, and put the magnifying glass away, shut back in the strange little cap, and set the nutcracker on the shelf where she could see its ugly little face every time she opened the door to her apartment.

Chapter Four

CLARA SPENT THE week leading up to the Christmas holidays working at a quicker pace than anyone else in the office—than anyone else, it seemed, in Paris. She pretended she was lucky, having no plans and no obligations for the holiday, so she could devote more time to the palace. In truth, she found herself stifling pangs of jealousy as she watched pedestrians balance parcels wrapped in brown paper and the lines at the greengrocer's and butcher's grow longer, full of people with Christmas dinners to plan and presents to wrap and parties to host.

Well, what did she expect? She had moved across the Atlantic to take a job where she knew no one, a grand gesture to launch a career. She had known it would be a lonely endeavor. And, she reasoned, Fritz had invited her for Christmas Eve, and Madame Boule for Christmas Day dinner, and that would be quite enough. As she packed up her papers in an otherwise empty office, however, she doubted that assessment for perhaps the first time, taking with her several cards and notes from colleagues who had diligently included her in their lists for Christmas greetings, a nicety she hadn't even considered.

A brisk wind had picked up, driving bitter snow across the sidewalks and forcing her to quicken her step. She collected her mail at the box. Letters from Mother and Louise produced a soft, sad ache, but she forgot that quickly as she opened a card from her office, a pale ivory envelope. There were no charming Saint Nicks or angelic choirs inside the envelope like the cards from her officemates, only a plain ivory notecard to match the nondescript envelope. She both hoped and worried it might be a work-related invitation to some party or dinner for the holidays. Instead, a few lines of confident cursive almost made her trip.

Dear Miss Ironwood, it read, *I have waited for your visit but have not heard from you. I am in earnest that it is of great importance that we meet. In the interest of candor, I forewarn you I will continue to seek you out until this matter is resolved.*

It was signed, as she knew before reading the name, *Nathanael Nussbaum*. With uncertain fingers, she folded the note and placed it back inside the envelope. She still had the hotel card tucked away in her pocketbook. Perhaps, she reasoned, after the holiday, she should seek Mr. Nussbaum out. After all, what harm could come of a chat with an acquaintance of Godfather's?

Plenty, she thought to herself as she dug out her notebooks and began to rework an equation she was convinced was not coming out right. Trust Godfather to find someone to nag her, to undermine her confidence, to critique her work all the way across the ocean. That music box she had made with the leaping stags, what had he called it? Awkward, yes, that was right, poorly proportioned. And her fishbowl with mechanical koi? Redundant, of course. She sighed. Right now she was the only one assessing her work, and she was a harsh enough critic. She scratched out a mistake in her arithmetic and started over.

A loud thump from next door interrupted her work.

She sighed, shook her head, and set to thinking again, only to be interrupted by another sound not unlike a sandbag dropped from the top of a ladder. Several staccato cracks and another whump.

Clara began to wonder, if she inquired at her neighbor's, whether there was any way to bury her annoyance under enough manufactured concern that it would be read in the spirit of neighborliness.

Another crescendo through the wall, and she decided she didn't care.

She rapped on the door of the next-door apartment, remembering belatedly that her French would only allow her the most rudimentary of inquiries and that miming *Why is there a rhinoceros dancing a minuet in your front hall?* was not going to be easy.

The door was flung open before Clara could either decide how to formulate her question in French or slink back to her apartment. A tall woman in a chinoiserie dressing gown and her fair curly hair bound in a thick braid answered. *"Bon soir! Je suis désolé, avez-vous—"* A lithe black cat darted into the hallway. "Shit! Hector, get back here."

Clara plastered herself to the wall of the corridor as her neighbor—who was apparently neither French nor a rhinoceros—pursued the shadow of a cat down the hall. Clara had just begun to wonder if it would be more polite to join the chase or to quietly slip back to her apartment when the woman rounded the corner, cat draped over one arm.

"Alors, qu'est-ce que vous—"

"You're not French!" Clara exclaimed, then recovered. "I'm sorry, you spoke English when the cat—and I'm not French, either, so—"

The woman deposited the cat inside with an inelegant thump. Hector slunk away with a disinterested flick of its tail. "Guilty as charged, not French. American, as I'm going to wager you are, too." She guarded the open door with a bare foot. "Come inside? Before Hector makes another dash?"

"I—well, thank you." Clara followed the woman inside. Her apartment looked as though dynamite had been exploded precisely in the middle, leaving a clear circle perhaps six feet in diameter. Everything outside that circle was chaos—clothes draped over chairs, opened letters and paper flowers and crumpled handbills on every surface alongside posters advertising various cafés and performers. Clara trained her eyes very deliberately on a nondescript spot on the far wall, trying to pretend she didn't see the mess. Surely her neighbor was wrought with embarrassment over the state of her apartment.

But no, the woman seemed blithely unconcerned with the fact that she had several half-full cups of tea balanced precariously on the edge of a desk or that there was a scarf tangled in the crumbling fronds of a dead potted plant. "I'm Annabelle," she said, holding out her hand. Clara accepted and was met with a firm grip. "Annabelle Forsythe. Or perhaps Belle Flora?" She waited for some glimmer of recognition. "No, didn't think so."

"I apologize, should I know you?"

"No, probably not. Belle Flora is my stage name. My most recent one. I'm a dancer," she added as an afterthought. "At the Jardin Vert? No, of course not—and yes, I'm aware how stupid the name is given the venue. Monsieur VanNeeve likes us to all have flower names, it's humiliating, really." She paused. "I'm sorry, did I catch your name?"

"Clara Ironwood," she said cautiously. "I live next door."

"Oh, right! Of course. I think I've seen you hanging out your laundry. You keep odd hours," she added. "Then again, so do I. Opposite ends of the clock, we are, I suppose—you're a dove and I'm a nightingale."

"A what?"

"An article I read in a monthly—there are doves, who wake up early, and nightingales, who keep late hours. But you're hardly ever home at all, it seems, except you must sleep sometime."

"I work long hours." Clara edged back but almost tripped over a stack of books. "I'm so sorry to be a bother, I was just—I heard a noise and I was worried—"

"Gosh! I'm sorry. I should have realized how loud I was being. Sorry about that, really!"

"What—what exactly was it?"

"Oh, I was trying a new routine. I've been just mad for Loie Fuller's serpentine dance, and thought maybe I could do a bit of a riff on it, anything to set me apart at the Jardin Vert and get a solo, you know—it's so tiresome being in the chorus. I studied dance for years, only to end up sharing the stage with some girls who rouge their knees and sweet-talk their way into the chorus."

"I see."

"No, you don't!" Annabelle laughed, and Clara found herself laughing, too, despite herself. "You have some respectable job in some respectable office, typing letters for some respectable lawyer or doctor or something."

"Not exactly. I—" Modesty forced a blush into Clara's cheeks. "I work for the Exposition. I design clockwork and mechanical features for one of the displays, actually."

"Well, I'll be damned. A real professional, that!" She swept a half a year's worth of magazines off the sofa and flopped into one corner, inviting Clara to join her. "How in the hell did that happen?"

Clara's exhale was thick as she sank into the decaying cushions of Annabelle's sofa. "That's a long story. Suffice to say, I did some work repairing a very damaged cuckoo clock for a Bavarian transplant back home—I'm from Milwaukee," she supplied. "It was really like a complete reconstruction." She still remembered it— the gears had been stuck fast and the little hunters and shepherdesses had ceased their merry hourly dance, the owner had been sure, for good. She had revived them within a day and a half. "His cousin's architectural firm had just won the bid to design the Palace of Illusions, and he recommended me for a job." There was more, of course—the portfolio mailed off without Godfather's blessing, the letters of recommendation from various clients who were, technically, Godfather's. That last awful day when he'd told her she'd never succeed in Paris.

"That wasn't a long story at all—why, it was hardly a story!" Annabelle laughed, not unkindly. "Though I can appreciate wanting to leave Milwaukee for Paris, given the opportunity. I outgrew Omaha and tried out Chicago, and then New York. But how does one outdo Paris?" She glanced at a mantel clock half buried by what Clara realized belatedly was a corset. "It's almost eight!"

"What's at eight?"

"Nothing is at eight. But I wanted to be dressed by eight so I could go down to the Folies—Loie is performing a new choreography, and I so want to see it before I invest any more in my own little experiment."

"Why?"

"Why! Because if what I've come up with is too similar to what she's doing, no one will hire me to do it! She's awfully jealous. A bit litigious, too. With fair reason—plenty of dancers have tried to imitate her. But no one would believe that I came up with it on my own, don't you see? I need to create something entirely new, entirely fresh. Something Loie doesn't do."

"I understand, I think." The world of clockwork had its form of creativity, but it didn't demand constant novelty as a defining feature.

"Well, I won't be going tonight, at any rate. I really ought to find an alarm clock, or something. I suppose I'll have to try for— oh, but she's not performing again until after Christmas." Annabelle stopped, a spark of a smile lighting her face. "You should come with me."

Clara balked. She'd just met this woman, and had little intention of accompanying her into Paris's nocturnal diversions. "I'm sorry, I don't think I could justify the money—"

"Oh, no money involved! My friend Jeanette's brother Matthieu works the door and he'll let me in to watch from the back, and if there are spare seats, he'll let us have at them. Especially if I bring a pretty American."

Clara was even less inclined to serve as bait for a doorman, but Annabelle pressed on. "Have you been to the Folies? Even once? You work long hours, yes, I know, but—it's Paris and you're here and the rest of the world isn't." She shrugged. "Take advantage!"

"I really oughtn't to impose—"

"Please! It's no imposition. You haven't seen Loie and you really, really must. Even if it doesn't do a thing for clockwork."

"My own work, you see, it's—"

"You can't possibly work all night!" Clara chose not to dissuade her. "Please? Besides, it's such fun to get dressed up and pretend to be someone important for the night. Should I wear the blue or the green—oh, I stained the green," Annabelle interrupted herself, tossing aside a gown in a vertiginous print that Clara assumed must look better under dim light.

"Well, that will be a problem. I don't really have evening clothes." Clara winced—that's right, she'd been told she'd need more formal clothing before the Exposition opening. There would be dinners, parties. Fritz was having his dinner jacket tailored.

"Why, who doesn't bring evening clothes to Paris! You're about Lucille's size," Annabelle offered, and before Clara could ask who Lucille was or why she had stashed a gown of mauve velvet in Annabelle's hall closet, the gown was off the hanger and the hooks unfastened. Annabelle had an irresistible sort of persuasive magic. She had Clara's shirtwaist and sensible wool skirt on a hanger and replaced with yards of mauve before Clara quite realized she had agreed to the entire production.

"That will do just fine. You take it home with you—Lucille won't mind if you borrow it. I'm afraid mauve isn't quite your color—I suppose you usually wear reds and peacock blue and emerald, don't you?" Clara didn't admit that her sole evening gown, left in the back of the closet in Milwaukee, was a nondescript chestnut brown she had hoped would render her invisible at the opera. "That dark hair and a complexion like winter and roses!"

"Thank you?"

"Now, let's see—I'll call for you at eight, the Thursday after Christmas," Annabelle said, imitating formality, and then laughed. "This will be fun! Don't you dare forget, and don't you dare bring work home instead."

Chapter Five

FRÄULEIN KRIEGER BUSTLED through the cramped parlor of the apartment she shared with her brother, a tray of gingerbread in each hand. Fritz and Alma Krieger had the same big, earnest eyes, but in other ways were almost comically opposite: he was dark-haired while she was blond, he seemed made of corners and angles while she was dainty and soft, and he was a trickster and tease while she exuded motherly concern. She had accumulated a parade of small children behind her, encouraged, no doubt, by the strong scent of cinnamon and sugar in the kitchen and the fact that every time she emerged, she was carrying a new plate of something their parents usually didn't let them eat.

The conversation around Clara ebbed and flowed in currents of languages she didn't understand, German and French and, she was fairly sure, Russian. She could pick out the occasional *sehr gut* and *très bien* and *mais pourquoi*, but the current ran too swiftly for her to keep pace. It was intellectually exhausting, being in a space where the words ran faster than she could understand them, constantly in a state of translation and half comprehension. By an hour into the party she felt like a clock whose gears needed oiling, moving laboriously and grinding uncomfortably.

Fräulein Krieger sat next to her, the soft cushions yielding with a *whumph* as she half fell into them. "What a party!" she said with a laugh. "So many children, more than last year."

"How do you know all of their parents?" Clara inquired politely.

"Ah, their parents—I know the children first! There are so many busy parents in our building, working, even the mothers, doing sewing, laundry—ach, we are almost into a new century and yet it is still so hard to make do, yes?" She watched a pair of little girls as they slowly circled the Christmas tree, her eyes reflecting their surprise and delight. "When they are home from school, or the little ones who do not have their schools yet, I say, 'Come to my garden, come to my house, we will play,' and so— you see, I make many friends that way." She leaned forward to chatter in French with a girl whose dark hair looped in braids over her ears.

"Here, Hélène, meet my friend Miss Ironwood," Fräulein Krieger said, switching to English. "She is a very smart lady—*très intelligente.*"

"Pleased to meet you," the little girl recited in deeply accented English. She had a missing front tooth. Clara smiled and took her hand, suddenly lonelier than she had been in months.

Hélène returned to her friends, who had gathered with their dolls under the Christmas tree. "Hélène's mother is a seamstress. She used to be quite in demand, working for one of the ateliers, making gowns and pretty things, but now she only takes in mend- ing for extra money. They are saving to buy a—oh, what is it, *klavier*—"

"Piano!" Clara supplied, a bit too eagerly. Some of the children glanced over their shoulders at her. She blushed. "That's lovely, does she play?"

"She would like Hélène to learn—Hélène has been practicing a bit with me." Fräulein Krieger nodded toward the slim upright piano wedged behind the Christmas tree. "It is too small, here, for the piano and the tree and everything else we've stuffed inside, but how else is one supposed to go about it? Not have a tree?" She laughed. "One must have a tree! And the nativity set, yes, and all of it. You do, don't you?"

That strange, nostalgic loneliness assaulted Clara again. Homesickness, she acknowledged to herself. "I don't have one here, no—I'm not home enough to enjoy it. But my parents—oh, they always had the grandest tree. To the ceiling, it always seemed to me." She could see it now, with the candles flickering in its boughs, and Mother's favorite clear glass ornaments, and the German blown glass ones Godfather had given them, and dozens of others, of stitched wool and beaded wire and glued tissue paper that she and Louise had made over the years.

"Ach, not even a little one? A few branches?" Fräulein Krieger shook her head. "That will not do! Next you will tell me you have no nativity and no gingerbread and no candles and—oh, this is a tragedy, Fräulein Ironwood!" Despite herself, Clara laughed. "Then it is good you are here, so you are not without something of Christmas. But look! Your cup is empty. More glühwein? I make the best glühwein. Come, come, with me."

She pulled Clara into the kitchen where a pot steamed gently on the stove. The counters were chaos and a pile of dishes waited in the sink, but Fräulein Krieger did not seem to notice or mind. "It is my own recipe—I use a grapefruit, not only oranges, you see, so there is a bit of bitter to offset the sweet—there!" She filled the dainty glass almost dangerously full.

Herr Krieger swung the door of the kitchen open, nearly colliding with his sister in the narrow space. "Miss Ironwood! And here I thought you kept Christmas as Ebenezer Scrooge did in the first half of the story!"

"Now, Fritz! That is rude, that is unkind—Miss Ironwood is too sweet a person to dish out to you what you deserve, but I will!" Fräulein Krieger snatched a wooden spoon from atop a teetering pile of dishes.

"Now, dear sister, I protest! I have done nothing to earn violence—ouch!" He unsuccessfully dodged a smack from the spoon. "I surrender! My apologies to Miss Ironwood!"

"Very well." Fräulein Krieger laid the spoon back on the pile in the sink with magnanimous grace. "I hope you have learned a valuable lesson."

"I doubt it," he replied with a sigh. "Now, Miss Ironwood—there is a one-week holiday until after the New Year. How will you spend your time, without work?"

Clara took a slow, deliberate sip of her wine. It was good—warm and sweet but with a strong undercurrent of spice and sharp citrus. "I suppose I might tidy up my apartment. I always like to start the New Year fresh."

"You will clean house? As a rest from work?" He held the door open for her. In the parlor, the bustle and laughter had only increased. "I confess, miss, that is the furthest thing from my mind."

Clara considered Fritz's cluttered desk at work. "You don't say."

"Come now! There will be concerts and parties and much else—not to mention my sister's cooking. You are always welcome here, of course, we will have a dinner for New Year's—"

"Thank you." Clara perched on the edge of the sofa. The children had settled into mostly quiet play under the tree, the girls rocking their dolls and speaking softly so as not to wake their cloth and porcelain babies. Two of the boys plucked a pair of candlesticks from the mantel and began to mock fence with them, drawing the ire of the girls under the tree and swift action from a father with a stiff bottle-brush moustache. Clara covered her laugh with her hand; Fritz didn't bother.

"What is this!" Fritz said. "Laughing at such miscreants?"

"They can hardly help it—it's Christmas!" She smiled. The Christmas Eve parties when she was a child—she could remember the feeling, bursting at the seams with excitement. There was a deep sense that the day was special, magic almost. It wasn't only the promise of Santa Claus filling her stocking—no, it was more. It was a deep, thrumming, beautiful anticipation that spilled into joy at the smallest things, at the candles being lit and the cousins arriving, at Mother serving the cake and Godfather putting on a puppet show. A lump formed in her throat—she had forgotten how to feel that way.

The boys had been roundly scolded and returned to the less dangerous activity of roasting chestnuts over the Kriegers' little stove. Clara had no doubt they would burn their fingers and barely notice.

"*Ich habe der kuchen!*" Fräulein Krieger called from the kitchen.

"And the coup de grâce—the cake!" Fritz stood to attention and hurried to open the door for the grand arrival of the cake. For a moment, Clara forgot where she was and expected Mother to emerge with her intricately decorated white cake, to the impressed applause of the gathering. But of course Mother wasn't here—she was probably still piping flowers in perfect snowy icing back home, awaiting the arrival of the guests and debating how long she would have to change into her party dress if she spent just one more half an hour on the cake. It was the same every year. It would be the same this year, except for one singular, glaring difference—Clara wasn't there.

The lump that had insinuated itself in Clara's throat swelled, intrusive and refusing to go away. "I'm so sorry, but I must be getting home," she said to no one in particular. She collected her coat from the overburdened coatrack by the door and slipped outside, not before noticing Fritz's curious expression following her.

Chapter Six

CLARA HURRIED HOME through nearly barren streets. A light snow fell and settled on the tops of streetlamps and in the crevices of gutters. Flakes caught in the lamplight, suspended for a moment as though caught in time, and Clara was surprised to feel a sharp point of cold where a tear slipped down her cheek.

She hadn't expected to miss home. It was silly, she chided herself, letting some children and the scent of gingerbread send her into homesick nostalgia. But Christmas had always been a happy time in the Ironwood house. No, it was more, she admitted as she allowed another tear to turn into a tiny icicle as it went its way down her face. When she thought of Christmas at home, she thought of before—before she had ruined things with Godfather.

In her gilded memories of childhood Christmases, Godfather was always there, mischievous, hovering on the periphery or inserting himself into the center of activity. And always with his gifts. Strange clockwork scenes and toys that jumped, flew, and even danced as if by magic. When she was eight, Godfather gave her and Louise two-foot-tall dolls in harlequin patchwork that, when properly wound, sprang over a yard into the air, arms and legs flailing comically. When she was ten, Godfather brought a pond of shimmering stained glass set with ornate metal swans. They swam on the surface of their pond, weaving to and fro and around one another in a complicated minuet.

She knew now how he made the toys—the patchwork dancers were loaded with springs, and the swans only danced because of magnets under the glass. But there remained a nostalgic enchantment to them. They had been magic to her, once. She wanted to create that feeling herself, and so she had apprenticed under Godfather and that—that had destroyed the last of the magic she might have harbored from childhood.

The apartments surrounding hers were lively, unsurprising as friends gathered and families celebrated. Foolish of her, to think she could capture some glimmer of those Christmases at home here, far away, among people she barely knew. At least her closest neighbors were quiet. Probably, Clara wagered, away for the evening, sharing bottles of wine and fruitcakes, or wedges of cheese— or whatever Parisians ate for Christmas Eve. She unlocked her silent apartment and sat with a heavy thump on the settee.

Godfather's nutcracker teetered on the shelf above her and fell. She lunged and caught it as it hurtled to the floor. She wondered if saving that hideous face was really worth the requisite athleticism as she propped the nutcracker on the settee beside her.

"Well, it's just you and me tonight. Do you have a name? I shouldn't wonder if you did—Godfather tended to name things. What was his clock's name—Hugo Hourly." The nutcracker stared back at her with unseeing though baleful eyes. "Don't blame me, I didn't make up that horrible pun."

She picked the nutcracker up again, opening the secret compartment under the cap. Inside, the delicate glass glinted at her as though asking her to pick it up. It was a pretty little thing, if nothing out of the ordinary, really. Just a magnifying glass.

She held the glass up, looking through it for the first time. The framed prints on the wall wavered and buckled through the lens, and the lamplight distorted and grew wan at the edges. Then the light seemed to press into the center of the lens, brightening to a warm white that pulsed gently.

She pulled the glass way, expecting to see the lamp blazing or even a small fire overtaking a corner of the apartment. The same dim light greeted her, cheerful enough but hardly brilliant. Tentatively, she looked through the magnifying glass once more. It must be bending the light in some unexpected way, she guessed, reminding herself not to hurt her eyes looking at an artificially intensified light. With deliberate care, she tilted the lens away from the lights, looking instead into the dark corner of the apartment where a largely neglected potted plant lived. It drooped, blurry, in the glass.

The light ebbed and lapped at the edges of the lens again, even though there was no lamp nearby. As it did, the plant seemed to change. Though it was difficult to see clearly, the flat leaves seemed to curve upward and brighten, faded green burning bright emerald as the stalks twined and grew. She squinted, wondering what properties of the glass could create such illusions.

The light unfurled toward the center of the glass again, softly warming like the horizon before the sunrise—a dramatic change from darkness, but not painful to look at. It drew tight toward the middle of the glass, an eye closing swiftly, and as the light coalesced it suddenly flared so strongly that Clara clamped her eyes shut.

When she opened them, the world had turned inside out.

Her dim apartment was awash with light from a brilliant sunrise—or perhaps it was a sunset, she couldn't tell—outside the window. It had been the depth of night just moments before, she was sure—had she fainted? That would explain the light, but it wouldn't explain the changes in her simple, spare apartment.

Clara was quite sure that the walls had never before been covered in pale blue silk, and the mirrors and picture frames had been in chipped dark wood, not gilt. The plant had grown into a topiary of a strange bird, graceful curves rendered in brilliant green leaves. The simple clock hanging on the wall had transformed into an intricate grandfather clock not terribly unlike Godfather's, but in paler wood and, she saw, featuring songbirds and vining flowers on its golden face instead of the stern owls and constellations Thrushman favored.

She blinked, not believing her own eyes.

She ran to the window and opened it, letting the pale pink light flood inside. It was not only faintly rosy in hue, it smelled of flowers—of rosewater and the tea roses in a summer garden. The harder Clara tried to catch the scent, the more it retreated, but when she paused, it rushed over her in a wave of sweet perfume and nostalgia. Outside, a light snow fell, swirling over a city she recognized only distantly.

She turned her attention back inside, letting herself adjust to the inversion of her own apartment. It was completely different and yet not strange. If she had imagined an apartment into being, she would have thought of something very much like this place— the colors, the delicately rendered details. She opened the door to her bedroom to confirm that her dented brass bedframe had been replaced by a sweeping four-poster with fluttering pale curtains. She was quite sure that her ceiling had been too low for it, before.

With shaking hands, she pulled her coat back on and opened the door of the apartment, tucking her key into a pocket, vaguely aware of how absurd it was to think about locking up when she had, apparently, broken reality. The stairs were no longer heavy dark wood, but a filigree spiral suffused with the rosy sunrise light. She clutched the glass in her hand, not daring to let it go.

She hesitated as she reached the street—was this safe? Probably not, she ventured. But it was impossible to resist. She had to know more, to understand, and to do so, she needed to see. Experience was, she had always felt, the best teacher. She didn't understand the mechanisms of a clock until she put her hands to the gears, and she knew without articulating as much that she could not understand the strange beauty she beheld until she moved among it.

The route Clara usually took toward the Seine was still familiar even though it looked entirely different, as though someone had stripped the wallpaper from the world and redecorated, the bones of the structure left intact but everything else completely altered. The soft fall of the land, the way it dipped slightly as she approached the river; a grand white dome rising on the hill in the distance where the incomplete Basilica of the Sacré-Coeur held court in the world she knew.

She passed buildings she had seen every day, now layered in absurd and confusing complexity. Some apartments yielded nothing but the same blank, dark windows; others blazed with multicolored light. Some building facades remained plain while others had turned into Gothic cathedrals in miniature or were overgrown with flowering vines. Some individual apartments' exteriors took on the look of baroque palaces or gingerbread cottages. At turns, however, some apartments sank into a clouded darkness.

One building, which she knew as a counting-house, was a thick smudge of near nothingness.

The courtyards were the most mesmerizing. Each held story-books in their four walls—evergreen forests with mushrooms as tall as a child, tiny but trim brown-and-white villages in orderly streets, or medieval castles with high towers. One was guarded by what Clara was sure was a dragon; on second look, it turned out to be a boxwood topiary of enormous size.

The sunrise light was laced with gold by the time she reached the river. She gasped—the Seine's brackish brown was now pale pink, as though the river had absorbed the color of the sky and held it. Fragrance bloomed from its waves, too, a stronger and more concentrated perfume than she had caught before, but in the same fresh rose. Clara wondered if the scent had come from the river or from the sunrise itself, and decided, as the current began to take on a pale golden hue, that perhaps it wasn't a simple answer.

As she watched the colors shift and change, she noticed a sound that seemed to emanate from the river. She walked closer, discovering as she did that the bridge she had taken every day had transformed from its pale stone to a web of spun glass suspended between spires of crystal. Fascinated, Clara examined it, the river's sounds momentarily forgotten. The bridge's nearest pillar was solid under her hands, but she had no idea how such a structure could have been created. The spires were intricately spun, as though a giant glassblower had wound them from the spool and planted them, still hot, in the riverbank.

She couldn't be sure if the color she saw in the glass was a reflection of the sky, the river, or both. As she brushed the glass, the pink hues intensified under her fingers. Startled, she yanked her hands back, and the color ebbed and crept under the surface of the glass, bleeding several feet in every direction.

Unnerved but even more curious than before, Clara turned back to the river. The sound was not quite birdsong, not quite the gentle rush of the water. It was musical, and intentionally so, Clara realized, recognizing the interplay of harmony and melody, deliberate crescendo and precise ritardando.

The waves were singing.

Clara stopped, jaw slightly unhinged, and stared. Of all she had seen, this caught her, shook her, insisted that the world she was moving through was not anything she had seen before, was nothing she understood. The waves were singing, and though the sound was not quite human, it belied an intelligent musicality. She edged away from the bank of the river, wondering what other secrets it might hide.

For the first time, it struck Clara that not only might this place not be entirely safe, but there might be something human—or not quite human—watching her, marking her movements. Was she alone? She couldn't see anyone else, but someone had made the wonders lining the streets and bordering the Seine. The thought was unnerving.

And then she realized she had no idea how to get back.

Chapter Seven

CLARA STOOD ON the banks of the transformed Seine, listening to the symphony of the water, and trying to decide what to do next. On the one hand, she couldn't shake the chill of realization—she was either trapped in some sort of alternate Paris or she had gone quite mad. It didn't feel like a dream, not at all—Clara's dreams were perfunctory recitations of memories and anxieties and never had the scents, music, and saturation of color of this place.

She had heard of people having terribly realistic illusions after drinking absinthe, but she had never touched the stuff, or anything else that might result in imagining herself in a fantasy of her own making. She hadn't had anything to drink besides the glühwein, and she didn't see how that could result in hallucinations. And when people went mad, she reasoned, they usually did so a little at a time, not all at once like Alice falling down the rabbit hole.

So this place had to be real. She stood stock-still for a long time, unable to quite fathom the only logical conclusion she could draw.

Real. The singing waves, the perfumed sky, the glassworks bridge that changed color when she touched it. *Real.*

Though caution nagged at the edges of her mind, the underlying fear that, unlike Alice, she wouldn't be able to get back home again, she yielded to wonder.

What else might she find? She made up her mind to cross the bridge.

The rose scent intensified and shifted over the water, brightening and unfurling until it was a garden of floral notes. The music, too, was louder here, but never coalesced into a melody Clara could follow. She paused in the middle of the bridge to look up and down the Seine, but the rose color hovered in a vapor like early morning mist, and only the faintest shapes could be seen struggling to take form. She thought she saw a grand structure where the Eiffel Tower ought to be, but couldn't be sure, and the shape seemed not quite right. She turned back to the far bank.

There was a sunrise on the other side of the bridge.

At least, that was what it looked like. The soft, shifting hues and undulating light were, Clara discovered as she approached, flowers and pale mist, a garden unfolding even as she watched. As the blooms opened, slowly and almost imperceptibly, the colors changed from the murky purples of predawn to gilded rose to brilliant saffrons and corals. Just as they had erupted in full color, they faded again. The entire garden rippled in variegated color. Clara moved through it in awe, appreciating slowly that the scent of the flowers matched the intensity of the light, musk brightening to citrus.

She emerged onto what should have been a street but was paved in what appeared to be tightly overlapped shells that shimmered opalescent in the light of the sunrise garden. She stepped tentatively, expecting to feel them crush under her boot, but her heel made a crisp rat-a-tat on the strange pavement. The Jardin des Tuileries was—should have been—ahead. Curious what its mirror might be here, she navigated toward it past buildings that must have been made of sandalwood, given the scent emanating from them.

The Jardin was where she expected it to be. Tall hedges still hemmed in the gardens, and fountains still burst to life within the green walls, but instead of the carefully trimmed ornamental shrubbery and wide avenues, the space was crowded with trees. Christmas trees, Clara realized, gently shaped of fir and spruce and even boxwood, but trimmed with candied fruits that shimmered with sugar. Gently flickering lights, warm and alive like candles but without the tapers or wicks, illuminated the depths of the boughs. Though she couldn't place it, the faint aroma of gingerbread hung in the air.

"Bon matin!"

A bright voice, too melodic to be quite human, pierced the quiet and nearly frightened Clara out of her skin.

"Bon matin! Et c'est vraiment un bon matin!"

She turned slowly, locating the source of the sound.

A tall woman, dressed as a shepherdess. No, Clara amended, the imagined ideal of what a shepherdess might wear, the sort of clothing suited to a porcelain figurine or a ballet costume, with full skirt and useless apron and a tightly cinched Swiss waist. The woman, too, was an oddly perfect ideal, with pale, smooth skin and abruptly rosy cheeks and lips. A pert tricorn hat offset perfectly coiled curls of dark hair. Her hands were poised like a dancer's, her stance an alert first position.

"Good morning," Clara managed to choke out.

"Oh! English! I am able to speak English." The strange shepherdess smiled brightly. "I am versed in French, English, and German. Is English your preference?"

"Yes?"

"Then good morning!" She dipped a curtsy that looked more like a stage bow. "Have you come for the ballet?"

"I'm sorry, I didn't—ballet? In a garden?"

"Oh, then I suppose you haven't. It's been a very long time since we had an audience. It has made some of us rather rusty, I'm afraid. Would you, do you think? Would you like to attend the ballet?"

"I—all right?" At Clara's timid acquiescence, the shepherdess took action. She produced a gilded chair with a velvet cushion from behind a stout spruce decked in sugared grapes. Then she clapped her hands, and a pair of huntsmen appeared, one with a violin and the other with an oboe. They did not greet her or even seem to acknowledge Clara's presence, but took their places in a small clearing.

The boy with the oboe began to play, and the violin chimed in, producing a gentle waltz that Clara thought she might recognize. The ballet began. The shepherdess who had spoken with her took the mossy stage as a soloist, each step and pirouette mesmerizing. When she leapt, she seemed to float, momentarily weightless and suspended only by the melody. Clara was not trained in the techniques of ballet, but the movements were all precise and crisply executed, in perfect unison with the music. Even Clara was fairly sure that the technical complexity of some of the combinations was of an exceptionally difficult level.

Then, suddenly, in the middle of a musical phrase, the violinist stopped, followed by the oboe player, and they wandered away into the forest, leaving only the shepherdess standing in the clearing.

She sighed. "And there you have it. Quite imperfect, unfinished really." She curtsied again. "But I thank you for your kind attention."

"It was magnificent!" Clara stood, applauding belatedly. "Why, you could have your choice of ballet companies!"

The woman laughed. "Oh, no! Quite impossible. We cannot leave, of course."

Clara paused, the trickle of fear returning. "Does that mean that everyone who...who finds themselves here is trapped?"

"Trapped! No, of course not. The craftsmen come and go as they please, of course. They're not like us, and neither are you, I presume—you are a craftsman, too? Craftswoman? Drat English, it hasn't got proper gendered nouns, you know."

"I'm a clockmaker," Clara ventured.

"Yes! A clockmaker! Our own craftsman was a clockmaker, a very good one. It has been many years since he visited us, you see, and left the choreography quite unfinished. A pity, isn't it? The ballet is so good up until the end and then—well. You saw." She paused. "Would you like to see it again?"

"Oh, no, not—not right now." Clara watched the woman as she picked at her skirt, the folds falling perfectly under her deft white fingers. "What is your name?"

"I am called Olympia." She smiled. "And you? You have a name, too, I would imagine?"

"Clara Ironwood." Clara searched the woman's pale expression. "I'm sorry, but this is all still very strange to me and—how is it that a ballet dancer lives in..." Should she call it Tuileries? "Lives in the woods?"

"This is where we were put, my musicians and I." Olympia shrugged.

"That's not quite what I meant."

"No, I suppose it isn't." The woman's face took on a thoughtful pout. "We are here because we were fashioned to be here. As you are fashioned to be, for the most part, elsewhere."

Slowly, Clara began to realize she hadn't understood at all. "Fashioned?"

"Of course. Made, created, crafted, produced. I don't know how you consider it—but a craftsman made us to live here in the wood. His mechanical ballet."

Clara stood for a long moment in stunned silence. "You're clockwork?"

"Yes." Olympia folded her hands with intentional politeness. "Now, I don't mean to chide, but it's a bit rude to balk at it. I don't make a fuss over your being flesh and blood even though that all seems quite strange to me."

"It's only..." Clara gathered her scattered thoughts. "It's only that...where I come from, clockwork can't talk."

"Oh, of course it could, if only you had the right mechanics to reproduce the voices—"

"No, it's not that the mechanics are too complex, it's that, well...you seem to be able to think and react to me. Clockwork only does the same thing over and over."

"That! Oh, that. Well. Yes. This place is different, you see. It's impossible to make a dead thing here."

"A dead thing?"

"That is what we call the poor crafts on the other side—dead things. That's not really fair, I suppose, because they don't know any better. They're quite oblivious to the fact that they are dead things." She wrung her pretty pale hands, hands Clara now saw as complex, perfectly attuned doll's hands. "Oh, how to explain! You make a garden, it grows, yes? It is alive. But if you pick the flowers and make a bouquet, it is very pretty, but it is dead. You make bouquets on your side. Here, you make gardens." She paused. "That's a bit confusing because even the gardens here are more alive, you know. But I suppose it catches the heart of it."

"And so a clockmaker, a craftsman… he made the woods here, and he made you?"

"Not the woods. The woods were here, before I was, a remnant from a daydream on your side, most likely. Probably a child—children are much better at that sort of thing." She strolled toward a fountain, beckoning Clara to follow. The fountain was as she recalled it from an abbreviated stroll through the Jardin some weeks earlier, except this one was wider and shallower and, running in a ring around its lip, a vine of crystal flowers sprouted. Cups, she realized as they drew closer—cups set into crystal petals that could be plucked. She held one up—it was so delicate she worried she might crush it.

"Have a drink," Olympia suggested. Clara had a brief moment of concern as she dipped the cup into the fountain—in her own world it would be quite unsanitary, and who knew what sort of magical danger might lie hidden here. Yet as she took a second glance, she noticed—the water was faintly lemon-colored and—she started—lemon-scented. "It began rather simply—years ago, I think, some little fellow playing on your side was thirsty and imagined the fountain made of lemonade." Clara stared at her, and she laughed. "And it's still here! Have a drink, then!"

She lifted the cup to her lips in wonder and tasted. The best lemonade, perfectly tart and yet tempered with a gentle sweetness, but more than that, it conjured instantly memories of picnics and a broad summer sun and the clank of ice in a tankard—memories she was not entirely sure were her own.

Olympia had explained the changes in her apartment, Clara

realized—she had imagined it looking the way it looked in this world and, without meaning to, changed this world's version of the rooms and furnishings. "Why him?"

"Oh, I haven't any idea how that all works. Why a place gets fond of someone and they get to paint over it whatever they fancy—people who come later refine it, of course, or layer over it completely. And sometimes the whole thing goes inside out. You could change it, if you wanted. It's easier to change things when you're here." She shrugged, then brightened. "Do you know ballet well? Perhaps you might finish our choreography!"

"I'm afraid I don't know ballet well at all."

Olympia's smile faltered, but she recovered. "Or even come and be our audience again. We do so love an audience—I dance properly when wound properly, of course, but never as well as when someone is watching."

"Of course, it was absolutely lovely—" A resonant bell tolled, startling Clara. Its bright peals reverberated under her feet, through her shoes, and sent a shiver up her back. Not entirely unpleasant, but uncanny, as though she were part of the humming cloche itself. "What is that?"

"*Orleans, Beaugency, Notre-Dame de Clery,*" Olympia answered in a singsong voice. "It's the bells, of course."

"Of course." Clara set the crystal cup back into its nest of petals. "I—what time, do you happen to know, do the bells ring out?"

"Why, at noon!" Olympia laughed. "Fancy not knowing that. *Vendome, Vendome,*" she sang along with the dying echoes of the bells. Noon! Madame Boule would be expecting her for dinner soon enough, and she had no idea how to get back. "Not that I have much need of that sort of time. Musical time, now, is a different matter—oh, do you need to leave?"

Clara forced a polite smile. "I'm very sorry, but I do. But do you happen to know—that is, how do I go back?"

"And I thought not knowing the noontide bells was funny!" Olympia laughed again; Clara tried to tamp back the anxiety that had remained, until now, buried under wonder. "Well, it's only"—Olympia hiccuped between giggles—"it's only that the craftsmen make their keys themselves, or at least they used to—at the very least, they're apprenticed and learn to use them properly! I've never heard of a craftsman who didn't know how the key worked!"

"Keys." Clara fished the magnifying glass out of her pocket. "I don't suppose they work both ways."

"How else does a key work? Don't you lock the one side of the door with the same key as you lock the other?"

"I suppose," Clara replied, "that you do." Without thinking, she held the glass to her eye. The fountain, the Christmas trees, the shimmering sugared fruit, and Olympia vanished in a blaze of white light.

Chapter Eight

CLARA BLINKED. SHE shoved the glass back into her pocket, realizing belatedly that she had just thrust herself through an invisible portal into one of the busiest gardens in Paris at the height of noon—and on a holiday, no less. The light still sparkled in her eyes, and she squinted, hoping she hadn't appeared like a ghost in front of a crowd of onlookers. How could she explain a sudden appearance in a public park, she wondered, as the glare finally receded and her eyes adjusted.

She looked out into a silent and deserted Jardin des Tuileries. The first gray light of dawn was creeping between the topiaries. She took a hesitant step forward, then another. She was met with the ordinary Jardin in ordinary Paris, not a Christmas tree wood hiding a mechanical ballet. The fountains had been shut off for winter.

She understood quickly that the passage of time must be different between both Parises. She kicked herself for not noting the precise time she had tried the key, but resolved to do her best to figure out the ratio; she assumed, of course, on first glance that time must run more slowly on the "home" side and more quickly on the "other" side, but then realized she had no confirmation of the fact that it had not been, say, two days. Or weeks. Or even—stories of Rip Van Winkle came careening out of her memory—years.

Before she could frighten herself into wondering if a century had passed while she had been watching the mechanical ballet and sipping fountain lemonade, she stepped out onto the street. Unless very little advancement in technology had occurred, a century had not slipped by. Not even a decade, she ascertained, fairly sure that even ten years would mark an increase in the auto-mobiles on the streets of Paris. A bell tolled, and then another—ordinary church bells this time.

Unless she had happened to stumble into another day known for bells at early morning Mass, it was Christmas. She had never felt compelled to go to church before, but this was an exception. For one, it would explain why she was wandering about outside in the last dregs of dawn. For another, it would give her at least an hour of anonymity in which to stop the whirling in her head. Saint-Germain was the closest church; she could hear its bells inviting all to Mass, and she accepted.

Like plenty of good Milwaukee families, the Ironwoods had attended the Gothic-esque Lutheran church downtown. She had thought the building imposing and grandiose at the time, stuffed in a pew between Louise and Mother while the choir intoned each step of the liturgy. The interior of this church disabused her of any notion that she had seen the height of church grandeur—and it wasn't even one of Paris's more famous cathedrals. She settled into a pew in the back, watching as droves of parishioners filed by her, realizing belatedly that she had certainly flagged herself as a tour-ist when she had failed to kneel and cross herself before entering the pew.

Fortunately, the Lutheran liturgy wasn't so dissimilar to the progression of the Mass that, despite not understanding more than a few words here and there, Clara followed the kneeling, standing, and sitting. She didn't even try to mouth the responses. Instead, she fell into deep thought.

Whatever she had encountered could only be described as magic.

Magic, therefore, was real.

A thin trickle of wonder bloomed into nearly uncontainable excitement. *Magic is real.* She stared at the polished wood of the pew in front of her, eyes unfocused as she let the strangeness, the beauty of that truth settle over her. *Magic is real.* Her hands quivered until she clamped them closed in her lap, but she couldn't stop her smile, impervious to any attempts to wrestle her face into somber submission.

Focus, she told herself, putting perhaps excessive demands on rational thought to consider the evidence and conclusions of her discovery. She was very sure that she was not mad, and very sure that she had not experienced some hallucination or sleepwalking phenomenon. The whole thing had made a strange sort of sense. It was all quite logical, if you could accept the facts as they stood. Clara was very used to collecting facts and then applying them, and so she found, with some surprise, that she could accept the whole picture drawn by the individual facts of this situation with very little resistance.

There was an alternate Paris—possibly, probably, she considered, an entire alternate world—running congruent with the one she lived in.

Godfather had known about this.

Godfather, she swirled the idea around her mind like wine

around the glass, *knew* about this. And not only that, he had wanted her to know, too. He'd sent her the nutcracker and prodded her into discovering the key. It would only be a matter of time, he must have wagered, until she would accidentally use it and slip into—what was she going to call the other place?

She shook her head. Alternate world nomenclature would have to wait. Godfather intended her to find the other place, and yet he had buried every clue she would need to do so. That, she reminded herself, was no surprise—Godfather never taught directly when he could make her teach herself through trial and frustrating error. And yet, how had he managed to avoid any hint, any mention of it for the many years they had spent together?

They had worked elbow-to-elbow for long days when she apprenticed to him, and he had never breathed a single word that suggested there could be a world mirror to theirs, full of wonder. Full of magic.

Or had he?

The priest raised his arms, and the congregation stood. Clara scrambled to her feet, but her mind was cast back into her childhood. She remembered a Christmas party, the tree trimmed in pink and burgundy ribbons that year, Louise in a brand-new dress, the grown-ups gathered around a bowl of punch, the children waiting for the cake to appear. Clara must have been ten— no, eleven. She remembered Louise's lavender gown, sprigs of flowers and a wide sash, the length brushing her ankles, and the disappointment she had felt in still wearing a shorter child's dress. "When you're twelve," her mother had said.

Eleven, just on the cusp of being not-quite-a-child, and yet far from being grown. Louise had seemed so old then! But when Godfather had asked if Clara wanted to hear a story, she had eagerly clamored for one. He had pulled the lake of dancing swans he had made down from the shelf—Mother always put Godfather's complicated and quite breakable toys on a high shelf, making Clara occasionally wonder why he bothered making them at all, as no one really got to enjoy them.

Godfather set the swan lake on the table and peered at it for a long moment, until Clara drew close and gazed into it, too, wondering what she had missed in the depths of the mirror lake or in the variety of the swans, who each wore a crown with colored glass gems. Finally Godfather spoke. "Do you know what this is?"

"It's a lake with swans, Godfather."

"Yes, of course. But do you know what it is, *really*?"

"You made it—so it's glass and metal and springs and wheels and—"

"Yes, yes, of course. That is what it is made of, but not what it really is." Usually when she answered his questions incorrectly, even as a child, Godfather would begin to get cross. That Christmas Eve was different; perhaps that was why she remembered it so well. He knelt beside her and looked at the mirror lake and the swans from the same perspective she had. He wound the key on the back, and the swans moved in orderly, graceful arcs. "This is the pond in the park. The one where you feed the ducks."

Clara looked at the lake again—the shape was familiar, a sort of squashed-heart shape that did follow the lines of the pond in the park. And the little palace on its shores—that was placed just where the bandstand was, only rendered here of white filigree and pink glass instead of brick and mortar. The path that wound around the pond—it branched in the same places, but it curved into flowers and spirals instead of ending at park benches.

"Except there are swans," Clara confirmed as she gazed at the toy, "instead of ducks."

"And much more besides. The lake is clear as a diamond, and you can see to the bottom, where it's all paved with mother-of-pearl. The swans swim all day and practice their dance. At night they go to roost in the little pink glass palace—you can see inside, it's all clear and clean and snug, and there is fresh golden straw every day for them to sleep on. On Sundays a girl comes down the path—it's all made of mother-of-pearl, just like the bottom of the pond, you see—and collects popcorn for the swans to eat."

"Popcorn! Where does she collect popcorn?"

"Why, from the popcorn trees!" Godfather laughed. "They are like our catalpa trees, with huge fans for leaves, and ancient-looking bark, except the bark, I think, is gingerbread. It smells like your mother's recipe. And when they bloom—pop! Instead of flowers, it's all popcorn balls.

"It's all there, you see. If you find the right lens to look through." And he'd twitched his nose so that his spectacles had waggled comically, and she had laughed, and thought it was a pretty story and nothing more.

It wasn't. Godfather had made her a facsimile of the "otherworld"—yes, that would work for it, at least for now, she decided. The duck pond at the little park up the street really was a lake of dancing swans with a pink glass palace on its bank, and Godfather had seen it. She thought of all his creations—dead things, as Olympia had said, created in their own ordinary world, but also inspired, she realized, by the otherworld. His skill and craft were his own, yes, but he was granted another gift, the vision of the otherworld. *The right lens to look through*—that hadn't been a pretty metaphor about imagination. He'd meant a very real magnifying glass hidden in the very real nutcracker they'd used to open walnuts a hundred times.

The congregation rose for the final benediction—they had received Communion while Clara had been thinking about pop-corn balls for swans—and she blended into the crowd as they filed outside.

"Miss Ironwood!" She turned at the sound of her name, jarred to be recognized in the real world after her thoughts had been so occupied with the otherworld.

Madame Boule waved at her from up the sidewalk. "And you said you would not come for Mass—and this is dawn Mass, you are up early for one who did not mean to come!"

Clara felt sudden, vague panic—she couldn't let anyone know about the magnifying glass or the otherworld. If nothing else, they'd think her mad. She was not used to lying—in fact, she'd always considered herself quite bad at it. "I woke up early," she floundered. "And the bells, I couldn't fall back asleep, but—"

"Oh, of course, and I am like a child on Christmas, too. I wake early, too excited!" Madame Boule laughed. "Now you must come home with me and help me make dinner, yes?"

"I'd be happy to," Clara said, grateful for the promise of something practical to do while her mind twisted over itself with wonder.

Chapter Nine

CLARA WAS AFRAID she was a terrible guest for Madame Boule, not only because most of Madame Boule's nieces and nephews and neighbors who crowded her apartment did not speak English and Clara fumbled through conversations in broken French, but also because she was distracted by sparkling, electrifying knowledge she couldn't breathe a word about, even if she had shared enough of their language to explain it. Who would believe her? Who wouldn't think she was raving mad, talking about a world of bewildering enchantment running parallel to their own?

Magic was real, and she had a key to a magical otherworld. The most ordinary moments—peeling potatoes in Madame Boule's kitchen, roasting chestnuts on the rug in front of the fire, stirring her coffee—were punctuated with memories of the Christmas Wood, the mechanical ballerina, the lemonade fountain, and Clara found herself startled into quiet awe.

She was grateful when the wan winter sunlight paled further and she could say her goodbyes and retreat to her apartment. The initial wonder of the otherworld had given over to a thousand unanswered questions. Questions wanted answers, and Clara was exhilarated by the prospect of investigating. Like picking the gears from a seized clock to find the root of the problem, only wider, deeper, and exponentially more complex.

She hesitated only momentarily before lifting the glass to her eye. She hadn't encountered any dangers in the otherworld, only gardens made of sunrise, singing waters, and of course, Olympia. But there had been shadows, too, she remembered. And if there were other craftsmen, as Olympia had suggested, might not they wander in that world of wonder, too? Was she, strictly speaking, allowed to come and go as she wished?

For perhaps the first time in her life, Clara decided she didn't care what the rules were. The questions were too compelling, the possibilities too captivating. She lifted the glass to her eye, and in a blaze of light, her own world was washed away and replaced with the other.

She thought, first, to go back to Olympia and the Christmas Wood, but she had the feeling that the mechanical ballerina had already told her most of what she might know about the otherworld. Clara wanted to know more, to patch together a clearer picture from the puzzle pieces Olympia had given her. People on this side affected the otherworld, created things without meaning to, that much she understood, and something else Olympia had said—it was easier to make changes while one was in the otherworld itself.

Make changes—Clara wondered what, exactly, that meant. Could gardens made of sunrises be planted and tended, or glass bridges spun across the Seine? Had the river been taught to sing? She shook her head—too many questions to answer all at once.

What she needed, she decided, were more observations. She resolved to take her usual route to work, comparing what she might find here to what she was familiar with from daily treks to and from her office.

As before, her path was a mirror of the ordinary Paris, buildings where she expected them to be, often taller or overlaid with blooming vines or painted in brilliant colors or taking on the facade of completely different architectural styles. One fairly typical apartment building had been replaced almost entirely by a sprawling oak tree. A bakery had been transformed with gingerbread and spun sugar. The courtyards of apartments delighted her; she realized that she was seeing children's imaginings rendered full-scale, the games they invented in their playtime unfolding in the otherworld.

Yet some buildings were as bland as they were in the ordinary Paris, or worse. Clara was surprised to find that her own office building was one of the sad, ordinary-looking edifices along the street. She gazed up at its blank front, windows and doors interrupting a facade so plain it looked as though it had been erased.

Inside, most of the building was dusky and thick with what looked like smoke but didn't have the right sort of smell. The shadowy grime that hung in the air had a stale, almost moldy scent, like bread gone bad at the bottom of the bin. Waving it away did no good; Clara began to feel that it was clinging to her clothes as she moved from office to office. Most of them were sterile spaces rendered in dull grays and beiges, devoid of the papers and models populating the desks and cabinets in the offices on the other side. Some others looked like tattered war zones of paper and balsa wood and plaster, as though all the frustration of creating a model in the ordinary Paris had exploded in creative shrapnel in the otherworld.

A very few were brighter spaces; Clara blushed a bit to peer into Fritz's office and see a brilliantly painted mural on his wall with soldiers on parade and prancing horses—they were, she saw with a start, actually parading and prancing despite their restriction to a mere two dimensions. Still, his papers were scattered and torn, far worse than his usual clutter, and a haze hung over his desk, too.

Clara found that her own office was one of these lighter spaces, with her desk nestled into an enormous clock. The gears were seized, however, and the space darkened by the same shadowy veil.

"What this place needs," Clara said to herself, feeling very much like her mother at spring cleaning time, "is a good airing out." She found the windows all staunchly closed, but with a little finagling, managed to open several and create a cross breeze of rose-scented air. The grimy film dissipated, and air grew lighter and fresher. Papers, especially the tattered shreds, lifted in the air in swirling clouds and, Clara saw with delight, disintegrated in the breeze and scattered into shimmering dust. She looked to her own desk and picked up discarded papers and broken pencils, depositing them into a bin next to her desk. They also dissolved with a faint shimmer. She turned her attention to the giant clock. A few adjustments, and the gears began whirring again with graceful precision.

Clara didn't feel that she ought to meddle with the other desks, but the lighter air and the cleared papers had a brightening effect all on their own. Like the first green of a landscape in the throes of spring thaw, the monochrome of shadow was lessened, and faint tints of color crept along walls and the edges of desks. The stale odor was replaced with rosewater, and the quality of the light was bright and clean.

The otherworld office was so welcoming, Clara found she could hardly wait to get back to work on her Palace of Illusions, the short week between Christmas and New Year now feeling interminably long.

Chapter Ten

AT EIGHT O'CLOCK that Thursday, as promised, Annabelle rapped on Clara's door. Clara was surprised, expecting the
dancer to be late or to have forgotten completely, even though she
had dutifully dressed herself in the mauve velvet gown and even
coaxed her hair into the soft waves favored by more fashionable
women instead of the simple knot she usually wore.

"Don't you look charming! You should really wear your hair
like that more often. Do you want a bit of carmine for your
cheeks? No?" Annabelle didn't seem to mind that Clara wasn't
very talkative; she produced enough conversation for two. "What
is that perfume you're wearing? Heliotrope? Guerlain makes the
best heliotrope perfumes." Clara didn't correct her that it was just
her cheap scented soap.

As Clara let Annabelle drag her down the street, listening to
a monologue of backstage gossip all the while, she felt a prickle
at the back of her neck and the strange conviction that someone
was watching her. She turned as surreptitiously as she could, not
wanting to alarm Annabelle—who, she admitted, seemed blithely
unflappable anyway. Her heart plunged as she registered a dark

shadow behind them, winding around the streetlights as they passed underneath.

But the shadow was nothing more than an ordinary man in a top hat and dark coat, she realized as he came beside them at a street crossing. He was striking, with silver flecks in his dark hair and an imposing profile, but not out of the ordinary. Just another figure on the street who ought to have blended in with dozens of others. She chided herself, behaving like every corner hid a Jack the Ripper or an H. H. Holmes. Did she want to seem like a nervous country cousin among the confident Parisians, or even Annabelle, who navigated the pastiche of streetlamp-lit shadows with aplomb?

Still, the fellow seemed awfully close, and matched every turn they took until the glitter and flash of the Folies came in view. Of course—he was on the same outing they were. Or, nearly so, Clara amended, as Annabelle steered her down an alley that smelled of disrepute to a heavy door set in the side of the brick.

She rapped three times with surprising force from her thin hands, and the door swung open. A bear-shaped man answered, red hair cropped short but a full moustache obscuring the better part of his face. *"Flora! Ma petite jonquil, et avec une autre fleur si belle—"*

"I'm not *your* little daffodil, Matthieu," Annabelle said, with a conspiratorial glint in her eyes and a hand laid on Matthieu's arm that suggested there might, someday, be a possibility of reversing that situation. "And you need to learn to be more polite on first meeting. Especially with Americans. They don't all find your sweet talk charming, you know."

"Particularly if they barely understand it," Clara added.

"Then I will practice my English." He turned to Clara. "What great happiness meeting your acquaintances. A lovely rose bouquet flower—"

"We don't say 'rose bouquet flower.' Honestly, Matthieu." She ushered Clara inside past him. "Don't you remember what we practiced last week?"

Even the unruly moustache seemed to concentrate. "It is a pleasure to meet you. May I inquire as to the health of your cactus?"

Annabelle burst out laughing. "Keep working on it."

"*Jeanette n'est pas ici ce soir, mais vous pouvez voir*—"

"English!" Annabelle sang with an impish smile.

"You are a strict schoolteacher! We are quite nearly sold out." He let Annabelle wait a long moment. She matched his stare with a patient smile, clearly enjoying this game. "But. Fourth row, two seats are empty."

"Are you sure these seats are free?" Clara asked as Annabelle ushered her through a labyrinth of back hallways.

"I'm sure. Matthieu checks the box office and swipes a seat or two off the cancellations if he can so they don't go back up for sale. It's a game he plays with the sales girl."

"But what if," Clara pressed, "someone did buy those seats?"

"We look innocent and Matthieu informs them that they are mistaken and they can watch from the rail. No one argues with Matthieu and those shoulders." She turned to find Clara, whose surprise registered, it seemed, quite clearly on her face. "Oh, don't look so moral about it! These fellows can afford good seats and fine caviar and Veuve Clicquot. If once in a while they stand so we can sit, so be it."

Halfway through a dizzying plate-spinning act, Clara sensed again that someone hovered at her periphery. Strange, given how crowded and lively the theater was, to sense one person, but she glanced around and found the same man from the street. His sharp nose and flinty eyes were unmistakable, even if he had eschewed the top hat she had first seen him in. He was handsome, but there was a distant stillness to him that sent a faint shiver all the way to Clara's fingers. The audience around him seemed to move, reacting to the performance in collective waves like a school of fish moving together. In the middle of the crowd, he stood apart, the obstacle that the fish darted around, unmoving and unmovable.

And Clara realized with a start that he was looking right at her.

She turned, cheeks reddening even as the crowd broke into applause for the act. She joined them belatedly, willing herself to look forward instead of finding the man's face again. Should she know him? Did he think he knew her? Was she being a country cousin again? She flushed—men looked at women for plenty of reasons outside of recognition, and gadding about Paris at night might send a particular message about the kind of woman she was.

Annabelle turned to her and grew concerned at her shaken expression. "Well, they were good, but they weren't that good," Annabelle said. "Whatever is the matter?"

"You wouldn't believe that I have a strong affinity for plate spinners?"

"No one has that strong of a reaction to plate spinners. Except perhaps china painters. Did that man next to you goose you? He has a look—"

"No, nothing like that. I—I thought I saw someone I knew."

"Ah," replied Annabelle with a knowing look. "What sort of someone? If he gives you any trouble, Matthieu will set him straight."

"He isn't—" Clara stopped. Actually, Matthieu wasn't a bad

sort to have around if the cold gentleman got any closer. "I'm sure it's nothing. Just mistook him for someone else."

"And now I'm left to my own inventions to figure out who the mystery figure is. A spurned lover? A jealous husband? Your long-lost twin..." She laughed. "I read too many penny dreadfuls, I know. Now hush! Loie's on next!"

Clara tried to turn her attention back to the stage, even though she felt a cold trickle down the back of her neck. She was sure the shiver was entirely her own invention, an overreaction to what was certainly an ordinary man. Still, every impulse she had begged her to turn around, not sure which was more unsettling a prospect—that he was still there, eyes fixed on her, or that he had disappeared. If there was a wasp in the room, Clara reasoned, it was almost worse not knowing where it was.

The stage lights dimmed and a single light wavered in front of a painted garden, the wrinkles in the fabric visible from Clara's seat. She wasn't sure what she expected; she was familiar with bal-let, but the set was nothing like the opulent stagings of *Giselle* and *Swan Lake* she'd seen even in Milwaukee. Still, a hush fell over the audience. The light faded, then flared, and in the center of the stage stood a woman in the most bizarre costume Clara had ever seen.

Loie Fuller was dwarfed by swaths of voluminous silk. The quivering yards of white fabric held its breath, kinetic potential in the white light. Then Loie began to move—at least, it was clear she must be moving, because the fabric took shape and became the undulations of a bird's wings.

The dancer onstage became a bird in flight, the lights shifting from pure white to a warm yellow as the wings morphed into the petals of a flower. Beneath the illusion, if Clara forced herself to look, Loie moved, molding her body into a frame for the shapes she created by manipulating the folds of fabric with the movement of her arms. Her feet stepped, turned, pivoted, but Clara barely registered these movements, all of her attention on the shifting images Loie painted onstage.

The flower petals unfurled, yellow brightening to pink and then red, a sunset of movement. Then the blossom folded back on itself, a column of shivering silk fading to pale blue, tightening and yet burgeoning with possibility. Clara forgot to wonder how Loie did it, even forgot to worry if the mysterious gentleman was still behind her, and let the illusion carry her with it. Slowly the silk unfurled again, colors shifting over it like a choreographed rainbow, until it was clear—Loie was a butterfly emerging from a cocoon, stretching her wings for the first time, becoming herself in the wash of prismatic light. She danced, wings of joy and possibility. Clara held her breath. The entire audience, she sensed, held its breath.

Then the stage went dark and Loie disappeared.

The entire dance lasted perhaps three minutes. It was probably less, Clara calculated, as the lights slowly rose and Loie took her bows. But in the moment, it had been timeless, transporting. She had not been a dancer on a stage, and Clara had not been a woman in the audience. Loie Fuller had turned them both into sheer possibility.

The audience roared with applause, Annabelle not least among them. "Well? What did I tell you! Isn't she an absolute wonder?"

"It was incredible," Clara replied. The footlights came up and the audience was released from the spell. "How did she do it?"

"Many have tried to answer," Annabelle replied with dramatic mystery. "None have succeeded." She paused. "Well, none have succeeded as perfectly as the Electric Fairy."

"Electricity." Clara paused. "There were lights, colored lights—I wonder how they did that."

"I've no idea," Annabelle replied with a shrug. "I'm always too busy watching *her.*" The aisles grew crowded as the rows cleared out. Clara ventured a glance behind them.

The man with the flint eyes stood alone in an empty row, as though waiting.

Clara swallowed, refusing to panic over nothing. After all, the man hadn't done or said anything. Men stared at women all the time, she reminded herself. They didn't tend to stare at her, but then again, she rarely wore ostentatious velvet evening gowns cut low in the front and back. She silently cursed Lucille's tastes in dressmaking, whoever she was, and then apologized to her. Lucille certainly had every right to wear whatever she felt was pretty.

"Do you think we might manage to look at the mechanisms Loie used? Maybe Matthieu could show us?" Clara asked, hoping to delay long enough for the man to leave, or at least to keep Matthieu nearby.

"Well, Loie is awfully secretive—but if no one is keeping an eye on them, I can't see the harm. Wouldn't it be just a delight to meet her? I have so many questions."

Annabelle managed to hail Matthieu, who was watching a row of dancers file into the dressing room. To Clara's dismay, he waved her over, and she left Clara standing by herself in the aisle.

Slowly, she turned, already knowing what she would see.

The man stood a yard away, eyes locked on her.

Clara sucked in her breath and followed Annabelle, and though she had disappeared down a dusty back hallway, she made herself small and tucked her skirts into a corner. She waited, cramped and awkwardly wedged where she didn't belong, as dancers and a pair of harlequin-patchwork acrobats walked past. One of the acrobats gave her a saucy wink, which she returned with a stiff smile. He merely laughed, showing a pair of missing teeth.

Annabelle finally reappeared, her face flushed. "I've just met Loie! I'm over the moon, I tell you—but that man! Your mysterious personage? Who was he? He looked an absolute gentleman, and my word, cuts a figure!" She fanned herself dramatically. "A bit older, perhaps, but there's no harm in that. The older ones know what they want, and they have the money to get it."

"I have no idea who that man was," Clara replied. "Just some well-dressed letch, and I suppose he's gone now, so it doesn't matter much. But you! You met Miss Fuller?"

"Oh! Yes, I did. Well, for a moment. In the hall. She was leaving with her mother. I was able to say hello and that I enjoyed her dancing very much before she was out the door. But her mother complimented my shoes."

"How exciting!"

"Not really, I suppose, but imagine meeting one of your absolute heroines! I won't sleep tonight, I'm sure." She stood for a moment in rapturous repose. "Matthieu says we can look at the lighting mechanisms now if you want."

In truth, Clara had forgotten about them, but her interest piqued as Matthieu showed them where the lights were controlled. There were general stage lights, but Loie used a more complicated system than mere white footlights, which cycled through different colors, allowing Loie to change her white garment into any hue she wished. Clara saw quickly that the man employed to run the lights could change concentration and brightness as well, permitting Loie to completely control the light and color, aiding in her transformations onstage.

81

"Someone must do this bit for her, though," Clara murmured to herself.

"Oh, yes, there's a stagehand specially trained to do Loie's lighting. She won't trust just anyone." Annabelle jabbed Matthieu in the ribs and burst out laughing. "He auditioned for the job and was quickly weeded out."

"It is not so easy!" Matthieu protested. "The time must be perfect."

"Of course," Clara said. "The timing of the lights and colors is just as much a part of the choreography as the movements themselves." The Electric Fairy, indeed. "Imagine if this was done with clockwork—you could set it up without another person. You could design the whole thing to work with a simple set of mechanisms—"

"Trust you to find some way to bring work into this!"

"But imagine, you could do something completely different than Loie does—but still use lights and colors."

Annabelle paused. "That is true. I've been so focused on her choreography that I didn't consider—just suppose." For the first time since Clara had met her, Annabelle was quiet, absorbed in her own thoughts. "I wonder where she had this—this thing made?"

"I have no idea," Clara replied, "but it's a simple carousel design, and if you had it timed with internal mechanisms, you wouldn't even need someone else to operate it." She gently prodded the prongs holding the colored glass. "These could be made with images or silhouettes," she murmured, thinking of the shadow puppets Godfather used to make for her and Louise. Still images could be overlaid on the plates, and though they didn't move, a dancer could interact with them. "You could dance with anything you wanted to."

"Now, that's an ingenious idea!" Annabelle crouched next to Clara, brilliant blue silk satin pooling around her. "Loie dances with lights, but I could dance with shadows!"

"You are finished yet?" Matthieu waited in the wings, nervously fidgeting with a pocket watch. "I have to lock doors."

"Lock them tight, Matthieu," Annabelle said, sweeping past him. "We've already stolen everything we need." He gaped after her in disbelief. "Oh, Clara! This is going to be fun!"

The Giant's Pocket
by Christian Elias Thrushman,
dated 6 July 1882

There was once a very nice little village that lived in the shadow of a very nice big mountain, in the hollows of which happened to dwell a very nice enormous giant. I recognize, dear reader or listener Louise or Clara, that this appears to be a terribly unusual situation, as most giants in stories are unkind brutes intent on grinding bones and stomping things and generally proving themselves a nuisance suited only to be struck down by young Jacks and brave tailors. This giant was an aberration from this pattern, appearing in a story and being very nice (and it must be noted for the sake of science that it is entirely possible that most giants, by simply not making nuisances of themselves, avoid being in stories altogether and the impression that most are wicked is false).

This was a very special village, as well, and not only on account of the neighboring very nice enormous giant. In the middle of the village was a well, just like the sort that is found in many small villages. This well, however, did not have a rope and bucket and could not draw water. Instead, it was a well of dreams. Good dreams, bright dreams, dreams that made people wake and wonder if what they had seen in their imagination's nightly wanderings might be possible. Dreams that made people keen for something they hadn't seen yet, dreams that spurred them to make imaginary things real.

Now, as I have said, there was no bucket to draw these dreams—they floated from the well of their own accord and no attempt to catch or control the effluence of dreams had ever been successful. Wise men and women from all over came to inspect the well and drew the same conclusion: All the bright and wonderful dreams anyone had ever dreamed originated from the well, so it must not be tampered with or closed. The general consensus (with which I quite agree) was that, if the well were harmed in any way, no one would dream such dreams again, and that such a loss would be of unfathomable detriment (with which I quite agree, as well).

(One particularly wise woman, however, advised that, as closing the well was impossible, it would behoove the village to build a high fence around the well to prevent small children and chickens from falling in, which was very good advice that the villagers promptly followed.)

Given the nature of the village and their duty of safeguarding the well of dreams, they made an alliance with the giant, which has, to my knowledge, not been duplicated in any other place. Simply having an alliance with a giant proved an excellent deterrent from most violence from abroad that might have threatened the well, and in return the village assisted the giant with such tasks as he was unable to complete on his own due to his enormous size, such as stringing popcorn to decorate his Christmas tree and making clove oranges for his punch. They lived quite happily for many years (giants live quite a bit longer than regular people), until one day something dreadful happened.

Now, ordinary armies were understandably afraid of the giant, who would have needed only to put on his good boots and go for a bit of a tromp about the battlefield to finish them off quite thoroughly, but a far-off kingdom had heard of the well of dreams guarded by the giant. This kingdom had in its court, unfortunately, a very wicked magician. His specialty was dreaming powders and sleeping potions, for which he had the name the Sandman, and given his interests, he was quite keen on exploiting the well for his own purposes. The wicked fellow had even thought of a cunning solution to take the village by force.

In the dead of night, he would mix a great draught of his strongest dreaming powder and release it into the air with the aid of a collection of fireworks. You see, dear listener, he had developed a terrifying array of projectiles the likes of which had never been seen in the world (though they are unfortunately now quite commonplace, and are perhaps the reason giants are far rarer than they used to be). His plan would have succeeded beautifully save for an old page who had lived in the village in his youth and, as all youths in that village had impressed upon them the magnitude of the responsibility of protecting the well of dreams, could not let such a threat go unopposed. Immediately after overhearing the magician dictating to his secretary (for he intended one day to write his memoirs), the old page set out at once to warn the village.

But the old page was not very quick of foot, and by the time he arrived, the village had mere hours to plan before the arrival of the magician. The old page had not developed on his hasty journey any plan by which to counter the wretched plot of the wicked magician, and the townspeople were quite in a state when they finally succeeded in waking the giant from his midafternoon nap and apprised him of their dire situation.

"Oh, ho," the giant rumbled (giants tend to rumble rather than laugh properly), "that won't be any fuss at all! Everyone knows that a sleeping draught can be countered by a tincture of edelweiss."

"Yes, yes," explained the beleaguered page, who was by this time working himself into quite a state, "but if everyone is asleep, who is to administer the tincture?"

At this they had to explain the entire situation to the giant again (it must be conceded that most giants are not of the most quick-thinking lot), and the caravan of the wicked magician was appearing over the hills when the giant finally ventured a question.

"It seems to me," he said slowly, "it seems that one must actually breathe in the sleeping potion in order to be affected."

The page nearly died of an apoplectic fit at this point, but the giant's assumption was confirmed.

"Why, then that is easy! I can hide you all in my pocket. Then you will not breathe the sleeping draught, which will be good for you, and one of you can then give me the dose of edelweiss, which will be good for me, and then finally I can put on my boots and stomp the wicked men, which will in turn be good for you again."

The villagers agreed hastily after the page suggested the slight amendment of the giant putting his boots on immediately for the sake of expediency in the necessary stomping upon his reawakening, which he agreed to, although he preferred not to sleep in his boots.

The Sandman, being a prideful fellow, did not for a moment presume his plan would not be successful, for after all, he had thought of it. He set off the fireworks and projectiles loaded with sleeping draught upon what he assumed was an unsuspecting village, noting with particular glee when the giant fell into a stupor. He deployed his troops immediately (having promised them payment of extra and especially pleasant dreams if they completed their tasks), but no sooner had they scattered through the town and found it quite deserted than the giant, revived by the tincture of edelweiss, stood up and made short work of them with his boots.

It's said that the wicked magician himself, in a panic, accidentally inhaled an excessive dose of sleeping potion and has been dreaming naught but terrible dreams ever since. And the well of dreams remains undisturbed to this day.

Chapter Eleven

AS THOUGH THE New Year heralded the official countdown to the opening of the Exposition, the pace for all the workers from the construction crews to the board increased rapidly as soon as the calendar turned over to January. Clara hardly had time to consider the otherworld, the magic key, or the strange meeting at the Folies, except to note that in the first week back at work she solved problems far more quickly, didn't trip over her own calculations, and left every day without a headache. She couldn't forget the mold-scented haze, the clutter and disarray of the otherworld's offices, or the fresh lightness that the rosy air blew in.

It wasn't just her work that flew by, either; Fritz commented on the increased energy that all the firm's employees seemed to have brought into the New Year. He attributed the change to a restful holiday, but Clara couldn't help but wonder. If the otherworld was bright, clear, and tidy, did it make for easier flow of the creative channels on this side? If it was overshadowed and cluttered on the other side, did this side suffer? And if so, how had it gotten that way? She filed all her questions away, determined to answer them soon, unsure how to balance exploring a mystifying otherworld with the deadlines and demands of her very real projects for the Exposition.

The mirrors arrived from the prestigious workshops of Saint-Gobain, and she had to supervise their installation. Fritz joined her as workers began to unload the great panes of glass.

"*Mein Gott!* How many years' bad luck would it be to break one of those!" He laughed, but Clara's stomach went into knots as she watched the delicate dance of the workers as they handled the huge mirrors.

"Too many," Clara replied. "I'm stepping out until they get them into place," she added, shielding her eyes as the corner of one mirror slipped slightly.

"Please, allow me," said Fritz as he opened the door for her. "The weather is quite mild today! One could almost imagine spring arriving, but not quite, not quite."

"Oh, don't say it!" Clara buttoned her coat, even though Fritz was right. The sun cast a mild warmth over the Champ-de-Mars and snow lingered only in shadows. "When it's spring, the Exposition will be almost ready to open! And I've still so much work to do."

"It looks as though the work is mostly being done by those strapping young French lads," Fritz replied with a cockeyed grin. "But oh yes—the lights."

"I won't be content until they've been installed and the timing all checked."

"You will be content then? Promise?"

Despite herself, Clara laughed. "No, I won't make a promise I can't keep."

"Then let us take a look at the progress of the pavilions instead of forcing your hand." He gestured toward the line of buildings built along the Champ-de-Mars, their grand facades mostly complete but, Clara knew, their interiors still under construction.

"Did they ever get the turnstiles for the entrance sorted?"

"You should see! They did, but then they installed several incorrectly and accidentally created a maze. The workers have been making bets on who can get through it the quickest, like a test for rats, you know."

Clara laughed again. Any annoyance she had once had with Fritz Krieger had dissipated into an easy rapport. "Say, Herr Krieger, I—"

"I hope I am not being too forward," he interrupted. "But we have been working together for many months now, and I have begun to consider you a colleague, and even a friend. Any other colleague, I would begin to call by their Christian name. Is it entirely inappropriate if we proceed in that fashion?"

Clara was taken aback, not so much by the suggestion as by Fritz's sudden frankness. She smiled to herself—in her own mind, he had been "Fritz" for months already. "I think that would be fine, Herr—Fritz."

The Palace of Illusions was dim when they returned. The lighting installation had begun, but as the wiring was still awaiting final approval, the lights couldn't be turned on. Still, the effect stopped her in her tracks. The mirrors, perfectly positioned, made the room look as though it went on into infinity. Dozens of Claras looked back at her, at different angles, moving when she moved, sliding toward her and darting away again.

"My goodness, what a sight! Well, you can certainly be proud. The name Clara Ironwood will be synonymous with 'brilliant design,' I am sure."

"Or it will be promptly forgotten once I'm off the payroll,"

Clara replied. Truth be told, she didn't mind that idea—she had always been more interested when the accolades focused on her work, preferring to retreat into the periphery herself.

"As much as I'd prefer to stay and gaze upon my reflection unto infinity, I'm afraid I have a meeting with the lads from Optics."

"Do you mind—that is, do you think it's all right if I stay a moment?"

"Only if it's to admire your work and not to check the electrical mountings again."

"I will make no such promises."

"Very well," Fritz acquiesced with a laugh. "Stay the rest of the afternoon, if you like."

Clara retreated into the labyrinth of mirrors. It was exactly what she had planned, what she had worked for. She imagined lines of people, waiting to see her Palace of Illusions and—

A noise from the hallway stopped her.

Surely, she rationalized, it was only one of the workers from Saint-Gobain, coming back to collect some tools, or the foreman making a final assessment about the wiring. Still, Clara was cautious, which was why she was hidden by the edge of a mirror when a man she recognized came into view. Nathanael Nussbaum.

From this corner of the room, there was nowhere to go that wouldn't immediately give away her presence—if not her exact whereabouts—in a room filled with mirrors. She watched the man for a moment. He wasn't terribly threatening, really, with his thin shoulders and unkempt sandy hair. There was even something gentle and inviting about his deft hands with long fingers, a craftsman's hands. But she didn't trust him—he seemed to find her when she was vulnerable, off guard. She didn't want him reporting their conversation to Godfather, either.

But where could she go? There was no way out of the building without being seen, reflected into infinity in the mirrors.

Her hand closed around the magnifying glass in her pocket. The key. She had taken to carrying it with her, appreciating its priceless value and feeling strangely attached, unwilling to leave it at her apartment unguarded. She took it out, tentative at first, but gaining certainty as it winked brightly at her. It reflected the warped lights of the mirror reflections as she lifted it to her eye, and then the thousand pinpricks of light coalesced and blazed open the door to the otherworld.

Clara hadn't had time to consider, before escaping to the otherworld, that she would emerge in the mirror of her own design, newly sketched into existence as the Champ-de-Mars transformed for the Exposition. She blinked, and a thousand crystalline mirrors blinked back at her. Even the famed workshops of Saint-Gobain couldn't produce mirrors like these, impossibly clear and yet with a depth like looking through a window. And in each of them, her face peered back slightly altered—all of them her own image, but in facets. It was as though she had been broken into a thousand pieces, each representing a single moment of emotion, reaction, thought, and then these images scattered across the grand hall of mirrors.

Her Palace of Illusions was, here in the otherworld, a palace of revelation, of precisely rendered reality.

She wandered slowly through the mirrors, marveling not only at the many faces returning her gaze but at the variable colors and lights. She had designed the electric lights in the real palace to cycle and change, but this light was not the artificial glare of electricity. It thrummed and grew and shrank to pinpoints and ballooned as naturally as breathing, innovating a dance it set in motion for itself.

Imagine, she thought to herself, *just imagine what it could look like were it crafted and refined intentionally, not just in complementary reaction to creative impulse on the other side.* She touched a mirror and felt, deep beneath its surface, a dormant warmth.

Though she could have spent hours poring over the details and making plans for how she could keep crafting what she half fondly, half sheepishly considered "her" palace, she was irresistibly curious to see what the other palaces and pavilions might hold. She followed the plans she had memorized for the doors and halls of the Palace of Illusions.

The landscape outside was changed entirely.

She had been used to a cacophony of half-finished buildings all coated with a generous supply of dust. Leaving the Palace of Optics, if she looked across the Pont d'Iéna, she expected to see the pastiche of pavilions representing the French colonies. Instead, the other bank of the Seine was shrouded in an ever-shifting quilt of cloud, fog, and glittering airborne sand. She could swear she saw mountain peaks protruding from somewhere near where the Palais du Trocadéro ought to have been.

Overwhelmed by the chaotic beauty across the river, Clara brought her attention back to the cluster of buildings under the shadow of the Eiffel Tower where she stood. It rose above her with a silvery sheen so sharp that she found it hard to look at. Next to the Palace of Optics, the pavilion for Morocco had been built. It was, in her recollection, a suggestion of a bustling marketplace, with an imitation of a mosque as its centerpiece. Here, however, the space was a barren skeleton. It was as though someone had drawn a life-size sketch of the pavilion on the Champ-de-Mars and then left it unfinished. Void of color and empty, the edifice reeked of the artificiality the Exposition had worked to avoid.

However, towering above all the other pavilions, the display for Siam beckoned from the other side of the Eiffel Tower—or, what the display had become in the otherworld. On the real Champ-de-Mars, the pavilion was, like all the other nations' buildings, constructed of cardboard and plaster, an illusion of permanence rendered in ticky-tacky.

Here, the staggering bell tower, higher than its counterpart, was certainly made of real wood, carved as though by hand, stretching hundreds of feet into the air. As the breeze stirred, a chorus of bells sang a sweet, strange melody. Inside the pavilion, she knew, the Exposition had endeavored to show the civilizing effects of European trade in Asia. The pagodas and murals were to impart a flavor of authenticity and exoticism while never forgetting the great riches that could be drawn from the modernization of trade.

As she peered in a shadowy door, she could see that none of this carefully curated impression remained. The interior highlighted the teakwood Siam was famous for, but not as a product of European trade. Instead, life-size figures Clara didn't recognize emerged from panels of wood, intricately carved and, she felt, nearly pulsing with life. Not quite, she knew—they remained motionless in relief on the walls. But they felt real, with a bare honesty of expression that the Exposition couldn't approach.

She drew back, staggered by the enormity of possibility that even mere suggestion, it seemed, had on the otherworld. Why had Maroc been translated here as a shell, while Siam had the same breath and life that her own Palace of Illusions had?

She remembered something Fritz had told her as they had toured the grounds—a minister from Siam living in Paris had been intimately involved with the building of the Siam pavilion, while Maroc had been conceived of almost entirely by Frenchmen. Could that account for the difference? Did belief in your creation make it real?

Stranger still, on a stretch of land near where the Quai des Nations was being built on either side of the Seine, there were holes in the landscape. Some were bland renderings, like Maroc, but others were darker, bleaker. Like scorch marks on the Seine, they seemed to draw light into them and churn with shadow. The effect was like a disorienting quilt, reminding Clara of the "crazy" quilts her mother made from a dizzying array of scraps. Except here, the quilts weren't made of scraps but of the space itself.

Clara was debating which to investigate first—one of the many varying patches of brilliant color and strange structure, or the eerie shadows or unnerving blandness that she intuited were wrong, somehow—when she saw movement. Someone near her Palace of Illusions.

She hid behind Siam's dark teak tower. Nathanael Nussbaum. Her breath caught. He had a key, too—he had to, if he could slip into the otherworld. That meant he did have some connection, perhaps, to Godfather. Did his presence here, she wondered, make her more or less inclined to trust him? She wasn't sure.

She didn't fancy finding out now, either, alone and with no recourse if he wasn't the friendly ally he claimed to be. She imagined, with a shudder, that if anything happened to her in this world, she'd simply go missing in the real world. A terrible experience for Mother and Father and Louise, never to hear from her again.

She stayed behind the Siam pavilion, ready to cross back where she expected no one in real Paris to see her uncanny reappearance. What did that look like? she wondered. How, exactly did it work—was there some balance of matter or energy or—no, there was no point in trying to parse the riddle created by a magic she had to assume was not of the material world she understood so well. Especially not now—Nussbaum was walking right toward Siam.

She used the glass and was borne by its brilliant light back into the real Exposition grounds. Fortunately, she had chosen a wise place for her reentry, with no onlookers to shock or amaze. She'd end up with her own pavilion at the Exposition, she thought with a nervous laugh, if someone caught her materializing out of thin air. Without any further delay, she hurried back toward the crowded safety of the Paris streets, away from Nathanael Nussbaum.

Chapter Twelve

"DID YOU KNOW," Annabelle said, pouring out another glass of wine, "that some people can see colors when they hear music? Isn't that just beautifully bizarre?"

Clara accepted the glass from Annabelle—a chipped Moroccan tumbler—and collected a chunk of cheese from the tray Annabelle had made for them. As it turned out, her neighbor's cooking habits and her own lined up perfectly. With meager kitchens and even more limited time, both grazed from the markets, boulangeries, and street vendors of Paris. Inviting each other over for dinner meant a bountiful spread of whatever looked good at the corner market and maybe a dented cake bought half-price at the end of the day.

"People," Clara replied, "are beautifully bizarre."

"Isn't that the truth!" Annabelle speared a dried apricot with a long fork. Hector picked his way through stacks of hatboxes and settled himself by the plate of cheese, just close enough to be a threat. "So tell me more about this magic lantern you've made."

"It's not exactly a magic lantern—"

"I know, I know. But it's basically a lantern and it sounds like it's made of magic, so I'm going to go with calling it a magic lantern."

"Fair," returned Clara. She shooed Hector away from the cheese and took a slice for herself. "It's not dissimilar to Loie's in that it's a focused light with different colors of glass, but with the silhouettes layered over the top. I've designed it to work on clockwork, and to overlay the panes of glass between colors. You remember your rainbow, right? Refracted light?"

"Sure, right. Prisms and all that."

"Exactly—colors that lie next to one another rather blend into one another. So that's what I've done—it's a full rainbow, with shadow puppets of butterflies. I couldn't think of anything more creative, but you see, after this first set, you could change them to anything you want."

"First set?"

"The glass panes and the cutouts are removable so you could change the order, remove colors, change the silhouettes—"

"Oh! Oh, that's brilliant. You could have...oh, goodness. You could have a fire dance with all reds and oranges and yellows, and dance with a phoenix, or something-something-water-something with blues and fish—or mermaids!"

Clara blinked—she hadn't even considered the actual application of the design, and here Annabelle was, from the distant look in her eyes and the movement of her hands, already choreographing a combination. "You certainly could. Or—that thing you said with color and music."

"Well, I don't see colors when I hear—oh! But I suppose everyone could, in a way." Annabelle cocked her head. "That would be the perfect first go with it, wouldn't it? A color dance, a whole prism dance. Because I suppose anyone could see the link between color and music, if I showed them what I thought it ought to look like with dance."

"Shall I set it up for you?"

"Yes! I want to play with my new toy right away, thank you." Annabelle settled herself onto the floor in a dramatic sweep of her jade-green dressing gown. Clara perched nimbly on a wobbly footstool and unveiled the lantern.

Essentially, she had mounted a kerosene lantern inside a carousel of frames for glass plates, each of which was interchangeable. The frames angled, allowing for overlap and blending of the colors when the lanternlight was projected in one direction, which she could do with a simple adjustment of the mountings.

"It's so pretty!"

Clara laughed. "It's not very pretty—my soldering skills could use work. But what it does—watch!" Hector sniffed the lantern with a judgmental twitch of his whiskers, and then leapt away as Clara wound the key at the back of the lantern. The clockwork tightened and then released into a slow spiral. The plates danced a stately promenade around the light, casting a glow on Annabelle's peeling wallpaper that began azure, slipped into violet, brightened to rose.

"It's a damn delight!" Annabelle clapped her hands as the rose bloomed into gold. "I could do so many things with this! However do you do it, though?" She waved her hands. "Never mind, I'll never understand it. Loie would pop a button if she could see this—she hasn't got her own private clockmaker!"

She stood with a sweep of her dressing gown and turned gently into the light, letting sunrise yellow wash the green silk pale, then pirouetted into cerulean blue and dipped into azure, arms reaching and back arched as violet settled her into shadow.

"Can you change the speed?" Annabelle asked, trying a soft leap into vermilion but overshooting and landing by the ottoman instead. "And the size?"

"The size is just how far away it is"—Clara pulled the lantern back a few feet—"and speed is a simple adjustment."

"Too fun," Annabelle replied, dropping onto the ottoman. "I'll work out some actual choreography and then we'll play with the speed, yes?"

"Of course."

"Oh, brilliant." She sighed. "I'll have to work on some sort of costuming—of course not what Loie does with the fifty-seven yards of silk or whatever the hell that is. Simple, white, of course. That's going to be the hard part—you can always scrounge something if you're not picky about the color. Speaking of, do you want a dressing gown?"

"What?" Clara had almost gotten used to Annabelle's abrupt changes in subject, but not quite.

"A dressing gown! Our dinners, you're always wearing... that." She plucked the stiff hem of Clara's serviceable wool skirt and gave it a shake. "It's all right for work, but land sakes, don't you get tired of being all buttoned up all the time?"

Clara picked at her skirt absentmindedly. Her high collar did have a tendency to itch, and sometimes the thought of flopping ingloriously onto a sofa, corset long forgotten, was rather appealing. "I suppose sometimes it feels a bit stuffy to wear this around the house," she admitted. "But I didn't bring much with me to Paris."

"Then you're going to love what I smuggled home. That soprano that the Jardin Vert hired on a three-year contract last month—it turns out she had a contract with some opera house in Austria and was just paying her way across Europe one job at a time. You should have seen VanNeeve's face, like a beet with some kind of fungus." She laughed. "Anyway. He changed the locks on her dressing room—the nice dressing room, you remember—and wouldn't even let her back in to collect her things. And she had the most ridiculous collection of dressing gowns!"

Annabelle flung open the battered steamer trunk that served as both breakfast table and ottoman and produced handfuls of multicolored silk. "I don't know why she had that many of them, but no matter—I thought they could serve for costuming. Or, well." Annabelle shrugged. "The pawnshop pays all right in a pinch." She rifled through several and laid them on the sofa. "Pick one!"

Clara hesitated—none of the robes had the tailored lapels and strict collar of her dressing gown from home, built thick against the cold Wisconsin winters. But also, she considered, tailored stiff against the risk of growing loose, careless. Louise wouldn't approve, she thought with a sly smile, of the parrot-blue silk with gold tassels, or the blaze orange smocked intricately across the back.

"Now, that's a very pretty one," Annabelle whispered as Clara lingered over a dark purple silk with peonies embroidered on the sleeves. "Would suit you just so, too."

"And what does that matter?" Clara laughed. "No one but you would see me in it."

"Maybe so, maybe not," Annabelle said with a teasing lilt. "Now—you mean to say you never consider...how does one say...entertaining at home?" She lifted an eyebrow at Clara's silence. "Come now, we're both grown women living in Paris, of all places!"

"Never!" Clara said, flushing hot. "I don't—I mean, I wouldn't—" She fumbled for words about something she had never even considered speaking about openly. "It's not safe, and it's foolish to get wrapped up in something like...that."

Annabelle grew uncharacteristically quiet. "I'm sorry, I didn't mean anything by it. It's just—it's 1900, and this is France. It's not Puritan New England, you know."

"I know. I didn't mean anything by what I said, either." Clara twisted her hands into the purple silk. She hadn't considered it— that on their own, away from the scrutiny of protective mothers and predatory gossip, women might . . . she shook herself free of the thought. "It isn't something my family was at all . . . open about."

Annabelle tried not to laugh and failed. "No one's family is! I didn't know what from what until I moved to Chicago and then— well! A dressing room is an education swifter and more complete than any college course, I imagine." She sobered. "It's better to be safe, I suppose. But oh! Sometimes it feels like such a racket that we women have got to do all the practical thinking."

Clara considered this—Annabelle said "practical" the way she might say "waste bin" or "chore" or "plumbing malfunction." She had never considered practicality a burden but suddenly saw what Annabelle meant. Caprice and passion were indulgences that came with unpredictable prices. It was true in romantic entanglements, but just as true anywhere else, really. Profession, family, even where to take an evening stroll. Practicality meant the costs were worked out ahead of time, ciphers tabulated and agreed to, but it could chafe, never deviating from it.

"I've made you go all quiet," Annabelle said, toying with the violet pane of glass on the lantern. "I'm sorry, I forget how to behave in polite company."

"Not at all," Clara replied. "I—I was just thinking about how very safe my life has always been. Always quite well planned, you know. Even coming here. It was the riskiest thing I've ever done— I ignored my godfather's wishes, I packed up alone, I crossed the ocean, and yet. I had a job with a good salary waiting for me, and the Exposition even arranged my apartment." She laughed rue-fully. "They made sure to find me a landlady—*lady*, mind you—who spoke English."

"You'd never make it as a dancer." Annabelle shrugged. "It's all uncertainty and chasing a job that might not be there. But there's nothing any better about that sort of unmoored life. It's silly, really—someday my feet will give out or I'll lose my looks completely and then what?" She danced her fingers from red to orange to yellow across the glass. "All on someone else's whim and I can't outrun time."

"Yes, but it seems you can also plan and scrimp and give up any little joys or surprises, and still end up alone in a cheap, drafty apartment infested with cats." Clara smiled softly. "I mean—after this job, who knows? Perhaps no one will want to hire me. And back to Milwaukee I go."

"Ah well. Eat, drink, and be merry, for tomorrow we return to Milwaukee. Or Omaha." Annabelle raised a glass and Clara joined the toast.

Chapter Thirteen

SOMETIME AFTER MIDNIGHT, Clara sat on the floor of her own apartment, the nutcracker in her lap. The conversation with Annabelle had unnerved her. She was entirely safe, entirely practical, and had always considered that a virtue—her German American family certainly did. Her physician father certainly did. Her orderly and mannered mother certainly did. She had assumed, always, that Godfather did, too—after all, clockwork was nothing if not practical. But now she wondered if the pragmatism of gears and clockwork might be too constricting in its safety.

She remembered once, overhearing a banker friend of her father discussing money over a bottle of port in the study, going into great detail about the concept of opportunity cost. If one was too safe, he said, in one's investments, one might actually be very unsafe. One might lose more money not dabbling in a bit of risk. "Every time you do something, you are quite obviously *not* doing something else. But people who leave their money in banks—or under their mattresses!—don't think of 'doing nothing' as a risk. Foolish thinking." And then he and Father had devolved into a conversation about whether investment in livestock or coal was more volatile, and Clara had slipped out of the doorway, bored.

She wasn't bored now. She was ashamed. She not only had all of Paris outside her door, she also had a gateway to another world sitting in her apartment. Why wasn't she exploring both of them, submerging herself in all that they each had to offer? What risks were there to using her magnifying glass whenever she liked? It appeared she could come and go at will. It seemed she couldn't accidentally harm either world by coming and going. And she didn't even lose time in her world—time, the most irreplaceable currency, was doubled, in her hands!

Why would she waste such a remarkable opportunity?

"After all," Clara said to the nutcracker, "you crossed an ocean to bring me this. I may as well make good use of it, for all your trouble." She set the nutcracker aside and lifted the magnifying glass. The room flooded with light, just as before, but this time she was prepared. She didn't shy away from it, didn't flinch, even as the brilliance washed over her. She blinked her way into the other-world, letting the lush apartment come to life as the light receded. Her apartment was already familiar in its otherworld iteration, but under the door of Annabelle's apartment, light shifted from red to orange and then toward green and blue—the lantern Clara had made finding its home here in the otherworld, too.

Time did run differently here, she thought—light flooded the halls as brashly as the noontime sun at midsummer, which, she acknowledged as she stepped outside, it certainly felt like. All of the chill and damp of winter was forgotten under a balmy blue sky and syrup-gold light. She made her way toward the Seine, where the Quai des Nations was blooming along the river in the real world and the patchwork of color and shadow had been when she viewed it from the Palace of Illusions. She had paused to listen to the river's song when she heard the last thing she expected.

"*Arrêtez! Halt!* Stop!" The voice rang out in three rapid-fire languages. Clara obeyed, heart pounding. This was not how she expected dipping her toe in spontaneity to go. Slowly, she turned toward the sound, not sure if she should expect an army of automatons or some other clockwork nightmare.

It was just a wiry woman in a well-worn cotton dress. Her iron-gray hair was wound into a crown of braids, and she was swathed in a voluminous apron. In any other situation, she would have struck Clara as pleasantly domestic, like a matron kneading bread dough in a cozy kitchen.

Except, of course, for the fact that she had a crossbow raised and leveled at Clara.

Clara held up her hands, shaking, to show she was no threat. "Please, I'm not trying to harm anyone." She kept her eyes trained on the crossbow, loaded, she was almost certain, with a vicious dart. A crossbow? The woman's dress wasn't fashionable, but she wasn't dressed in medieval getup, either.

"I don't know you. I know all the craftsmen."

"I'm sorry. I'm...new."

"There have been no new keys wrought that I don't know about. They are all accounted for." The woman's voice was clipped, her accent faint but clearly German. "Sit down. Hands stay up."

Awkwardly, Clara obeyed.

"And your name?"

No point in lying, Clara ascertained quickly. "Clara. Clara Ironwood."

"I don't know that name. It's not one of the old families.

But—she is a girl," the woman said, as if to herself. "Maiden name?" she barked.

"Ironwood. I'm not married."

"Mother's maiden name, then."

"Zimmerman."

"She was German." The woman waited, as though this were a question.

"Yes. My father's family was, too, but his folks changed their name when they immigrated and I suppose—"

"How did you get in here?"

Clara hoped the answer to that question would alleviate, rather than raise, the old woman's suspicion. "I used a key. It's a magnifying glass. I could show you."

The woman sucked in her lips, considering. "Slow. One hand. Show me."

Clara reached into her pocket and produced the lens. It gleamed in the light, almost seeming to wink at Clara, reassuring her it was all right.

"Hand it over."

Fear surged in Clara's chest. If she lost the key, she couldn't get home. She hesitated. She wouldn't get home if the woman shot her, either, she reasoned. Reluctantly, she held out the key.

"*Mein Gott.*" The woman turned the glass over in her hand. "I'd written it off as lost. Haven't seen Elias in decades." She locked her eyes on Clara. "Where did you get this?"

"My godfather sent it to me." She swallowed against a dry throat. "Christian Elias Thrushman."

"Thrushman, is it? Ha!" The woman sat down hard on the lip of the fountain, hiccuping with laughter. "Thrushman!" She set the crossbow down. "All right, girlie. Here's your key. For now."

Clara accepted the key and slipped it quickly into her pocket. "May I—may I ask your name?"

"You can ask whatever you want. Whether I answer is a different story. I'm still not entirely sure I trust you, even if you say you know Elias." She watched Clara intently for a long moment, as though she could read deceit in a person's eyes. Who knew? Clara considered. Maybe she could. "Magda. My name is Magda."

"Pleased to meet you, Magda," Clara said, knowing the polite exchange was a bit absurd.

Magda barked a short laugh. "Wish I could say the same, but truth be told, I don't know. Yet. Tell me what Elias has been up to."

"My godfather?"

"No children of his own?"

"No, he never married. He was very good friends with my parents, they asked him to be my godfather. I—what else do you want to know?"

Magda shrugged. "What *do* you know?"

Strange question. Until that moment, Clara would have said she knew her godfather well. They had spent every holiday and nearly every Sunday together when she was growing up. She worked alongside him for years. And yet now she found herself unsure of what to say. "He's a brilliant clockmaker," she began. "The most respected in Milwaukee."

"Milwaukee?" Magda interjected. "Fucking Milwaukee?"

Clara froze, completely out of her depth with this iron-haired spitfire rattling off a trail of German that she assumed were mostly curse words.

"I've been looking for him on this side of the Atlantic. Even sent some inquiries to contacts in New York. But godforsaken Milwaukee?"

"It's not that bad—" Clara began, wondering if this woman believed everything west of the United States' Eastern Seaboard to be a frontier hinterland.

"It's ridiculous, is what it is. But I suppose I see his logic, now that I consider it. Start over. Reinvent himself—well, halfway. He was always a good clockmaker." She pursed her lips. "Go on."

"He has a very nice little house near the lake. It's all full of things he's made—they're really works of art, toys and gadgets and things." She paused. "I apprenticed with him."

"And there it is." She nodded. "And he taught you how to use the key."

"He didn't teach me anything of the sort," Clara retorted, surprised by the vehemence in the words. "He sent me the key with a cryptic note and that was that. I didn't even know what it was."

Magda nodded again, slowly. "You weren't ready. Or he thought not—he was always so particular. God, no one ever lived up to the standards of Christian Elias!" She laughed ruefully, and Clara realized with a start—she really did know Godfather. "But for some reason he thought you needed it, and now. Or." She sucked in a long breath through her nose. "Best not to consider that. At any rate. How many times have you used the key?"

"Only a few times before."

"Thank God, I thought I was getting loose in my rounds. And not for long, those times?" Her eyes narrowed. "If Elias invited you in, you've as much right to be here as anyone. Once a craftsman, always a craftsman, and we've got no veto rights on anyone's apprentice. Always been that way."

"How long have you been here?" Clara asked.

"Me? Oh, I was even younger than you when I apprenticed and made my key."

"Then you don't...you don't live here."

She smiled strangely. "I go in and out. To be honest I'm here more often than not nowadays. Someone has to keep an eye on the place, to keep it safe."

"I'm sorry, I don't understand—"

"Of course you don't. Elias didn't bother telling you. Damn his eyes." She said it half annoyed, half amused, as though she really couldn't begrudge him anything. "This place is only for craftsmen. That is, the actual visiting it—it's for everyone, of course, whether they know it or not."

Clara shook her head. "Please, slow down—what do you mean, 'whether they know it or not'?"

Magda sighed. "I could strangle Elias for not training you properly, really. Selfish old fool. He always was, you know." Clara opened her mouth, then closed it again, not sure if she ought to agree or argue. "This place, the *anderwelt*, carries on a sort of relationship with what you'd probably call 'the real world.' Excepting, of course, that this world is maybe a lot more real than the other, come down to it." She paused, thoughtful. "At any rate. Creativity flows both ways. Things we do in our world show up here—you go visit the fairgrounds sometime and you'll see what I mean, new things sprouting up like mushrooms every other day. But you also visit the anderwelt mirror of a textile mill or a prison or a battlefield and you'll see that, too—this place holds all their dark ghosts."

"I think I saw—well, some apartments are like a slice of a fairy tale, and others are dark or plain and feel sad. And the fairgrounds—I've seen them, there's color and then there's blank space, and there's also a darkness like a shadow. Is that what you mean?"

Magda eyed her carefully. "Mostly, yes. Most of what you saw is what people on the other side made, and it's mirrored here. But sometimes a certain type of craftsfolk make things here that only exist here. I am one of those craftspeople, your godfather was one—is one still, I suppose. We curate this place so that it can hold all the dreams and imaginings of the rest of the world. We make things, refine things. Test out ideas and concepts where they can be real and alive instead of dead things." Dead things—Olympia had said the same thing. "Give ideas life here so they can become something over there, someday."

Clara let this idea roll around in her mind for a long moment—understanding with growing clarity the importance of this place beyond a mere fairyland for her to explore. "Then this is a sort of reserve of...ideas?"

"More like a reserve of the stuff ideas are made of. We tend to believe that nothing new or wonderful would ever be made again on the ordinary side without this place. Just think—all the Rembrandts and Beethovens and Edisons of the world relying on an old hag with a crossbow!"

Magda laughed, picking and then tossing a white stone flower growing out of the pavement. It burst into brilliant blue butterflies. Clara watched them scatter against the golden sky. "I apologize if I was a bit rough in my introductions," Magda said, gesturing to the bow. "Something's happening, with the Exposition. You said you saw blank space—that's normal. It's not good, but it's normal. But the shadows, the dark spaces—that's not normal. I had to make sure you weren't involved in it. That you weren't doing anything you weren't supposed to be doing."

"You mean...I shouldn't be here?"

"No, you're one of us. You apprenticed with Elias, even if he didn't train you right. He gave you a key. You can come and go as you please. But someone, or a few someones, must be doing something, something very wrong in the anderwelt here in Paris, and it's causing those black spots you saw. Like I said—coming here is only for craftsmen. Not businessmen or politicians or any of those donkeys' asses. They'd try to use it. Gain from it. That would ruin it. There are places that have been ruined already," she added ominously.

Clara waited, but the woman didn't continue, even though what she alluded to felt very important. She needed to know more, to fill the holes in her understanding. Tentatively, she asked Magda another question. "Do you have an apprentice?"

"Hell no."

"All right, then." Clara folded her hands, not sure what she was supposed to say, or do, next in this absurd conversation. She was sure Magda had plenty of answers to her questions about the otherworld—what Magda called the anderwelt—but she seemed loath to divulge anything. Was that because she didn't trust Clara, or some other reason? Without any way of knowing, Clara fell back on the one thing she knew Godfather had always appreciated. "Would you care to show me what you've been working on?"

The old woman's eyes lit up. "Are you sure? It's not quite finished."

"I'd love to!"

"Well, all right." She caught up her crossbow again and, seeing Clara's eyes follow it warily, cackled. "It can't hurt you anyway, girlie. See?" She lifted the weapon to show Clara a tightly wound metallic netting where the bolt should have been. "Can't harm anyone in the anderwelt—that's a hard and fast rule we follow—but I've rigged this to fire a net and hold any miscreants I come across."

"Does that happen often?" Clara asked, peering at the ingenious design, relieved that she had been mistaken and the old lady couldn't have skewered her after all.

"Nope." Without another word, Magda slung her crossbow across her back and marched off along the river. Clara ran to catch up.

Chapter Fourteen

"I'M QUITE NEARLY done," Magda said. She knelt next to a carousel perhaps two feet high. Clara didn't show her disappointment. She had expected a wonder like those she had already seen—the glass bridge, the sunrise garden, the mechanical ballet. Instead, this was a child's toy, beautifully rendered, but nothing she couldn't have found in a finer workshop in the ordinary world.

"You see," Magda continued, "I like working in wood—all sorts of wood. You've probably found that Elias preferred, often, to combine materials, to play with all sorts of stone and metal and glass, and weird stuff, too. Gingerbread. Marzipan." Magda laughed. "Things you never would have thought of. But wood here—it breathes. It takes longer than other materials. It's very demanding, but I like it."

Clara nodded again, even though she wasn't quite sure what Magda meant. The old woman plucked a figurine from the carousel and showed it to Clara. It was a leopard, a perfect miniature of a sinuous cat, lithe form and thick muscles carved expertly into the wood. Magda had painted it with exceptional care, each spot a constellation of black dots. Clara accepted the figurine.

It was warm. Not just from Magda's hand—the figurine exuded its own heat. Though perfectly still, the leopard was the same temperature as a kitten curled in the sunlight. Clara peered at the cat, even more surprised by what she realized next. Magda had not been speaking metaphorically—the wood breathed. The leopard itself didn't breathe, not through its partially open jaws or minute nostrils, but the wood had a gentle pulse of breath in her hands.

"I'm just fiddling with the details now," Magda said. "Really, it could be finished. Shall we? I really ought to finish it."

Clara handed the leopard back to Magda, fingers trembling a little. She didn't know what Magda meant by "finish" as the carousel looked complete. Perhaps some last touch of paint or an adjustment to the finials. Magda fitted the leopard back into place, and then turned the carousel gently on its base, revealing the mechanism to wind it. So it was just a toy—Clara hid her disappointment as Magda wound the carousel.

It began to spin, the familiar up-and-down and roundabout of carousel rhythm. And then, slowly, almost imperceptibly at first, it began to grow. Clara blinked—was it possible? Like a flower unfurling in the sunlight, but far faster, the carousel expanded. Soon the leopard was the size of a house cat, then a greyhound, and then finally, as the mechanism slowed and the carousel came to a halt, it was life-size, along with, in proportion, every other animal in the carousel's menagerie. Horses, zebras, an elephant, a lion, a pair of ostriches—all grown from fitting in Clara's palm to far outpacing her.

More miraculous, they were alive.

She noticed the lion first. He stretched, though rooted in place by the pole, and shook his shaggy mane. The wooden rivulets

Magda had carved broke into thousands of individual honey-colored strands. The elephant tested his trunk, and the ostriches both discovered that their necks would allow them to turn and preen their feathered rumps. Clara stood still as a statue, eyes wide in utter disbelief.

"Well, it's finished now, anyway. I always have the hardest time deciding when I've fiddled around with the details enough. I'd go on forever, probably, if I didn't one day just say, 'Enough!' to myself." She chuckled, then glanced at Clara, who felt as though all the blood had drained from her face. "Oh, dear. You must think me horribly cruel!"

Magda stepped through the menagerie to the inside of the carousel and pulled a rope—brilliant scarlet and tied in a huge knot at one end. Clara recognized it from its miniature, a bit of embroidery silk. The poles retracted into the ceiling and the animals were free. "You see, I wouldn't cage them permanently. How awful! No, this is just their roosting place."

Clara's heart went into her throat as the lion took a grand leap from the carousel.

"Don't fret, they don't eat meat!" Magda called. "They don't eat at all. And they're made to be quite tame." She patted the flanks of a jet-black horse with pink feathers in its mane. "Given I meant them to be ridden, they'd have to be."

"Of course," Clara managed to say through near-frozen lips.

"Oh! Oh, you've never seen—" Magda cackled. "Your face, it's like—how do you say? Spun sugar. Those little sugar dolls they make at Christmas, all white!" She slapped her knees.

"How does it work?"

"What do you get if you cross an elephant and a rhinoceros?"

"What? I—what?"

"Ele-phino!" The old woman laughed again. The lion, seated next to her, tossed his mane, annoyed at the sudden sound. *"Hell if I know?* Get it, it's a pun, in English—I've been waiting to use that one."

"Right." Clara wondered, for the first time, how long Magda had been on her own in the otherworld.

"I don't know," Magda continued, more soberly. "I don't know how it works, not the way I know how the gears of a clock go together or how a mill wheel turns. I just know how to use it. This place takes good workmanship and—well, you see."

"It brings it to life?"

"Not precisely." Magda stroked the lion's mane, settling him. "The materials here are alive already. They're just waiting to be…let out, so to speak." The lion emitted a loud rumble not unlike a purr. "I figured if I was going to make a lion, I'd want him to purr like a kitten," she explained. "See, if you look closely—he's still made of wood."

Clara approached the huge cat with faltering trepidation. It watched her with large golden eyes but let her lay her hands on his flank. Sure enough, her fingers met textured wood, not a feline's fur.

"You can't tell anyone," Magda said quietly. "That's the hardest part. You have a husband, you have children—you can't even tell them. It's to be kept absolutely secret. You find an apprentice, and that's the only person you ever tell." She scratched behind the lion's ear and he flopped onto his side like a kitten, great padded paws in the air. "Elias always was a fool, but to send you the key without telling you a damn thing—that was the stupidest thing he's ever done." Still, she didn't sound angry, exactly. Lines of worry formed between her dark brown eyes.

"I haven't told anyone," Clara said hurriedly. "In case you were concerned—anyone out there would think I was crazy, anyway."

Magda barked her short laugh. "That they would, too. Most of them. But there's some, some who have heard legends of a place where wood and metal come to life, where time stops, where you can drink light and eat the scent of springtime and well..."

"I'd want to go there, too."

"You'd want to come for the right kinds of reasons," Magda answered. "I can see that already—you want to make your own creations, let life spring under your hands just for the joy of it. You like the work. Hell, some people would just want to see it and that's a beautiful thing in its own way, too. But other people." She shook her head.

"The donkeys' asses?"

"Those ones. There are people in this world who only see it for what they can beat out of it. What every corner of the world is worth, how much silver they can wring from every rock or hunk of wood." She sighed. "They wouldn't get what they want out of this place, but they'd chew it up and leave it for dead." She stood up suddenly. "Let me show you something."

She didn't wait for an answer, but Clara followed anyway. Magda didn't slow down, even as they passed marvels that Clara could have spent hours gawking at—medieval towers made of thick vines instead of ordinary apartments, waterfalls of silk, a garden of glass. The lion trailed them, as though not sure what it was supposed to do with itself.

Magda finally found territory Clara recognized, even on this side of the veil. The Seine, for one, meandered on its way through the otherworld in an identical footprint to the everyday map of Paris. Even clearer an orienting landmark, a silver spire rose toward the sky, the Eiffel Tower mirrored and magnified, both more delicate and more imposing, glistening like a spiderweb coated in dew.

But Magda wasn't interested in the tower; instead, she pointed to a scorched shadow that took up at least a city block of Exposition grounds along the Seine. It was one of the dark spots Clara had seen the last time she had been in the otherworld. The decaying gray landscape strained against a golden haze where it ended. A sour smell wafted from the dusty gray mounds in front of her, displacing the pleasant lemon-and-mint scent that had filled the air moments before.

"What is this?"

"It's dead." Any joking in the old woman's face was gone. "Someone killed the anderwelt here. It's not the first time, of course. These kinds of blights have been appearing in the anderwelt since *handwerkerin* first started recording, but they were rare. Always tied to specific kinds of *incidents*. But seeing landscape like this just dotted with blights, it's new."

"Blights?"

"You got a better name for that?" Magda threw an angry hand toward the desolation in front of them. "It lasts for years. Decades, sometimes. The anderwelt itself is injured and takes a long time to repair. And it affects the other side, too. Where the anderwelt is maintained, cared for, it feeds the other side. I reckon nothing would ever blossom over there if the ground wasn't fertile here, if that god-awful metaphor makes sense."

"It does," Clara said slowly, appreciating with growing clarity that this place wasn't merely a place at all, nor was it simply reflection. It was a source, a spring, and its effects on the world she knew ran deep.

"Someone is doing this. There are only a few ways—" Magda sucked her lips over her teeth, disgusted. "You can't harm anyone on purpose, here in the anderwelt. Spilled blood, it blights the land."

Clara recoiled. "I—I wouldn't, but—that means someone did that, here? Someone killed or—"

"Maybe. But there's two ways of killing something here, and the other one is more likely what happened in this case." Magda turned suddenly and looked her full in the eyes, startling Clara with her intensity. "What is made here cannot be taken back to the other side. It must stay here." She paused. "Do you understand? You cannot take anything with you that you make here."

"Yes," Clara said, "I understand. Anything I make here—it stays here."

"Nothing of the anderwelt can cross over. If it is taken back, it's a dead thing, and the anderwelt is blighted by that action, too." Magda glared at the darkened expanse in front of her. "They don't just happen out of nowhere. Someone did this, and it has something to do with the Exposition. It must. Why and how is what I can't gather."

"Now I understand the crossbow."

"I had to be sure about you. I'm still not sure you're *not* involved, in some convoluted way, but I'm pretty sure you aren't intending to be."

"Never," Clara whispered, horrified by the scene in front of her. She took a step toward it, and Magda grabbed her arm and yanked her back.

"Don't. It's poison, not just for the land but for people. It's chaos inside a blight—looks static from the outside, but in there it's waves tossing time and space and, right quick, your sanity along with it."

"I can't imagine anyone doing this on purpose," Clara said. "This place is—it's—" She found herself entirely without words.

"I don't know who would be a big enough fool, either. But I need to figure it out, and soon." She glared at the formless shadows pulsing as though barely contained. "There's a delicate balance, and if too much of the anderwelt is blighted, it starts to spread. It could ruin all of Paris, all of—who knows? I sure as hell don't know."

"*You* need to figure it out?" The anderwelt was still new to Clara, and only partially understood, but she felt an overwhelming protectiveness as she began to understand it could be harmed. "Isn't there anyone else who could help, or—"

"I don't know who to trust!" Magda half shouted. "The person making these blights has got to be a handwerker, or maybe a group of them—hell, a whole guild could be involved, I don't know." She turned solemn brown eyes to Clara. "Be careful. Careful who you trust with anything. The world is changing out there and it's rippling through into this place."

Clara nodded, appreciating the gravity of a situation she had never meant to tumble into but unsure what role she was supposed to play in it. "I should go soon," she said. "I haven't quite figured out how to mark time here compared to out there."

"You probably never will," Magda said. "You know how time passes like water, like sand through the hourglass, unnoticed, when you're deep in your work? Best I can figure it, that's how time works here, too."

"I want to learn how to make things," Clara ventured. Godfather had sent the key, but she wasn't officially an apprentice—at least, not in the way Magda seemed to suggest the process worked.

"You have a key. You're allowed."

"Yes, but am I... is it..."

Magda softened. "You're allowed. Don't go trying to make anything big or difficult right away, you might royally botch it. Start small. At any rate, I'm here almost all the time now. Like I said, keeping an eye on the place. But here." She dug a wrinkled card from her pocket. "My address in Paris."

Clara decided that was as close to an invitation as she would ever get, and left Magda playing tug-of-war with her lion.

Chapter Fifteen

CLARA FOUND THAT she couldn't stay away from the other Paris. She wouldn't have said she neglected her work for the Exposition, but she didn't bring it home with her any longer. Instead, she had the key out of her pocket almost as soon as she was through her door, slipping into the otherworld.

At first, she observed. This was her usual method—on being presented with a broken clock or a set of plans from Fritz, she pored over what she could see first. And there was no shortage of things to see in the other Paris—even in her own apartment building, jungles flourished, castles grew, gardens bloomed out of stones.

Feeling like an intruder, but supremely curious, Clara let herself into Annabelle's apartment. Locks rarely seemed to occur in this world, she noticed—perhaps craftsmen could fashion locks, but they didn't tend to show up on their own. She gasped as she opened the door—while her own apartment had stayed roughly the same size, with somewhat higher ceilings, Annabelle's spread before her, an entire sunbathed estate. All of Annabelle's characteristic chaos and color sprawled over a spacious piazza and gardens.

Two constants seemed to emerge—first, most of the creations were unintentional, brilliant projections of what people imagined in their ordinary lives. Few seemed to be creations of craftsmen, even the fortress made of stones and seashells in the courtyard below, which Clara guessed was the fancy of the children in the apartment two floors below her, whom she had often seen building with castoff bricks and a bucket of shells from a trip to the shore. Second, the spaces of blank plainness were few but seemed tied to particular places—spaces Clara realized were empty and stale in the real world. Out of one apartment where, in the ordinary Paris, she often heard shouts and long silences, a thin gray pallor sifted like a fog.

Finally, she had to reconcile herself to the fact that she would never see everything and if she ever wanted to learn to craft as Magda did, she would have to begin sometime. She began simply. Sitting cross-legged in the courtyard next to the shell castle with tools that she found in the same place she stored her tools in her ordinary apartment, she fashioned a small bird of waxed paper and wire that had appeared in a cabinet, right where she would have stored them had she bought them herself. She gave the bird a simple mechanism at its heart so it would flap its wings when wound.

It was a design she had made before, several times, with Godfather looking on. He'd been pleased at first, at the taut wings fluttering the little bird upward and then allowing it to gently settle on the table again. Clara had swelled with pride that he had looked on it with any favor, and had promptly made several more, in varying colors of marbled paper. Like little jewels of sapphire and ruby and emerald, they had cluttered her worktable for days as she refined and tuned each one.

But when she had suggested that they might put them up for sale in his little shop, Godfather had grown cross and shaken his head. "Stuff and nonsense!" he'd growled. "I don't sell novelties for idle people to gawk at."

She could still remember the tight shame in her chest and the heat that spread across her cheeks. She had shoved the birds into a trunk, hidden in her room.

Clara held her breath as she wound the iridescent purple bird in her hand. The ones she had made in Milwaukee could only rise and gently fall, the mechanics allowing for no variation in that singular trick. She turned the pin on this bird and let it fly.

The bird whirred to life under her hands. The sheen of the paper shifted as the bird took to its wings, flexing the wires and bending them under its own volition. Before she could let out her breath, it darted upward and arced over her head. Then it swooped toward her, barely brushing her outstretched hand with its paper wing before flying off again. Clara laughed out loud.

In the days that followed, she made a few more simple designs, copies and variations on things she had made before. She was grateful for the slow progression of time while she was working, or she would never have had time to sleep at all.

Work for the Exposition accelerated, and she found that the bursts of making "live" things in the other place only made her more inclined toward solving the many riddles of her own Palace of Illusions when she returned.

The morning after she had made and planted an orchid out of silk and copper wire in the anderwelt, Clara set to work on the revised lighting plans for her palace, hoping she had read the particulars on the electric bulbs correctly. She ran the math—the voltage should be correct, unless they had ordered the wrong size bulbs. They'd done that for the exterior of the Palace of Optics, and the whole schematic had to be reworked. Clara would have pitied the poor bent-shouldered Parisian man who had spent the past week reconfiguring wiring except he had once stolen her sandwich from her desk and had never apologized.

"Fräulein! You may thank me later. I may have just arranged a job interview for you." Fritz dropped a neatly folded piece of paper on her desk.

"Herr Krieger." Clara unfolded the paper—an address in Fritz's clipped handwriting. "What is that supposed to mean?"

"While you were out this morning—"

"I was in a meeting with the electrical workers, not 'out.'"

"In any case. While you were out, a fellow came in looking for you, and I arranged for you to meet with him later."

Clara's stomach clenched. "Who was this—this fellow?"

"Why, a countryman of mine!"

"You knew him?"

"No, he's from Nuremberg, and I am from…" He waited. "Heidelberg, dear Miss Ironwood, I have told you a dozen times."

Clara forced decorum. "Of course. Was he about my age, pale green eyes, a little squirrelly?"

"I do not know what it means to be a squirrel in your manner of speaking, but yes. The same young man, in fact, who we saw at the fairgrounds some time ago. He left his card—well, his hotel's card. He said he assumed work and the holiday had gotten in the way of your meeting with him."

"Not exactly," she said. "I have no interest in meeting with him. He's an acquaintance of someone I really prefer not to associate with any longer."

"He said it was quite important. Now, what you do with your

time is not my business, but I have already accounted for your being gone all afternoon. So." He dropped the card pointedly on her desk. "There you are."

Clara considered ignoring the summons completely, but Nussbaum represented the specter of Godfather and a tangled knot of unknowns about the anderwelt, and she let curiosity win out in the end. She found the hotel so easily that she didn't have time to consider what she would do when she got there. She couldn't very well loiter around the lobby waiting to see Nussbaum, or prowl the hallways for some sign, lest he surprise her and force a conversation. No, she was completely unprepared for that. Movement by her foot startled her—a mouse skittered into an alleyway. Perturbed, she went into the hotel's lobby.

It was a nice enough establishment, not opulent but not run-down or dodgy, either. The sort of place middling businessmen might frequent, or students with a bit of money.

The front desk was unstaffed, but a maid dusted the mantel and shelves in the adjacent parlor. "Pardon," Clara began, stumbling through her French. The maid stopped and waited. *"Pardonez-moi, savez-vous un homme? Un homme*, um, named, *nomme?* Nussbaum?"

"Vous cherchez quelqu'un?" The woman watched her with a quizzical expression, waiting for Clara to continue.

She had to talk again. Damn it. *"Je suis* looking—I, um. Nussbaum?" she repeated.

"Il y a un homme qui s'appelle Nussbaum ici, oui—voulez vous parler avec Nussbaum?"

"Nussbaum, *oui*, Nussbaum!"

The maid sighed and set down her dusting cloth. *"Un moment, s'il vous plaît."* It was only when the woman disappeared up the stairs and Clara heard knocking on a door that she realized that she had entirely misunderstood the maid.

She ducked around the corner into a cloakroom just as Nussbaum appeared, following the maid down the stairs. The maid sighed the loud exhalation of the beleaguered and explained what Clara could only assume was some variation of "an insane woman came in babbling your name but she's gone now."

To Clara's horror, Nussbaum didn't immediately return upstairs, but settled in the parlor, picking up a newspaper. He unfolded it and apparently found some article worth reading. Clara bit her lip. Someone, at some point, was bound to come into the cloakroom, and if Nussbaum was still sitting right outside, Clara wasn't sure what she would do.

The front door of the hotel opened. Clara had a single moment to decide—make a dash to slip out behind whoever came in or shrink back into the cloakroom and hope the person entering didn't need to hang up his hat.

She waited too long and was forced into the latter choice. Fortunately, the man who entered bypassed the cloakroom and made for the parlor.

Where he stopped and greeted Nussbaum. Curious, Clara edged toward the front of the cloakroom, hoping to overhear some hint of who the man calling himself Nathanael Nussbaum might be. Unfortunately, the conversation was carried out entirely in German. She sighed. If she was less than proficient in French, she was useless in German. Still, she kept her ears tuned to the conversation, which sounded, to her estimation, professional and clipped.

She edged out of the cloakroom, hoping for a look at one or both of the men. She saw the back of Nussbaum's head, his light brown waves combed carefully into place, and an older man—

She yanked herself back into the forest of coats before he could see her. Sandmann. Her godfather's awful pustule of a friend from—from where, exactly? From Germany, from Nuremberg like Godfather, she'd always supposed. What could he be doing here, and how did he know Nussbaum? Well, she reasoned, it did suggest that, after all, Nussbaum really did know her godfather.

Suddenly Nussbaum's voice rose a step and, she thought, sounded firmer. The other man volleyed a return, more agitated in tone. The maid hurried from the room. Clara heard her footfalls on the staircase. In the confusion of voices, she was sure she made out a word she knew—*anderwelt*. And another. *Clara*.

She pulled back into the coats, black wool obscuring her from a casual glance into the room. She waited until she heard the entry open and close again, Sandmann departing, and then footfalls on the stairs. Quiet. Then she crept to the doorway and, assured the parlor was empty, slipped out into the street.

Heart pounding, she pulled gloves over shaking hands. The appearance of Sandmann in Paris shouldn't have bothered her so much; he'd never done anything untoward or criminal. He just looked like someone who might want to. At any rate, affiliation with him did not endear her to Nussbaum—though at the same time, it seemed they were not on entirely friendly terms. Perhaps, she thought, she should return and meet with Nussbaum, at least to hear what he had to say. As she left the door and swept around the corner, her foot caught the umbrella of a passing gentleman and the two of them sprawled, altogether indecorously, on the sidewalk.

Chapter Sixteen

THE CEMENT BIT into Clara's elbow and she blinked back tears brought on not only by the sharp pain, but by humiliation. *"Excusez-moi,* I was in a rush—I..." She trailed off, swallowing actual sobs that threatened to emerge and embarrass her further.

"Mademoiselle!" The stranger reached down a gloved hand and took hers. "It was entirely my fault! And I am terribly sorry!"

She let the stranger lift her from the ground—his arm was strong, she noticed, though he was dressed in a finely tailored suit and an expensive-looking overcoat. A young man, she realized as they found themselves face-to-face. "No, it was me, I wasn't paying attention."

"Hardly, I am—oh no! You are bleeding, here." His hand brushed her elbow, where she was managing to bleed through her sturdy wool dress. He gestured toward the hotel. "Please, let me help, we could step inside and—"

"No!" Clara half shouted, then flushed. "I'm so sorry, there was a man there, I was trying—"

"Say no more." The stranger put a finger to his lips and shared a conspiratorial smile. "I see precisely what has occurred. You are entirely the victim here—of some blackguard's harassment and of my innate clumsiness. I cannot make amends for the former, but for the latter, please." He held out his arm.

Clara's thoughts raced. She glanced back toward the hotel. The door hadn't reopened, Nussbaum hadn't emerged—but perhaps, she reasoned, remaining in the company of another person wasn't the worst idea.

"Very well," she replied. "I would be much appreciative of a few minutes to catch my breath, at any rate."

"There is a very nice—and quiet—little place I know. Just around this corner."

"That would be perfect, thank you." Clara allowed him to lead the way to the next cross street. "I didn't catch your name."

"I, being a boor as well as a clumsy lout, didn't give it. Edouard Gagnet." He bowed his head slightly. He was rather nice-looking, Clara thought, if she let herself think it—thick dark waves and eyes that couldn't decide if they were gray or blue. He had a sharp nose and an easy smile, and she found herself smiling along, which was quite out of character.

"Clara Ironwood," she returned.

"Here it is," Edouard said, steering them into a narrow café with a bottle-green awning. "I will ask after some clean cloths for your arm, yes?"

"Yes, thank you," Clara said, sitting in a half-hidden corner and unbuttoning her sleeve cuff. She rolled up the sleeve to the elbow, wincing as the fabric separated from the large scrape.

"Ah, that looks wretched." Edouard returned and, without another word, gently took her arm and pressed a cool, damp cloth to the battered elbow. She flushed, but he didn't seem to notice as he deftly washed the blood from her arm and dressed it with a bandage.

"Thank you," she stammered as he withdrew his hand. "They were quick with the bandages."

"They know me here," he replied. "Ah, that makes it sound as though I am always in here needing to clean up blood—no! They know that I am a doctor, that makes far more sense."

"I had assumed you were a boxer," Clara joked. "Maybe a bull-fighter? Something requiring plenty of bandages."

"Skills far beyond my scope," Edouard said with a laugh. "I am merely adequate at patch and mend work, I'm afraid."

"You seem more than adequate."

"And this was a very complicated case, yes," he said, knitting his eyebrows together. "You're very lucky I came along when I did."

"I can see that now," Clara said. "Is this how you get all your patients? Trip them on the street and then offer assistance?"

"Hardly! You wound me!" He laughed brightly, then sobered slightly. "No, typically I work in the public hospital, l'Hôtel Dieu. The poor and infirm of Paris require very little provocation before requiring medical aid, unfortunately."

"I'm sorry, I didn't mean—"

"Not at all! My work is a dismal affair, what can be said? It's why I spend so much time in the cafés and the parks instead. It's good to see people happy, in good health, enjoying all that this life has to offer." He leaned toward her with an impish grin. "Which is why I think we ought to split a bottle of *good* wine instead of merely acceptable wine."

"Oh, I couldn't, I have to get back to work—"

"Work! With such an egregious injury! What sort of charlatan do you work for who would make such demands?"

"The Exposition," Clara replied with a smile.

"Surely they can spare you for an afternoon—wait, what do you do, exactly? There are no dancers, no actresses, yet needed at the fairgrounds?"

"You assume too much. I'm not nearly that interesting. I'm a clockmaker."

"That is sufficiently more interesting!" He flagged the waitress and rattled off an order for what sounded like significantly more than a bottle of wine. "You will tell me all about the intricacies of clockwork and how it brought you here."

Clara listed the reasons she shouldn't concede in her head— work waited, she didn't even know this man, what would people think—but she remembered the chagrin she had felt while talking with Annabelle. All the caution in the world didn't guarantee any happiness in the end, and who could tell what the chance not taken meant forfeiting, really? In any case, Edouard Gagnet— *Doctor* Gagnet, she amended—seemed an upright sort of fellow, and this was lunch in a quiet café, not a midnight tryst.

Which was how Clara found herself whiling away an afternoon over a bottle of Bordeaux, telling Dr. Gagnet about everything from the intricacies of music boxes to the progress on the Exposition pavilions.

"I have heard—there are many mechanical marvels to be unveiled at the Exposition. Are my sources correct?" Dr. Gagnet refilled her glass.

"All sorts, I suppose—there are pavilions for agriculture and industry and the military, beyond of course what the individual nations will provide as displays."

"Certainly, yes, like the last Paris Exposition. Of course, I was young then! But the Galerie des Machines was a wonder. Have you heard of any more unusual or novel plans for this Exposition?

There are rumors of clockwork creations, which is why I ask you," he added, but the question seemed almost forced.

"No, not anything beyond what one would find in the most up-to-date industries—that is the point of the displays, isn't it?"

"Of course, of course!" He prompted her with more questions about her work, and she didn't consider until the bottle of wine was nearly empty and the waiters had moved the awnings to block the late afternoon sun that he had given her hardly any information about himself.

"Have you lived in Paris your whole life?" she asked, guessing this a fairly innocuous question.

"Me? Oh, well, yes," he said, startled, it seemed, to have the conversation turn to him. "Do you enjoy it? People have such diverse opinions, I find, about large cities."

Clara paused. A month ago, even, she might have said she found Paris tolerable, pleasant on occasion, but nothing she would seek out intentionally. Now the city had begun to creep into her bones. She found she looked forward to her walks to work, watching the city unfold in the mornings. She wondered how much of this had to do with seeing the mirrored magic of otherworld Paris, and how much was simply getting to know the real face of the city.

"I didn't think I would like it," she confessed. "But I find that I do."

"There are such a great many things to do, I find I cannot make up my mind and wander about the park instead!" He laughed. "Do you ever do that? Just wander along the Seine or through one of the gardens?"

"I can't say that I do," Clara replied. It seemed the sort of thing a young man was able to do that roused suspicion when a woman did it.

"Then you must allow me to call on you sometime and take you for a stroll. That is what Americans do for socializing, as well, yes?"

"I suppose that would be rather nice," Clara stammered, shocked both that he offered and that she was inclined to accept. She fished a card from her pocketbook.

"What about Tuesday next? I have—" He glanced at the card. "Oh, but this cannot be your residence! It is practically inside the Grand Palais."

"Practically," Clara said with a wry smile. "It's my work address. I'm there far more often than I'm home."

"Ah, I see." A troubled look crossed the young doctor's face, but he quickly pocketed the card and resumed his pleasant smile. "Tuesday next, at four o'clock. And now I am afraid that work calls to me, as well—I am required in the ward tonight." He dropped several more francs than were necessary on the table.

"Good luck," Clara said.

"And *bonne santé* to you, mademoiselle!" He dipped a quick bow and left Clara with her sore elbow quite forgotten.

Chapter Seventeen

A LATE WINTER evening had already begun to creep around the corners and behind the trees when Clara left the café. The wan light made the streets look softer and seemed to slow the pace of the Parisians walking home or to early suppers. Soon the deepening chill of night would speed their steps again, but Clara enjoyed the easy, contemplative quiet.

She couldn't help but smile to herself. Doctor Gagnet. That would shut Mother up if she dropped one more time into one of her letters that Paul Howard, who had called last spring, was getting married in June and wasn't it too bad she hadn't spent more time with Jeremy Blanding as he was starting to take Maisie Cartwright out for drives in his new surrey. Of course, there were far better reasons to enjoy the company of a handsome young Frenchman. Beginning, she allowed herself to think with uncharacteristic abandon, with the way his thick hair waved over his ears.

She caught herself laughing a little, and buttoned back up. No need to wander the streets looking like a madwoman, she chided. And then she noticed something that erased the last hints of a smile from her face.

A thick, dark shadow oozed from around the corner, pooling in the pavement cracks and sidling up the wall.

Clara slowed her gait even more, trying to ascertain what exactly she saw. Nothing seemed to be casting the shadow—that was impossible, she insisted to herself, even as the shadow began to splay out along the wall and move upward. It reminded her of a reptile, spastic motion on first one side and then the other, and capable, it seemed, of moving far more quickly than she was.

She glanced around—no one else had come down this side street, no source for the shadow and no chance of help, either. She edged toward the main thoroughfare, and the shadow dribbled down the wall into a puddle at its base.

She nearly ran to the relative safety of the easily flowing crowd. Looking back, she saw the puddle begin to roll in thin waves, lapping at the edges of the wall, slipping into a storm drain bit by bit. She restrained her speed, not wanting to look desperate or attract attention, but she willed the pedestrians around her to move faster, faster damn it all, before that horrific black thing sprouted up again.

As she approached her apartment building, she broke and trotted through the archway into the courtyard. She looked from side to side like a hunted deer, wondering if she could scent the awful shadow, what it would smell like. As she reached the stair, she spotted a dark patch growing beneath a gutter downspout.

With crawling horror, she watched as the formless shadow grew legs, no—fingers, long deft fingers. It gripped the wall and the downspout and began to climb.

Clara ceased caring what she looked like. She didn't stop to calculate how quickly it could move in relation to her footfalls. She just ran.

Her feet smacked the steps and the stairwell echoed—for the

first time, she hoped she might bother the neighbors, that they might come out and yell at her. The shadow kept pace with her, snaking its long tendrils upward.

Halfway to her apartment, she realized what a very stupid mistake she had made. What assurance was there in going into her empty apartment? What would doors and locks do against a shadow? It might seep under the door. It might drip through the keyhole.

Panic rose like bile in her throat as she reached Annabelle's apartment and pounded on the door.

The shadow's tendrils slipped over the railing at the far end of the hallway.

The door swung open. Annabelle raised an eyebrow. "What in God's name, Clara? You look—"

Clara hushed her. Fearing the worst, she turned and looked down the hall.

The shadow froze. Then, faster than the blink of an eye, it retreated down the wall again, out of sight.

"What in the world?" Annabelle let Clara push her inside, but not without several protestations. "You look like you've been stalked by the devil himself."

Maybe that's what it was, Clara thought. The devil himself—to hell with all the horns and pitchfork rigmarole, nothing could be as terrifying as that black shadow. "I don't know," she finally said. "I—"

Clara stopped herself and took a steadying breath. She couldn't go telling her neighbor that she had been followed home by a shadow. "I had lunch with a man," she finally stammered.

"Yes. You're right. That's horrifying." Annabelle slumped against the doorframe. Clara noticed that her eyes were rimmed red.

"I'm sorry, I came at a bad time."

"No, no, it's—" Annabelle paced across the room, dodging a stack of magazines as she raked her fingers through her hair. "You tell me about what happened."

"There's nothing to tell, really. I just—it was after that, I..." Clara hesitated. "I thought someone was following me."

"Same fellow?"

"I'm not sure." Clara considered this. She had no idea what the shadow was, let alone if it had some connection to Nussbaum or, she considered, Sandmann. Certainly it had nothing to do with Dr. Gagnet—it was related, somehow, to the magic of the other-world, but bent horribly wrong.

"You're going to have to grow a slightly thicker skin if you're going to get along swimming in this sea of cads." Annabelle flopped on the sofa, startling Hector. Not only had she certainly been crying, Clara noted, but there were dark circles under her eyes.

Clara bit back a retort—of course she looked oversensitive, had she been this distraught over a mere leer from an untoward man. But of course she couldn't explain that she had been stalked by a sentient shadow. Instead, she sat gingerly next to Annabelle, so as not to upset the tower of teacups on the sofa's arm. "What happened?" she asked softly.

"Oh, more of the same." She sighed. "You don't want the whole sordid thing."

"But I do."

"You don't! No one does. No one wants to see what happens when the curtain falls, when the lights go out. Everyone *knows*. But all those people with all their money, they pretend they don't know. Maybe if you pretend you don't know something long enough, you forget it even exists, I don't know."

"A man, then."

"Men! Plenty of them." Annabelle kicked the steamer trunk that served as her table. "No, not like that. You *don't* know, do you? How it works? All the theaters do it, all the way up to the Paris Opera Ballet. Special receptions for the subscribers, the expectation to go make nice with them in the salon after the show. Let them have a look up close at what they saw onstage. No changing out of the tulle and corsages, no sir. Give them a nice personal show. And if they like that show, they'll pay for more. Some ballerinas live in the nicest apartments in Paris. Kept very well, all quite high-end. For a time, anyway."

Clara's stomach turned. "You mean you have to—"

"Oh, it's all up to our discretion, so they say! That's the worst part of it. VanNeeve knows who does and who doesn't, and if you're resistant to the point of offense, well." She pinched her lips together and took a long breath through her nose. Clara waited. "He was a lawyer. Not a terribly unkind fellow, but there are limits of what I will entertain. He complained. And I'm fired."

"Fired! Annabelle, that's awful—that can't even be allowed, it's not part of your job…" She stopped herself. It was, she realized, fully part of Annabelle's job to carry on the facade of the danseuse backstage, in the patrons' salon, to allow the audience their continued fantasy. "I'm so sorry. If you need anything—"

"I don't know what I need. I need to spit in VanNeeve's eye and I need to burn down that damn salon and I need to have a good cry—another one—and I need to find a new job and I need to make every degenerate in this city regret ogling my calves and…" She stopped. "I need a lot of things, I suppose."

"We all do," Clara replied quietly. "But I suppose we can start with a cup of tea and some ginger cookies Herr Krieger sent home with me. Fair?"

Annabelle forced a small smile. "Fair."

Chapter Eighteen

CLARA WORRIED THAT the shadow—or something worse—could return as night fell and she went back to her apartment, tin of ginger cookies thoroughly demolished. What if it found her sleeping? she wondered. What if it found her alone at all?

There wasn't, she reminded herself, much to do about it. She took stock of what she knew, as though some pattern or solution would present itself. Godfather had introduced her, albeit in an unorthodox manner, to a secret otherworld. No one outside a very small circle was supposed to know about the place. And yet a creature made of shadow—that had to be of the otherworld, not this one.

She sighed. There were only two people she knew and trusted who she could talk to. Godfather, and that was impossible. And Magda.

She sat up straighter. Magda—of course. The appearance of a living shadow stalking her would certainly fall under the umbrella of strange dealings when it came to the anderwelt, and Magda would surely want to know about it. After all, why would the magic of the anderwelt be following Clara home?

She pulled Magda's card from her pocketbook. She wasn't sure if Magda would even be there, in the same Paris she was; the old woman had mentioned spending much of her time in the other Paris. Under normal circumstances, she wouldn't have minded the short walk to the address on the card. Tonight, however, the darkness pressed against the windows and Clara shivered. Did shadows prefer the dark? she wondered. What if that thing got more powerful in the absence of light? After all, it emerged in the evening, with the wan light and lengthening dusk. Her throat tightened.

No, she wasn't leaving her apartment.

Unless.

There was one way to leave her apartment without really leaving at all. She pulled the lens from her pocket. With the now-familiar blaze of light, she turned the world inside out and emerged in the otherworld.

It was night in the other Paris, too, but a soft, welcoming night. It always felt to Clara that the streetlamps bordering the walkways of the city pinned back the night. Here, a serene blue darkness lapped right up to her window.

Unlike the ordinary night, there was a clarity here, as though darkness was only a different quality of light. She could still see each cobblestone in the courtyard, even lacking any kind of source of light, a lamp or even a full moon. The landscape held its own diffuse light, blue and gentle. She was sure, as she scanned the view from her window, that there were no shadows out in the open under the night sky.

She remained unsure whether there might be dangerous creations lurking in the otherworld. She doubted, having met Magda, that homicidal craftsmen would be allowed to free-range any mechanical atrocities, but that didn't mean that all of the otherworld was completely toothless, either. Nearly anything people created, she reasoned, could be either good or bad, depending on how it was used, and plenty of things intended for good use could turn dangerous with neglect. She considered Olympia, created in a celebration of art and movement, and wondered if, left unfinished long enough, she might grow restless, unfriendly.

She would ask Magda, she resolved by way of ignoring, temporarily, the discomfort raised by her own curiosity.

Magda's address was on a familiar street, and Clara wove her way through night-blue avenues and across the star-strewn river. She paused on the glass bridge to appreciate how the stars seemed to dance in the clear waters beneath her—far clearer than the Seine in ordinary Paris. A school of fish sent ripples through the stars; Clara glanced up and saw the waves mirrored in the sky.

A deep, almost unsettling scent wafted over the water. Sweet, but not cloying like vanilla; spicy, but not warm like cinnamon. In contrast to the drowsy light and calm quiet, it dug into her blood, awakened her. She felt, when she inhaled, that she could stay awake forever. It sharpened her vision, made her hands anxious, longing for their tools and work to do. Lacking that, she let the scent roll over her and almost shuddered with the strangely willful ecstasy of it.

As she approached the workshop on Magda's card, she considered what she would do if Magda was asleep, or simply not there. After all, it was night—the middle of the night, it seemed, the very breath of the world slowed in slumber. The thought of settling in and waiting for dawn wasn't entirely unappealing. The soft contours of the midnight-blue world were peaceful in a wholly restful way, like waking sleep. In fact, there was a hammock made of honeysuckle vines where a park bench could have been, and Clara made note of it to come back to, should the search for Magda need to wait.

When she approached the building, however, the windows were blazing with light. Clara knocked and, when no one answered, tried the door. It was unlocked and swung open without a sound.

"Hello?" Clara peered into the brightly lit atelier, cluttered, as she had expected, with sketches and tools and projects in various stages of completion. "Magda?"

No answer. Clara tiptoed across the floor, avoiding a half-carved wooden block and a crate of chisels. A single piece of pink paper stood out from the chaos, pinned to a beam near the stairs. A note; Clara muddled through translating the French. *On real Paris. Change you if you have emergency.*

That was probably not quite right, Clara acknowledged, but she got the gist. This counted, she wagered, as an emergency, even if it wasn't quite at a critical level yet. She pulled the key from her pocket and held it to her eye.

Clara's eyes hadn't adjusted from the wash of white light when her arm was seized in a viselike grip and she felt the cold bite of steel on her neck.

"*Achtung, ich habe*—oh hell." Magda's voice, inflected first with anger, dropped in pitch quickly. She released Clara's arm and let the knife drop. Clara caught a glance of it—mother-of-pearl inlay and a wicked double blade. "What in God's name are you doing here?"

"I saw the note," Clara replied, half stupefied by the rapid transition from the otherworld. Her head swam and she felt a keen emptiness.

"You saw the—all right, that explains you showing up here.

Except it doesn't explain why you were out in the middle of the night, or why you were looking me up." She sheathed the knife. "Is this an emergency?"

"Yes, of a sort." She blinked, still feeling strangely dull, like a murky film had settled over her vision and muddied her thoughts. What was the trouble again? She couldn't quite remember—it was all so long ago, so long ago.

"You were by the river, weren't you." Magda sighed. "One more reason to blame Elias—he should have warned you not to breathe the night air."

"What?"

"What's the word in English—*drunk*."

"I'm drunk?"

"In a manner of speaking. The night air is very strong. I'll make you a cup of tea, that usually knocks it out quick enough."

Magda bustled into the back of her atelier—just as cluttered and busy here as it was on the other side—and Clara could hear her clattering about what must have been her kitchen. She felt a surge of exhaustion, the sudden return of any tiredness banished by the perfume of the otherworld. She found she was quite content to let her hands lie still in her lap and her eyes fix themselves on an ornate cuckoo clock hanging on the opposite wall. The regular tick and clack was a different sort of intoxicant, producing a stupefying fascination. It seemed to sing, gently, *The pendulum swings, to and fro, and to and fro in dreams we go. In and out and cuckoos shout but never leave a farthing.* Wasn't that Godfather's old clockmaker's song? She couldn't remember. Her eyelids fluttered and almost closed.

"Drink it up, girl—oh, wake up!" Magda shook her shoulder, not entirely kindly. "Damn Elias, I'm always cleaning up his messes." She set a large cup of tea on the table next to Clara. "Drink up!"

The tea was almost too hot to drink, but Clara wasn't going to argue with Magda. Brewed strong and heavily flavored with lemon, it cut through the fog behind Clara's eyes and dissipated the shroud around her thoughts. Magda waited until she'd drunk half the cup. The dullness dripped away.

"Ginger tea with lemon," Magda supplied an answer to her unasked question. "Well then. There's an emergency. Of a sort?" Magda leaned forward.

Clara shook her head, clearing the last of the cobwebs. An emergency—yes, she remembered now.

"I'm being followed," Clara said. "But it—" She paused. She had assumed it would be easy to say something that sounded like a madwoman's ravings to Magda but found it was, in fact, still difficult to put it into words. "It wasn't a person following me. It was a shadow. Like a black blot."

"*Scheisse.*" Magda sank back into her chair. "That is—that is not good."

"I had assumed," Clara replied dryly. "But what is it?"

"You oil the gears, yes?"

"I'm sorry?"

"When you build anything, fix anything. You oil everything well."

"Of course, but—"

"In the other place, that is the oil. The grease between the gears. It has will and life in it. It is the only thing that retains any life when brought to this side. But it is a shadow of its life, and its will is bent to a craftsman." She shook her head. "It is a great abomination, to bring anything back to this side, but to create a *schattenhund*, that is—that is a crime I cannot even begin to fathom."

"So another craftsman," Clara tried the word. "Another craftsman must have made it and sent it to follow me?"

"Most certainly, yes." She refilled Clara's tea and poured some of her own. "Do you know any?"

Clara paused. "Does the name Nussbaum mean anything to you?"

Magda set her cup down roughly. "I knew Nussbaums in Nuremberg. Yes, at least one craftsman. But it's impossible it would have been the man I knew. It was years ago."

A flinty edge to Magda's voice told Clara not to press—at any rate, Nathanael Nussbaum was too young to have been an acquaintance of Magda's "years" ago. "What about Sandmann?"

"Knew one once. Handwerker, not a very creative one. Good at clockwork."

"He knew my godfather?" Clara asked. Magda nodded, didn't elaborate. "Do you think he could be—?"

"Tracking you with a schattenhund? I doubt it. He wasn't the ambitious, clever sort who would do a thing like that. No, there's something bigger than Elias's and my old acquaintances can explain. Elias had enemies—well, he had a way of making people angry, I'm not sure it's the same thing. Someone could certainly think you were worth checking into, given your affiliation with him. But to use a schattenhund—this is outside the guilds and outside the rules." Magda sucked in her lips and cursed again. "And with the blights, too? I don't like it one bit. Could it have something to do with your affiliation with the Exposition?"

"I don't know. I feel quite behind at understanding any of this, to be honest," Clara confessed. "I suppose one question is, who is gaining, and how?"

"You might know better than I," Magda said softly. "The blights—they suggest that things have been brought from the anderwelt and into the Exposition specifically."

Clara considered this. "It does, at that." She paused. What additions to the Exposition might have had their origins in the anderwelt? And under whose direction? Nothing she knew of, that was certain. The displays and wonders were firmly creations of real-world craftspeople. Her head swam. "But what do I do now?"

"Well, the schattenhund itself is easy enough to manage—they won't let themselves be seen by anyone but their mark, and they can't stand light. Just keep the lights on. Even a lantern will do it, though it will come snuffling right up to the edge of the light."

"All lights on, full blaze, got it."

Magda laughed. "Can't blame you." She pinched her mouth shut, thinking. "Finish your tea," she said absently.

Clara obeyed. She wondered if she should say anything to Godfather. It was doubtful, but not impossible, that if the blights on the anderwelt represented a larger conspiracy, her mail could be intercepted, but she wasn't sure what good it would do to send a missive to someone thousands of miles away anyway. *Thanks awfully for the key, the otherworld sure is dandy, oh and by the way, I'm being stalked by a shadowhound. Also do you know a Nussbaum chap?*

No, that wouldn't do at all. She sighed. Godfather had no idea, she was sure, the trouble he'd plunged her into, and there was no good way to tell him.

"What was my godfather like," she asked suddenly, "when you knew him?"

"The thing you have to understand about Elias," Magda said

slowly, "the thing you can't ignore, is that he was a genius. One of the once-in-a-generation types."

"What makes you say he was a genius? That is—I saw what you did with the carousel."

"That was nothing special. Elias wasn't content to make bits and bobs to set about like that." Clara balked at considering the carousel a knickknack, but didn't argue. "He remade parts of the anderwelt itself—if he wanted a mountain, he'd build one of crystal. If he wanted a forest, he'd plant one of gingerbread. There have been very few who could achieve that kind of creation. He learned quickly, and surpassed what anyone could teach him. And then—" She shook her head.

"What?"

"You know your history well enough—war and more war, isn't that the way of it? Men and their squabbles." She sighed. "The war of 1870 eventually came along and, more than that, all the little kingdoms and duchies in Germany unifying—what a word! They came together like puzzle pieces jammed together by a toddler. There were arguments among the craftsmen how to proceed—many of the guilds were very tied to those old states."

"I can't imagine Godfather caring much for politics."

"He didn't, and that was the trouble for him—he couldn't be bothered by it. We had a strict prohibition on forays into the anderwelt anywhere near the battlefields—political ones or the guns-and-horses types—and he flaunted them."

"Now, that sounds like Godfather."

"And what was worse—well. This world affects the other. War is destructive here, and it taints the creative breath of the anderwelt. Makes it uncooperative, unpredictable. I think—well, I think we drag our fears and hungers along with us, though no one's ever listened to me." She stared into her tea. "But how could it be any other way, that what we are afraid of, what we're denied, what we thirst for would spill out into what we make? There even more so than here.

"Anyway. He went into the anderwelt when and where he wasn't supposed to. Something he did while he was there—and no one knows what, though there are plenty of theories—created a nastier blight than even the one you saw. Elias was, you might say, excommunicated—even though no one could ever prove what he'd done." Magda pursed her lips and added quietly, "Or even that it really was him." She shook her head. "But it had to have been him after all. Damn Elias."

Poor Godfather, Clara thought, then chased the thought away. It made sense, didn't it—that his pride would have been his undoing. "And he came to America then, I assume."

"I assume. I could never find him after that. You can't take a handwerker's key, not without a very lengthy trial and all kinds of fuss—it's only been done a handful of times. I've found things I'm sure Elias made. No one else works in marzipan, that's for certain. Spun sugar towers and that kind of thing. But no one heard a thing from him on this side or the other, not until you came along." Clara was fairly sure she saw a pair of tears glistening in the corners of Magda's eyes, but she only said brusquely, "Well, finish your tea and then we will send you home. Trust Elias to deliver this sort of problem to my doorstep."

Chapter Nineteen

FRITZ LEANED OVER Clara's desk, extending his hands in a supplicant's prayer. "I do hope I'm not interrupting your work—"

"No more than usual," Clara replied briskly.

"—but I have a favor to ask."

"This should be interesting," Clara said with a smile. "More lights on the Palace of Illusions? Something gone wrong with the mirrors?"

"Nothing of the sort! In truth, it is not even anything you were hired to do. One of the exhibits has hit snag after snag and I've been asked to consult. Care to join me?"

"Care to tell me what exactly you're asking me to consult on?"

"I'd rather keep it a surprise." Fritz grinned impishly. "I promise it's worth your while."

"I've got to be back this afternoon," Clara said, remembering her appointment with Dr. Gagnet. "For a—a meeting."

Fritz raised a curious brow but didn't press. "We'll be back well before that. Wrap up, it's cold out."

"Very well." Clara gathered her coat and followed Fritz, trying not to show just how curious she was. As they passed several couples on the sidewalk, Clara cleared her throat. "I was wondering, as a—well, a recent arrival in Europe. Is it—is it acceptable for an unmarried young lady and unmarried young man to take a friendly walk together?"

"Now, we are colleagues, no one should think poorly on that!" Fritz began to laugh, but stopped himself. "But of course you would be concerned about when people are not thinking, only reacting. No, there is nothing untoward as long as the couple is not—oh, you know. Canoodling in the shadows."

Clara flushed, the pale sun hot enough to redden her ears. "I was merely curious about the protocols. Socially speaking."

"Why, Clara—you are blushing! Don't tell me some Frenchman has caught your eye." He grinned wickedly. "Or, oh no— you have probably caught some Frenchman's eye."

"I wouldn't think anything strange of it if some young lady caught *your* eye," Clara replied.

"You wouldn't, would you?" His grin didn't fade. "Well, you and my sister could contrive to introduce me around a bit more, I'm finding myself quite at loose ends." As if to demonstrate, he tipped his hat to a fashionably attired young woman, who reinforced his point by ignoring him. "Socially speaking, it is quite acceptable for unmarried young people to take a stroll in a public park, attend an art museum, or go to Mass and happen to share a pew."

"Well, thank you for the information," Clara replied stiffly.

"I won't pry," Fritz added. "Your social life is entirely none of my business. I'm just rather pleased you have one." He nodded toward the red canopy of a café. "Right here—yes, and then down the stairs."

"A restaurant?"

"Do you think I would lead you astray?" Fritz held his hand to his heart in mock dismay. "You wound me! No, the Messieurs Lumières contract with the café to host exhibitions of their films in the salon downstairs. Though perhaps we could stay for a late lunch after, do you think? I have heard exceptional things about the fish."

Clara followed Fritz down the stairs without responding to his suggestion of lunch—even if the faint scents emanating from the kitchen were, she admitted, enticing. The basement salon was draped in velvet curtains and lit dimly by globe sconces. It seemed better suited for card games and cigars, in Clara's estimation, than anything else. Rows of rickety folding chairs had been set up in front of the centerpiece of the salon, a temporary white screen that nearly glowed in the gloom.

Fritz abandoned her immediately to greet—Clara squinted— one of the draftsmen from another project. She didn't know anyone's name. No one had bothered to introduce her around when she'd arrived, and she was rubbish at remembering that sort of thing anyway. Instead, she folded her overcoat around her arm and tried to fade into the velvet curtain at her back.

"Miss Ironwood! Do come sit with Mr. Gregory and me." Fritz waved her over. "Mr. Gregory is American, like you. Do you know each other?"

"No, I'm afraid—" Clara paused and Fritz laughed. "That was a joke, wasn't it?"

"Yes, I am quite aware that America is a very large place."

"Weston Gregory," the American man said, offering his hand. "And you must be the Miss Ironwood I've heard so much about."

Clara remembered her manners and took his hand, meeting any expectations he had with a firm shake. "I'm afraid you have me at a disadvantage," she demurred. She shouldn't be surprised that people knew her name; she was, after all, the only woman working on the mechanical designs. Still, it was unnerving. She wished she could be as anonymous as a man was allowed to be, for people to remember her designs, not the immaterial fact that she was a woman. "Have you been in France long?"

Mr. Gregory shook his head. "Only since last summer. From North Carolina, originally, though I can't admit I miss it much—not when there's all of Paris at your doorstep! You?"

"I'm from Milwaukee," Clara said.

"So not from the same hometown," Fritz interjected. "What a shame. I was hoping to hear stories of your childhood exploits."

"Are you always like this?" Clara asked.

"Only when left unsupervised," Fritz replied. "Now, I will behave and you can enjoy the show. But they've asked us to consider how we might contrive a display, so see what you think—we're quite counting on you." He winked.

Clara rolled her eyes and pulled her overcoat closer. A man stepped in front of the screen and began to explain the projector and its mechanisms, but entirely in French. Clara gave up trying to follow him. Instead, she watched as a waiter from upstairs turned off all the lights in the room one by one, each increasing the dusk until it was nearly full night in the windowless salon.

And then the projector whirred to life. Clara blinked, adjusting to the light as images appeared on the screen. They began to move. Clara started—though rendered in black and white, they looked entirely lifelike. A woman and a man and a baby, having breakfast, ordinary hot cereal and coffee. The mother's frizzled hair shifted with her movements as she sipped what must have been strong coffee from a tiny cup. Behind her, leaves swirled in a stiff breeze. The man gave the baby a teething biscuit, and she seemed to look right at Fritz and offer it to him.

Clara glanced at Fritz, who was mesmerized by the display. His dimple deepened as he laughed at the baby, white ruffles of her dress blowing in her face.

Clara was surprised to realize that she was laughing, too.

They were shown several more films, including scenes from the streets of Paris that Clara recognized: boys sailing boats in the park and horses drawing carriages down wide, dusty boulevards. Clara watched with the same rapt attention she used to give the shadow plays Godfather made for them on long winter evenings. She almost forgot that she was supposed to be considering technical questions and mechanical realities as a snowball fight broke out on the screen, white snow playing against dark overcoats and hats, powder exploding in fine clouds.

Then the projector stilled again, and the globe sconces flared bright against the walls.

"Well?" Fritz waited.

"Remarkable," Clara replied softly. This was a new kind of magic, one beyond even clockwork.

"We have rendered her speechless, Mr. Gregory—quite an accomplishment."

Clara blanched. "*You've* done nothing of the sort, Herr Krieger."

"Ah, now, give me a bit of credit for bringing you!" Fritz stood. "Now, I do want your professional opinion, and I will not even steal it and pass it off as mine when I present it to the Messieurs Lumières."

"Very kind of you," Clara said. She took a breath, an idea born of a certain kind of mechanical magic blooming in her mind.

"Can you imagine it, if we combined their projections with the Palace of Illusions?"

"Ah, Miss Ironwood! You have already outpaced every expectation the Exposition has for the palace. And to change our plans now—and you have only just managed to hide the clockwork, think of trying to hide a projector as well!"

"But imagine it," she countered. She could envision it already, mirrors tilting to catch the moving images and send them bouncing around the room, faces growing and shrinking and blinking out of existence, horses and carriages trotting from one corner to another, jumping from mirror to mirror, snowballs sailing toward the spectators—

"I think I can imagine it," Fritz answered quietly. "But I am quite sure that the management of the Exposition cannot even begin to match your imagination. So we must reduce your capabilities to meet theirs. And besides, Monsieur Lumière will surely want to be presented on his own. He is quite proud of his work, and it would not do to relegate him to a supporting figure in our own designs."

"I suppose that's true," Clara conceded. "Though I do wish—" She stopped herself. Working for the Exposition meant bringing their visions to life, not her own. She squinted at the screen, estimating its size and how many people had comfortably been able to see it. "Unless the exhibit will be quite exclusive, they will need—"

"Much more space, yes." Fritz appraised the screen with a tilted head. "And that is apparently the trouble. Nothing has worked so far. All of the plans drawn up look fine, but when they're installed, nothing functions correctly."

"Where are they being displayed?"

"There's a niche along the Quai des Nations." Fritz shrugged. "It's nearly impossible fitting everything in, of course—"

"Where, exactly?" Clara asked, her curiosity piqued, remembering the crawling dark patch near the Quai in the anderwelt.

"I can pull up the plans—not far from the United States, I believe. Which may be part of the trouble, of course, as the layout didn't originally have a spot for you upstarts—ah, Monsieur Lumière," Fritz interrupted himself and turned to the man who had introduced the films. "Is it true that you're set on a hundred-foot screen? The discussion has moved, I understand, to installing it on the Tour d'Eiffel itself."

"A hundred feet! By Jove." Clara considered the scale. "And of course housing for it and the projector as well and—"

"And it must be kept wet. Auguste Lumière," he added, offering his hand. "The screen must be kept wet, for the optimal brightness of the *actualités*."

"Well, then you certainly don't want it outdoors," Clara said blithely, forgetting who she was talking to and that her opinion had not actually been asked.

"And why not?" The Frenchman raised an eyebrow.

"The dust! Have you ever been on the Champ-de-Mars on a dry day? Your shoes are coated within a minute, and you have to beat your coat afterward. Your wet screen would be mud by the end of the first evening, I wager."

Monsieur Lumière's smile faded, but then he laughed. "You could not be more correct! Now, why hadn't I considered that?"

"If you want cold water on your hopes and dreams, ask Miss Ironwood," Fritz said. Clara flushed hot and began to back away. "But, if you want pragmatic solutions, she cannot be bested." Clara blushed even deeper but let Fritz draw her into the conversation.

"We have had nothing but trouble. The mechanisms jam, the first screen ripped, and the workers have been..." Lumière shrugged. "I do not like to tell tales, but things have come to fistfights."

"My goodness," Clara murmured. "Are you all... quite set on the space itself?"

"Hardly!" Lumière laughed. "As long as there is room somewhere, it needn't be in any one building. Provided, of course, that the actualités can be viewed by as many people as possible, that is."

Clara laughed politely, but she saw instantly the difficulty. The Exposition wanted to keep the celebrated Lumière brothers happy, and display their innovative work, but the practicalities were no small thing. Housing and mechanics for projector and screen, and a hundred-foot screen at that. Enough room for a large audience. And darkness, of course.

Clara smiled as the complexities piled one on top of the other. A puzzle. Just what she liked.

Chapter Twenty

CLARA RETREATED TO the workshop, considering the problem of where to display the Lumières' actualités. She pored over the map of the Exposition grounds, keying on the Quai des Nations and overlaying it with her memories of the anderwelt's light and dark patterns. Yes, the scrap near Italy that the Lumières had been given was, she knew, awash with dim shadows in the anderwelt.

She caught her breath. It seemed entirely likely that the blight that Magda had warned her about was the cause of the Lumières' difficulties. If that was true—but of course it was, she reasoned. It was precisely as Magda had explained, except that Magda didn't have a specific example. Clara did. That shadowy blight was getting in the way of building something new, something unique.

Curious, she decided to investigate the site for herself. Knowing how they had attempted to leverage one space for the actualités could only help, she reasoned—and she was curious if she could see any signs of the broken anderwelt. Magda's warning reverberated through her thoughts—that the blighted land was toxic, dangerous, that someone should never enter a blight. But that was on the other side, not here.

The Quai des Nations was crowded with replicas of other countries' landmarks, their imposing size and detail belying the fact that they were mere plaster and cardboard. The little hall originally set aside for the actualités was, Clara gauged quickly, not only too small for the grand design the Lumières had in mind but also underwhelming for the technology that the board wanted as a centerpiece of the Exposition. As she explored the exterior, she didn't notice anything different or unusual—perhaps a general disquiet, but she was fairly sure that was her own memory of the landscape of gray ash in the anderwelt. Then a pair of workers passed by, their discussion devolving into a shouting match in French Clara didn't understand. Unease settled around her, and she wondered if the poison of the blight had provoked them.

She tested a side door and was a little surprised when it opened easily. No one was around, no workers carting supplies or building up the currently half-finished plaster veneer. The space felt in limbo, not distinctive enough to be any particular exhibit but not a blank canvas, either. Clara wondered what it would become, now that the Lumières had relinquished their claim. She traced a plain column with a tentative hand, and pulled back quickly as a loud clank interrupted her.

The empty interior left no place for anything to hide, but narrow hallways ran behind the open areas, like so many of the Exposition buildings had behind displays and facades. Clara hesitated, then crossed the empty floor to explore one of the access hallways. Before she reached it, movement in the shadows stopped her. She ducked behind a pillar, and a nightmare plodded out of the hallway.

It was a tin soldier, rendered larger than a human, cast like the toys that sold nine for a shilling. Another followed the first, and another, the trio standing in an intentional formation blocking the hallway. The toys for children had more detail than these monstrosities; usually someone carefully painted the faces and uniforms onto toy soldiers. These were blank metal, glinting dull in the sun that filtered through a dusty window. They passed for humanoid only in that they carried themselves on legs and swung heavy arms by their sides; their faces were punctuated by round black eyes and mouths in brash gashes across expressionless faces.

Clara clung to the pillar, unable to fathom the horror she saw in front of her. They were surely from the anderwelt—crafted there and then ripped from it, creating the blight. But why? Had someone brought them here as guards, some kind of security detail? There was plaster dust on their hands—were they pressed into construction service, or was that merely from storing them in the unfinished building? Or were they meant as public displays for the Exposition? She shuddered. They were ugly, horrid creations, and whatever craftsman had made them didn't deserve his key, she thought with disgust.

But someone had made them, certainly. And brought them here. And now—now she had to get away from them. Their heavy hands and bare metal boots could crush her, she realized with growing fear. There was nowhere to move where she wouldn't be spotted, and though they were clunky, ill-made things, she had no doubt that those huge legs could cross the room in a few strides, far faster than her. No one knew she was here. No one would find her. She squeezed herself tight against the pillar.

Voices in the back hallway—she strained to hear them. She knew the presence of other people could either mean rescue or the situation growing much worse. The voices were too low for her to understand, but she knew they weren't speaking English.

French—no, German. Suddenly, the soldiers turned about-face and marched back into the hallway.

Clara didn't wait to see if they were gone for good. She ran for the door and burst into welcome sunlight. She wandered her way back toward her office in a half daze, lost as to what to do next.

Magda—Magda would know what to do. She hurried to her friend's workshop, but Magda wasn't there, nor was she in her workshop in the other Paris. Clara drummed her fingers, frustrated.

Surely there were other craftsmen about, even if their numbers were small. How did they find one another? How did they meet, talk, solve problems of small and grand scales, from gears that stuck to—well, to someone creating blights? Someone other than Magda surely cared. She knew Nussbaum and Sandmann were craftsman, as well, but she didn't trust either. Magda had mentioned guilds, but Clara had no idea where they were or how they worked, let alone how to contact them.

She found herself frustrated not with Magda, who had every right to come and go as she pleased, but with Godfather. He had neglected to teach her so much—if he had given her even the simplest of orientations to this brilliant, beautiful world, she wouldn't have been floundering in what was shaping up to be a serious and seemingly dangerous mystery. Just a few straight words, instead of riddles and fairy tales and hidden compartments in ugly nutcrackers.

Clara sighed. There was one thing for certain—a pile of very real work waited for her in her very real office, all under very real deadlines. If she couldn't do anything to solve the puzzles of the otherworld, she could tackle the ones waiting for her on her desk.

Chapter Twenty-One

CLARA SPENT THE rest of the day trying to compartmentalize everything being asked of her—completing work orders on the Palace of Illusions, researching the specifications for the Lumières' screen, and relegating the monstrous tin soldiers to a place in her mind she could force to wait until later.

And then, of course, was her scheduled walk with Dr. Gagnet. She tamped down the flutter of nerves as she wrangled her arms into her coat and skewered her hat in place. If Dr. Gagnet didn't come, what of it? A chance meeting and a nice conversation, it didn't mean they were fated for each other. Still, the brilliant elation she felt at seeing his figure come around the corner sent another set of butterflies loose in her stomach and spots of color to her cheeks.

"Miss Ironwood!" Dr. Gagnet greeted her with a slight bow and the offer of his arm. "I hope I did not keep you waiting long."

"Of course not, you're right on time."

"I'd rather lost track of time—such a day in the ward today! But I will not trouble you with those details. Very unbecoming to a lovely day such as this."

He steered them toward the Jardin des Tuileries, and Clara couldn't help but feel a pang of disappointment as they entered that the trees were perfectly normal instead of a Christmas forest and that the fountains didn't spill over with lemonade. She wondered what Olympia did while she waited for visitors to impress with her dance.

"I prefer coming here in the summer," Dr. Gagnet said. "The children sail boats on the fountains, and it's such a pretty scene."

"I arrived at the end of summer, but I confess I didn't spend much time in the park."

"Your work must be quite fascinating. And with the Exposition coming so close to the open!"

"Don't remind me!" Clara laughed.

"You cannot be behind, though, can you? You seem so diligent!"

"No, it only feels overwhelming when I forget I've got it all quite well planned out." She hesitated, then told him all about her method of scheduling her own work hours, building in time to revise her plans and of course for delays from the various contractors. He listened intently, pausing to ask questions about how much control she had over which contractors were chosen and who was hired to work on her designs.

"Hardly any—it's all meant to show France at her best, of course, so the decisions about which factories and workshops to employ are made far above my head. Take the mirrors—Saint-Gobain has been in business since the Sun King, so of course they got the contract." She paused, then laughed. "But of course you can't be interested in any of this!"

"Believe me, Miss Ironwood, I am!" He led her toward a bench, washed in the last of the afternoon's sunlight. "You see, my work is—it is very necessary, of course. But it does not have the same sort of excitement and promise yours does. It is fascinating to hear how a thing is built, created from a vision."

Gagnet sat down, and with a flush of excitement, Clara sat next to him, far enough for decorum. "But a doctor—you must have rather exciting days, too. And fulfilling—making people well!"

"Perhaps, in another manner of practicing medicine. Were I a private physician, for example, or a country doctor. But in the public hospital, oh, that is another matter entirely."

"I'm sorry, I didn't realize."

"No, it is not something that Paris wants to highlight, to put on display, you know. Not with the grand Exposition of the new century, especially!" He smiled ruefully. The expression hollowed out the curve of his jaw, and Clara caught her breath. "But the truth is, by the time the poor come to the hospital, they are often beyond the skill or craft of medicine to help. They are battered by neglect, often malnourished. The ravages of disease—"

He stopped abruptly. "This is entirely inappropriate, I am sorry."

"No," Clara said quietly, something in her stirring at seeing his righteous indignation and bare compassion. "I am sure it is like this in every city."

"It may well be. I will spare you the details of alcohol and opium and the rest, but it is horrid to see. Young women, aged to twice their years, and there is nothing we can do but give them a place to die."

Clara's breath stalled in her throat. "I had no idea, I—" She reached impulsively for Dr. Gagnet's hand. It stiffened in surprise under hers, then relaxed. A warm joy flooded her at that reciprocity of touch. "I am glad they at least have someone like you to care for them."

166

"You are kind. And I am sorry, I have monopolized the last of the daylight with my depressing thoughts." He stood, still holding her hand in his. "May I walk you home?"

Alarm rose in the back of Clara's mind—walking in public was one thing, but taking a man back to her apartment was certainly not decorous, even if she trusted Dr. Gagnet. Perhaps even having him leave her at the door would be considered inappropriate. She withdrew her hand and rearranged her skirts. "Thank you, Dr. Gagnet, but I'm afraid I've left some paperwork at my office that I will need. Perhaps you could accompany me?"

"Certainly! We can return along the Seine." He offered an arm. "We can each pick our own barge and decide where we shall sail it. A game I used to play as a child."

Clara agreed, and let her companion fancy himself captain of a barge en route to Egypt where he could sail down the Nile and see the pyramids. "I am quite keen to see the exhibits from Egypt and other lands of antiquities at the Exposition, but I have always had an itch to see them for myself." The Exposition again—Gagnet seemed even more intent on the workings of the world's fair than the average Parisian. Or perhaps, Clara allowed herself to wonder, he was simply interested in her. "Tell me—does the Exposition hold magic for you any longer, now that you have seen her from the inside?"

Clara started a bit at the word "magic." Yet it was surely only a figure of speech. She looked back over the water. They had wandered near the Quai des Nations, landmarks of dozens of countries rendered in miniature along the bank of the Seine. She tamped down a shudder as she remembered that at least one building housed tin monstrosities. "I am sure," she said instead of answering directly, "that I will be just as dazzled by the lights as any fairgoer."

Gagnet seemed dissatisfied by her hedged answers, but pivoted back to the Seine. "Ah, there it is again—my ship en route to Egypt!" He gestured toward a stout barge designed solely for river sailing.

"And what will you name your boat?" Clara asked.

"Ah, she is the loveliest ship on the water," he said with a softness to his eyes that made Clara wonder for a brief breathless moment if he would name his imaginary vessel for her. "So I shall call her ... *Helen*. And what for your ship?"

"She's the fastest," countered Clara, "so I shall call her *Atalanta*. And now we are back where we began, and I have a pile of paperwork to look at."

A shadow of disappointment, or perhaps even frustration, passed over Gagnet's face, but it passed quickly. "Of course! I cannot keep you from such important work. I shall call on you again, yes?"

Clara could not help a genuine smile as she agreed, readily, to meet him again the following week.

The Queen of Mice
by Christian Elias Thrushman,
dated 23 March 1881

You must know, of course, that mice are rather remarkable creatures, who can fit into the narrowest of spaces between wall and trim and slip between the laths behind the plaster. And in doing so, they can move unnoticed between all sorts of places. For the most part they sneak between rooms and between rowhouses and apartments, but sometimes they can disappear into other places entirely. For you may not realize, esteemed reader or listener, that there are cracks and gaps between our ordinary world and others so astonishing as to be beyond even your imagining, clever Clara or Louise. Even the loftiest of human intelligence cannot comprehend what the humblest of creatures might discover, all for looking in the strange and low and forgotten places in the world.

Such was the case of the Queen of Mice.

The Queen of Mice, of course, lived in a castle—most specifically, behind the stove in the expansive kitchens on the lowest level of a great stone castle in which resided a human king and queen. She had several hundred subjects who also lived behind the stove. From her throne set near one of the stovepipes, the Queen of Mice could see the entire kitchen. This not only made her subjects' stronghold in the wall secure against invaders such as the small army of cats that roamed the halls and the little turnspit dog who snuffled along the baseboards when off duty, but also allowed her to see where the best scraps fell.

The most celebrated day in the mouse calendar was not, as you might guess, Christmas or even the queen's birthday, but Sausage-Making Day. For on Sausage-Making Day, the entire kitchen was in a bustle and blur of crispy fat, and crispy fat is chief among dishes favored by mice. By a long-standing arrangement between the Queen of Mice and the head scullery maid, the mice were given free license to dine on any scraps that fell to the floor on Sausage-Making Day.

One particular year, however, the head scullery maid was indisposed (some say it was a migraine, while other sources point to an attack of arthritis). When the mice emerged to collect their annual due, they were met with sharp resistance, including a contingent of the spriest of the palace cats, a phalanx of tabbies led by a notch-eared old tom. Several dozen mice were killed within the first moments of the melee, and the rest retreated swiftly behind the stove.

The Queen of Mice was of course irate, but what could she do? The truce had been broken, and she had no recourse with which to mount a counterattack, especially as the little turnspit dog had joined the troops guarding the baseboards against incursion, a rare parlay between himself and the cats. She and her subjects were forced to remain behind the stove, their situation swiftly revealing itself as a siege, as the cats and the turnspit dog did not intend to leave their quarry at peace, setting up a schedule of sentries.

The row in the kitchen emanated through the entire castle, attracting the attention of even the king and queen. The king had a good chuckle at the thought of the dog and the cats united in battle against the mice, but the queen was horrified, having never before realized that her castle might harbor uninvited residents. She called an all-out war against the rodents, insisting that even the stove be removed from its base and the cats allowed to exterminate the mice living behind it.

Plans were made immediately to remove the stove, but it was such a hulking beast that it could not be accomplished right away. The court engineer, the head cook, and the privy astronomer all had to be consulted. The engineer devised a system of pulleys and pallets for moving the stove, the cook devised a menu that would not require the use of the stove, and the astronomer searched his celestial tables for days most auspicious to avoid being squashed by large objects.

This gave the Queen of Mice time to plan. She sent runners in all directions to find an outlet by which they could escape, but they soon discovered that each mouse hole was watched by a member of the squadron of tabbies. They searched the entire castle, high and low, and no exit point from the walls could be found that did not lead directly into the claws of a feline, and the Queen of Mice began to grow disheartened.

She remembered, then, a secret passed down from mouse monarch to mouse monarch—a strange little cleft in plaster at the corner of the kitchen, a strange little dent in the wall that no one had explored in many mouse generations.

The Queen of Mice determined to test the little hole for herself. It did not lead out into the kitchen, nor deeper into the castle walls, nor to another room, nor even to outdoors. It led—precisely back to where she had begun, but the tunnels behind the plaster, the laths, the entire kitchen appeared the same, and yet different. Perhaps it was backward, or inside out—the Queen of Mice did not know. Men far wiser than any mouse, the Queen of Mice included, had failed to discover precise geographical coordinates for the inimitable place she found herself.

The Queen of Mice made no such attempts at academic inquiry, quite confident she lacked sufficient philosophy to understand and vocabulary to explain this phenomenon, but she was observant of the most important facet of this strange development—in the mirror kitchen there were no cats and no turnspit dog. She scurried back to her subjects, delighted to offer them an escape route even if it was into an unknown otherworld, and only just in time, as the pallets and pulleys were already in place to move the stove.

The mice therefore evaded extermination, the cats and turnspit dog eventually grew bored of waiting, the queen was assured that there were no mice present in the kitchen, and in short order, the head scullery maid was back on duty so that the next year, Sausage-Making Day could be celebrated in appropriate fashion.

Chapter Twenty-Two

A SHARP RAP on Clara's door interrupted her evening spent working equations on the ratios of projectors and screen sizes. Annabelle practically skipped inside when Clara answered. "It's going to be another couple months of lean living, but then have I got a job, have I got a job!" She dropped a package beside the door and then clasped Clara by the hand and swung her around.

"Tell me all about it, then!" Clara extricated herself from Annabelle's impromptu polka around the room.

"The Exposition, of course!"

"That's grand! A bit of a wait, if you need a loan or anything—"

"I'm no idiot, I've always got a bit of money socked away. Just guess what the job is. But no, you'll never be able to guess."

Clara considered what she knew of the Exposition's displays. "Underwater ballet in the aquarium." Annabelle shook her head. "Waltzing with the steam engines." Another head shake. "Dance of the Seven Veils in the textile exhibit."

Annabelle laughed. "Now, that would be a way to get the fellows to accompany their ladies to that display, for certain. No—the

Palace of Optics will have a demonstration of phosphorescence. I'm going to actually glow in the dark!"

"How in the world are they doing that?"

"I have absolutely no idea. All I know is that the choreographer loved my 'Prism Dance with Birds of Paradise'—oh," she added, "I spent last week cutting out new silhouettes and choreographing a new dance."

"You must show me!" Clara replied.

"Of course, yes, but I'm not finished with my story! The choreographer is a distinguished sort and he said I was just the kind of talent they wanted for—and I quote—this 'bold experiment in kinesthetic expression.' I've never been just the kind of talent anyone wanted for an experiment of any kind, let alone a bold one!"

"You'll be the boldest experiment in talented kinesthetics—no, wait, none of that was right, was it?"

"I don't think so, no," Annabelle said. "I find I won't need the magic lantern for quite some time in any case. I thought perhaps you might have use for the parts—you were so kind to make it, I don't want to take advantage and not even use it."

"Oh, thank you but—" Clara considered the way the lantern cast a beam of light and how, with minor adjustment, it could create a halo of soft glow instead. Perhaps just the thing to ward off a schattenhund. "You know, I think I'll find a use for it."

"Brilliant!" Annabelle handed her the cardboard box with the lantern stored neatly inside.

"We ought to celebrate somehow." Clara considered the depth of night outside—but Magda had said the schattenhund wouldn't reveal itself when she was with other people. With Annabelle, she would be safe. "Perhaps down to Horace's for mousse au chocolat?"

"Your French is getting better!" Annabelle laced her fingers through Clara's. "Dessert and coffee is perfect. I know I ought to play the part of the irresponsible danseuse and drag you to the Moulin Rouge instead, but frankly I am worn out! Job hunting is exhausting."

After a shared mousse au chocolate turned into two éclairs and another mousse, Annabelle and Clara tumbled through the door of Clara's apartment. Clara was laughing so hard her sides hurt, her corset the only thing keeping her upright. "Hold on, let me get the light—"

"Well, I am surprised to see you out so late. Not like you at all, not a bit." The female voice was familiar, but entirely jarring here in her apartment, so far from Milwaukee. Clara turned back to the hallway.

"I am sorry to startle you," Madame Boule said, ushering in a second woman. "But I was not sure what else to do, when Miss Ironwood arrived and you were not home."

"Louise."

Her sister stepped from behind Madame Boule, her traveling suit a bit wrinkled, but her hat at a perfect angle above flawlessly pinned hair. "Good evening, Clara. I would make pleasantries with your friend, but I find I'd very much like to move my valises inside and take these boots off. It has been a very long day."

Annabelle gave Clara's hand a sympathetic squeeze and faded into her own apartment's doorway. There was a slight scuffle as Hector attempted to escape, followed by a sharply hissed, "You little shit!" Clara kept a straight face as Louise raised an eyebrow.

"Of course," Clara said, taking the valise from Louise's hand and gathering several more. "Thank you, Mrs.—Madame—Boule, for helping with my sister, I think we—that is I—"

"*Merci beaucoup pour votre hospitalité gentille. Et pour le gâteau, bien sûr!*" Louise shook Madame Boule's hand warmly and then followed Clara inside.

"I'm sorry," Clara said, out of breath with surprise. "I had no idea you were coming. None at all."

"Mother wrote." Louise peeled her gloves off one by one. They were unspotted pale gray, matching her dove-colored suit perfectly.

"I'm sure she did." Clara felt tips of color rising in her cheeks. "Didn't you wait for a response?"

Louise shrugged. "I don't suppose we thought we needed to—you wouldn't turn down a visit from your family, would you?"

"Of course not, but—"

"Then least said, soonest mended." She unpinned her hat. "Mother would have come herself, and maybe she will, later. If the crowds aren't too bad."

Clara sighed, exasperated. "It's going to be the Exposition Universelle. Paris will be one giant crowd."

"I figured. That's why I wanted to come early."

"There's nothing open yet, and, Louise, I am working, all the time, every day—"

"Paris is open," Louise answered dryly. "There's plenty to see in Paris, you know. And I assumed you wouldn't be at my beck and call. You always work. Every day. Remember last New Year's when you missed—oh, but never mind."

"I just mean, I won't be free to take you around. I'm going to be a terrible hostess."

"I know, I know. You're very important and very busy. Don't fret over it—we'll have time once the fair opens, I'm sure."

"I'll still be working then—yes, I'm sure," Clara amended. "And I'm sure you're tired."

"Not terribly." She seated herself on the edge of the sofa, as though she worried the upholstery might stain the pale gray of her suit. "I can stay up a bit, until you sober up."

"Sober up! Louise, my friend and I were getting coffee and dessert at a little café—why, if you're hungry, I'll take you there, too!"

Louise cocked her head. "I'm sorry, I didn't mean to imply anything. It's only, I have never in my life seen you...giggle. Not like that."

"Maybe you're just not very funny, Louise."

Louise cracked a smile. "I know I'm not. Not like that—what is she, honestly? A cancan girl? A barmaid? Someone's kept dame?"

"Louise! She's..." Clara threw her hands in the air. "She is a dancer. But she's respectable!"

"She does not," Louise said, "look very respectable."

"Did Mother send you here to keep an eye on me? Answer honestly."

Louise sighed. "Not precisely. Well. Yes." She raised a hand, holding back a stream of protest from Clara. "Not the way you think. All of your letters were about work, about the project, about...honestly, Clara, I lost track of what you were talking about half the time. Mother worried you were working too hard." Her voice softened. "Like before."

"That wasn't overwork, it was—" Clara didn't want to rehash the whole thing again, that the break with Godfather hadn't been because she'd worked herself too hard. "It's not like that here. It's not like working with Godfather."

"He's not well."

"What?" Clara's heart constricted and then plummeted. "Louise, no one told me, is he—"

"Oh, he's all right, I suppose. But he closed the shop after Christmas and says he won't reopen until after Easter, maybe later. Maybe never, I say. He looks tired, Clara. For the first time, I feel as though he looks a bit...old."

Clara sat next to Louise. "He didn't say anything to me."

"Of course he wouldn't. You're his favorite, his *apprentice*. He wouldn't want you to worry. And to be fair, he didn't say anything to any of us, either. He just seems worn out, somehow."

"When did that start?" Clara asked.

"Before Christmas—before Thanksgiving, even. The day he dropped off his Christmas gift to you, actually, that was the first I really noticed it. Bags under the eyes, seemed a bit stooped. Now that I say that—honestly, I shouldn't have worried you, he hasn't gotten any worse. I imagine it's just age catching up to him." She paused. "What did he send you? He said it was a surprise. How he loves his surprises."

And how Louise hated them, Clara recalled with a slight smile. "That ugly old nutcracker," she replied.

"Why in the world would he send you that old bit of bric-a-brac? Did you ever even say that you liked it?"

"I suppose it was meant to be sentimental."

"Oh, he's worse off than I thought, then!" Louise rolled her eyes. "Godfather getting *sentimental*."

"A certain sign of his impending demise, most definitely." Clara didn't belie that she did, in fact, worry, knowing Godfather's choice to send the key accompanied a sudden downturn in his health—or, she considered, knowing Godfather, a sudden uptick in anxiety. "But at any rate, you'll be wanting a bed, I imagine."

"That is preferable when lodging somewhere, yes."

"And I don't have a spare. So you may take my room—no, I

insist on that point—and I will sleep on the sofa. I get up early, that way I won't bother you."

"Well, if you insist," Louise said, already moving her cases into her room. "The rest will be delivered tomorrow," she added.

"The rest? That's not—that's not your entire wardrobe?"

"Of course not! And I'm under strict orders to take you to have new dinner and evening gowns made for the Exposition." Louise paused. "She may be thousands of miles away, but Mother will still get her way."

Chapter Twenty-Three

ONCE LOUISE WAS settled in the apartment's bedroom, Clara set up a bed for herself on the sofa. It was just like Mother and Louise, she thought with a sigh, to orchestrate everyone else's lives for them whether they wanted the intrusion or not. And though she was usually reticent to invite their opinions on how she conducted her affairs, now was the absolute worst time for Louise to arrive with a fresh set of expectations.

She had the palace to finish outfitting with electric lights. She had a new project for the Lumière brothers. She had the mysterious German, Nussbaum, needling her. She had—did she have?—a beau. She had a world of wonders beckoning her every spare moment that she had to keep absolutely secret from her observant, discerning sister.

And she had a hound made of shadows stalking her. Clara searched the darkened windows, looking for the schattenhund. She unpacked Annabelle's lantern and set it on the table. She had made it able to affix to mountings onstage, but a very minor adjustment created space for the little kerosene lamp and resetting the panes of glass allowed an arc of light to protect Clara's humble sofa.

Clara turned the light down, and her throat clenched as she saw it—a darker blot creeping against the soft black of the window. Hurriedly, she turned the light back to full blaze, and the shadow retreated.

"Damn it." She stood in a face-off with the window, accepting finally than an interrogation from Louise about her nighttime light was better than inviting the schattenhund into her apartment.

Even with the hound kept at bay, Clara did not sleep well. She rose in the soft gray of a damp morning, left Louise a note that she would come home from work early, and walked to work as the street cleaners finished their morning's pass of the city.

She dedicated her morning to the Lumières' screen. What building, she wondered, could host a hundred-foot screen and a crowd of people? She returned to the plans and maps of the entire grounds, hand deliberately covering the blighted corner that held the monstrous tin soldiers. Her gaze fell on the Galerie des Machines. The Festival Hall inside was large enough, she reasoned, and nothing had been permanently established there—yet. She tested her memory of the anderwelt against the map in front of her, and that sector of the fairgrounds was unmarked by blight. The filing cabinets held interior plans and photographs of all the buildings, and she thumbed through the thick folders until she found a stack of Festival Halls in various stages of construction, from the 1889 fair and through the changes that had been made to it. She began to sketch out a few ideas, interrupted by the sonorous bells announcing that noon had snuck up on her entirely unprepared.

"Take credit for it all, I don't care," she said as she dropped the sketches on Fritz's desk. "I still haven't quite figured out the mechanism to keep the screen wet."

"Take credit? I would never," Fritz replied with feigned affront. "I'll insist you're given all the credit, and all the work."

Inwardly, Clara both glowed and grimaced. She had no more time for more work—and yet, to solve the puzzle of the Lumières' screen! To be part of one of the most anticipated displays at the Exposition—if she hadn't been caught up in the anderwelt, too, it would have been the most exciting thing to happen to her since arriving. As it stood, she wasn't sure how much more she could take on. "Their old building," she inquired, trying to sound light, "is it being used for anything new?"

"Haven't the faintest," Fritz replied. "But it's far too late to reassign any of the spaces on the Quai des Nations now, not without risking an international incident." He laughed. Clara hadn't expected him to be aware of enormous tin soldiers prowling the grounds, but she had held on to a thin hope that anyone might be able to tell her anything useful.

"I have to leave early," she said instead of voicing everything she was really thinking about. "My sister arrived in town last night."

This confession led to an enthused Fritz insisting they join him and Alma for dinner within the week, but he didn't begrudge her the afternoon off.

Louise waited at the apartment, sitting primly on the sofa with a magazine and a cup of tea. "You haven't a thing to eat in this house," Louise said. "How do you manage it?"

"There's no point in buying croissants ahead of time," Clara said with a smile. "Just pop round to the bakery on the corner next time you're hungry."

"I won't report your bohemian grocery habits to Mother," Louise promised.

"Go ahead," Clara replied. "Even Mother couldn't argue with fresh croissants."

"And why in the world do you keep that strange lantern on all night?"

Clara paused. She had concocted the kind of answer that would appeal to Louise's sensibilities, but the delivery had to be on point—a dose of anxiety, a bit of naivete. "You might think me silly, but Paris is a very big city and who knows what sort of people might be about. I feel a bit safer, with a light."

Louise, to her relief, merely nodded sympathetically. "I suppose that's fair. I've never lived in an apartment building before—it must be a bit unsettling, not knowing all your neighbors, and I'm sure some of them are not the most savory sort of people. It isn't like home."

"Don't get too snobby about the good character of Midwesterners," Clara retorted. "Remember that H. H. Holmes was American born and raised. The terror of the Chicago World's Fair, remember?" To her surprise, Louise laughed.

"Now then." Louise set her teacup down with the pronounced finality of a judge leveling a gavel. "I would like to see the city. Do you propose we start with the Eiffel Tower or Notre-Dame? I'm given to understand they are at opposite ends of the city."

"Yes, I—you want to see the entire city this afternoon?"

Louise shook out her skirt as she stood. "I'd like to have a bite to eat first, and then I thought you might show me..." She searched awkwardly for the right words. "Some of your favorite places. You know, your view on Paris."

"I see. All right, well." She thought for a long moment. She had been buried in work, she wanted to say, she had hardly noticed—but she had, of course, found landmarks she appreciated. It was only that it felt strange revealing them to Louise. They hadn't, she acknowledged, been close in years. They played together as children and, with only two years separating them, were the best of friends until they were ten or twelve. And then—what had changed? Clara struggled to put into words the frustration she felt with Louise, and the embarrassment Louise seemed to feel with her.

This request, to see Paris as Clara enjoyed it, wasn't just a request for a tour guide. Louise was asking to get to know her better. An olive branch, so to speak, to begin to close the gap an adolescence spent drifting apart had rent.

"There is a café down the street with very good soup—different every day, if you don't mind a surprise. And then—" She steeled up the strange sort of courage required to open oneself to another person. "The Grand Palais and Petit Palais are not open yet, but are beautiful buildings. They're part of the Exposition, and I work nearby. And just beyond is the Jardin des Tuileries, which I rather enjoy."

Louise cocked her head. Clara had the sense she was holding back from critique—that these weren't on the front page in whatever guide she had purchased, and Clara's taste was bound to be suspect. But she decided to choose the olive branch. "That sounds lovely."

The air was cool, damp with the early whispers of spring but still standoffish. Soup was a welcome lunch, and Louise praised the potato and leek recipe the café used. She listened as Clara described the architecture of the Grand Palais and Petit Palais, interested in the displays planned for both spaces. And she praised the Jardin as beautiful, even under the pallor of a retreating winter.

"I think you're quite right," Louise declared. "Not that I don't want to see Notre-Dame, of course, but this feels like—oh, like I've seen the real Paris."

Clara wondered what Louise would think of seeing the Folies or the backstage at the Opera Ballet if she wanted to see the real Paris, but didn't say anything.

"Now, you tell me—what are the most interesting exhibits they'll have at the fair?" They had just passed the Grand Palais on their route back to Clara's apartment. "I can't wait to see it all!"

The realization settled around Clara that, yes, Louise intended to stay for months. She had known, instinctively, from the moment Louise had arrived, but she felt it, deep in her weary bones, the dread of making conversation over breakfast and being expected for dinner and sleeping on that lumpy uncomfortable sofa. Months.

She forced a smile. "The Avenue of Nations will be spectacular. And of course all of the pavilions of science and innovation." She began to tell Louise about the enormous telescope and the underground aquarium, but something felt strange. A tickle at the back of her neck, as though she was being watched.

"I read about the kerfuffle with the United States being excluded from the Avenue of Nations at first—the nerve! Though all's well that ends well. America and France always have been friends, haven't they?"

Suddenly Clara noticed that the walls themselves seemed to be moving. With slowly creeping disgust, she made out dozens—no, hundreds—of tiny bodies, eyes sparkling black and whip-thin tails in constant motion. Mice. Hundreds of mice, swarming along the alley and into the gutter, thronging in half-hidden corners.

Louise appeared oblivious. "I would like to see the art exhibition, too. I was reading about how the impressionists are going to get a larger slice of the space than some critics think is appropriate. Now, if you ask me—I say, Clara, what is the matter?"

Clara turned her blanched face away from the vermin quivering in a mass. "Nothing. I just—"

"You're overworked, aren't you." Louise had the habit of asserting things in the form of a question with the intonation of a definitive statement that usually meant she was convinced she had accurately perceived a situation. It didn't matter what the reality was, Louise had declared it so. "You work far too hard. No man in your office works half so hard, I would guarantee—"

"Well, of course no man works as hard as I do!" Clara retorted, grateful for an outlet that didn't involve confessing to seeing swarms of mice. "They don't have half as much to prove. You have no idea, really, Louise, what it's like to work, especially what it's like to work in a man's profession."

"Oh, this old number again. I don't know what work is, I'm just a spoiled lady of privilege—it's not as though I sit about all day eating sugarplums and tatting antimacassars, you know."

"Yes, you keep yourself very busy, I'm aware." Clara glanced back. The sides of the street teemed with mice. They ran up drainpipes and scurried along the gutters. Did no one else notice? Not Louise, she ascertained quickly, who was working herself into a true state of pique.

"I keep myself busy! You act as though everything I do is just some mindless hobby, that I've never had a single thought in my head. I'll have you know that the board said that our fundraising was absolutely necessary to funding the orphan's home, and—" Louise heaved a sigh. "You never did understand. You never could work with other people. Everything had to be your way, your pace. You would never let me help you tinker with your contraptions, even when we were children."

"It isn't tinkering!" Clara half shouted, then reined in her voice. "Why would I let you help? You didn't know what I was doing most of the time, and you slowed me down. You had your garden and your flower arrangements and all of that—you didn't need me!"

"Because it might have been nice to do something together once in a while," Louise answered, "and you never had any interest in what I liked to do. Dance lessons, gardening, piano, even the photography club. We tried everything to get you to take some interest in doing something with other people."

"We?" Clara halted. Behind her, so did the mice. The nearest ones stood on their hind paws, whiskers quivering, as though watching how the scene would play out.

"Mother and Father and I." Louise smoothed the trim on her coat, avoiding Clara's eyes. "Once we were older, you didn't want to play with me anymore, and you didn't make friends at school. I thought—we thought—maybe you just needed an extra nudge."

"Did it ever occur to you that I was perfectly happy—what was it?—'tinkering' with my 'contraptions' by myself?"

"Were you?"

The question hung in the air, suspended like frost. Clara's gaze darted to the mice, who had faded back against the walls. Was she happy? Was she happy when she was a child? Was she happy now?

"That is an impossible question," she snapped, "and one I am not interested in dissecting right now."

"All right," Louise said. "But honestly, Clara. You've gone on acting as though everyone in the world was your adversary long enough. It is forgivable in an adolescent, but for pity's sake, you really have to give it up."

Clara didn't reply as they hurried inside, closing out the night air and the hundred pairs of eyes following them.

Chapter Twenty-Four

ALL NIGHT, CLARA heard the skitter and rustle of mice in the walls. More than once she found a pair of eyes peering out from a slim gap in the molding, disappearing as soon as she moved. She barely slept, and when she did manage to fall into a brief doze, she started awake again, imagining tiny paws running over her. Sometime before dawn, the noise abated, and Clara slept fitfully, waking far later than her usual schedule.

Bleary and fumbling, she escorted Louise to a nearby café for café au lait and a croissant, as she didn't trust herself to even boil water. How had her sister missed the scuttling in the walls all night? Had the mice left her alone and focused solely on her?

"You seem distracted this morning," Louise said, sipping her coffee. "Anything wrong?"

Oh, yes, Clara thought, only a shadowhound and an army of mice and no way to explain why either was following her. Clara stared at her coffee with dry eyes still scratchy from lack of sleep. Beyond that, she felt the pull of the anderwelt—she missed it. She couldn't think of a way to use her hours after work to slip into the anderwelt without Louise noticing—and resenting—her absence, and the brief time she had spent there had already woven itself into a habit. More than a habit, she realized. It was closer to a vocation, or a love affair.

"Nothing, nothing. I just didn't—" Clara stopped herself. If she admitted she hadn't slept well, Louise might take offense, having accepted the offer of Clara's bedroom. She sighed. Why were people so complicated, with their inconvenient emotions and illogical reactions? Louise no more than most, she amended guiltily, taking a defensive sip of coffee. It wasn't her sister's fault Clara didn't have the mental dexterity for dealing with delicate, easily bruised things like emotions today.

"You're not unwell, are you?" Louise leaned toward her. Clara wanted to stay annoyed, but there was genuine concern in her sister's eyes.

"No, I'm fine. I was just thinking about—it's not important. Work problems." Louise raised an eyebrow but didn't argue. She must look a fright, all dark circles and bloodshot eyes, Clara thought. What a silly thing to fuss over, she chided herself, when she was stalked by rodents—but she did want to look her best when she met with Dr. Gagnet for their promenade in a few days' time.

Clara wasn't sure why she hadn't told Louise about Dr. Edouard Gagnet. She wondered how Louise would react if she knew about him. Surprised, certainly, but would she be pleased or appalled? Concerned or relieved? Perhaps, Clara thought, a bit of everything. Louise had always been the more sociable of the two, but Clara knew that Louise carried a few deep wounds she didn't speak of, all due to a Mr. Henry Foster, who had called regularly for years and had been expected to propose but never did. The last Clara had heard, he had married Blanche Kingston, the prettiest and also blandest girl in Louise's class in school.

There was time for that, Clara decided as she gathered her coat and hat and left Louise happily sipping coffee and paging through one of her guidebooks. It might even, she conceded, be rather nice to confide in Louise over that sort of sisterly talk. She made her way to work still bleary despite the coffee and started on the simplest task she could, to avoid botching anything complicated in her sleep-deprived state.

"I've brought you a present!" Fritz's voice just behind her chair nearly startled Clara out of her skin. "*Mein Gott*, you're like a jumping jack!"

"Have you ever considered not sneaking up on people?"

"Have you ever considered that you have absolutely no awareness of the outside world when you are working?" Fritz laughed.

Clara had to admit that usually his assessment would be correct, even if today she wasn't solely thinking about work. "You said you had something for me?"

"My sister's famous *apfelkuchen*. She insisted I bring you a nice big slice. We are so looking forward to having you and your sister for dinner this week—she'll bake another big *kuchen* and make you take half home."

"That's very kind." Clara accepted the half-smashed paper packet. It did, she had to admit, smell divine.

"And I hope it makes up for this?" Fritz gingerly handed her an envelope. "Picard himself was so impressed with your work on the lighting that he said whoever designed the Palace of Illusions lighting should fix the design for the exterior of the Palace of Optics. Monsieur Blanchard has, between you and me, failed quite completely to rectify the problem."

"And after he stole my sandwich," muttered Clara. "Fine, fine, what does it look like?"

Fritz dropped the papers into her hands and retreated. "I am merely the messenger!"

"It's all right, Fritz, I—" She began to scan the papers. "This is a complete mess."

"I know. I know! I will happily do whatever I can to help, but I have four other projects. Lavallé keeps dropping more adjustments on projects we've completed already, and then pulling other projects from us. I don't know who he's getting to finish them, but I don't want us to look as though we're slacking on the job, you know—"

"Yes, yes, I know. I can already see how to fix one of these errors. And what's this?" She pulled a note from the stack of papers, handwritten on good ivory stationery. An invitation— no, more like a summons. "You could have mentioned it would involve a dinner with the board."

"Ah, well. I thought that was a nice bonus?" Fritz grinned wickedly.

"I don't want to have dinner with the board! Will you be there? Please tell me you will be there."

"I will be there, and I will endeavor to ensure that you are seated near me so that I can save you from both the horrors of speaking French and of the French speaking horrors to you."

"Very funny."

"You say that, but Messieurs Mercier and Lavallé are absolute letches."

"Lovely." She glanced again at the date. It was the same as her next arranged walk with Dr. Gagnet. She suppressed a groan. Of course—and she had, foolishly, never gotten his calling card to send him a message in case she had to reschedule. That had seemed both highly unlikely and very forward. It presumed treating their meetings as anything other than chance encounters. Now Clara wished she had been just a bit bolder.

The thought of Dr. Gagnet waiting for her, pacing the steps in front of the Grand Palais, believing she had forgotten their meeting or, worse, chosen to ignore him—it settled like lead in her stomach.

No, she would have to track him down.

But first, work. She pulled the blueprints for the Palace of Optics, the plans that had been made thus far, and began to draw. The ideas flowed from thought to pencil, scratching into her notepad with a bright rhythm. Within an hour she had found the source of the original design flaw—a miscalculation with the wiring— and had begun to work new schematics. And better ones, she thought as she checked her numbers, that would allow for the lights to change and shift, to seem as though they were dancing along the grand fluted shell of the exterior of the Palace of Optics.

She realized with a start sometime after four o'clock that she was hungry, and after leaving her preliminary designs on Fritz's desk, she decided to solve her problem with Dr. Gagnet and get a sandwich in one outing.

She recalled what he had said on their first meeting—that he worked in one of the public hospitals, l'Hôtel Dieu. She found she knew without having to consult a map which tram to take—a great improvement in her skill, she congratulated herself. Soon the great white facade loomed before her. It was quiet, but not entirely peaceful. Instead, the entry felt hushed, stifled. Men in white smocks and nuns in full habits moved like ghosts in the hall just past the entryway. Clara realized she had no idea how or where to find Dr. Gagnet or anyone to help her.

Luck was on Clara's side—the Augustinian nun occupying the

entryway happened to be Irish, which Clara ascertained quickly from her accent even when she greeted her in French.

"Good morning!" she almost shouted in relief, and then recovered her decorum, blushing. "Good afternoon, I mean."

"May I help you?" the nun sighed, as though this was only the latest in a series of trials to befall her lonely post.

"I'm very sorry, but I am trying to find a particular doctor employed by the hospital," Clara said.

The woman looked at her as though assessing a new hired girl and finding her entirely disreputable. "Well—do you know if he's a ward surgeon or a staff physician?"

"I—I really don't know, I'm sorry."

"What do you need him for?" She drummed the cover of a book on her desk. "We don't make appointments that way, you know."

"No, it's not—it's of a personal nature."

"Oh, I see." She raised an eyebrow. "Bold of you to come here. Usually they secret their...mistakes away somewhere else to get things taken care of."

Clara felt as though she had been submerged, suddenly and cruelly, in cold water. "No, it's nothing like that at all! Dr. Gagnet and I are...friends. Merely friends. I needed to contact him to break an engagement." She paused. "Not that sort of engagement, I mean a meeting."

The nun's thin eyebrow remained arched with suspicion, but she turned back to the book, which appeared to be a directory. "Gagnet, you said? Is that G-A-G-N...?"

"Yes, yes. Edouard Gagnet."

The nun flipped through the book. "Awfully sorry, miss, but he's not listed here."

"Are you quite sure? He told me he is employed by this hospital."

"He did, did he." She quirked a smile, not entirely nice but with a faint hint of knowing sympathy. "Told you it would be all right, he'd take care of you if anything happened, because he's a doctor?"

Clara felt the warmth go out of the room. "No, no, he said nothing of the sort. And I—I wasn't—" She faltered. Had Dr. Gagnet lied to her? It seemed impossible. "Perhaps I misunderstood him—my French isn't very good. Maybe he is employed at a different hospital."

The sister gave her a look that told her she thought that as likely as finding a pair of porpoises dancing a minuet down the hallway, but shrugged. "I have a directory of all the licensed doctors in the city. I'm afraid I don't have a compendium for all of France," she added with a mild snort. She dragged a large book out from a drawer. "It's G-A-G-N...all right, here we are."

Relief flooded Clara, but as the nun rattled off a list of names, it was clear Edouard was not among them. "Philippe Gagnet, Simon Gagnet, Jean Gagnon..." She waved her hand over the book. "Anything familiar?"

"Thank you for your time," Clara mumbled, tears spiking her eyes.

The woman softened. "Look here, love. Chin up. It seems you didn't make too grave an error with the fellow, whoever he was. Just got a bit heartsick, that's all. It mends right quick."

Clara nodded but didn't feel any better. Her error, she worried, might have been graver than the nun could realize. There was only one good reason she could think of that a man would lie to her to get close to her. The key.

Chapter Twenty-Five

CLARA WALKED HOME half numb, knowing it would be far faster to take a tram but preferring the time to sift through what had happened and sort out fact from speculation.

The waters of the Seine lapped against the bulwarks below her, and she bit back unexpected tears. Why, of all the far more important things to consider, was she most affected by the dawning realization that Dr. Gagnet's interest in her had been fabricated? She felt incredibly stupid, to have believed that she might hold some attraction for a handsome, successful man. She had been taken with him, flattered, begun to foster feelings—and it was all a lie.

Then, of course, there was the real problem. If Gagnet had lied to get close to her, and it had something to do with the anderwelt, how did he know that she had Godfather's key in the first place? And who was he? Could he be a craftsman, Clara wondered—or part of the conspiracy Magda suspected? One bright spot, Clara considered—he had no idea she had found him out. She weighed what to do with this information but, given she had no way of finding him, decided it was ultimately of little use in the immediate sense.

She climbed the stairs to her apartment slowly, dreading the cheerful chatter Louise was sure to pepper her with, all the while pretending she hadn't just discovered another threat stalking her through Paris.

Louise was waiting for her and didn't seem to notice that Clara's mood was more melancholy than usual. "I've managed to get us into an atelier for gowns—not one of the best, but it came recommended. You're rather later than I expected, so we do need to hurry."

"Louise, I—I'm not sure I'm particularly up to an errand today."

"An errand?" Louise laughed. "Hardly! This will be fun!" She pinned her hat into place and pulled on her gloves. "And if we've time, I'm determined to take you somewhere to get proper gloves and shoes."

"What's wrong with my shoes!"

"Did you buy them in the men's department?"

"No," Clara replied, not inclined to tell Louise she had accidentally procured them in the boys' wing of a French department store because she had misread the signs. "They're nearly new. I don't need any others."

"Indulge me," Louise said with a smile, and Clara found she had no good excuses—at least, none she was willing to share. The thought of admitting what had happened with Gagnet to her sister—she felt a deep, cutting shame. Of course Gagnet wasn't really interested in her. Louise would have seen right through him, Clara thought. Louise understood people in a way Clara only understood gears and cogs.

Louise navigated them to the atelier with the skill of a homing pigeon; Clara wondered how her sister had memorized a map of

Paris so quickly. She introduced herself to the clerk at the desk and promptly rattled off a conversation in French that left Clara's head reeling. The clerk left them with a pile of swatchbooks.

"Now, Mother insists you're to have an evening gown—you'll need one for Exposition things, yes? And after seeing your wardrobe, I'm going to insist on at least one afternoon dress, too. And—"

"Louise, stop," Clara said. She drew her voice low and close between them. "I don't have the money for this."

"Mother said she would pay." Louise turned back to the swatchbook. "This moiré silk—I'm not sure I could, do you think? It's almost too modish, but it is pretty—"

"I am not letting Mother pay for my clothes," Clara replied, voice still a whisper. "I'm not a child."

"Neither am I," Louise replied blithely.

"You know what I mean, I—"

Louise closed the swatchbook with controlled precision. "Yes, I know exactly what you mean. You're a modern, independent woman who doesn't need anyone or anything. You live in Paris by yourself and pay your own way. And I am—well. Your dullard sister who is still setting her cap for a nice young man to marry." She leaned closer to Clara and lowered her voice. "But you are wearing boys' shoes and you don't have a stitch to put on if you're expected at any evening events. For your job. At which, may I remind you, you are so very independent and modern."

Clara seethed but didn't reply. She'd been humbled by the false interest of Gagnet, and now her sister's assessment was far too accurate for comfort. For the first time since she came to Paris, she felt like a fool.

"So please, Clara, accept a little help. I'd enjoy seeing you wear something that showed off how pretty you are, fair enough? And it would make Mother very happy to know she could give you a useful gift." She turned back to the swatches. "People like feeling useful, and it's a kindness to let Mother give you a gift."

Clara wanted to blame Louise for the uncomfortable swamp of emotions she found herself in. But it was hardly Louise's fault— no, it never had been Louise's fault, she acknowledged. "All right," she whispered, then, louder, "Yes, all right."

"Thank you," Louise said. "Now. Do you want to select your own fabrics or should we let the dressmaker pick for you?"

Clara reluctantly took a swatchbook and thumbed through it, to Louise's well-hidden frustration, pointing out several wools and a cotton that wouldn't do for evening gowns at all. "What colors do you like?" Louise finally asked after Clara got lost in a page of black crepes.

Clara paused and thought. She usually chose colors that were practical against stains and that would blend into a room of men in dark suits. She stood out enough being the only woman in a man's job, and she didn't feel like drawing more attention to herself. The atelier's clerk sat tabulating some figures; her dress was a rich cranberry. Louise wore a walking suit of robin's-egg blue, enchanting little notches cut out to show her pristine white blouse beneath. It was as though neither woman had ever considered *not* being seen.

"I like blue," she finally said. "Not light blue like your dress but darker. Kind of green and blue, maybe."

"Good, that's good. Blues and teals, we can work with that. What else?"

"I don't like red." She wasn't sure what made her say so with such finality, but it felt right. "I don't like any shade of red, really. I do like brown, but I don't think that it likes me, particularly."

"No, it does not," Louise confirmed. "What about pinks, or purples, or—"

"Maybe dark purple? Is it called plum, maybe? I don't know if I like pink." She found herself smiling. "I never tried to like pink."

"Well, that's something, anyway." The dressmaker called them in, and Louise conversed comfortably with her as an assistant measured Clara and decisions were made about her wardrobe, chiefly the addition of one afternoon gown, a walking suit of deep midnight-blue wool, a dinner dress in forest green, and an evening gown of an arresting indigo that Clara was sure was a few shades too visible for her comfort.

"That wasn't so bad, was it?" Louise asked.

"How do you—" Clara paused. Louise waited. "How do you know what to choose? What will look nice, what colors will look best together?"

"How do you know how to fix a clock?" Louise laughed. "I suppose there's some knackiness to it, an instinct—but really, Clara. I just read a magazine now and again."

Chapter Twenty-Six

SHE NEEDED TO tell Magda, Clara resolved, staring at the ceiling as mice played staccato rhythms in the walls behind her. If Gagnet wasn't who he pretended to be, if someone had lied to get close to her—she needed help.

Clara sought Magda out the next morning, before she even went to work. She didn't care that it was far earlier than acceptable for Parisian social calls when she banged on the door of Magda's workshop. Fortunately, it appeared Magda kept early hours—or hadn't gone to bed—as she answered the door promptly, her leather apron smeared with fresh grease and a pencil protruding from her frazzled bun.

"Must be important," Magda said as she held the door open. "Come on in."

"I think I might know something about the person following me." Clara shucked her coat and waited for Magda's reaction, which she assumed would be alarm.

"Well, that's broad," Magda replied with irritating calm. She shoved a stool toward Clara. "Sit down, I'll make coffee." She glanced at Clara. "No, tea. You're too wound up for coffee, you might bust a gear."

"Aren't you worried?" Clara asked, ignoring the stool to follow Magda into the ramshackle kitchen off the workroom.

"I've been worried for about three decades," Magda muttered. She set a kettle on an ancient potbellied stove. "Well, who is he?"

"I don't know. I don't know anything, really. Only his assumed name." She handed Magda the tin of tea sitting in a basket of odd pantry items next to her. "He told me his name was Edouard Gagnet, and that he was a doctor. One or both of those things is not true."

"Now that's a fun riddle!"

"I—I tried to call on him at the hospital he said he worked at, but there is no doctor there by that name, or anywhere else in the city."

"Tried to call on him?" Magda's eyebrows shot up.

Of course that was what Magda picked up on. "Yes. He had—befriended me."

"Oh, that's the oldest trick in the book, isn't it!" She laughed, not cruelly, but Clara's ears reddened. "He acted like he was smitten, did he? And you fell for it, as you would—he was probably quite charming. Quite handsome." She waited, and took Clara's silence for an affirmation. "Ha! Well, let me tell you, it's only age and wisdom and plenty of disappointment that blunts the edge of that particular weapon."

"I didn't tell him anything."

"You sure?"

"I'm sure. I was cautious, even if I didn't have any reason to suspect him at first—our meeting seemed so accidental! But I'm used to keeping Exposition plans under wraps, so I was careful about what I was saying."

"I'm sure you were."

"What's that supposed to mean?"

"It doesn't take a psychoanalyst to discern that you're rather cautious as a rule." Magda snorted, and her cup clattered on her saucer. "He could be connected to the blights. Very well could be." Magda added a chipped teapot to the mismatched array of china. "Found another yesterday on my rounds. Out in the Bois de Vincennes. Small, but I swear the others look larger this morning."

"What do you mean by that?" Clara asked, startled.

"It's all theoretical, of course, because you can't just run experiments on blighting the anderwelt, but the reigning theory is that blights can feed one another. You add one, it strengthens or expands the others." She fiddled with the burner on the stove. "Darkness begets darkness, chaos begets chaos. The whole of anderwelt could fall into blight and the world out here would be as dull and gray as ash..." Magda paused, seeing Clara's eyes widening. "I don't know, I don't deal in the theoreticals much."

Implying, Clara ascertained with growing frustration, that there were people who did deal in the theoreticals. She wondered if she should perhaps ask for a reading list. A syllabus, as it were, on the anderwelt. It would have to wait, Clara knew, which was too bad—she needed to know far more than she did.

Magda tasted her tea and made an approving face. "The really useful bit is—he doesn't know that you've found him out, best as we can tell. So if he comes sniffing around again, maybe you see what you can learn from him."

"I couldn't!" Clara paused. "Wait. I'm supposed to meet him for a walk soon—don't give me that look, Magda—but I have to be at a dinner for the Exposition. I couldn't find him to tell him." A plan formed quickly. "You could go and see if you recognize him."

Magda sucked her lips around her teeth, the idea clearly sour tasting to her, but she didn't produce an argument against it. "I doubt anything will come of that, but you never know. Could be worth a try—anything is, really. Paris is filling up with all kinds of interesting sorts these days. There are handwerkerin all over the world, you realize that, don't you?"

"I suppose I would have realized it if I'd given it a thought. I've been a bit busy worrying over schattenhunds and my sister showing up and my very stressful job."

"Don't get pert with me, child." She smiled as she sipped her tea. "It could explain that faux physician. You and I are far from the only people in Paris who know the anderwelt exists, and it's certainly possible other people know who you are."

"I don't particularly like that thought."

"Who would?" Magda reconsidered. "Except for narcissists and politicians and actresses, I suppose."

"What am I supposed to do?"

"Keep on with it."

"That's your advice?"

Magda shrugged. "I'm old, what do you want? I've been on my own for years. I've gotten patient."

Clara felt an ember of frustration, and more than that, something almost like betrayal. Magda was her only ally, and if she wasn't going to take the mysteries and threats surrounding Clara seriously, what was Clara supposed to do? Godfather had cast her to sea alone, and Magda's plan of nonintervention left her adrift. There was a time for patience, but this was not it. This was the most significant and terrifying thing to ever happen to Clara.

She considered what she knew so far. Blights plagued Paris and seemed to be spreading; she had no idea who caused them.

Godfather had sent her a key, so perhaps he knew something was afoot, though he'd told her nothing. Disconcerting, there were clearly others who knew far more than Clara herself did. Gagnet was not who he claimed, but could certainly be a craftsman, a conspirator, or both. Nussbaum and Sandmann were both in Paris; what one or both knew of the blights, or her key, was still unknown.

Clara recognized with new clarity how very limited her understanding was, and that Magda was not entirely reliable for providing more information. She trusted Magda, but the woman was fiercely independent and seemed to have divorced herself from not only the business but the society of other craftsmen. There could be plenty that she simply wasn't aware of.

Which meant, Clara decided as she said her farewells to Magda, that she would have to forge ahead on her own. Starting with one of the easier questions to answer: Who was Nussbaum, really?

Clara didn't have time to answer that question immediately, she acknowledged. She was late to work already, and a pile of revised plans waited on her desk. She had promised Louise they would make dinner together—a proper dinner, not half a baguette eaten on the sofa. She had neglected the laundry for weeks and a stack of letters from Mother and Father and several distant family members waited to be answered. Clara closed her eyes and, for a long moment, let herself feel utterly overwhelmed. Then she caught the next tram to work.

The next morning she traced the route back to Nussbaum's hotel, stopping a block or so from the entrance and turning into a quiet alley. She swiftly pulled the key from her pocket, braced herself for the rush and blaze of light, and found herself in an alley made not of brick but interwoven tree branches and foliage.

There wasn't time to admire the masterwork of topiary that had overtaken most of a city block. Instead, she moved quietly and quickly through the streets. Deserted, as she'd expected.

Except. There was movement near the hotel, a rustle and a repetitive tap that could have been footfalls. Clara peered around the corners, hiding herself as best she could behind a thick cascade of foliage from one of the trees. Someone was just inside the entrance of the hotel, and the doors were growing.

Clara blinked. The doors had grown to twice the height of their counterparts in the ordinary world, and seemed thicker and broader, with a slim, barred window set high in the left panel. In fact, all of the windows had narrowed, and many of the lower windows were barred in delicate wrought iron. A fortress—the hotel had taken on the aspects of a medieval castle.

Before she could wonder what that meant, Nussbaum stepped outside. He ran a hand through his disheveled hair, glancing at a piece of paper and muttering to himself. Clara watched him, his attention entirely absorbed with what she assumed might have been a schematic as he referenced it and then set his hands to the lowest window and drew it narrower—how? She squinted. He didn't hold any tools and the window frame was made of dark wood as hard and unyielding as stone, but he seemed to pull it closed as easily as a voile curtain.

He repeated the adjustment on the other side of the door, and then stepped back to assess his work. Clara leaned forward slightly, hoping to see what was in his hand, and the branch under her hands snapped. She pulled back, but the damage was done— the sound rang out like a shot and, worse, the curtain of leaves swayed as obviously as a flag waving at her precise location.

Nussbaum turned instantly, eyes wide with suspicion and body taut with the tension of a cat ready to pounce. Clara did the only thing she could think of—she turned and ran.

The avenue of trees hid her movements at first, but when it ended, she was in the open, on a large thoroughfare with ironwork lampposts shaped like stern giants holding candles. They seemed to point at her as her footfalls scrambled on the stones.

"*Pardon! Arretez-vous, pardon!*" Nussbaum's voice followed her. Why hadn't she slipped back into the ordinary world when she had the chance? She chided herself for her rash decision-making—in Paris proper she would have blended in with a street full of people, and anyone witnessing a man chasing a woman was sure to side with her. Here, she was alone—and Nussbaum was gaining on her.

Just ahead, the Jardin des Tuileries opened from the street. She knew that space better than others, and perhaps, she reasoned, she could lose Nussbaum in the Christmas Wood long enough to use the key. Her shoes scattered pearlescent dust from the pavers under her feet as she dashed past the first fountain. She chanced a look behind her—Nussbaum was still in pursuit.

Worse, he had seen her face. She was sure there was no way he didn't recognize her. He called out, confirming her fears.

"Miss Ironwood, please! I'm not going to hurt you!"

She found enough breath to yell back. "Then why are you chasing me?"

"Fine! Fine, I'm slowing down!" She glanced behind her and saw Nussbaum check his pace and hold up his hands. She took the opportunity to duck into the Christmas Wood, spreading dark and thick and richly scented before her. "Damn it!" Nussbaum shouted behind her.

She dodged tree branches and plunged deep into the wood,

flattening herself against a deep green fir tree to catch her breath. Hands shaking, she pulled out the key.

"Hello again!" Clara nearly yelped, but it was only Olympia. "I knew you'd be back, but oh dear—what is it? You look all out of sorts!"

"I'm sorry, I can't talk now!" Clara brought the key to her eye.

"I can help, I'm sure! You were so kind—" Olympia reached for her hand just as the blaze of light overtook her and the anderwelt melted away.

Chapter Twenty-Seven

CLARA FOUND HERSELF in an underused corner of the Jardin, blinking away the last of the key's light. She had to move quickly, to get to a busy street where she could lose herself in the bustle and flow of Paris, before Nussbaum popped out from the anderwelt and—

She realized there was a taut grip on her wrist.

Heart racing, she looked down. Olympia sat on the ground, one hand clutching Clara. Her legs were splayed at haphazard angles, dancer's turnout and posture abandoned.

Her eyes were blank and dead.

Clara's stomach dropped. The figure next to her was nothing but a life-size, lifeless doll. Olympia was as perfect a replica of a human as Clara could imagine, but the breath and pulse of life she had in the anderwelt were gone. Clara pried her hand from her wrist—it was harder than she expected, as she had to release each finger one by one. She set the hand in Olympia's lap, nausea stirring at manipulating the shell of the dancer.

"Oh no." Nussbaum. Clara leapt back, tripping over a curb and nearly falling. "What happened to Olympia?" He knelt gently by her side and checked her limbs, turning her wrists and ankles deftly. To Clara's horror, but also curiosity, he unscrewed one of her hands and checked the functioning of the gears hidden inside. He looked to Clara with shock drawing his face white. "Why did you do this to her?"

"I didn't!" Clara backed away farther, more terrified than ever. "She grabbed my hand just as I came through, and—"

The tension didn't leave his face. Clara felt the direction of suspicion shift suddenly. It wasn't merely that he recognized Olympia. Anyone who had visited the Parisian anderwelt might have become acquainted with the dancer in the Christmas Wood. No, it was the dismay clouding his expression, the strain of grief on his voice. He was who he said he was—a handwerker who knew the value of the anderwelt, not someone with an aim to exploit it.

"Please," Clara whispered. "It was an accident. Is she—can she be brought back—or is she—" She caught her breath. "It was an accident."

Nussbaum met Clara's eyes. "I believe you. For a moment I—I wondered if it was worse than just Olympia, that you were the one who's been blighting the anderwelt."

"I'm not!" Clara retorted. "This was entirely unintentional. I have never brought anything back through, and I'd never blight the anderwelt."

Nussbaum rocked back on his heels and sighed. "You didn't intend to, but you just did."

Clara felt sick. "I didn't mean to," she protested.

"I can see that." He smiled tersely.

Clara forced herself to look at Olympia's blank, lifeless face. "Can she be fixed?"

Nussbaum nodded. "It can be done, though it will be difficult.

I do not know why you ran from me, or why you were spying on me, but I am afraid I am going to have to trust you now. We have to take her back through to the other side so I can repair her, but we can't do it here."

"Why not just go back right now?" Clara raised her key. "I'll just—"

"No! The other side, this spot, is blighted. Because of what you—" He paused. "I know it was accidental. But ripping any creation from the anderwelt creates the blight, and I promise that you do not want to end up in the middle of one."

"Like the ones along the Seine, in the Exposition grounds."

Surprised, Nussbaum nodded. "Then you've explored more than I anticipated already. Yes, like those." Nussbaum seemed to run a quick calculation, ticking off a few numbers on his fingers. Clara found herself uncomfortably disarmed by the distant look in his green eyes and how his teeth caught his lower lip as he thought.

"We'll just need to move her a short distance, but how to do so without being seen, that's the trouble."

"What can I do? I didn't mean to hurt her, really I didn't. She was so sweet, and such a beautiful dancer."

"You've met her before?"

Clara nodded.

"It seems we have quite a bit to discuss. But first we have to—"

The chatter of a group of small children interrupted them. Nussbaum fell silent and bit his lips close together. His hair was still a mess of honey-brown waves that fell into his eyes. Clara was struck by the way he looked, not imposing, but vulnerable. Scared.

The children, followed by a pair of nuns, scampered into view. Nussbaum watched them, careful assessment in his clear eyes. "That complicates things." He swallowed, hard.

"I have an idea." Clara watched the children, who had gathered around a fountain and had no intention, it seemed, of leaving. The morning was bending toward noon, and plenty of people would soon fill the park. "Can you trust me?"

"It seems I have no choice."

"Well, consider the feeling quite mutual. Pick her up. Follow me. And oh—you'd better catch on quickly, because if anyone has to do the talking in anything but English, it's going to have to be you."

Nussbaum didn't argue, but his face didn't get any less pale, either. He gathered Olympia in his arms as easily as if she'd been a pile of laundry. Clara nodded firmly and, she hoped, confidently, and marched straight past the children.

"*Bon matin!*" she said brightly. "*Vouz êtes*…um…excited… *joyeuex pour l'Exposition*… soon?"

The nuns swooped in closer, ready to protect their charges from Clara's baffling mix of French and English. They didn't have time to question her before Nussbaum followed, carrying the lifeless Olympia. They all gasped, and the children crowded close. "*Qu'est que c'est?*" the youngest of the nuns stammered, eyes wide under her starched wimple.

"*Une nouvelle attraction de l'Exposition!*" Clara said. "Ah, tell your friends?"

Nussbaum caught on in a flash. "*Ca, c'est un merveille, une invention moderne! Une automate! Elle est une danseuse, voyez!*"

The children clamored to see Olympia better, interest piqued by the mention of an automaton, and the nuns didn't bother holding them back. Nussbaum cleared his throat and, Clara assumed, said something about the marvelous automaton they might see at the Exposition. One child shouted a question and then several others chattered in agreement.

Nussbaum glanced at Clara, apology in his eyes, and then set Olympia by the fountain. Beneath her left shoulder, there was a delicate brass lever that Clara now realized, as Nussbaum turned it twice, was a key. It settled strangely in Clara's stomach, seeing Olympia treated like a toy—a life-size, impossibly complex toy, but a toy nonetheless.

With no warning, Olympia jettisoned into movement, perfect feet laying a perfect pattern across the pavers. Clara was no dancer, but she thought it was the same choreography she had seen Olympia perform already. It was changed, somehow—no mistakes were introduced, no imperfections, but it lacked any artistry or expression. It was lifeless.

The children and the nuns did not share her reservation. They watched, eyes widening in joyful amazement, as the clockwork slowed and Olympia came to a stop mid-pirouette. Gently, almost reverently, Nussbaum straightened her legs and arms and invited them to visit the exhibits at the fair. Then he and Clara hurried away.

"All right, I admit—that worked rather well." Nussbaum shifted Olympia's weight and began walking.

"I suppose, but I wish—" She paused, the wish half formed. That she hadn't seen Olympia's perfect and yet almost ghoulish dance?

"I would have warned you, had we the time." Nussbaum sighed. "They will still work, the things made in the anderwelt, if they are brought here. But—"

"But you wouldn't want them to, once you've seen how they work." She shivered. "It was—I read this awful penny dreadful once, with voodoo and reanimated corpses. I would never have imagined describing a piece of clockwork that way, but it was like watching some dead, empty thing."

"It was," Nussbaum replied softly. "There is no crime one could commit in the anderwelt as deeply offensive as robbing a creation of that spark of life which makes it whole." He paused. "I did not mean that as an accusation. I know you did not mean to do it, Miss Ironwood."

"We need to get back," Clara said. "I—I suppose I'm not going into work today," she added with a laugh.

"It's not necessary." Nussbaum hurried to reassure her. "I can make the repairs myself."

"No, I—I want to, if that's all right."

"Of course it is all right. I would welcome it." He smiled, and Clara found she had hoped he would say so. "Now. Saint-Roch ought to be fairly deserted this time of day, and far enough from the ... site itself, so I think we can find a quiet corner somewhere to cross back over."

Clara nodded agreement, and furtively the trio made their way to the church's white facade. The baroque church fit into the street like a jewel box and, as Nussbaum had predicted, was vacant save for a priest tidying the altar. He didn't look up as they came in.

"Now then," Nussbaum said, sidling into a chapel lit with a few candles. "It might be easiest if we hold hands." He blushed at the suggested. "I don't mean to be forward—"

"Not at all. If it's the most practical, we ought to be practical." Yet she found she didn't mind that Nussbaum took her hand in his and let her hold Olympia around the waist. His grip was firm and yet gentle. She felt quite suddenly much safer, even as he pulled a button from his pocket, threaded through a string of blue silk. The button began to swing. His key, Clara realized, only seconds before the anderwelt settled around them like snow blanketing a field.

Saint-Roch's counterpart in the anderwelt was filled with light, which reflected off nearly every surface in dazzling, brilliant jewel tones. In the anderwelt the church did not merely resemble a jewel box, it was one. The walls and soaring ceilings were filled with frescoes rendered in sapphires, rubies, and emeralds, and translucent statues incandescent with the planes and angles of cut diamonds filled every corner.

Nathanael Nussbaum struggled with Olympia's lifeless form, scraping her limbs against the floor with a chilling echo, and Clara scolded herself for gawking. "It's all right," Nussbaum said. "The lapidary who worked on this church—he found ways to grow rubies and sapphires and the rest from seeds and then carved them into the statues you see there. Truly remarkable work."

"Did you say *grow* rubies and—" Clara shook her head. "No, not now. Olympia first."

Nussbaum nodded. "We'll take her to my apartment." As they left the church and skirted the Jardin des Tuileries, Clara forced herself to look at the blight she had made, the disease she had inadvertently spread across the anderwelt.

It wasn't there.

"Herr Nussbaum," she whispered urgently as he rearranged Olympia's limbs. "I thought—I thought I would see the damage I did from here. I—"

Nussbaum stopped mid-step and set Olympia down. "You should. You should be able to see it. It ought to be black from— from those gates inward, at least. But the Christmas Wood—it's still there." He took a step toward the park and then paused. "It's impossible. The wood should be all shadow, the trees wilted and decayed, the fountain—but it's still lemonade, from what I can see!"

"I didn't ruin it?"

"I don't understand how you didn't."

"Is it because I didn't mean to?" Clara asked.

"No, accidents have happened before, and always result in blight. This—I have never heard of this." He caught Clara's hand in a firm grip, holding up the key she still clutched between her fingers. "Unless it's something about your key." He met her eyes. "But it isn't yours, is it?" She shook her head. "It's Uncle Elias's key. I should have guessed."

Chapter Twenty-Eight

"ALL RIGHT, HAND me that screwdriver." Nussbaum beckoned with his left hand while the right held Olympia's blank face steady.

Clara passed him the tool, the handle carved of pale wood and the metal carefully polished. Everything in Nussbaum's anderwelt apartment was clean and spare. Unlike the soft tumult that had emerged into Clara's anderwelt apartment, layers of brocade and silk, texture and color, Nussbaum had pared his space into a haven of light and utility. It gave her room to breathe. Even though it was not terribly spacious, the tall windows spilled wide pools of light into every corner. A pale beechwood screen carved with trees and animals separated what must have been Nussbaum's bed, or some other space he preferred to keep private, from the rest of the room.

Nussbaum's tools reminded her of her own, a set both practical and beautiful. She wished she had her kit with her; but no, that wouldn't be helpful. She had no idea how to help repair Olympia. She wished she did, that she could peer over Nussbaum's shoulder and offer useful suggestions. Instead, all she could do was hand him instruments.

And watch him work.

He had thin hands and long fingers; Clara had noticed that right away. Now she saw that he had the calluses of a craftsman on his fingers, and the precise, quick movements of someone well practiced in his art. He had already removed Olympia's hands and feet and checked all the mechanisms housed in her minute joints. In his concentration, his loose waves had fallen into his face; absently, he tucked a strand behind his ear. Carefully, almost reverently, he removed the plate with Olympia's beautifully rendered face. Like a mask falling away, it revealed a web of complex wheels and gears underneath.

"There. Set that on the towel—" Clara had the plate carefully wrapped in white linen before Nussbaum could finish. "Thank you. See, this mechanism seized when she was brought through the veil. Now, if I take these gears out, can you oil them while I recalibrate the main springs?"

"Of course!" Clara said, too eagerly. She laid out Nussbaum's tools on a clean tray, hoping he would notice how orderly her methods were. Even for something as simple as oiling gears, Clara was nothing if not professional.

"Here." He barely glanced at her while handing her the pieces, one by one, but his fingers brushed her palm and her breath hitched a little. Working together with Nussbaum, shoulder to shoulder, was strangely intimate, nothing like working with Fritz. She thought about it; aside from Godfather, she had never worked in such close physical proximity to another person before. She laid out the gears to oil and began to work, pretending that she had answered the question of why Nussbaum's brief brush of a hand registered with her emotions at all.

She busied herself with the work, stealing glances at Nussbaum's progress. He had removed several large pieces and was refitting them into the frame, expertly fine-tuning the gears with his smallest pair of pinchers. He caught his lower lip between his teeth as he concentrated. Clara smiled, warm at the unintended intimacy.

"Do you have those pieces ready?" He didn't turn away from the dizzying array inside Olympia's head as he spoke. Clara returned them to him, one by one, remembering where each had gone and in what order.

"All right. I will try the mechanism and then we will put her all back together." He turned a few screws and the wheels sprang to life. He stopped just as quickly, made a few adjustments, and then tried again.

"Is it working?" Clara asked, nervous again. Nussbaum had been confident he could fix Olympia, but what if he couldn't? He would be well within reason to hate Clara for what she'd done to the dancer.

"Yes—at least, mechanically." He set his pinchers down and brushed his hair out of his face, as though he had just realized how untidy it had become. "Would you like to replace the facial plate?"

Clara flushed like a girl at a cotillion who had just been asked to dance for the first time. "Yes, I'm happy to." She positioned the finely carved face back into its setting and, reaching for the screwdriver, felt it placed firmly in her hand. Nussbaum's fingers rested briefly on hers, a moment unmoored in time, and then she was weaving minute screws back into their threads.

She had scarcely set the last screw in place when the vacant blue eyes under her hands blinked several times. Clara jumped back, nearly upsetting the table with Nussbaum's instruments still laid out with surgical precision.

"Oh, it's you!" Olympia pressed a hand to her chest. "You're the last thing I saw, and then—then here I am." She shook her head. "Something feels strange—oh, that's better," she amended, loosening a screw in her right temple with her fingernail. "What happened?"

"I'm afraid there was an accident," Nussbaum said.

Olympia turned to him and broke into a radiant smile. "Nathanael Nussbaum, as I live and breathe!"

"Not precisely accurate," he replied with a gentle smile.

"Come now, close enough!" She cocked her head. "Though I am curious what breathing would be like. Do you really fill your chests with air? Like...balloons?"

"We do," Nussbaum said, laughing now. "Almost precisely like balloons. Now. How do you feel? Does everything seem in order? All the gears properly aligned?"

"Yes, everything feels—why, I feel even better than usual!" She hopped down from the table and turned several perfectly executed pirouettes. "But what happened? An accident, you said?"

"It's entirely my fault," Clara rushed to explain. "I was just about to use my key to return to—well, the other Paris, you know. And you held my hand—"

"Oh, and I tumbled right through with you!" Olympia, to Clara's surprise, laughed. "How I wish I could have seen it! But I don't remember a thing."

"You wouldn't—the spark of the anderwelt left you the moment the key turned," Nussbaum said in a tone like an apology.

"I understand. I was told under no circumstances could I ever cross to the other side. That's the first rule, of course." She waited for their agreement, as though everyone had been trained in the same finishing school for life-imbued mechanical dancers that she had. "I'm awfully sorry for you, though, that must have been a terrible shock."

"It was," Nussbaum said softly. "And Miss Ironwood should not take all the blame. I was not behaving entirely rationally with her, and I frightened her." He met Clara's eyes over Olympia's carved wooden waves. "And I am sorry about that."

"It's all right," Clara said, finding herself oddly shy under his intense gaze. "Though I admit I am curious as to why."

"I'm curious about you, as well." Nussbaum smiled. A prickle of heat returned to Clara's cheeks.

Olympia watched the exchange and clasped her dainty hands. "I shouldn't bother you both any longer—I can make my way back to the wood. It's where I belong, and I feel a bit out of sorts anywhere else."

"Are you sure? We could accompany you, or—"

"Oh, it's not necessary at all! Not a bit. No, you two work out whatever you need to work out. People are so complicated that way."

"Now, no putting on airs, miss. We have just seen your very complicated innards."

"Why, Nathanael Nussbaum! How very gauche! To mention a lady's innards!" Olympia swatted his arm playfully.

"I will be sure to visit in the next day or so, to make sure that everything is in proper working order."

"I appreciate that, monsieur, but you know as well as I—if it were not, I'd be quite useless. Just a stringless marionette sitting on your floor, really." She smiled blithely, but Clara remembered, with a pang of guilt, Olympia as she had appeared on the other side—a puppet was an apt description. "*Au revoir*, friends!"

"Well." Clara glanced about the spare space, the open reaches of the floor and the abundant light making her feel exposed. "I suppose we should sort out what we need to say to each other."

Chapter Twenty-Nine

NUSSBAUM CLEARED HIS throat. "We do indeed. Taking a seat might be in order." He invited her behind the screen with a wave of his hand. She was relieved to see it wasn't a bedchamber after all, but a quiet sitting area with a pair of soft armchairs in airy gray and a low table already set with tea service. A stack of books sat nearby—ordinary, worn books with battered covers. She read the title of the top copy: *Hard Times* by Charles Dickens.

"Can I offer you tea?"

"I wouldn't want to be any trouble—"

"None at all," he replied, pouring a hot cup of perfectly brewed Earl Grey from the pot on the table.

"How...?" Clara accepted the cup and saucer. "I ought to stop asking that at some point, really. I know, I know. Anderwelt."

Nussbaum laughed. "A simple manipulation I would be happy to show you, if you like. But I think we have more important things to discuss. Sugar?"

"No, thank you."

Nussbaum took a small lump for himself. "Apologies first, then. Awfully sorry about the rodents."

"The rodents—you?" Clara pulled back as though one of the mice had appeared in front of her. "The mice came from you?"

"I confess it and I apologize for it."

"And the shadowhound?"

Nussbaum stopped mid-sip, spilling a bit of tea on his trousers. "Schattenhund? Never, no. You've been followed by a schattenhund?"

His shock seemed earnest. "Yes, before your rats, even."

"Mice only. I do not, mademoiselle, deal in rats." He broke, briefly, into half of a smile. "In any case. I had to know you were who you seemed to be, especially as you refused to meet me yourself. The mice watched your comings and goings and reported to me. I am sorry, but I had to know you weren't involved with the blights."

"I—I am to understand that not only do you control large groups of rodents, but they can talk to you." She held up a hand. "No—no, don't try to explain it, I find I'm forced to believe you."

"It's simple—mice are the only creatures that can come and go between the anderwelt and the regular world without a key. No one quite knows why—there's a lovely story that the first mice were actually born in the anderwelt and then infiltrated ours." Clara thought of another story—Godfather's "The Queen of Mice." Had he tried to tell her, in that strange little fairy tale, that mice were messengers between the worlds? "I doubt it's true. At any rate, it's a useful trick on occasion."

"But you . . . talk to them?"

"Not exactly. More like simple, tiny telegraphs from simple, tiny minds. There is magic in the anderwelt stranger than that. This is but a parlor trick, really. And, I might add, one that your godfather knows how to perform, as well."

"I should be shocked by that, and yet it does seem rather in character." She sighed. "What else does my godfather know how to do?"

"Juggle, hide things in a void of his own making, and make the most wonderful candied hazelnuts I've ever had."

"A void."

"Yes, and only he seems to have figured out how to do it. It's a bit like palming something using sleight of hand. But instead of slipping a coin in your pocket, he could slip it into the otherworld."

"Fascinating." She shook her head. "I'm sorry, but this is all rather new to me."

"I understand. Uncle Elias—he should have begun training you earlier. I cannot imagine he had intended for his line of craftsmen to die out with him." He set his tea down, waiting intently for her answer.

"I think—" Clara stopped, suddenly angry. She brought her voice under control, and the result was tight and short. "I think he decided I wasn't good enough. To risk training any further."

"I do not believe that to be the case." Nussbaum hesitated, then pulled a letter from a leather case he kept beside the tidy stack of books. "He wrote to me about you."

"You know, if you had led with a letter of introduction that first time we met, I might have been more willing to trust you."

"Consider it my mistake. We wrote in English so that I could practice—I had the idea he might at some point send for me." He handed her the letter, the familiar thickly formed pen strokes clearly written by none other than Christian Elias Thrushman, dated over a year earlier. She read it, breath catching.

I have found an American for an apprentice. This girl is quite extraordinary, and as you have already gained your key, it would be a terrible shame to waste the potential to bring new blood into our little family. I have silly dreams, an old man's fancies if you will indulge them, that you might find her an intriguing and charming girl if you were to meet her yourself. At any rate, she has progressed more quickly through the rudiments of clockwork, wood-work, and metallurgy, and I shall begin to advance her studies. I do hope you will meet her someday, either here or in the anderwelt.

"Godfather must have changed his mind," Clara replied, handing the letter back. "He never did advance my studies. He just put me to work in his shop, repairing clocks and making little things for sale. Music boxes, timed toys."

"Yes, but when you decided to come to the Exposition, how did he react?"

"Terribly! He railed about how I wasn't ready, I was a petulant child, I—"

"He didn't want you to go. And he refused to tell you why. It was because he wanted you to stay and realized he may have lost the chance to train you properly." Herr Nussbaum took the letter back, folding it precisely along the creases. "He had merely delayed your true apprenticeship, though as to why I can only guess."

"What do you guess?"

"Now that I've seen what his key does, it has to do with my guess as to why he sent it to you." He stood and paced slowly, fingers tapping against one another as though he were counting out a math equation. "When did it arrive?"

"With my family's Christmas package. Which would have been—oh, late November, I believe. He hid it in an old nutcracker."

"I see. I think that he sent it to you for safekeeping. Which means that he was afraid to have it with him. And I suppose you found the key at some point, and then—"

"No, I didn't," Clara interrupted. "I never liked that nut-cracker. I thought it was ugly, and a little creepy, to be honest.

I always had—I couldn't imagine why he sent it to me. I put it away and sent him a note thanking him. He must have sent me a telegram immediately after reading my note and realizing I'd found nothing out of the ordinary. So it's clear," she said, piecing together the edges of the puzzle, "he wanted me to find the key. He wanted me to make my way into the anderwelt. Whether he was afraid to have the key in America or no, he didn't merely send it to me in the nutcracker for safekeeping."

Nussbaum considered this. "He told you how to find the key in a telegram? And how to use it?"

"Not quite—he used a phrase only I would know, to make me keep looking. And I suppose he figured I would be curious enough at that point that I would eventually stumble on how to use the key. Which, clearly, I did."

"Yes, you did. Uncle Elias certainly intended to make you an apprentice, and I suppose we can say you are one now." He dug another paper from his case. "He was worried about you. I don't know if Paris concerned him, or the Exposition in particular, or if he only knew that you might be in danger from your association with him. But he sent me this." A small notecard, scuffed a bit around the edges, but with Godfather's broad handwriting on the back.

The lehrlingerin *is coming to Paris. Keep an eye on her. Make sure the rats don't follow her. Whatever you may think of me, protect her.*

Clara pointed to the unfamiliar word, and Nussbaum laughed. "It's the feminine version of the word for apprentice. I suppose he thought he was being clever. But it tells me clearly that he still believed you to be his apprentice—even if he did not hold up his end of the bargain as your teacher yet. It also tells me that he was afraid."

"And you have been acting—well, if it is not untoward to

suggest a gentleman is afraid." Clara set her tea down having barely touched it. "When I saw you, before you saw me, you were making the facade of your hotel into a fortress."

"I don't know for certain who to trust or what is happening here, but I do like having a bit of security. The anderwelt isn't dangerous, but craftsmen could be."

"You seemed suspicious of me."

"Not suspicious of you, exactly."

"It's perfectly all right. I was quite suspicious of you."

Nussbaum acknowledged this with a nod. "I was far more concerned that you, without realizing it, might have aligned yourself with—well. It sounds overly dramatic, but the anderwelt has enemies. In the Exposition, most of all. Someone is using the anderwelt for their own advantage, and the blights are increasing."

"I've realized." She glanced at the notecard again. "Why—why did he say this? 'Whatever you may think of me'?"

Nussbaum laid his hand over hers, covering the paper. Its loose edges fluttered lightly. "Because I was once supposed to be his apprentice."

"Oh, I—" Clara flushed. "I didn't mean to pry. If it's not—if it's not polite."

"He didn't dismiss me, if that is your concern. No, it's much stranger than that."

Clara remembered what Magda told her. "He was—well, kicked out, wasn't he?" For disobeying the rules, for ignoring the human side of the equation. Sounded exactly like him. "So he lost his chance at having an apprentice, then, too? Or—"

"Or I would have disowned him? Yes, I probably would have, given the choice." He sank into his chair, pensive. "You might as well have another cup of tea, the story is a long one."

"If you'd rather not," Clara began, but Nussbaum lifted a hand to stop her.

"You must know, at some point. You were told about his indiscretions, but not the extent of them, I presume."

"With the war on and the unification—there was a ban on going into the anderwelt, and Godfather did anyway. He—I don't quite understand entirely, but he spoiled a part of it."

"Correct. But there's a bit more to it. He was a well-intentioned man, always. He was younger then, and thought he could help, somehow. He figured if he used the anderwelt trick of hiding things in the void, he could prevent an entire battle, and the ripple of that would force the French into a détente—I'm not sure I followed the whole logic of it, but he truly believed he could stop the war."

"I'm sorry, how would you prevent a battle by hiding something in the anderwelt?"

"Not in the anderwelt itself, in a void—never mind, we'll go over that some other time." Nussbaum bit his lip, breaking into a smile. "Rather simple, really. Uncle Elias thought that if he hid an entire army, no harm would come to anyone."

"An entire army? In his…void?"

"To hear him speak of it, there is little difference between hiding a coin and hiding an army. The trouble was, as the tribunal assessed later, when he attempted to pull the army into the void, he hadn't considered the effects on the anderwelt itself. Or," he added, "on the young man who had tagged along."

"You were there."

"I was there. And then"—he laughed ruefully—"I wasn't. Uncle Elias must have lost control and the anderwelt rippled, collapsed— I am not sure how to explain it. It was the only explanation the tribunal could offer. And I was drawn into the anderwelt, out of

Uncle's control or my own. Whatever happened caused the ander-welt to be blighted instantly."

"Godfather, he—he left you there?"

"He didn't know I was drawn in, too. He hadn't asked me to come along—quite the opposite. And once in that realm of ash and dust—no one would stay long. You must understand, it was as though a thousand mortar shells had gone off at once in the anderwelt—it was a wasteland. I landed several miles from Uncle, and he was disoriented and, of course, of only one mind— to get out. He used his key within minutes, only to be immediately remanded to the guild authorities and summarily banned, as I later learned."

"He didn't try to find you afterward?"

"When I didn't write, or try to find him, he naturally assumed I had chosen to take an apprenticeship with someone else and didn't want to speak to him." His gaze lengthened as though he were looking far back into the past. "But as for me, I was trapped in the blighted part of the anderwelt, and no one was going to find me. I didn't know it then, but no one was allowed into the ander-welt within miles of what has come to be known as Elias's Folly. I was trapped," he repeated.

"Surely the guilds ought to have allowed some sort of rescue."

"They didn't know I was there, either—they thought I'd cho-sen to follow your godfather. You can't imagine the mess I had to untangle when I did return," he said with a weak smile. "For one, given the situation, I was allowed to become a craftsman without a formal apprenticeship, once everything was finally sorted out."

"Finally?"

"You have seen, I'm sure, how time works differently in the anderwelt. And space?"

"Time, yes. But space?"

"It can bend, or fold—under the control of a handwerker, usually. But in the blighted area, it did it on its own. It kept bending and folding and dropping me at its fringes, only to throw me back into the middle. And it was a far larger blight than any you've seen in Paris."

Slowly Clara began to appreciate the horror of what Nussbaum was describing. "When you say were trapped, you mean..." Suddenly she considered the decades that had passed. "How long were you there?"

"Nearly twenty years."

"My God."

"It didn't feel real, the passage of time in the blight. And," he said with a wry grin, "I didn't age much, did I?"

"No, you look—well, if you say you were a young apprentice in 1870, I'd believe that twenty years got lost somewhere in there." It seemed impolite to say aloud, but Nussbaum looked thirty at the most.

"If I say I spent twenty years in the anderwelt, you might imagine a prisoner marking days off on the walls of his cell. But I didn't know how many days had passed. For a very long time, all I knew was the ever-changing nightmare of the blight. But I couldn't get back without a key. It took me much of the time I was trapped to learn how to make my own. I could barely think in the darkness and confusion of the blight—and a key is no easy thing to make."

"But you made one."

"I did." He pulled a button from his pocket, threaded on a faded blue ribbon. "Simplest-looking thing I've ever made, and it took longer than your Palace of Illusions."

"How does it work?" She reached a tentative finger toward it, then retreated. It seemed oddly intrusive, as though she was prying into something intensely personal, not merely someone's work.

"The same way yours does. It captures and inverts the spatial and temporal fields of our world. Simple stuff, clearly."

"Yes, but I mean—I hold mine up and look through it. Yours—"

"Every key works differently. Strange, but if you try to copy a key, it never works. Here." He twisted the ribbon until it was taut, and the button began to spin. The ribbon twined and the button thrummed along its length and suddenly Clara was aware that, as she'd watched the button dance on their string, they had returned to the regular world.

No great flash of light, as she'd come to expect. No shaking or shedding of the old world, no fanfare. It had merely settled around her. She sat in an armchair, but it was situated in the corner of an ordinary hotel room, cramped between a dresser and a valet stand. "That was—it was entirely different. I wasn't paying attention, before, with Olympia."

"Elias always had a flair for the dramatic," Nussbaum replied. "I didn't have the luxury even if I had possessed the same theatrical leanings."

"Someday, if I want to keep going back and forth, I'll have to make my own key, won't I?"

"That's the way it has always been." Nussbaum tucked the key into his pocket. "I would help you, if you would like."

"I think I would." She smiled, then remembered where she was. "Though I probably shouldn't take my lessons here."

Nussbaum blanched. "I am sorry, I hadn't considered—well, you can rest assured that no one of any import comes in or out of this hotel who would see you."

Clara paused, remembering one person she had seen in this hotel. "One more thing. Herr Sandmann—do you know him?"

Nathanael's brow creased. "Why, yes, he's an old acquaintance of Uncle Elias, and we're in the same handwerker guild." He hesitated, then added with diplomatic neutrality, "He's not a very close friend, I must confess."

Clara had to laugh at the polite sidestep she would have made herself. "I remember him from his visits to Godfather, when I was a child. Age doesn't seem to have improved him, or I miss my guess." Nathanael shook his head. "Do you think...he couldn't be involved in any of this, could he?"

"Sandmann? No, I doubt that. He's a second-rate craftsman, and he tries to make up for it by worming his way into friendships with the right people. He's unpleasant, but harmless, I'd wager."

Clara nodded, not entirely convinced. Still, she reminded herself, childhood fears didn't constitute grounds for suspicion in the real world of adults. She glanced at the mantel clock. It felt like it had been days since she'd been home, and between the time that had passed in the anderwelt, perhaps it had been. As it stood, it was merely noon, but Louise would expect her home for lunch. "I have to be going," she apologized. "May I—may we continue our discussion another time?"

"Tomorrow, perhaps?"

"I wouldn't have dreamed of imposing so soon," Clara demurred, but when Nussbaum's face fell, she added, "but of course. I have so many questions. I've a dinner obligation tomorrow evening, but after—would that be too late?" Nussbaum shook his head with an eagerness that put a blush of color on her cheeks. "Nine o'clock, in front of the Grand Palais?"

Chapter Thirty

CLARA ATTEMPTED TO avoid Louise after lunch, which was, as Louise occupied her bedroom, entirely impossible. Clara had completely forgotten that they were expected at Fritz's for dinner, but for better or worse, Louise had never forgotten a social obligation in her life. "Are you going to change for dinner? I think I am—well, I haven't decided. Is this a more formal dinner, do you think, or—"

"It won't be formal," Clara almost snapped, then recovered herself. "It's just Fritz."

Louise assessed her with a single long glance. "You seem awfully out of sorts. Are you all right?" She pursed her lips. "Do you need a rest? Perhaps lie down a bit before we leave for dinner? I wouldn't want you to overwork yourself—"

"No, I am perfectly fine. I promise I am not overworked." In fact, work was the furthest thing from her mind. For once.

"You say that, but I wouldn't want anything to...happen. Again."

"Again?

"Oh, well, I don't—when you stopped working with Godfather.

I wouldn't want you to be…overworked." She paused. "You know."

Clara eyed her sister, taking in her concern, her averted eyes, and her sudden inclination to fuss with the antimacassar on the sofa. "Louise, why do you think I stopped working with Godfather?"

Louise paused. "Well, we all knew."

Clara bit her tongue. "What, exactly, did you know?"

"About your nerves. That you were…well, understandably, of course, it's nothing to be ashamed of." Louise reached out for a hand that Clara refused to give. "That you had a bit of a breakdown."

"Did Godfather," Clara asked slowly and very deliberately, "tell you that I had a breakdown? Did he say that to Mother and Father?"

"I don't know," Louise replied, eyes on the crocheted doilies decorating the sofa arms. "He wrote to Father that you were coming home, he must have—well, I don't know what he said, exactly. But Mother told me you had a bit of a collapse. She must have read between the lines, if he didn't say it explicitly, and of course why would he, he would be terribly uncouth to simply spell it out."

"Louise." Clara made her sister meet her eyes. "I did not have a breakdown. I do not suffer from anxious nerves. I don't know what Godfather said, but I am quite sure that he does not have sufficiently refined social graces to dance around saying as much if I *had* suffered a collapse of some sort."

"That is probably true," Louise mused. "Then why did Mother think so?"

"Because she's never understood—" Clara cut herself off. "It doesn't matter, and I don't know. But I assure you that I did not, have not, and am not in any current danger of having an attack of nerves. At least not due to work," she added in a muffled whisper.

"But if that wasn't the reason, then why did you stop working with Godfather? I thought that was all you ever wanted to do."

Clara exhaled. The answer to that question had grown more and more complex the more she learned about Godfather, and the anderwelt, and the key, and everything Nussbaum had just told her. She couldn't explain it all to Louise, that her concept of being an apprentice barely touched what Godfather would have eventually expected, that he was especially demanding given the nature of this responsibility. That something had happened to make him retreat from telling even Clara the secret. That Godfather might have gotten a little paranoid. But also that mysterious craftsmen in Paris did appear to be out to get her.

"He was a very difficult man to work with," she finally answered. "He was demanding. Nothing I did was good enough. I'm sure he had his reasons." She sighed. "But in the end, I wanted to go back to being simply godfather and goddaughter, and I'm afraid I ruined that."

"Oh, Clara, I'm sorry. I didn't realize. I thought—oh, I thought everything about working with him must have been perfect." She paused. "For you, anyway. I would have hated it."

Clara laughed. "As it turns out, so did I. He was such fun when we were children, though, wasn't he?"

"Yes. Though strange, and sometimes he almost frightened me." Louise's face settled into thoughtful softness. "Funny how the people we like best as children might not be the best sort of people to deal with as adults."

"Speaking of dealing with adults," Clara said, "though that term may not be entirely apt for Fritz Krieger, we should go." She stopped Louise's next question with an upheld hand. "And your hair is fine."

Fräulein Krieger greeted them with her usual warmth. "Miss Ironwood, it is such a delight to meet your sister! I do hope you won't mind if I resort to first names, so as not to confuse myself with two Miss Ironwoods."

"Of course not," Clara replied.

"After all, you have been in my home once already, and to come back is to let me fold you into our family. And then your family is my family, too!" She laughed and directed Louise to sit in their most comfortable chair, an overstuffed wingback with fading purple velvet upholstery. "So please, call me Alma."

"With pleasure," Louise replied, shifting in the chair against the springs Clara knew were hidden by lumpy batting.

Alma smiled. "Now, Clara. Would you be so kind as to assist me in the kitchen?"

"I would be happy to." Clara left Louise to banter with Fritz. He seemed delighted to have a conversation companion who relished it as much as he did.

"Here, take an apron. My, that's a pretty blouse!"

Clara had never been complimented on her everyday attire before, but she had let Louise starch and iron her blouse and change out the buttons. "Thank you. Should I chop the cabbage, or—"

"Don't worry about that just yet. I wanted to speak to you privately."

Clara's hackles raised instantly. Surely Fräulein Alma Krieger—sweet, gingerbread-scented Fräulein Krieger—couldn't be a person she should suspect? Did she need to be wary of every human in Paris? And the mice and rats, too, she amended.

Alma saw her reticence and rushed to reassure her. "It is not a bad thing, no! I am sorry if I alarmed you. It is only, I am returning to Heidelberg after the commencement of the Exposition."

"Oh, I'm sorry to hear that—or perhaps I'm not, if the circumstances are good ones?"

"Quite good, actually—I was engaged to be engaged, you might say, before I accompanied Fritz here." She handed Clara a towel embroidered with strawberries on the hem and they dried the dishes waiting in the sink as she talked. "I delayed in order to join Fritz for the past year. It was...important to him." She set the glass she was buffing down with a gentle smile. "You might not realize, but Fritz is a bit...uncomfortable with new people, in new places."

Clara raised an eyebrow. She wouldn't have described Fritz as uncomfortable at all, but she was comparing him to herself. "I wouldn't have guessed."

"He doesn't always get along easily. I came to keep house, yes, but he could have found a cleaner. Or just lived like an unkempt bachelor!" She rolled her eyes, then her face softened. "He needed me. He—well. He has never courted a young lady, and he has always found groups of men a bit hard to break into. He is so very sociable and outgoing but—"

"But he often feels rebuffed." Clara sighed, knowing too well what Alma couldn't articulate. "He isn't quite sure how to fit in."

"Precisely!" Alma handed her a large bread bowl to dry. "I do not mean to be forward, but—if he had interest, would you..."

"Alma Krieger, are you playing matchmaker?"

Alma blushed. "Well, not in any formal sense. I just worry that when I return, he'll be quite alone. I do so wish to see him set up his own household, find a nice young woman—I'm sorry if I am too forward, but I had to ask."

"I must confess," Clara said slowly, setting the bowl down with her towel still draped on its edge, "that I have not thought of your brother in such terms. And if he attempted to...pursue such interests, I cannot say that I would return those intentions." She avoided Alma's eyes. "But I do consider him a friend. At this point, a very good friend. The best friend I have here."

Alma stopped her with a wave. "I understand. There is no need to explain further. I just—I hoped, you know. He may never marry without some push, some miracle!" She laughed, but the laugh was hollow. "It is good to know he has a friend here. That is perhaps all I could really hope for."

Clara helped Alma slice cabbage and mash a pot of boiled potatoes, wondering all the while what Fritz would think of his sister's matrimonial schemes. Louise and Alma would probably have plenty to talk about, if they had the chance—comparing siblings who didn't seem to want to find a match and set up housekeeping. She was content with her work and her interests, or at least, she had thought she had been. She hadn't turned down the interest of a handsome French doctor, though. She had enjoyed their time strolling Paris's avenues, warmed under his kind questions, enjoyed the stupid flutter of her stupid heart at the way his eyes crinkled at the corners when he laughed, at the angle of his profile.

A sharp sensation in her eyes—dear God, was she crying? She set the knife down and rapidly wiped away the evidence that she had actual feelings for the facade of Gagnet. She'd been wrapped up in what his deception meant—for the key, for the anderwelt, for possible ties to the plague of blights—but this emotion was beyond the pale. She named it—sadness. Loss. What had she lost? She admitted it to herself—Gagnet had been a lie, but the warmth she felt, the hope she had put into his interest was real. Now she felt really and truly stupid. She shook her head and brought her focus back to the cabbage and the hefty knife Alma had given her.

And who knew what Fritz even wanted? He seemed happy enough. It certainly wasn't something she was going to discuss with him.

That was that, really—unlike Louise and Alma, she wasn't going to meddle. If Fritz wanted to find a bride, it was going to have to be on his own terms.

Alma was a wonderful cook and surprised them with a gloriously sticky marmalade roll after dinner was over, which Louise protested she couldn't be expected to eat but took a sizable slice of anyway. Fritz proposed a round of charades before dessert, which Alma readily agreed to. By the time they had cleared the dessert dishes and finished their cups of coffee, it was nearly nine o'clock.

"I could not in good conscience let two ladies go home alone at such an hour," Fritz apologized. "I will go with you. Now—yes, the tram is still running."

"How do you memorize the tram schedules?" Clara said. "There are so many different lines—I get them all jumbled up."

"No need in a year or so—the metro will simplify everything just beautifully."

"I won't be here, so that hardly helps," Clara said with a laugh, but the statement struck an uncomfortable chord. Where would she be in a year? The Exposition would run through October, and she had counted on making contacts that might lead to another job. But now every new acquaintance, every card slipped in her hand, every suggestion of employment was tinged with sour suspicion.

"Couldn't you be convinced to stay? I thought Paris might

finally have gotten into your bones." Fritz tilted his hat to a jaunty angle and opened the door for them. "They say it enchants everyone eventually, but I suppose you were a hard nut to crack."

"I have to go where I have a job," Clara demurred. It was dark, and unusually foggy, the streetlamps weak punctuations in the gloom. A single shadow, darker that the rest of the street, glowered in the recesses of a gutter. The schattenhund. Clara tore her eyes from it and turned back to her friends. "Do you have one of those to further the Parisian enchantment for me?"

"If ever I could offer someone a job, Clara Ironwood, it would be you." He turned to Louise as they sidestepped a puddle together. Already the schattenhund had receded in her vision, huddled in its oily corner. It wouldn't reveal itself to the others, and an oddly comfortable feeling of safety settled on her. Louise and Fritz—their trustworthy proximity made her feel safe. "She has the best head for mechanics of anyone I have ever met. I shall show her off accordingly at our dinner tomorrow and see if anyone can entice her to stay."

Louise looked taken aback for a moment, then beamed. "Well, I for one am quite proud of my sister. Just look at her—lighting up the fair with the *fée électrique!*"

"Ah, and you are the linguaphile of the family, then!" Fritz winked. "I must keep Clara's head from expanding, you see—so I will remind her that her French is atrocious. Did you quite understand what your astute sister said?" he asked with a teasing smile, turning to Clara.

She flushed pink. "Electric...something."

"The fairy electricity, it might best be translated. I've heard speculation already—it will be the displays incorporating electricity that will be the most astonishing. That will be remembered."

He laughed. "I should have hoarded all of those projects for myself, but no, I was a good manager and assigned them to my best employee."

"It is strange—a rather nice sort of strange, but still very odd—to think that in mere weeks thousands of people will see something that I helped make. That I will be able to point to the Palace of Illusions and say, 'I designed that bit of it. That part is mine.'" Clara smiled softly. "I don't mind that no one will know it was mine—I'll know."

"Yes, I'm afraid that Saint-Gobain will get the credit for the mirrors, and you and I will fade into obscurity." Fritz shrugged. "That is the way of it, you know—the art lives on and the artist is forgotten. Better to enjoy the work in the moment than aim for immortality, for it will surely pass you by."

Chapter Thirty-One

"WHY, MISS IRONWOOD! I had no idea you could look so charming." Fritz offered Clara a reassuring smile as he took her arm. What a difference a day made, Clara thought, feeling a bit disoriented at the sharp contrast between the Kriegers' cozy apartment and a supper of cabbage and potatoes and this, a formal dinner in the soaring hall of the Grand Palais. And yet, she realized, she appreciated more than she'd admit how Fritz hardly changed at all. "You really ought to wear colors more often, you know. All that gray and black is well and good for pragmatism, but it makes you look like a cranky old spinster."

"Who says," Clara said, poking Fritz in the ribs, "that I'm not a spinster? I like gray. It matches everything." She had to admit, however, that the dark green Louise had talked her into selecting for a dinner dress caught the light from the chandeliers in a fetching way. An exorbitant sum in rush fees to the atelier had ensured it was ready for this, her first formal Exposition affair.

"Gray does not match everything!" Fritz clapped his hand to his head in mock agitation. "One kind of gray does not even match all the other kinds of gray. You don't know the first thing about colors, do you?"

"I know how to wire several different sets of colored lights to the satisfaction of even the exacting Monsieur Picard, so there."

"Ach, and I've been wounded, fräulein!" Fritz laughed. "Now, may I offer a bit of advice, as a long-suffering veteran of these types of gatherings?"

"By all means." Clara surveyed the gold-rimmed china, the chandeliers dripping with crystals, and the abundance of silk velvet and taffeta swirling around her, feeling a bit dizzy.

"The higher-ups like to show off their best architects and engineers, but they don't actually like talking shop. It makes most of them feel rather stupid, in the end, as they don't understand the technical bits, so if they ask questions, answer simply."

"Got it. What else?"

"Avoid the oysters. They've been sitting out too long."

"Is that it?"

Fritz shrugged. "The champagne is good, but if you want to make a good impression, don't drink too much of it."

"I wouldn't anyway!"

"Of that I am quite certain. Ah, Monsieur Lavallé!" Fritz turned, pasting on a broad smile while he whispered to Clara, "Escape while you still can."

Clara followed his gaze and gasped. The man who had trailed her to the Folies, who had frightened her with his insistent gaze—there he was, in sharp evening dress, staring at the low-cut pink corsage of a woman standing nearby. She remembered where she was and closed her gaping mouth. Was that all there was to it? she wondered. Lavallé was a cad in expensive clothes, plying the same tired schemes men had employed for generations? She'd simply been leered at by a man well known for doing so? Yet it didn't quite fit—she was so sure he had followed her.

She retreated across the room, feeling both grateful and entirely alone. Which was worse, she wondered, being set adrift in a sea of strangers or enduring a few leers from Lavallé? His gaze crept back toward the woman in pink, and Clara decided that it was in fact better to ebb in a solitary tide.

She drifted toward a table set with dozens of coupes brimming with pale champagne, less because she desired a drink and more because it provided a point to anchor herself while she looked over the rest of the room. There were certain to be a few people she knew, acquaintances from previous meetings, people who she knew more from their names on reports than actual interactions. At least, she would have assumed so.

In a far corner, a more animated knot of people gathered around a man Clara quickly recognized—Auguste Lumière. She considered making her way over to him, as she hadn't found any other familiar faces in the swarm around her, but it seemed awkward to trek all the way across the room for—what, exactly? He was unlikely to remember her, after all. She hovered uncomfortably close to the tidy rows of champagne, debating if picking one up would make her look more or less pitiful.

"Clara! Thank goodness—someone I can actually talk to!" Clara turned, surprised, and nearly knocked into the table. The waiter minding the coupes shot her a glare that could have melted ice, but she swiftly forgot him as she saw Annabelle.

"What are you doing here?" Clara said, forgetting polite small talk and low volume entirely. The waiter sighed audibly.

"They wanted a few of the danseuses to come—you know, so that the party wouldn't be just a bunch of boring mathematician types." Annabelle winked. "Present company excluded—that dress is just delicious, why don't you wear that color more?"

"Present company very much included," Clara replied. "I haven't the slightest idea what to do, who to talk to—I'm a terrible dullard at parties, I'm afraid."

"Nonsense! Now, what you do," she instructed, swooping toward the table, "is you take a glass of champagne." She plucked a coupe from the table and beckoned Clara to do the same, the waiter still eyeing them both suspiciously. "Now you have something in your hands, something to do, you see? And then, well, simple. We feign nonchalance and we meander toward the only area of any interest in this barren wasteland—that fellow looks like he knows how to tell a story." She gestured toward Lumière with the coupe.

"Oh, that's Auguste Lumière," Clara supplied. "I had thought to say hello, but he seemed rather busy."

"You know Auguste Lumière? What about Loie Fuller, have you met her since we chatted last, too? President McKinley?" Annabelle rolled her eyes. "Or maybe just the vice president."

"I didn't say I *knew* him," Clara replied. "We talked once and I helped design the casings for his film projections at the Exposition. That hardly constitutes knowing someone."

"In Paris, that's all relative," Annabelle replied.

Before they could immerse themselves in the lively crowd gathering in the vicinity of Lumière, Lavallé stepped up to a podium that had been placed awkwardly between a pair of windows, as though the sweeping velvet curtains could form some facsimile of a stage. Clara and Annabelle found themselves near the front of the crowd that shifted into an audience.

"*Mesdames and messieurs d l'Exposition,*" he began. "*Je suis très heureux, très fier d'être avec vous ce soir.*"

"I'm not catching any of this," Clara whispered to Annabelle. "Except something about happy something."

"Hush, he's talking about some secret addition to the Exposition," the dancer replied. "And I don't understand the technical terms very well, so you'll have to translate into pedestrian once I translate out of French."

Annabelle pursed her lips as she listened, hips listing toward the podium in a fetching pose. Clara noticed Monsieur Lavallé's eyes graze across them both as he spoke, and she stiffened, turning away. She had lost entirely what the speech was about, besides hearing the occasional word she thought she recognized. Exposition. Dance, that was clear. Animal? Automatic?

Automaton.

Her head jerked back to the podium as Annabelle squinted. "He can't possibly have said what I thought he did—there were rumors of an automaton in the streets?"

Clara's mouth went dry, and she unwisely took a sip of champagne to alleviate it. She coughed against the dry wine as bubbles infiltrated her nose. She choked out an affirmative whisper. "I heard something... I think." She should have expected rumors to spread; if anything, it had been part of her ruse.

"Well, I'll be. He says—oh, Clara! Why didn't you say there would be automatons in the Palace of Illusions?"

"I didn't say, I—" Clara's jaw felt loose. She tried again to listen to the man's speech.

"*...mais c'est un merveille moderne, pas seulement une rumeur!*" Not merely a rumor, he said. This Clara understood, and her eyes widened with disbelief as a trio of petite human figures were marched in front of the curtains. Mannequins, she scoffed internally, not true automatons—each was maneuvered by a broad-shouldered man in unassuming black. A stage trick, she dismissed it.

And then, from the piano in the back of the room, a set of chords rang out and, in unison, the dolls came alive.

Not true life, Clara knew—they weren't Annabelle in her living room or Olympia in her Christmas Wood, moving with self-possessed energy and identity. They were automatons, capable of movement only on a clockwork cycle. But they were exceptional automatons. She pinched her lips together and watched, heart accelerating at each dip and turn.

"The mazurka from *Coppélia*," Annabelle whispered. "They'd never make it at the Mariinsky, but whatever they are, it's impressive."

"It's impossible," Clara replied in a whisper. And yet, it wasn't entirely impossible. She had seen dancing like this once before—Olympia, stripped of the anderwelt spark in the real-world Jardin des Tuileries. Annabelle raised an eyebrow at her as the short performance concluded, the music a crescendo toward a final ringing chord. Clara blinked as the automatons were shuffled away again, reduced to awkward puppets without adequate strings. "Excuse me."

She followed the strange parade of handlers and machinery, but a fourth man, hovering by a service door, stopped her. *"Je suis désolé, mais personne n'a la permission—"*

"I work with the Exposition," she protested. "I work with—with mechanics. Those are part of—"

"I am sorry, madame," the man replied, accent thick. "These were not produced in our Exposition workshops."

There was only one place, Clara was certain, that those dancers had been produced. The anderwelt. She watched as the trio were manhandled through the doors, wishing desperately for a look at their mechanisms. Her hands clutched into her skirts, and she backed away from the door and directly into the waiter who had given her a hot glare near the champagne. "So sorry," she muttered, scanning the crowd for Fritz even as Annabelle found her and clutched her hand.

"Clara! What has come over you?" She pulled Clara toward a quiet corner occupied only by a large potted palm. "I know you said you're not an exceptional party guest, but—"

"I'm sorry, Annabelle, I just—that was impossible, what we saw. I wasn't—" She paused. She couldn't explain the dancers' provenance to Annabelle, so she skated back to another rationale. "This is my field, this is what I do. I was aware—or thought I was aware—of every project requiring this sort of clockwork. Especially involving the Palace of Illusions." She paused. "I need to find Fritz. Herr Krieger."

She spotted him with a small group of men comparing notes, it seemed, on the show. She sidled close to him as Annabelle hung back, then, after giving Clara a conspiratorial smile, launched into conversation with the other men, providing a natural segue to their attention.

"Fritz!" Clara caught his sleeve. "What was that?"

"I don't know," he said, staring after the closed door. "I wish I knew. No one consulted me." He shook his head. "I am sorry, Clara, it was absolutely rotten of them to spring a change to the palace on you like this."

"Oh, hang that." Clara pulled harder on his sleeve. "It's more than who was consulted about what. Those—those things were impossible, Fritz, you know that as well as I do."

"Were they? And here I was just considering what to put in my resignation letter as I'm obviously not up to snuff any longer."

A mad idea came into Clara's head. "We should get a look at them, Fritz. Between the two of us, I'm sure we could figure out the trick."

"Trick?"

"Surely it's a trick—that kind of clockwork isn't possible, you and I both know that. But some sort of trick—puppetry, maybe."

Fritz's lopsided grin returned. "I suppose we could. That big chap isn't guarding the door any longer."

"And if he was..." Clara beckoned to Annabelle. "Are you up for a bit of espionage?" she asked her friend.

"Always." Annabelle produced a petite hand. "Hello. Annabelle Forsythe."

"Pleased to meet you." Fritz bowed slightly, resulting in a broad smile from Annabelle. "Fritz Krieger."

"Now—Annabelle, that door they took the automatons through. No one's really watching now—do you think you could slip through ahead of us and distract anyone guarding the way?"

"I have never been more sure of anything." Annabelle grinned. "And this party had been so dull!"

Chapter Thirty-Two

THE HALLWAY WAS deserted, and so Fritz and Clara found a bored Annabelle leaning against a dinged shelf stuffed full of table linens. "Nothing but a service hallway," she complained. "And here I thought we were in for a bit of adventure."

"Don't discount the possibility yet," Clara replied. "Any noise, any idea which way they went?"

"I've been in my fair share of service stairs and halls," Annabelle said, returning Fritz's amused look with a laugh. "What? It's true. One finds oneself in the back hallway for a fair number of reasons, Herr Krieger!" She winked. "That way"—she gestured right—"only leads to the far service entrance into the hall. But that way"—she pointed left—"is an exit, by way of storage rooms and the kitchen."

"That sounds more promising." Fritz took the lead, with Clara close behind and Annabelle scanning behind them.

"Do hurry, though," Clara said. "They might be gone already, or—"

A heavy door opened just ahead of them, scraping hollow on the worn wood floor. Fritz stopped abruptly and Clara nearly collided with him. Annabelle tripped lightly into Clara, catching herself with a dancer's grace.

Low voices conversed in German—no, Clara corrected, it wasn't a conversation. One voice ordered, the others murmured assent. Even without any fluency in the language, Clara could tell that much.

Fritz advanced alone. Any other time, Clara would have laughed, his lanky frame suspending itself over his toes like a disjointed marionette. Instead, she bit her tongue and tried to subdue the shaking excitement in her hands.

Suddenly, a man barreled out of the room and had Fritz by the collar. Clara stifled a scream; Annabelle froze beside her.

She could only assume that the torrent of French was made up largely of accusations and threats; she was fairly sure many of the words weren't available in her primer of language study. Other men emerged—the ones she had seen before, manhandling the automatons. Her breath hitched. They didn't seem interested in Clara or Annabelle, or perhaps hadn't yet seen them, huddled behind a shelf teeming with crates.

"Come on," Annabelle whispered.

"What?" Clara pulled back. As frightened as she was, she couldn't conceive of retreating, abandoning Fritz. "We can't leave him—"

"You wanted to see those puppet things, right?" Clara blinked. "Then come on—they're busy, you can slip in. I'll make sure of it."

Clara's eyes widened, realizing what Annabelle was suggesting. She counted the men—unless there were more she didn't know about, they had all left the room to join their leader in the hallway. Annabelle gripped her hand and pulled her into the open with exclamations in high-pitched, panicked French. She kept tight hold of Clara's hand until they joined the fray near Fritz, then shoved her into the room while she loosed a resounding smack on the ears of the nearest assailant.

All eyes turned to Annabelle, and Clara retreated into the dim storeroom. Just a closet, really, lined with stacks of plates and crates of silverware. And three automatons piled like discarded furniture against the far wall.

She didn't have much time; she had that much intuition even if she didn't usually engage in back hallway espionage. The figures were as bereft of life as dolls. She avoided their eyes—they looked right through her, dull smiles pasted on their faces. Like Olympia, they had brass keys set into their backs. Life on demand, she thought with a shiver. She turned one of the dancers gingerly, searching for panels to reveal the mechanisms. Almost hidden, they were set into the backs, where ribs on a human would have been. She prized one up with a fingernail. The nail cracked as the panel gave way; she wished, absurdly, that she'd thought to bring her tools.

Who takes tools to a formal dinner, you goose? she chided herself, then forced herself to focus. The interior of the dolls looked disconcertingly like Olympia's—too finely wrought, too perfect. The shine of the anderwelt was absent, but the hallmarks were there. She gently prodded the gears—they whirred briefly to life, raising a mannequin arm, then settled again. She caught her breath—no one had noticed, the guards still absorbed in the ruckus in the hallway.

No, the gears, the workmanship, the design itself—it wasn't of any normal origin. It was anderwelt. It had to be—the daintiness of each mechanism, the way they fit together, the principle was built of that foundational otherness. It required the spark of magic provided only by the anderwelt, and then that spark had been stripped to bring the dancers here.

She thought quickly, landing on a plan before she was sure it was the wisest one. She prized up the other panels, and from each, removed a single gear, memorizing which one it was. "I'm sorry," she whispered to the automatons. She knew they couldn't hear, but she added, "I'll try to take you home and repair you someday."

The noise outside was dying down, so Clara slunk back to the door. She hovered there, playing the part of frightened lady until Fritz noticed her. He took her hand, swinging his body in front of hers in a brotherly, protective gesture.

Annabelle had a few more sharp words for the balding man with his hand on her elbow, and then all three of them were released. They clattered down the service stairway and out into a narrow alley in the shadow of the Grand Palais.

"That was embarrassing," Fritz said, aiming for good-natured humor, but a tremor in his voice betrayed him.

"What, you're embarrassed? To be seen in the company of a common danseuse like *moi*?" Annabelle laughed. "Is it too indecent for you, my good sir? I had to concoct a story as to why we were in the hall, and well, the most convenient one..."

"You didn't!" Clara blushed.

"No, we didn't *actually* have a fumble in the hallway. You were there, remember?" Annabelle bit her lip in a coquettish facade. "Too bad, really, having the row over it without the fun. Wouldn't you say, Herr Krieger?"

"I—I had never—" For the first time since Clara had met him, Fritz was speechless, his ears turning pink with embarrassment.

"Come now! A handsome devil like you, I wouldn't have been embarrassed." She sighed theatrically. "But I am just a common danseuse, of course. Then again." She lit on an idea that made her grin. "I wonder—what did they think when there were three who left instead of two?" She burst into peals of laughter.

Clara couldn't help herself. "Well, Fritz is a terribly handsome devil," she added, unable to suppress laughter of her own.

"I protest! I am not nearly handsome enough to accomplish such a thing!" Fritz couldn't keep the stern line of his moustache from trembling and breaking, either.

Clara sobered slightly. "We can only hope they're sufficiently amused instead of questioning it further—and I do hope we didn't put you at any professional risk, Fritz."

"Hardly," he replied. "We've got the blessing and mercy of the great Picard and the board—the word of a few henchmen won't affect that. But what did you find?"

Clara hesitated. How to describe it to Fritz? She settled on, in essence, the truth. "Nothing that could have been made in any workshop I know. The mechanisms were too delicate, too precise."

"Couldn't they be from somewhere else?" Annabelle asked. "I mean—not that you aren't the best, but...maybe someone else has some method, or..."

"No, it's—it's that the technology doesn't exist. Shouldn't exist. We simply don't have tools to make anything like that." She paused. "It's as though...as though it would have to participate in its own making, if that makes any sense at all."

"Strange." Fritz shook his head. "I confess I do not know what to make of it. This is not within the typical protocol at all, to introduce some new development without the cooperation of the divisions undertaking the work. Very strange."

"It is strange," Clara said, knowing only one thing—someone had brought back a bit of the anderwelt, stripped it of its spark.

Had they sold it to the Exposition? Or was someone hired by the Exposition to exploit their own key? The latter made more sense, with the preponderance of blights on Exposition grounds.

"I don't suppose any of us wants to go back for dinner," Fritz said with a twitch of his lip.

"It's free dinner," Annabelle countered. "I don't know what that means to the two of you, but it's nothing to sneeze at for me."

"I need to fetch my hat, at the least," Fritz said, "and once I'm obliged to go all the way back inside—"

"You should just stay for dinner, yes," Annabelle supplied. "I can probably connive to have you seated near me, would that suffice?"

"I don't suppose I'm left with much choice," Fritz replied with a laugh. "You would be better company than Mercier. What a boor." And, Clara added silently, Lavallé, who had seemed to orchestrate the performance she had seen. Following her to the Folies, his proximity to the automatons—there was too much to ascribe to mere coincidence.

"Miss Ironwood?" Clara started. On the other side of the street, Nussbaum waited. "You're early."

Fritz appraised Nussbaum as he crossed the narrow street, took in both Clara's recognition and her surprise, and broke into a broad smile. "Miss Ironwood, do introduce your friend."

"Yes," Annabelle added, nudging Clara in the ribs. "Do!"

Clara saw both potential disaster and escape in Nussbaum's large green eyes. "Nathanael Nussbaum, this is my neighbor Annabelle Forsythe, and Fritz Krieger, with whom I work." She gestured weakly. "And I am early, but I fear—I will make my regrets for the rest of our evening," she said to Annabelle and Fritz, who watched her with infuriatingly knowing expressions. "Enjoy your dinner."

She waited in stubborn silence until they had gone inside. "Something's happened," she said breathlessly.

"You look pale," Nussbaum replied, catching her hand. "And you're shaking."

She was taken aback. She hadn't expected her own well-being to matter, not at this moment. "It's not important. I have to tell you—"

"You can tell me over a cup of hot coffee—or better, soup." He paused. "Where is your coat?"

"I left it inside," she replied, stomach sinking. Nothing could compel her back inside, not now. She wanted nothing to do with the Exposition, with its deceit and whichever handwerker they were scheming with.

"Take mine," he said, shucking his overcoat and draping it over her shoulders. Clara felt immediately warmer, and not only from the thick wool of the coat. "And I know it's not entirely orthodox, but there's a little café around the corner with excellent cream of chicken soup and a healthy dose of discretion."

Clara's mouth twitched into a smile. "You need that often?"

Nussbaum flushed. "Not me, but I'm given to understand it's so."

Over matching bowls of chicken and wild rice soup, Clara recounted the presentation and what she had encountered in the service closet.

"I disabled them," she finished, fishing the gears from her handbag. "I don't know if that was wise or not. At the worst, I figured it could buy some time."

"Yes, and they would have to go back into the anderwelt to repair them. Unless…" Nussbaum shook a bit more pepper onto his soup. "Unless they have means I'm unaware of."

"Is that likely?"

"Not very." He tasted the soup. "Very few know the anderwelt or its ways better than I do."

"Modest, aren't you?"

"I believe in honesty, especially in situations like this," he replied with a quirk of a smile. "You did the right thing, I think."

"You think?"

"Honesty again, Miss Ironwood. I can't know the future. Or all of the variables." He set his spoon down. "Damn it all, I wish I knew more."

"I might have one more snippet of a clue," she offered, and explained how Magda was waiting for Gagnet. "Come with me to meet her tonight."

"Very well, Miss Ironwood."

"Clara," she said impulsively. "Call me Clara. It seems odd, after all that we've seen together, otherwise."

He smiled gently, his eyes lighting with a soft-kindled joy. "And you may call me Nathanael."

Chapter Thirty-Three

MAGDA DIDN'T ANSWER when Clara rapped on her door, but the workshop was unlocked. Tentatively, she pushed the door open and walked inside, Nathanael just behind her. He laid a protective hand on her shoulder. It was warm and made her shiver, all at once.

The room was dimly lit, but Magda sat on the stool by her workbench, apparently waiting for them.

"Magda Metzger." Beside her, Nathanael Nussbaum stopped and planted his feet firmly in the doorway. "Why, I had never expected to see you again."

"Wait, you know each other?" Clara's brow constricted—Magda had brushed off her inquiries about Nussbaum, leaving her with the impression that if she knew him at all, it had been a passing association of little import. But the color draining from Nussbaum's face suggested otherwise.

Magda shook her head, a firm scowl on her face. "Should have guessed," she said.

"What do you mean, I—" Clara managed to reply before a figure emerged from around the corner. Gagnet—or whatever his

257

real name was—impeccably dressed as always, but he held a thick silver needle with a wide eye, just out of Magda's reach.

"Let us all remember to keep our heads," he began. "I have a few very simple questions and then I should like to make it to a late dinner."

"Didn't need to interrupt your dinner at all," Magda muttered. "Just hand my key back and move along."

Gagnet ignored Magda. "First. Miss Ironwood. We had a standing appointment, and I found this lady waiting for me instead."

"Is that a question?" Clara replied, more tartly than she intended. She eyed the key, keenly aware of its glint under the lamp on Magda's workbench. "First tell me why you have Magda's key."

"Simple. Collateral. She wants to keep it, certainly."

"You can't take a handwerker's key," Nathanael replied. "Not without a trial."

"Of course. But it can be held in evidence. It can be held a very long time, can't it, Magda?"

"Fuck right off."

"Lovely. Well. To expedite this process and get your key back swiftly, you could all cooperate. So, Clara. Our meeting. Would you care to elaborate on why I found Magda instead of you?"

"I was otherwise engaged." Clara decided to play the card, even if it was perhaps not the right turn of the game. "And when I attempted to reach you to inform you of this unfortunate quirk of my calendar, I discovered that there is no Dr. Edouard Gagnet in all of Paris."

She expected some sort of reaction, but he merely smiled. "No, there isn't."

"Would you like," she essayed, "to alleviate this awkwardness and give me a real name to work with?"

"Andrès Saint-Luc, and no further discussion will be necessary about me. The real questions all center on you, Miss Ironwood. I would have been wounded, of course, had you simply broken our appointment with no notice." He smirked and Clara's hands itched toward fists. "But you send this funny little agent of espionage instead."

"That would imply," Nathanael said, "that you know who she is." His voice was remarkably level, Clara noted. She let his calm steady her. "Otherwise, why would you suspect her?"

"Magda Metzger, the Hand Without a Guild?" The smirk broke into a full laugh. Not a nice laugh, Clara thought. There were too many teeth in it. "We all know who she is."

"We? What sort of 'we' do you mean?"

"Don't jump to hasty conclusions, Miss Ironwood. I'm not suggesting some secret cabal. My, what an imagination!"

Clara channeled enough anger into power for her own voice. "Forgive me. My friends and I are coerced by a man whose name is a lie. It wouldn't seem entirely out of the realm of possibility that you're not working alone."

He held her in a stony stare. "More than you know. Herr Nussbaum and Frau Metzger are both well aware of the guilds; they are hardly a secret. I only mean nearly any craftsmen you meet must know the infamous Magda Metzger, the lady who eschewed the guilds and lived a thousand lifetimes in the otherworld."

"You flatter me," Magda said. "Hardly a thousand. Barely a dozen if we do the math properly."

"That isn't important right now," Nathanael said. "What is important is why you lied to Clara, and who you really are."

"You forget that I am holding the power, so to speak." He played with the silver needle—more like a lacing bodkin for a corset, Clara thought, realizing it was covered with a pattern of vines. Fear rushed back over Clara, sweeping away any confidence she had built in the past minute's exchange. What would it do to Magda to lose her key? She didn't seem to doubt that he could, if he wanted, rob her of her ability to travel to the anderwelt.

"You have your answer already," Clara said. "I discovered you weren't who you claim to be. My friend offered to see if she might shed some light on the question. Clearly, it was more than we bargained for."

"Clearly." He glanced at Magda, who merely scowled back at him. "You may wish to discuss these matters with your *friend* in more detail."

Nussbaum glanced at Clara, lips tight. "If you have other questions, Saint-Luc, you better ask them."

Saint-Luc looked sharply after Nathanael. "You are quite invested, aren't you? Is it in the girl, or the old crone? Or in something else?"

"In getting out of here without running afoul of the guilds," Nathanael replied. "As you said, you hold all the power here. I'm just trying to expedite the process."

"Do you still have the key?" Saint-Luc asked Clara abruptly.

Clara started. "What key—"

"Don't bother. Is it still in your possession?"

Clara glanced at him, then at Magda, and finally at Nathanael Nussbaum, before deciding that she was not a good enough liar to risk much of anything. "Yes. I would never dream of selling it."

"Good," he said. Clara started. She had expected further inquiry into its whereabouts and probably insistence that she forfeit it. "Keep it, learn to use it. Next. Who else have you spoken to in Paris? Craftsmen, I mean."

"None that I know of, besides those of us here. I assume you are one, as well."

He nodded in affirmation. "Wise answer—no others that you know of. There is more afoot than you know, Miss Ironwood. The anderwelt is not safe. Neither are you."

"You're doing a very good job of reinforcing that point," Clara said, heat rising in her voice. "Lying to me, carrying on—and then intimidating Magda like this."

"I felt it all quite necessary to protect the anderwelt," Saint-Luc said, suddenly entirely earnest. "Someone is causing blights in Paris. It appears they are working with the Exposition in some way. And an unaffiliated apprentice shows up with a long-lost key, and coincidence upon coincidence, she is working for the Exposition. What were we supposed to think?"

"'We'? Who is this 'we' you keep coming back to?"

"The guilds. Most craftsmen—aside from our Hand Without a Guild here, Frau Metzger—are part of a guild, and the guilds form a consortium. It's necessary, for the protection of the otherworld."

"Have I been on the agenda of your most recent meeting?" Clara snorted.

"Yes," Saint-Luc replied, softly serious. "Yes, you were. It was determined that we had reason to be concerned. Surely you understand why we all feel so strongly that the anderwelt must be protected."

"I do," Clara conceded. "Frau Metzger has made me . . . familiar with the issue of the blights."

"If there is one thing I am sure of, mademoiselle, it is that Frau Metzger takes the issue of the blights just as seriously as I, and the guilds, do. We've tried to determine what has been causing them—or, rather, who."

"She hasn't made a key yet, Saint-Luc." Magda raised an eyebrow. "She's still an apprentice. There are things you can't tell her."

"Of course, of course." His brow constricted. "If you discover anything—do come to the guild of the Sacré-Coeur first, please."

"You mean before hamstringing the bastard myself? No promises," Magda muttered.

Saint-Luc ignored her, turning instead to Clara. "I had hoped to convince you to align yourself with our guild, but if you are safe in the keeping of Magda Metzger, I need not bother." He handed Magda her key. "I apologize for the inconvenience."

He donned his hat and greatcoat and swept past them, a shadow leaving more questions than answers.

"Don't let the door pinch you on the way out," Magda shot in reply. She heaved a sigh. "Well, that went well."

Clara blinked, clearing her head. "Are you all right?" she asked first.

"Yes, fine. That man was more bluster and cologne water than real threat."

"You know him."

"Never met him before, but Andrès Saint-Luc is the head of the guild of the Sacré-Coeur." She barked a laugh. "One of the newer guilds, but very straitlaced. Currently elected the judicial arm of the handwerkers' consortium of guilds, and Saint-Luc is their brightest up-and-coming managerial sort. And Nathanael Nussbaum." Her attention turned quickly. "Never expected to see you again."

"Frau Metzger," he replied, inclining his head in deference. "I confess the same assumption."

"You said you didn't know him," Clara said.

"You were asking around about me?" Nathanael interjected.

"Of course I was, you cornered me at work, I had no idea—" Clara saw that he was joking and dropped her defense. "Yes, I did. I asked Magda, who *said*," she emphasized as she turned back to her friend, "that she didn't know you."

"I said I knew Nussbaums. Never denied having knowing Nussbaums once."

"You implied—"

"You said 'said.'"

"Magda!"

"Fine, fine. Yes, I knew the little whippersnapper back when he was going to be Elias's apprentice. After the guilds stripped Elias of his membership and banned him, I—" Her voice broke off. She looked directly at Nussbaum. "First, you disobeyed him. Your presence there may well have caused the rift in the first place. You know that, don't you? Extra power and pull on the anderwelt? From a handwerker Elias didn't count on?"

"It's highly unlikely. The guilds investigated and cleared me of involvement. You know that as well as I do. The break occurred because of his choices, his arrogance. Because of your Elias, a swath of the anderwelt was ruined, perhaps forever. Worse than any other blight in history."

Your Elias? Clara watched the exchange, reading the unspoken truths between the words.

"And then?" Magda's voice cracked. "You left him. You could have at least helped him, spoken in his defense. But no."

"Unless you've forgotten, I was trapped in the anderwelt during his trial."

"He could have been reinstated! After you returned. Your silence cemented his reputation."

"He didn't want to be reinstated, any more than you do. And I doubt he's concerned over his reputation."

"You left your guild?" Clara asked. "I'm sorry, I don't—I don't really understand much of the system, but to leave the guild seems...a rather strong statement?"

Magda snorted. "It was, and I'd do it again. Pompous stuffed sausages, all of them. Leadership all like Saint-Luc. Yes, I left. Resigned my membership, if you will, in my own guild and the entire consortium. I thought the punishment for Elias unjust. There were unanswered questions, and I was the only one asking them. The blight was never properly explained, but they were content to let Elias take the fall. I was disgusted with the whole business."

"Well, I'm sure you two have quite a bit to catch up on," Clara said, deadpan, "but I want to know what Saint-Luc was going on about, and why he was so interested in me."

"He could give two figs about *you*, girlie." Magda rolled her eyes. "He cares about the blights, especially as it's happening on his watch as security official. Wouldn't want to lose his next election in the consortium."

Clara grew impatient. "Magda! You've hardly explained what the guilds do, let alone how they might be investigating the same thing you and I both want to stop—the blights!"

"Because it doesn't matter! It's all politics with them, all factions and jockeying for power. Their fights are always the same. *Modernity*, Clara!" She spat the word as though it was sour. "*Tradition*, Clara!" That word was treated no more kindly. "The new century! The centuries that have come before us! Why we can't just go on like we have been! Why we have to go on precisely as we always have! Waste of damn time, all of them!"

"Magda Metzger, as pleasant as ever," Nathanael muttered. "It's all well and good for you to run about the anderwelt with no ties to anyone, but there has to be some structure, some rules—the guilds are necessary for that."

"And I'm afraid," Clara said, remembering three automatons in a storage closet that were likely pertinent to the conversation, "the guilds have bigger problems than they might realize." She recounted for Magda what she had seen at the Exposition Board dinner.

A torrent of German profanity flowed from Magda with all the ferocity of the gutters after a rainstorm. "Why didn't you say so right away?"

"Because we were being interrogated!" She scattered the pieces she was clutching in her mind and then rearranged them, making sense of the disparate bits of information into a more cogent whole. "I think—I think it might be time to formally meet one of these guilds. Maybe they could tell me what my key and Godfather have to do with all of this."

Magda rolled her eyes, but Nathanael nodded. "I'm inclined to agree. There's more going on here than we know."

The Clockwork Daughter,
by Christian Elias Thrushman,
dated 29 September 1881

Once upon a time there was an old couple who lived in the last house on the last street of a pleasant little town. They had a delightful garden and several very well-fed and contented cats, but no children of their own. Though this grieved both, they endeavored not to speak of this sad fact very often, and set aside one night a year to properly weep for their misfortune.

They debated long before settling on Michaelmas, for the old man found that the bitter blackberries on the archangel's day matched the bitterness in his heart, and the old woman found that the pale blue daisies that bloomed on the saint's day matched the pale, faint hope she still held that some miracle might bring a child to their house.

One year as the sun set on Michaelmas, they were startled by a rap on their thick wooden door. The old man rose and, in surprise, let in an old peddler whose pack was nearly falling off his shoulders.

"Pray mercy, good people," he said, holding his hands before him like a supplicant. Yet in spite of this contrite position, the peddler seemed a shrewd fellow, his eye roving over the couple's cottage as though reading it to determine what it had, and what it lacked. Besides this, he was a very ugly man, with a large red nose and eyes that nearly bulged from his head. But the old woman was kind, and in spite of the traveler's appearance, she took pity on anyone out on such a chill night.

"Come in and rest by our fire," the old woman said.

"No, no, I have work to attend to," the peddler answered. There was something sharp, almost greedy about his manner, the old man thought. "I have fine things, pretty things—rare and strange things, and all for a fair price."

"There's nothing in your bag that would interest us," the old man said, sighing with regret as Michaelmas slipped away.

"Or are you quite sure?" the peddler asked, a keen glint in his eye. "For I collect items from near and far, and most especially from the land beyond the sea of light. It is a strange continent of many countries, lands of sweets and lands of delights and lands of dolls."

The old man and the old woman might have wished to ask what sea that might be, but as they had no wish to appear ignorant before the stranger, they did not. (I have no doubt, curious reader Clara, that you would not have been so hesitant, and there is a good lesson therein—for you will see what happens when one accepts gifts from provenances unknown. One should never fear looking foolish more than they fear their own ignorance.) Before they could protest again that they had no need of the peddler's goods, he had produced from his bag a box of wood so dark as to be almost black.

"We are but poor folk," the old woman cautioned. "Please, do not waste your time on us, for we have little coin to our names, and even less that we can part with."

"I do not desire your coins," the peddler said. "I desire only such payments as one cannot buy with coin."

At this strange statement, the old woman nearly regretted having invited the peddler inside, but she was beginning to grow curious. The box was carved all over with ornate designs and inlaid with something that she thought at first reflected the light, but then wondered if it was perhaps glowing on its own. "I don't know what we would ask for," the old woman ventured to say.

"Oh, don't you?" The peddler laughed. "You needn't ask at all. This box knows already. And the payment is quite simple—your fondest wish, your dearest hope. That is," the peddler said by way of clarification that was hardly clarifying at all, "your very best and brightest daydreams. To accept the bargain, simply open the box."

The old woman did not quite know what this strange man meant, but her fondest wish and dearest hope was plain to her, and she felt she would rather give up the futile pain of her daydreams than let them continue to haunt her. She let a wild hope seize her, that perhaps the box could yield what she wanted and she'd have no more need of daydreams. Before her husband could stop her, she laid her hand on the box and opened it.

But inside the box there was nothing but a doll.

Other esteemed readers perhaps may not care about such things as dolls, and I cannot blame them for turning instead to their books or their sweetmeats. But oh, Louise or Clara—think on your last Christmas table, full of lovely gifts, and think of the dolls that the Christ Child may have left you. No matter how lovely they were, how detailed, how fine their wee little frocks and bonnets and parasols, they did not compare to the doll inside the peddler's box.

She was so lifelike as to look like a tiny girl, a girl of perhaps three or four. She was almost life-size, too, so perfect that the old woman fancied she might be alive if only she would open her eyes.

Then, to her astonishment, she did.

The old man bellowed with fear while the old woman gasped in wonder, and the peddler slammed the door behind him. The old man insisted on a complete review of the doll child before he would let it out of the box, revealing that it was in fact a complicated work of machinery.

Though the old man had his reservations, the old woman began immediately to fold the doll child into the rhythms of the household as though the appearance of a lifelike doll with such complex clockwork that it could walk and skip and respond to questions and sing five complete nursery rhymes was the most natural thing in the world. Each morning the doll child was served breakfast on a plate with blue flowers that the old woman had bought and set aside for if she ever had a child; the girl did not eat, of course, but she praised the breakfast nonetheless. Then she helped the old woman with the daily chores, excepting of course anything that would involve washing or water. For the old couple knew, though *the little girl did not, that her mechanisms might rust and seize if she was splashed by even a little bit of water.*

At night the old man played his fiddle and the old woman told stories and they had never been happier than with their clockwork daughter. However, the sudden appearance of a child in their house, and one so strange in appearance as the doll-like girl, meant that the old couple had to become near recluses. For as lovely as she was, and as much as they enjoyed her five bright songs and her two short dances, she was, after all, clockwork. The old couple knew that the village would never consider her real, or alive, and their disapproval would break the old couple's hearts. One of them at a time would go to the market; only one would attend Mass each week. The women in town began to gossip. Even the priest, who was a levelheaded fellow not inclined to gossip, began to wonder. Were they ill? Had they been caught up in some illegal scheme? Or, as the priest suggested gravely, was the devil tormenting the poor old couple?

On a rare day that all three traipsed into the forest to look for mushrooms, several of the townspeople gathered and snuck into the house. All was as it had been for years, save a large box of midnight-dark wood covered in strange sigils. With the devil on their minds, the townsfolk took it to the priest, who, not recognizing the symbols but being, as I said, a levelheaded man, determined to send it onward to his superiors who knew such languages as Greek, Hebrew, and even English, and conveyed it by post that afternoon to Munich.

The townsfolk were not appeased, however, and waited for the couple to return. Upon their arrival, they saw the clockwork daughter and were first amazed, then curious, and finally suspicious of the lovely child. They began first to question, then to shout, and finally moved to grab the girl and take her, part and parcel, to the priest, as well. It would have been better if they had, for he was, as I say, a level-headed man and though he would not have allowed the clockwork child a First Communion or a Confirmation, he would have been pleased with the joy she had brought his kindly old parishioners. Instead, they got into a scuffle on the doorstep of the cottage. No one saw if the old man struck first or if one of the townspeople did, but the child was knocked over and her mechanisms became so rattled that they seized instantly.

The old man concealed that he was, in truth, relieved, the clockwork repetitions of the doll child having revealed themselves wholly unsatisfactory compared to the unpredictable caprices of a real child, but the old woman was more grieved than her husband, for she did not even have her daydreams left to her. For that is the trouble, dear reader or listener, that when we trade the best of our dreams for hollow things made of gears and wheels, we have given a live thing for a dead one and will never find it satisfactory.

Chapter Thirty-Four

"THE THING TO consider," Nathanael said, voice low as they wound their way up a steep Montmartre street in the clear air of the crisp spring morning, "is that Magda's impression of the guilds is rather biased. Understandably so, but it's perhaps better to keep an open mind, now that you're going to meet some of the leadership."

"They haven't started off very well in contradicting that impression," Clara replied, "considering how Saint-Luc chose to go about making introductions." Clara knew that Magda, as well-intentioned as she was, was insufficient as an army of one against whoever was causing the blights. Meeting with the guilds was necessary, so she had allowed Nathanael to make the arrangements.

Still, Clara couldn't shake her anger over Saint-Luc's intrusive and presumptuous interrogation the other night, even after a good night's sleep and a good breakfast made by Louise. Her sister had been disappointed when Clara had claimed she needed to go into the office, ruining their sightseeing plans for Clara's day off, but had perked up considerably when Annabelle had popped by with an invitation to lunch. It had taken Louise only a few days to entirely reverse her position on Clara's bohemian neighbor, now spending afternoons with Annabelle over tea or out on strolls in the parks while Clara was at work. She even developed a fondness for Hector, claiming the intractable tom was a charming gentleman of a cat, with his sleek black coat. She felt relieved, particularly now, halfway up a Montmartre hill on the other side of the city from Louise, to divest herself of some of her hosting duties.

"The other thing to consider," Nathanael added, "is that every guild is different in—well, in personality, one could say. The Sacré-Coeur is nothing like my own guild, the Nämberch. For one, none of us is nearly so sharply dressed as Saint-Luc," he said with a rueful grin. "All of the variation of the rest of the world, you'll find in the guilds and among craftsmen."

"Mere months ago, I had no idea that there was an anderwelt, keys, guilds, or craftsmen of your sort. And now you tell me there's an entire society I need to learn about." This felt more daunting to Clara than the rest of it; keys and mirror worlds she could comprehend, but learning new social mores and memorizing who thought what about whom—the prospect was heavy with overtones of headache.

"It makes sense—we are all just men and women, living in the real world, too, you know. We share the anderwelt, but that doesn't mean that the anderwelt erases every other belief and connection we have. Now, Andrès Saint-Luc and the rest of the Sacré-Coeur, they are dedicated, clearly, to the Catholic faith and particularly a devotion to the Sacred Heart of Christ—a rather new development in the long history of the Catholic practice itself."

"Raised Lutheran, remember," Clara said, jabbing a thumb at her starched blouse. "I have no idea of the ins and outs of Church practice. Does that put me on the outside here?" They passed a side street that offered a view of the new basilica of pure white stone.

"Only among the Sacré-Coeur and a few other Catholic-centered guilds. I forget, you are American, too—the Church in France is a complicated story that is best left for another time. The Nämberch is not so very religious. Some are tied very closely to a place; the Bavarians are a rather insular lot, and so my guild tends to be residents of Nuremberg. That's all the name means, in an old Frankish dialect," he added, and Clara felt a strange strain against her tautly controlled emotions at his intent interest in the subject. "Some are geographically diverse but hold to one philosophical truism or another."

"How do you choose?"

"You would think it a serious matter of conscience, wouldn't you?" Nathanael laughed. "But aside from some of the newer guilds that form membership from current craftsmen, most of us just follow our masters as apprentices."

"Then your guild was Godfather's, too."

Nathanael hesitated. "Yes, it was."

Clara took a breath. From what she had heard of Godfather's banishment from the guilds, she could find no fault in their decision. His plan had been arrogant and disastrous, a combination she could very much believe of him. Still, an ember of loyalty burned deep and inextinguishable—she knew Godfather could never have intended to harm anyone or the anderwelt.

"Finally, the politics of the guilds are just as bureaucratic, petty, and often underhanded as the rest of the world's politics. The main thing to know is that each guild governs itself, but they exist together in a sort of consortium and elect which guild will take on what roles and functions."

"The Sacré-Coeur, Magda said they were the judicial arm, didn't she?"

"Yes, which I suppose gave Saint-Luc the idea he was justified in playing interrogator. Elections are on a rotating triennial cycle with various fiscal, executive, and other roles determined by the electorate, which are selected from the guilds by an annual election—"

"Do I have to learn all of this?"

Nathanael stopped. "Not right now," he said. "I'm sorry, I find the whole thing quite interesting, really. The opposite of Magda—I feel that the best way to protect the anderwelt is the proper functioning of the guilds, not the rejection of them." His cheeks and ears had grown flushed with earnest intensity, and Clara didn't bother quelling the pleasant stir in her chest at seeing his enthusiasm. "I came to Paris not only because of your godfather's letter, but because the leadership of my own guild wished additional presence in the city after the first blight was discovered. I volunteered, as I am, as I said, interested in the workings of the guilds. And fortunately for you, we are here, or I could go on for far too long."

Clara wasn't sure what she had expected—a crypt beneath an ancient church, a labyrinthine garden, an attic secreted behind a hidden library. Instead, she found a simple office under the sign of an ornate key. She paused a few yards from the building, taking a deep breath. "Sorry, but I'm a bit nervous," she admitted. So much at stake, and yet the anxieties swirled mostly around meeting who knew how many new people and adhering to what she was sure must be a slate of new social norms and expectations.

"There's nothing to worry about," Nathanael reassured her. "Yes, Saint-Luc will be there, but he's more well-dressed bark than bite."

"I've never known any other craftsmen, other than Godfather. And Magda." She made a face. "And Sandmann, I suppose, but thinking of him doesn't help matters much."

"Lucky for both of us, he won't be there. Last I heard he was buttering up the head of the Nämberch guild for an administrative position, with no success. I'm sure he's still oozing around Paris somewhere, annoying someone."

Clara had to laugh. "That sounds about right. All right. Let's go in."

Andrès Saint-Luc and an older woman with bright silver streaking her ebony hair waited inside. The woman took Nathanael's hand in a firm handshake and greeted him with a stream of German, but he stopped her. "Frau Schwann, this is my friend, Clara Ironwood. Miss Ironwood, Hilde Schwann, the current electoral representative of the Nämberch guild."

"Very pleased to meet you, Fräulein Ironwood," Frau Schwann said. "Very good to see you, Herr Nussbaum. I trust all has been well?"

"Thank you for your willingness to help," Saint-Luc added, in a reserved tone that Clara was unsure how to read. Was detachment his typical demeanor, or was he uncomfortable at seeing her again? She hoped it was the latter—he had every right to squirm a bit.

"Shall we go into the meeting room?" Frau Schwann said. Clara glanced around—the tidy, spare office seemed private enough, but the other woman gestured toward a door in the wall, set centered in the paneling. Saint-Luc opened the door and held it, letting first Hilde Schwann and then Clara and Nathanael pass through. Clara couldn't see anything past the door before stepping through, just a clouded haze and a dim light. She reached for Nathanael's hand and was relieved when he gripped it firmly, entering before she did.

Stepping through the door felt like passing through a bright spring rain, the illusion so convincing that she felt she needed to shake herself dry when she emerged. She was glad she resisted the impulse when she looked around her.

They were under a huge dome like the inside of a pure white shell, the air still and calm, sounds diluted in the enormous space despite robust chatter rising from all sides. Men, women, young, old, dressed in all manner of styles plain and eccentric, workaday and fine, bright and sober. The press of people could have been lifted from a busy, cosmopolitan train station and deposited here. And here? What was here, exactly? "This is—this is the anderwelt, isn't it?" Clara whispered to Nathanael, who looked only slightly less stunned than she did.

"Yes, but we didn't—"

"There are several doors between this world and that," Hilde supplied quickly. "Uncommon, and as they require great skill and cooperation between many handwerkerin to make, only accessible to the guilds themselves."

"Doors between worlds. Of course there are doors between worlds," Clara said with a dizzying shake of her head. She noticed that, since their arrival, the hum of activity and chatter had slowed and stilled. No one was rude enough to stare outright, but she couldn't mistake the subtle angle of dozens of heads and glances from dozens of lowered pairs of eyes.

"Given that craftsmen live in every corner of the world, we required some expedient way to gather the leaders of guilds together. This is our solution to that problem—there are doors in most major cities, and all of them lead here." Hilde smiled at the assembly as though she, personally, had gathered them like chicks to the roost.

"Now, look here," Nathanael interjected. "We've come to you to compare information, voluntarily. This looks a bit like a public hearing."

Saint-Luc raised a deft eyebrow. "Why, have you something to hide, Herr Nussbaum?"

Clara paled. "I thought we were done with any accusations or—"

"No, no, Monsieur Saint-Luc has the tact of a wild boar," Hilde rushed to apologize. "This is a regular meeting of guild leadership, not an inquest gathered on your behalf."

Clara's throat tightened, thinking of all the people in the room watching her, staring at her. "We are not meeting with all of them, are we?"

"We had thought to, yes," Frau Schwann replied. Clara looked to Nathanael, the only person in the cavernous meeting hall who she trusted at all.

His ears were already red, and he squared his narrow shoulders against Saint-Luc. "She doesn't have to answer a thing. She's not a member of a guild, and so all the rules of order or parliamentary procedures you can throw around don't mean much—she can just leave."

"If she did, we could invoke our right to confiscate the key as evidence." Saint-Luc didn't seem perturbed at all, a man who knew all the cards in play and had counted the aces. "Now, there are a few—"

"Aren't we all on the same side here?" Clara interrupted. "Something is happening to the anderwelt, and it's bleeding into the other world, too, and no one wants that to happen, isn't that right?" Hilde rushed to answer, but Clara spoke again, more loudly this time. "I'm happy to share anything I know to stop the spread of the blights." She strode resolutely to the one place in the room she would have preferred to avoid—the dais, raised and centered and completely exposed. She took a deep breath and stepped onto the dais, where no one could avoid seeing her. "What do you want to know?"

The room was silent for a breathless moment. Clara's hands began to sweat, and her legs felt as though they'd been replaced with the wretched aspic her mother made when she wanted to impress someone. She forced herself to stop quivering, and before they could ask, she told them everything she knew about the clockwork dancers and the giant tin soldiers, rattling off the facts as dispassionately as possible to an audience that listened with an attentive horror.

Hilde spoke first. "We know that you have your godfather's key. And that you came to Paris last year—that is correct, isn't it?"

Clara nodded, and someone with a thick Scottish brogue called from the back of the room, "Who hired you?"

"I was hired by Fritz Krieger, to work for the architectural firm—"

"Does he know?" The man was thickset and had white whiskers and tiny glasses, hardly a threatening figure. Clara began to relax slightly. These were just people, mostly a little odd, just like her.

"Does Fritz Krieger know about the key, about the anderwelt?" The man nodded. "No, I am quite sure he does not. I do not believe," she added, anticipating the next question, "that anyone I know or work with closely is aware." She paused. "But I have been tracked by a schattenhund and I've gained your attention, so clearly it's not exactly a secret."

"A schattenhund!" a woman in pale green gasped. She reminded Clara of the ladies Mother used to invite over for garden club, dramatic and gossipy, and she had to remind herself that of course the anderwelt might have people of all kinds folded into it. "You're quite sure?"

"Quite."

"I wish I could say I was surprised," Hilde said, shaking her head, "but given that someone would denigrate the anderwelt and strip the life from its creations, I cannot say that I am shocked that whoever it is resorted to using a schattenhund."

"Does that narrow it down a bit?" Clara said, mind connecting that dot to the mystery at hand. "Someone within the Exposition, and someone who knows the anderwelt—couldn't that be the same person? And that person knows how to create a schattenhund. Doesn't that tell us who it might be?"

"Oh, dear." The gossip in green waved her hand as though feeling faint. "Oh, dear, no! It's a simple construct that anyone would know how to create. Anyone, really. Oh, dear." She tapped her handbag, which produced a mechanical box of smelling salts and began to waft them toward her on demand.

Saint-Luc rubbed his temples with a look of such withering contempt that it was quite nearly elevated to an art form. "No, we've made no progress in determining who the traitor might be, Miss Ironwood. The connection you suggest, that it is someone within the Exposition, was why we suspected you."

Clara blushed. "But there are so many involved in the Exposition, couldn't one of them be a craftsman—"

"No, it's quite impossible. We've investigated that possibility fully. You were the only employee, board member to construction crew, who was an unknown quantity."

"You're quite confident?"

"You wouldn't be here if I was not," Saint-Luc replied. "I realize you are not happy with the methods with which I conducted that investigation. Trust me that we, all of us, felt it necessary, and moreover, it is imperative that we accelerate our progress. Mr. Song, would you please show Miss Ironwood your map?"

From somewhere to the side, a man in a pale gray suit gathered a stack of paper. "Mr. Song is a brilliant mapmaker," the woman in green added. "He's created a map of the current blights and the timeline."

Before Clara could ask how the map showed a timeline, the mapmaker had set his papers on a table near her. "This," he said, "is a map of blights worldwide." Clara peered at the paper. It was blank. She blinked, confused. Then the man tapped his pen several times on the paper and a globe appeared above the paper, spinning slowly. There were very few black specks on the shimmering green-and-blue surface. "The Ceylon Incident, the Lake Baikal Plot—" He paused, realizing, clearly, that Clara had no idea what he was talking about. "At any rate." He slowed the spin of the globe with a pinch of his fingers. "You can still see the effects of Elias's Folly," he said, pointing to a spot that looked like a worn inkblot. Nearby, in what Clara realized was Paris, she noticed pinpricks of black. Mr. Song took the map in closer, and Clara saw with a gasp that it depicted the landmarks of anderwelt Paris itself—no, not merely landmarks. In gossamer miniature, the entire anderwelt unfolded before her.

"Now." A few more taps, and the landscape changed, rippling. The black marks disappeared. "Thirty years, in thirty seconds." First black bloomed at the edges of the map, what Clara recognized with a wince as "Elias's Folly." It slowly faded but did not disappear completely. Then, suddenly, the slow wash of the large blight was interrupted by sparks of jet black in Paris, tiny dots along the Seine, in the Champ-de-Mars, in parts of the fairgrounds she had not visited in the anderwelt. Clara squinted—it seemed that Elias's Folly stopped its slow fade as the new blights appeared, and even began to grow darker.

"Thank you, Mr. Song. Now. You see?" Saint-Luc turned to Clara. "The blights appear suddenly in Paris, all within the past several months. All, it seems, associated with the Exposition. And the presence of these blights has strengthened the one that already existed."

"But it was healing before, wasn't it?"

"Yes. Over time, they do heal. The Lake Baikal Plot took nearly three decades, but even it has begun to resolve." Mr. Song began to gather his map, but Saint-Luc stopped him.

"We don't understand everything about the anderwelt, or how it works, or its blights. This number of new blights is unprecedented, and is clearly causing something far more serious than we understand." Saint-Luc scrutinized the map. Clara could almost forgive him his callous demeanor as deep furrows creased his brow.

"What we're worried about," the man with the thick brogue said, "is that this could become something far more serious than isolated blights."

"If damaged areas in one place affect the damage in another, that could be bad. Very bad," a plump, nervous woman with a live bird in her hat added.

"I am concerned," Mr. Song said, "that there may be some balance point, some amount of damaged space in the anderwelt where a certain area becomes irrecoverable or even spreads." He paused. "My calculations are very rough at this point, as I have very little information to work with, but any more new blights concentrated here in Paris, and we could reach that tipping point."

"I don't have any answers," Clara said again, aware suddenly of the number of people in the room, watching her reactions.

"No one expected you to have *answers*," Saint-Luc said. Clara winced under the acid in his voice. How could she have fallen for his debonair act? She felt, again, like a fool. Beside her, however, Nathanael laid a hand on her arm, and she recovered her poise. "But what you might know is what connection these places have to the Exposition—who might be consistent across projects in all of these spaces, or what they might have in common," Saint-Luc said.

Clara turned back to the map, surveying the flecks of black. "These are all vastly different projects. Different architecture firms won bids for different buildings—I don't see any consistencies here." She paused. "If there is a common thread, it's someone who has their hand in almost everything." She thought of Lavallé. She didn't want to rely solely on the cold feeling he left in her stomach or the hard glint in his eyes when he'd found her at the Folies, but he was high-ranking enough to be involved in nearly anything he wished to be. "You're looking at a member of the board, not an individual architect or manager."

"And you're perfectly positioned to figure out who," Hilde Schwann said brightly. "Whoever hired them in the Exposition may lead us to the traitorous handwerker, and that is our real interest of course."

The seriousness of the request settled heavy on Clara. "I don't want to promise that I can—that is—I want to help! But I hardly understand anything about the anderwelt, or the guilds, or how any of this works, and—"

"Yes, but you can move freely about the Exposition grounds, and you know the firms and the architects and the projects well." Saint-Luc paused. "No one is expecting you to solve this mystery by yourself," he added, "but if you would offer your assistance, it would be most appreciated."

"There's one more thing," Nathanael said. "Your key."

"What about my key? My godfather's key," she amended.

"We haven't told them about Olympia. Or what your key does." Nathanael quickly recounted the story, putting far more blame on himself than on Clara. When he explained that the Christmas Wood had not been blighted, that Olympia had come out on the other side a dead thing but the anderwelt remained unharmed, there were audible gasps of disbelief among the crowd.

"This must be a mistake," Mr. Song interjected. "It is impossible—I have made a study of the blights, and the incidents causing them, and never have I found an incident of this sort that did not result in a blight."

Someone spoke a language Clara did not recognize, and the woman with the live bird in her hat translated. "Perhaps—perhaps the accidental nature of Miss Ironwood's action has something to do with it?"

"The otherworld does not care about intention when it comes to ripping its creations from it," Saint-Luc retorted.

"Yes," Mr. Song added, "though there are incidents when spilling human blood was completely accidental or even intended as beneficial—such as the custom of bloodletting—that did not result in blights, but in every mistaken transference of an anderwelt creation recorded, a blight was created. There was one episode in which a man forgot about several beetles he'd made of jewels and carried them home in his pocket. The disturbance resulted in a characteristic blight." Mr. Song paused. "As a bit of trivia, the beetles are in the British Museum."

"Then the key itself is the anomaly," Saint-Luc said. "The key itself was made differently, somehow."

"I don't know anything about how Godfather made the key, or if that was intentional at all." Clara fought back frustration, yet again, at Godfather and his secrets. "I wish we could ask him."

"At some point, I'm sure we will," Saint-Luc replied. "Until then, he entrusted it to you. God knows why, but I will not question a fellow handwerker in the allocation of his own key." He leveled his dark gaze at her, and she felt the solemnity of the charge as he said, "Keep it safe. For all of us."

Chapter Thirty-Five

FRITZ FOUND CLARA hard at work on purchasing orders the next day. She wasn't sure how she was going to keep her mind on work, either her Palace of Illusions or the Lumières' screen, after realizing the danger that the anderwelt and her own key were in. She was sure Fritz was about to chide her for inattention. Instead, he crooked a finger, calling her into a private meeting in an underused hallway. "I asked about the dancers in your Palace of Illusions. They will not be featured."

Clara remembered in time to react with surprise—of course, she thought, they wouldn't be featured, as they wouldn't work any longer. "Thank you for asking! Why, that must have been a fight."

"Hardly—I asked Lavallé why we hadn't been consulted and he simply said that they had never intended for them to be featured at all, it was just some sort of publicity stunt."

"Does that sound as strange to you as it does to me?" Clara asked.

"To be honest, yes, it does—not a very good stunt, if there are people expecting to see them. But then again, there have been rumors floating around of an automaton dancer in one park or another and I've no idea what that was all about, either." Clara carefully schooled her face against any reaction to the reference to Olympia. "Maybe someone knows more than I do."

"That is usually the case," Clara teased. She considered—Fritz regularly met with Exposition higher-ups, including the board. She feigned casual interest. "Say—how much do you know about Lavallé?"

"Aside from the fact that he personally invited me to partake in some very off-color entertainment after the dinner the other night and I had to feign a headache?" He made a sour face. "Not very much. Why? Did he say anything to you? I can't say there's very much I would be able to do, given how much higher in the chain here he is than me, but—"

"No, no, nothing like that." Clara hesitated. "That is—I could swear that a couple of months ago he . . . followed me."

"Followed you? You mean, around the offices?"

"No, I was out with a friend—" Fritz's moustache twitched, and Clara smacked his arm. "Yes, I have friends! Annabelle, with whom you are already acquainted, to be exact! He seemed to follow us all the way to the show we went to, and then he—he seemed to be watching me."

"Do consider, Miss Ironwood, that you are a lady worth watching," Fritz teased, then paused, more somber. "I have no idea how that could have happened, Clara, but from what I know of him . . ." He took her arm as a janitor began swabbing the hall with a battered mop and guided her around the corner. "He's a rather ruthless businessman. He looks like a starched dandy, I'll grant him, but I've heard he's a dangerous man to cross. Apparently he climbed over several colleagues to get his position with the Exposition, and several others lost their jobs under rather cloudy circumstances."

"Sounds like a delightful person."

"Which is why I most certainly did not want to go to Madame Gigi's with him, if I had wanted to go to such a place at all," Fritz agreed. He lowered his voice. "I wanted to talk to you, as well—perhaps here isn't the best place—but I've been approached by the Lumières about the possibility of joining their company, designing projection equipment. They see quite a future in moving pictures and intend to expand the business. I wonder if you might have any interest in coming along?"

"Oh, Fritz, I—" Clara caught her breath. This was what she had hoped for, in coming to Paris—that someone would see her work and appreciate it, that she would be able to stand behind beautiful, functional designs. Here it was—and she found herself unsure. Did she want to stay in Paris? And the Lumières' cameras, while fascinating, weren't what she had ever intended to work with.

Fritz must have seen how overwhelmed the suggestion made her. "It's nothing official, just a general expression of interest at this point. I'm not sure I'll take it, you know. But with Alma going home, and this job ending—well, by Christmas next, I'm sure, even with all the paperwork and wrapping things up—I suppose I am looking for a bit of a fresh start." He looked strangely lonely, but just then a trio of workmen came down the hall with a dolly of crates and she didn't press further.

Nathanael was waiting on the sidewalk when Clara emerged from the office after noon, her eyes crossing with calculations for maintenance plans for the Palace of Illusions over the six months it would be open. A strange protectiveness settled on her, when she thought about her creation—after only six months, it would be dismantled. But until then, she would make sure it was a marvel, a wonder for every minute of its existence.

"The automatons won't be featured in the palace," she said. "They claim it was a stunt. Aside from that bit of news, I haven't given a thought to anything except light bulb suppliers in the last three hours. I don't have any insight, ideas, or intelligent remarks on the anderwelt, its blights, or anything else."

"No one," Nathanael said, falling into step beside her, "expected you to solve this riddle in a day."

"I do have a—well, a suspicion, I suppose." Nathanael raised an eyebrow. "There's a board member who would have access to all the projects associated with blights. He's far from the only one, but he—he followed me once, I think. Monsieur Lavallé."

"Enough for me," Nathanael replied, but Clara stopped him.

"The trouble is, I don't know if I'm being...swayed, I suppose, by my opinion of him. He's an awful letch of a man, and his business dealings sound rather underhanded. I've got nothing firm whatsoever."

"So you'd prefer not to go to Saint-Luc just yet. Fair enough. Instead, fancy a jaunt with me in lieu of lunch at your desk?"

Clara could have claimed that her feet were tired and she was beginning to get a headache around her temples and that it was too chilly a day to enjoy a walk, but she didn't. She could have argued that she owed Louise more of her attention than she had given her recently, but she didn't. She even thought to protest that it was barely one o'clock and she had plenty of work she could do, should do, but she didn't say that, either. "Did you have somewhere in mind?"

"I thought," Nathanael said with exaggerated diplomacy, "that you might show me how your key works."

"Oh, I don't know," Clara replied, affecting modesty to match Nathanael's game. "That seems so very personal, and we've only just met!" She fanned herself with her hand, turning her face away as though affronted.

"Now, then, I've shown you mine."

She laughed, a short little yelp that set Nathanael into spasms of laughter and earned the indulgent looks of several older passersby, seeing a young couple in the first fits of springtime love. "Fine, fine!"

"If you don't mind a bit of a walk, I know just the spot to cross over. Have you seen Sainte-Chapelle?"

"I admit that I haven't played the tourist," she replied.

"This is more than a mere stop in the guidebook. I can promise that much."

He offered his arm and chatted amiably as they kept the Seine on their right and then crossed onto the Île de la Cité. Clara had only once come this far east, on Louise's insistence that she had to see Notre-Dame. Yet Nathanael did not make his way toward the grand cathedral and instead turned down a shaded avenue just west of it.

"Here it is," he said, in an almost reverent whisper and led her through a courtyard bound up in stone and into an old church—a chapel, really, in the lower level of the building. With the low ceiling it felt close and thick with old incense. It was nearly deserted, and she understood why Nathanael would choose the place—no one would notice them snap out of existence.

She pulled out her key. "No, not here," Nathanael said. "There."

He pointed to a spiral stair that she hadn't noticed on her first survey of the chapel. The steps were narrow and she had to keep sweeping her skirts out of the way, so she was only half paying attention when she emerged into such captivating wonder that she stopped abruptly and Nathanael collided with her back.

"I don't think I need to use my key," she whispered. The soaring walls around her were lined with stained glass, bands of ruby and sapphire melting in the afternoon sun. At first her vision swam only with color, and then pictures coalesced—each pane of glass was a story in miniature. Dozens, hundreds, each wrought in tinted light.

"You should see the other side," Nathanael encouraged her. "And we should do so rather quickly, before someone else comes in."

She recovered herself. "Of course," she replied. She pulled the key from her pocket and lifted it, letting the colors wash over the diamond-clear glass. "Ought we hold hands?" she asked, blushing slightly.

"I think that would be best, yes," Nathanael replied, a smile breaking his serious tone.

She took his hand in hers and lifted the glass to her eye.

The first thing Clara noticed when the flash of the anderwelt faded was that Nathanael was gripping her hand tighter than before and blinking like an owl at the wash of white light. And then she looked around her.

The walls of the church were gone, but the stained glass remained—the air itself woven in panels of brilliant color. The scenes, static though beautiful before, were now brimming with energy, the pictures shifting as the colors bled with every slant of a shadow or turn of the breeze. Clara moved closer to one, drawn, without meaning to. She didn't dare touch the pane, an image of trees and human figures, though she lifted a hand, wanting to. The trees shimmered, grew, bloomed, as the sun brightened and then slid behind a wisp of cloud.

"How..." she whispered.

"I don't know. This has been here for centuries. Elias said..."

He paused. "Your godfather said it had faded, but when they undertook the restoration, the colors all brightened again. Almost as though the care put into the work on the other side bled over and made this."

"Doesn't that always happen?" Her fancy and poor attempts at decoration had caused a transformation in the anderwelt, and parts of the Exposition ground thrummed with creativity on the other side.

"Not always."

Clara recalled the Moroccan display, rendered in pale ticky-tacky in the otherworld for all its pomp and glitter on the Exposition grounds. "It has to matter," she murmured. "Is that it? It has to be the work of someone's... heart, I suppose." She stumbled over the words, failing to find something more technical.

"God forbid we bring sentiment into this," Nathanael teased her. "I think you've got it. It's been studied, of course, and reams of paper in the personal libraries of many a handwerker, but the general consensus is that the anderwelt is a mediator between the self and the work, and carries a reflection over to this side."

"God forbid we bring philosophy into this," Clara countered. They lingered in the wash of watercolor around them, letting the light slanting through living color paint them rose and blue and gold. It was like playing with a rainbow and living in a painting, Clara thought.

Finally they turned back toward the Seine, which sang with an old melody like the pealing of bells deep within the waters. Clara slowed her gait. It was an incredible privilege, to see this, to be allowed to glimpse the depth of art and craft of so many others. Ordinary Paris had museums and the theater, but museums and the theater could only be a dim mirror to this.

And yet, she considered, mirror it was—a bright mirror show-ing contour and line, shade and hue, movement and expression of the essence of the ideal left pinned behind the veil. Did she do this, she wondered, in her own work? Did the Palace of Illusions, though made of mirrors, truly reflect what she wanted to show? She had tried to make magic, a little spark of magic, to make the Exposition visitors feel as she had felt when Godfather made one of his mechanical wonders for her.

Here, in the anderwelt, arm in arm with Nathanael, she knew what changes she would make, if it wasn't too late for them.

"Would you—would you like to see what I've been working on?" she asked.

"I would like nothing more," Nathanael answered.

Though the walk to the Exposition grounds was a long one, Clara didn't mind. They had time, she realized, feeling freed from the constraint of ticking minutes by the unformed time of the anderwelt. She let Nathanael tell her about the strange his-tories of the creations they passed, mirrors of landmarks and unique embellishments to the anderwelt landscape, crafted over centuries. She wondered how he knew all of them, appreci-ating that his education might have been significantly different from hers.

"And that," he said as they passed a fountain alive with stone merfolk diving and careening amid the spray of pale water, "was added sometime in the late seventeenth century. It looks like marble, but the mermaids are all formed out of mother-of-pearl. No one has ever been able to figure out how it was made."

"It makes me so curious, wondering what might have been behind the curtain of my own backyard all along!" She paused. "Well, I can imagine a few things, if Louise and I had any effect on it. She was very fond of playing princess, with all kinds of castles and enchanted gardens."

"Do you plan on going back to America?" Nathanael asked.

Clara paused, the answer stuck in her throat. She had avoided plans, as long as the Exposition took up her attention, and she had avoided the idea of returning to work for Godfather or trying to fit her eccentric ambitions into her mother's perfectly ordered house and her father's perfectly respectable reputation. "I'm not sure," she said. "There could be a job here, when I'm done. Or maybe there won't." The uncertainty unnerved more than it had before; she felt, keenly, that she had something she might lose.

"I don't suppose—wait a moment." Nathanael paled as he looked across the river.

Clara followed his gaze with growing trepidation, but she wasn't prepared for what she saw. A blight, far larger than the ones that had dotted the Quai des Nations. A wide band of the Champ-de-Mars was swathed with a creeping blank gray, as though the scene had been sketched on a giant's chalkboard and then erased. When she stared into the echo, lines and forms appeared, only to fade into flat fog when she tried to picture them more clearly. It pitched and thrummed, making her feel dizzy the longer she looked at it. Her eyes hurt, and she blinked back a headache.

"That wasn't there," Clara insisted. "It wasn't there yesterday." Nathanael gripped a lamppost made of twisting vines. It quivered under his weight, and Clara caught his arm. "Are you all right?"

He swallowed, his face taut. "No, it's—" He steadied himself. "It's the same as where I was trapped. I am sorry, it's too much like that."

"It isn't affecting the Palace of Illusions," Clara said. "But the other projects I've been working with—I say, it's—"

Nathanael fumbled for her hand and pulled her back with the urgency of a man hauling someone back from the edge of a high cliff. "We should—we must—"

"Now then." Clara squeezed his hand tightly. "It's all the way over there, and we're here," she said, trying to sound patiently rational even though she was beginning to feel nauseated with fear herself.

"I know. I know, it's not logical, I know. It can't hurt us." He repeated it in a whisper to himself, several times.

"It's near the installation of the Lumière brothers' screen," Clara finally added. "The other project I assisted with. I know right where it is, on the other side. I think the only thing to do is cross back over"—she hesitated, not wanting to commit to the next part but feeling it quite necessary—"and investigate." Once they left the anderwelt, the hours of the afternoon would begin ticking away again, but Clara didn't care if she was missed at work. This was more important.

"Yes." Nathanael nodded, pulling back from the sickly gray panorama. "Yes, that is wise. But first, let's get a fair bit away from this dead space. I wouldn't want to invite any interference with your key."

"Good idea." How strange, Clara thought, to be speaking about this as though deciding which tram line to take to the picnic grounds. As she and Nathanael sought a quiet place to cross over, she realized that they were still holding hands, and didn't want to let him go.

"Do you suppose it's safe here?" Clara pulled her key from her pocket as they found a dead-end alley. Nathanael nodded, and the brightness of the key transported them.

Nathanael hadn't dropped her hand. "It really is a remarkable key," he said. "The brightness, like opening a curtain first thing in the morning." He looked as though he wanted to say more, but only bit his lip instead.

"What now?" Clara said. "Do we—do we really go investigate?"

"I think that's the only thing for it," Nathanael said. "And besides, there's really very little risk in it—not like on the other side."

"Very little?" Clara replied.

"Well, there's no fun in it unless we're in some danger, right?" He essayed a smile, but Clara could see that he was afraid. Deeply, keenly, afraid.

Chapter Thirty-Six

CLARA COULDN'T BE sure, as she and Nathanael surveyed the perimeter of the Galerie des Machines, but it felt as though the fairgrounds here were dimmer, paler. It wasn't only the shadow of the Grande Roue de Paris towering over the huge building or the clouds skidding over the Champ-de-Mars. It felt as though a pallor had settled over this sector.

"I'm only imagining it," Clara chided herself as they circled the perimeter of the Galerie des Machines.

"Imagining what?" Nathanael followed close behind.

"That it feels different here, dark or quiet or—I don't know."

"I don't think it's just you," Nathanael said. "It feels heavy, somehow. Like the air before a storm."

Clara shivered. There was nothing and no one unusual around the exterior of the huge building. "I think we need to go inside," she said, not without some trepidation. This was not her palace, and she did not know it well. Besides, she had no business being here.

Nathanael nodded. "Have we considered what we'd do if we caught someone in the act of—oh, I don't know—blighting the anderwelt?"

Clara pushed against the heavy doors. They yielded, and she was almost disappointed. "I'll rely on your quick wits," she answered, the thought catching in her throat as thick as the plaster dust in the air.

"Wait," Nathanael said. He closed his eyes, his hands tensing at his sides. Clara was about to ask if he was all right when she saw movement along the building's perimeter. Mice. "I'll send them in first," he said.

"So we just—we wait? For them to . . . ?"

Nathanael didn't answer, concentrating instead on the mice. Clara waited, keeping an eye out for workmen or, worse, someone she knew, but this corner of the fairgrounds was deserted as evening settled over Paris.

"No one's inside," Nathanael said. Clara nodded, wondering how one thanked rodents for reconnaissance work. She led the way through the building, still under deep renovation and filled with choking clouds of dust.

"The dome here—" Clara sidestepped a pile of lumber as Nathanael led them toward the towering central dome. "This is where the projector and screen will be installed. The housing for the screen is complicated. There's a basin below for water, and the mechanics have to raise and lower the screen without being a distraction."

"How big is this thing going to be?" Nathanael stepped through the unassuming entrance to the dome, stopping abruptly to take in the scale of the space.

"They initially wanted a hundred-foot screen, but it's been redesigned to about seventy feet." Clara watched her step, looking for mice, as she followed Nathanael. The mice were keeping to themselves.

"Is that—it?"

"No, it's not supposed to be installed for several—what!" An enormous white screen took over the center of the space, the stained-glass dome above scattering broken colors over it. "This is my design," Clara muttered. "But it had not been begun. It would take weeks—" She blanched, remembering suddenly how Magda had built a miniature carousel and then used the ander-welt to grow it full-size. "Could someone have brought this from the anderwelt?"

Nathanael did not move for a long moment, observing the screen, the complex housing, the winches and pulleys. "It's entirely possible. The size would explain the size of the blight."

"It was dreadfully behind," she mused. "What if someone used my plans, built the thing in miniature, and then—"

"Yes," Nathanael replied. "What a trick—of course. They would finish the project far more quickly, with less materials. Less cost. Some of this work is so delicate—I don't know how it would have been made at this size." He shook his head, disgusted. "Who would have had access to your plans?"

"Too many to narrow the field very much," Clara cautioned. "My entire office, the board, anyone employed by the board to liaise with the Lumières, the Lumières themselves..." She sighed. "It doesn't rule out Lavallé, but it also doesn't prove anything."

"And no closer to figuring out which handwerker is actually doing this." Nathanael bit his lip, frustration and powerlessness clearly written on his face. Impulsively, Clara reached for his hand. He smiled, and her breath caught.

Then his hand constricted around hers. "We shouldn't neglect the rest of the space," he said. "This is—well, impressive," he said with a laugh. "What else may be hiding here?"

As the mice hadn't warned them of encroaching outsiders, Clara and Nathanael thoroughly pored over the expansive Galerie des Machines, picking their way through the upheaval of renovation. Discarded materials from the 1889 Exposition cluttered long-forgotten hallways, and sawdust from new installations coated every surface. Nothing else seemed unusual, as Clara remembered enough of the blueprints and plans to confirm to make comparisons. They circled the building and returned to the central dome unsure of what to do next.

"What's this?" Clara knelt near the screen. A few cards lay scattered on the floor, all, curiously, for the same café in a neighborhood not far from the fairgrounds. "Do you think this means anything?"

"Not terribly likely, but we have nothing else to go on. It's worth taking a look. Someone carrying multiple copies of a restaurant's card would suggest they go there often, and take meetings there."

"And someone of the sort who takes meetings in cafés is unlikely to be an ordinary workman," Clara said. "It could be one of the men we're looking for. And I suppose," Clara added, "the best way to investigate a café is probably to have supper there. I'll tell you what—my sister is always asking to try different places. I'll tell her this one came highly recommended."

"I don't know that I like the idea of you coming alone."

"I won't be alone," Clara answered dryly. "I'll have Louise."

"You know quite well what I mean."

"Yes, I do, and Louise is really quite formidable, I can't imagine anyone crossing her."

"I'll go, too. I insist. I'll eat alone if you—"

"No, we'll meet you here. It will be a happy surprise"—she gritted her teeth—"except that Louise will see right through it and assume it's a lovers' tryst, the sort of clandestine thing she reads in those damnable women's magazines…"

"Yes, it would be truly horrific for anyone to assume anything of that nature," Nathanael said, a smile itching at the corners of his mouth. "You'd never recover from the humiliating association with me."

Clara blushed. "Not that, no—it's that Louise will be so, so… *knowing* about it. It's intolerable. But," she added, "I can bear up well enough for the sake of the anderwelt."

"Very well. Meet there at eight?"

"Eight sharp," Clara agreed.

By the time Clara arrived home, she had gone over a dozen lines for luring Louise to a particular café that might or might not have been in her guidebooks, and had developed a convincing script, but it turned out she needed none of it. The cupboards had a packet of water crackers and nothing else, and Louise was hungry enough not to care which bistro Clara might suggest.

"I think I do know the name. It's supposed to be quite highly regarded for chicken, I think," Louise prattled as they walked through busy evening streets to the tram stop. "I had a lovely day—I made myself a little walking tour of the bridges on the east end of Paris, and I crossed all of—why, Clara, it's as though you're not even listening!"

"What?" Clara's thoughts were tangled in blights and keys and, irritatingly enough, Nathanael Nussbaum's thoughtful eyes and capable hands. "I'm sorry, it was a very busy day at work," she said absently.

"I should say!" Louise laughed. "If it was so absorbing, let me in on the story. What was so exciting about the Exposition today?"

"Light bulb orders for the Palace of Illusions," Clara lied

seamlessly. When had she acquired that ability? she wondered. But it was, she conceded, easy to lie to Louise about work. She might ask a few perfunctory questions to be polite, but she wouldn't understand the answers anyway.

"I can't wait to see what you're working on. Oh!" Louise stopped, turning to Clara with uncharacteristic mischief in her eyes. "Do you think I could, sometime? Perhaps you could, you know, sneak me in!"

"I'm not allowed!"

"Oh, come now—how strict are they, really? There must be people employed by the Exposition coming and going all the time. They wouldn't notice us among all that!"

"But they would," Clara grumbled. The hundreds of people coming and going, as Louise had said, were all men—workmen, yes, but also the dozens of male engineers and architects employed by the Exposition. Two women would stand out like an elephant. Probably, she thought, they would stand out even more than an elephant. People would assume the elephant was part of a menagerie exhibit. "I can't risk my job on a lark, Louise."

Her sister pinched her mouth closed, wanting to say more. "I just—you are in Paris and have access to the one thing here everyone wants to see and can't. Isn't that at least a little fun?"

"It's fun. It's all very exciting. Really."

"You sound like it's as exciting as peeling potatoes." Louise sighed. "Well, I suppose—oh!" Clara started as Louise waved at a crowd of people.

Then she picked out a face she knew. Fritz.

He ambled over, leaving a gathering that Clara now saw included his sister and a couple of the people she had met at his Christmas Eve party. "Good evening, the Misses Ironwood."

"Good evening, Herr Krieger," Louise said.

"Yes, hello," Clara said, already reaching for her sister's hand to pull her away. "We're just off for dinner now, rather late..."

"Miss Ironwood, I am glad to see you up and about," Fritz continued, willfully ignoring her silent pleas to go their separate ways. "I worried when you left work early today."

"I'm fine," she said, smiling wanly. "I felt a bit unwell at midday, but it was nothing."

"Nothing, you say? Well, that is good. I hope to discuss some plans with you tomorrow." He tipped his hat and returned to the group. Clara pulled Louise down the sidewalk before Fräulein Krieger could overtake them and extract more painful conversation.

"What in the world was he talking about, Clara? You were gone all day! Why, late even!" Louise resisted Clara's firm hold on her arm and pulled free, facing her. "You were lying! Oh, I see it—yes, there it is. That little frown when you're thinking what to say."

Perhaps Clara wasn't as good at lying as she'd thought. "Yes, I had...errands. That took me away from work. I should have simply told Fritz, but I—I don't know why I didn't." Clara tried to resume walking.

Louise stood firmly planted. "What sort of errands?"

"Nothing important."

"Important enough for you to miss work." Louise crossed her arms. "So it must be important. Some other girl might ditch work for a seamstress appointment or the like, but not you. You must be in some sort of trouble, is that it?" Her eyes widened, possibilities inserting themselves. "Oh, Clara, what kind of trouble?"

"I'm not in any trouble at all, most particularly not *that* kind," she retorted.

"Clara Ironwood, you tell me what is happening or—or—or I'll write to Mother!" Louise finally levied the one threat that she held, always, in reserve.

Clara exhaled through her nose, slowly, meeting Louise's eyes as she decided what to do. She couldn't think of a single lie her sister would believe. Unfortunately, she wouldn't believe the truth, either.

"It's about Godfather," she finally said. "He is...he was... involved with some people here. In his work, I mean."

Louise narrowed her eyes. "I suppose that aligns with what we know of Godfather. Why would you miss work on that account?"

"These are people with whom he, well—he had a falling-out. They have, um, well, like unions, but not quite unions—at any rate, there are people he wasn't on good terms with."

"But what does that matter to you? Clara, he treated you rather awfully in the end. I know you nearly worshipped him growing up, but for goodness' sake. He isn't worth your consideration now."

Clara paused, taken aback. Of all the arguments she had expected in response to her half-truths, this surprised her. She had considered pragmatism, timelines, precise types of clockwork— but Louise jumped right to the part she always skipped over.

"I know, Louise. I suppose—it was my work, too. For a couple of years. I had questions. Perhaps because I can't ask him. I want to know how he learned, why his work was always so..." She sighed. She knew, now, why Godfather's work always seemed imbued with magic. He carried the inspiration of the anderwelt into every one of his clockwork creations in the ordinary world. "You remember what those toys he used to make us were like. These people, they make things like that. I couldn't help my curiosity."

Louise's smile unfolded despite her best stern defense against it.

"I shouldn't be surprised. All right, mum's the word. I won't tell Fritz a thing."

Louise linked her arm through Clara's. Out of the corner of her eye, Clara noticed a shadow flanking them. At first her breath caught, thinking it must be the schattenhund, but the light was still too strong. Clara refused to turn and see who or what it was— Sandmann? Saint-Luc? Some enemy as yet unidentified?

A tiny pair of gray mice sprinted past her on the curb, then stood at attention to watch her pass. Nathanael's mice—a sense of calm settled on her, and then she nearly laughed, earning a curious glance from Louise. Who would have thought that an escort of mice could put anyone at ease?

"I don't know how you'll follow me into the restaurant," she muttered to the rodent guards who hid themselves in the shadow of her skirts.

"What's that?" Louise asked. "Here it is—Clara!"

Clara tore her attention from the mice at her feet. Behind her, she was sure a single figure had left the crowds on the sidewalk and fell into step just out of her peripheral vision. As she followed her sister inside, she scanned the crowd and spotted one familiar face.

She almost wished for Sandmann. Instead, Fritz briefly caught her eye and then faded into the press of people ebbing away toward dinners and shows and bottles of wine at cafés.

Chapter Thirty-Seven

NATHANAEL WASN'T IN the café. Clara noticed this immediately. Despite the fact that they were five minutes after eight, given the unexpected chat with Fritz on the way, Nathanael Nussbaum was not waiting for them.

Clara pushed her nerves down, her sister blithely chattering at the waiter as they were seated. A small mouse kept pace with Clara, staying in her shadow. *What do you want? What do you know?* she thought to it, wishing it could read her mind. It watched her with plaintive dark eyes, but of course it couldn't understand or answer.

"I think I'll have the trout," Louise was saying, but Clara wasn't paying attention. She pretended to read the menu, but instead she continued to scan the restaurant, hoping at any moment to notice Nathanael. "I believe the waiter recommended it, but he was rather quiet! I wonder if they have a good white wine that will pair with trout." Clara let her continue translating the menu out loud as she realized with mounting trepidation—Nathanael wasn't there.

Clara's eyes came to rest at the far end of the café, only two people at a table for six, as though expecting a larger party. Both were familiar—with her stomach tightening into a knot, she recognized Monsieur Lavallé. The other was Frau Schwann, the elected head of the Nämberch guild. Her pulse increased, and she hoped her face had not betrayed her. Perhaps it was coincidence, she hoped weakly, but logic wouldn't allow her to accept that explanation.

"Now, what are you having? I know you don't prefer fish, but the chicken sounds rather good—oh, with capers!" Louise said.

The mouse began to climb Clara's skirts.

"You know, I think we ought to go," Clara said abruptly. "I have a bit of a headache, and something in here is bothering it, and—"

"Clara! Why, you never get headaches."

"That's not entirely true—"

The mouse, very gently but insistently, clamped down on Clara's finger, and then pawed at her pocket. The pocket that held the key.

Clara swallowed. "Louise. If I tell you something that sounds strange in the next few minutes, please don't ask any questions, and please do as I say."

"Why, Clara—" Louise blanched as she absorbed the gravity of Clara's words. "All right."

Lavallé rose from the table for six. She watched him warily, refusing to give him any reaction beyond annoyance as he approached her and Louise. "Good evening, Miss Ironwood." His voice fell like cold steel, clattering on the quiet.

"Good evening." Clara folded her hands to keep them from shaking. "I'm afraid I don't recall your name," she stalled. Next to her, Louise moved closer, reaching for her hand.

His moustache twitched a bit, surprised by this slight. "Etienne Lavallé."

"Oh yes. Thank you." Clara didn't look away. What would a man do, she thought, in the same situation? Fritz, Nathanael, neither would look away or blush. "Very nice to see you again, but my sister and I—"

"I must insist that you join me and my associate," Lavallé interjected. "It's only polite." The hard glint in his eyes was not courtesy, Clara knew, but something else. Avarice. Power.

"I'm terribly sorry, but my sister and I were just leaving. You see," she said, looking pointedly at Louise, "my sister gets awful migraines, and she feels one coming on." Lavallé hesitated a moment, clearly planning the next play on the board, but Clara had already seen his objective, at least one of the checkmates he hoped to extract from the game.

It was her. She would have to place herself in a position of some vulnerability to draw him out any further.

"However," Clara continued, "I do think she can manage to get home on her own, if you are so insistent that I stay for a chat with you."

"That would be most appreciated," he said. He glanced at Louise, who cooperated with the ruse by giving him a pained smile. "In fact, I insist on paying for a hansom to take her home."

"That isn't necessary—" Louise began.

"Oh, I'm sure it is," Clara replied, quickly resetting the pieces of the game to her liking. "I'll arrange it with the manager," she explained, picking up Louise's pocketbook along with her own. She wasn't going to have Lavallé calling for the cab, perhaps having Louise followed. To her surprise, the mouse settled into her pocket as she rose to make the arrangements.

She ushered Louise out of the café, whispering, "Just go right home. See if Annabelle is about, or Madame Boule. Stay with them."

"Clara, what is all this? What—"

"Please don't argue. I don't think these people mean you any harm, but they also—" She glanced at Lavallé, holding court as his table. "Monsieur Lavallé also isn't used to being argued with." Frau Schwann seemed equally formidable, quiet but clever. And why was she here? That question frightened Clara more than any other uncertainty at that moment.

With Louise safely sent home—Clara hoped—she turned back to Lavallé. "Well?" she said. No point in niceties. She didn't even sit down in the offered chair. "Where is Herr Nussbaum?"

Lavallé seemed genuinely surprised that she had gotten straight to the point, but she didn't release him from her gaze. He coughed and then recovered. "I assure you, Miss Ironwood, we only wish to talk to you, and—"

"Hardly." The mouse was climbing back down her skirts, and she hoped it was planning to crawl under Lavallé's trouser hem and bite him. "I was to meet Herr Nussbaum here this evening and when I arrive, I find you instead. You cannot convince a woman trained in as much mathematics as I am that this is a coincidence."

"She is not as placid as you suggested, Frau Schwann." Lavallé raised an eyebrow.

"Thus far the encounter has been less than entirely comfortable," Clara countered. "You haven't even the courtesy to make polite introductions or tell me why you wish to meet."

Surprised, he laughed lightly. "I presume you already know Hilde Schwann. And, of course, you and I are already colleagues, in a sense, working for the grandest Exposition in history."

"I do indeed know Frau Schwann." She glanced at the woman, who maintained a neutral expression that refused to yield her position. Was she a prospective victim, or an accomplice? Either could be true. "But, monsieur, what business do we all have with one another? I'm afraid we are quite past dancing about with chatter about the Exposition." She finally sat down, sweeping her skirts out of the way now that the mouse was clear.

"I wouldn't say that," Lavallé replied. "I am still, in a manner of speaking, here on behalf of the Exposition. I am quite fascinated by what Frau Schwann tells me about the particular work your godfather did."

Clara thought her insides might actually freeze. She feigned disinterest, but her breath hurt in her chest. They were about to ask outright. Frau Schwann essayed a glance at Clara, asking her to admit everything with a placid nod.

Fine.

"My godfather was a handwerker in one of the guilds, yes. And he made a key and apparently you would like to know where it is." They both flushed, surprised that she was suddenly forthcoming. "I see no point in pretending otherwise, do you? You are after my godfather's key."

"Now, fräulein, we said nothing so—" Frau Schwann interjected.

"You don't need to say it. I'm not stupid. But you must think me an absolute weakling if you think I'd talk without some negotiation first." She leaned forward. "You'll let Nussbaum join our conversation."

"I'm afraid," Lavallé said, voice cooling, "that is not possible right now. He isn't here—"

"Why, then, we'll have to relocate to join him." Clara crossed her arms and waited. "I shan't even consider showing you the key until we do."

This seemed to do it. Lavallé held her chair and Schwann went toward the door—not the front door, but a narrow entrance to a back hallway.

Well, Clara Ironwood, she thought to herself, *you've really gotten yourself into it now.*

Chapter Thirty-Eight

A TRIO OF mice followed Clara, Frau Schwann, and Monsieur Lavallé down a hallway cramped with old crates the sour smell of spilled wine. More mice joined on the stairwell. Clara found it oddly heartening—these were Nathanael's mice. If they were still his eyes and ears, he was still all right.

The stairs opened onto another long hallway, and the turns and corners soon had Clara somewhat lost as to their orientation to the outside world. The thick sourness grew and then faded into the scent of dusty roses and spent lilacs as the hallway ended in a large attic. What an odd smell, she thought, blinking at the brightness of dust motes swirling in the open space.

Nathanael sat on a broken chair in the middle of the room.

"Evening," he said, hiding any surprise he felt. "I'd offer you a seat, but this is the only one available, and as you can see, someone felt it necessary to restrain me with it."

Clara looked more closely—a matted rope held Nathanael's hands to the chair frame. She turned to her hosts. "This was hardly necessary."

"Perhaps it was. He was trespassing, you see." Lavallé's moustache twitched with irritation. "And he was quite belligerent."

"You ought to see what they've got downstairs, Clara." Nathanael's voice was deadpan. "Explains a lot, actually. You can see most of the operation from that balcony."

"Now, you've seen that Nussbaum is just fine," Frau Schwann said. "Terribly regrettable, I did not want to resort to such measures." She looked to Lavallé with a pained expression that Clara couldn't decipher—was it an act, or was she actually questioning her involvement in this plot? "As for the key—"

"I don't have the key," Clara replied blithely.

"You suggested she kept it with her," Lavallé said to Schwann. "You all but promised she—"

"Well of course! A handwerker usually keeps the key on them, at all times!" Frau Schwann held up her hands in a mime of innocence. "And you said—" Schwann turned to her.

"I didn't say I had it." She forced her voice steady. "You can search me, but I haven't got it. And I've a feeling whatever I'm about to see will make a very poor impression about you. About both of you."

Before they could speak, she strode to an overlook bordered with a rail of spindle-thin wooden slats. She laid a shaking hand on the splintered wood.

The disused warehouse below was littered with boxes of glass and the rusted innards of machinery—a perfume bottleworks, she realized from posters on the wall, defunct. Dead scents hung in the air. She caught her breath. In a haphazard heap next to a set of barrels leaking something onto the floor—automatons.

At least a dozen, she calculated quickly, and all alike. They were unclothed, but that didn't reveal anything untoward; they had been made nearly featureless except for blank gray eyes and slits of mouths.

She fought back horror at seeing something so close to human and yet not human, stripped and devoid of individual traits or personality. "What are they?"

Frau Schwann sighed. "They are not my work, and I cannot answer any questions about their provenance." She turned her face away as though the scene were distasteful. Distasteful, Clara amended, but necessary. "They are automatons."

"Clearly," Clara replied with more acid than she intended. "But they aren't dancers."

Lavallé took up the explanation with more robust enthusiasm. "They are intended to work in a fashion similar to factory employees, but without the inherent risks to the men involved in such industrial spaces. It's meant as a more practical display. Right at home with the exhibits on modern machinery and factory operations."

Clara saw the tin soldiers' featureless faces reflected in these automatons. "These aren't the first you've brought over, are they?"

Lavallé raised a brow. "No, but it seems you know that already. The giants—we put those to work already. You must have seen, yes?"

"I wish I hadn't." Clara's mouth went dry. "It seems you don't need a key," she finally said. "The dancers at the Exposition dinner, too?" she asked.

"No, they weren't," Nathanael called from behind them. "He hasn't got the imagination to make dancers. All he can come up with are cogs in a machine—of course, that's all people are to him, too, just cogs that have the indecency to require food and water and—"

Lavallé looked like he was ready to strike Nathanael, but his clenched hand stayed next to his belt. "That's quite enough."

"Why did you even bother making those things down there with mouths?" Nathanael retorted. "Seems you would have preferred them mute."

"I'll take that into consideration for the next exhibit we make." Lavallé turned back to Clara, who was beginning to feel the precarity of her position. She moved away from the rickety balcony railing, scanning the room for some means of escape—but that would have left Nathanael alone in the loft, defenseless.

Frau Schwann stopped her. "You can understand the problem, though, can't you, Miss Ironwood? This process, of making creations and bringing them here, it has caused blights. But it doesn't have to be that way."

"Yes, you could stop this abomination right now!" Clara replied.

"No, you don't understand. I am not the one making these—these creations." Frau Schwann wrung her hands. "But a member of my guild is. I am almost certain— After we spoke with you— But that does not matter."

"If you know who it is," Clara said slowly, "you could tell Saint-Luc. You could tell the guilds." She backed away slightly, appalled by the lies the demure figure before her had been clothed in. "You could have said something at that meeting, instead of dragging out that charade, pretending you needed my help to identify who was behind this!"

"I cannot do that!" Frau Schwann lowered her voice. "I confronted the man responsible for the blights as soon as I suspected. He denied it—of course he did—but I knew."

"Then you should have ended it. End it now, take it to Saint-Luc."

"No! That pompous religious zealot, no. He would never understand the circumstances—it is my responsibility to protect my guild, and its members." She paused, tension drawing her face into a taut mask. Perhaps Magda was right, Clara reflected, to be so circumspect about the guilds. They could leverage their cooperation and strength to solve problems, true, but they could turn the same authority into an obstacle. "The man responsible will be dealt with, but I wish to keep it within the guild."

"I'll be transferring my membership," Nathanael muttered.

Frau Schwann looked suddenly flustered. "You all have no idea what it is to lead a guild. No idea. And this is more complicated—" She waited until Lavallé paced toward Nathanael, and then lowered her voice so only Clara could hear. "You know your Monsieur Lavallé's reputation, yes?"

Clara recalled what Fritz had told her. "To some degree, yes."

"Then you will believe me when I say that I wish to protect the member of my guild from—retribution, that is the correct word, yes? From the results of crossing such a man as that."

"He made his bed, climbing into it with Lavallé."

"There is a way for him to complete his contracted work with the Exposition, and for the blights to stop." Frau Schwann hesitated. "The key. Your godfather's key."

"I won't give it up. No one would." Clara shored up her courage. "No one who truly understood the anderwelt would exploit it like this."

"No one? Your godfather brought the dancers you saw at the Exposition," Schwann said.

Clara fell silent. "What did you say? My godfather would never have—would never—"

"But he did." Schwann stepped toward her. She looked, almost, sympathetic. "I'm sorry you held such a high opinion of him only to have it challenged now. But I knew, and I have held on to that secret for many years."

She was almost certainly lying. Almost certainly. Clara kept Nathanael in her line of sight, not moving any closer. She saw figures scurrying along the shadows—more mice.

"My godfather is not here to answer for himself, so there's little point setting up a defense," Clara said instead of debating the point. That was what they wanted—to push her into the negotiation they wanted, one that resulted in yielding the key. She wanted only one thing—to leave. And she saw how to accomplish that.

"What do they do?" she asked abruptly. "Your automatons? Would you show me?"

"Of course!" Lavallé snapped. "The craftsmen hoard their skills to make—I don't know, novelties and toys, but these are truly remarkable. The uses of such a creation are nearly limitless, and beneficial to all mankind."

"You are interested, then, in mankind's problems?" Clara said, a tart bite to the question. Play nice, she reminded herself. "That is to say, you are a theorist, a philosopher?"

"No, I hadn't meant to imply any such thing." Lavallé was flustered by the suggestion—interesting, Clara thought.

"More of a numbers person, then," Clara said with a kind smile that hurt to paste on. "Or management? You're a man of business, I mean."

"Yes, precisely. I am interested in the success of the Exposition, first and foremost." Lavallé glanced at the automatons. "I suggested that it might be best to find some use for the automatons beyond entertainment, and we thought a model factory within the Galerie des Machines made great sense."

Clara didn't answer right away, forcing aside acrid distaste. "Perhaps you could show me," Clara said, gesturing toward the abominations on the first floor. She met Nathanael's eyes briefly, and he gave her a silent nod.

Lavallé brightened, believing himself, clearly, on the verge of making the sale. "But of course, of course," he said as he led Clara down a staircase in nearly as poor repair as the railing. Her fingers left a trail through the dust on the banister. She steeled herself against seeing the automatons more closely.

"Who designed them?" she asked lightly.

"I'm not for blind trust until you've earned it," Lavallé retorted quickly.

Frau Schwann joined them. "I will tell you who he is only if you give me the key. It's the only way I can protect him and my guild."

"Then I suppose I don't need to know," Clara said, evasive. She picked up a dented screwdriver from an abandoned crate, wishing she had her own tools. "Monsieur Lavallé, you misunderstand me. I figured you must have had a hand in the design process itself, deciding about—oh, color, for instance." For some perverse reason, the automatons had been rendered in a mute shade of grayish beige, neither light nor dark, neither cool nor warm. "And what functions"—she swallowed the sterile vinegar of that word—"you wanted them to perform."

"They're meant to be able to replace over a dozen vital functions in factory work," Lavallé said. "Each plausible from the articulation of fingers, hands, all that, able to be selected by a foreman."

"And knowing what precise jobs you wanted them to do—why make them, you could ask, humanoid at all?" She winced as she unscrewed a panel at the wrist of the nearest automaton.

"That was my idea," Lavallé said. "I thought it was the most appealing for the Exposition audience. The effect is better if they looked like people, rather than machines. Seeing machines proper replace human workers might have an unsettling effect, which I wanted to avoid." Clara bit her tongue to keep from arguing—as though these waxen mannequins were somehow anything other than horrifying.

"We chose the color to keep them from looking too much like any one group of ethnics," he added. "Particularly for the American audience. They can be so sensitive about such things—we did not want their Irish or Italians or Negroes thinking they were getting a direct replacement!"

What an absolute tick of a man, Clara thought as she examined the inner workings of the automaton. She could tell immediately that the intricacy of the mechanics was not as complex as Olympia's or the dancers at the dinner, but still expertly crafted. Familiar, even, the mark of the same craftsman's process on each. With more time, Clara knew she could have discerned more of the design and the intended movements of the arms, legs, fingers.

"They'll be installed in the Galerie des Machines?" she asked, screwing the panel back into place and moving on to one on the back of the neck. *By Jove, Nathanael is taking his time*, Clara thought.

"That is the intention," Lavallé said. "In fact, I had it in mind to bring the project to you, Miss Ironwood, given how helpful your plans for the Lumières' screen have been." Clara bit the inside of her lip to avoid responding. He'd used her, used her designs, used her creativity—and then used the power of the anderwelt itself. He'd blighted both of them. She could have slapped him.

Instead, she pretended to prod the automaton's mechanisms while watching the back of the warehouse, the figure she anticipated finally coming down the stairs. "Well, this is all quite fascinating, really. What other projects do you have in mind?"

"Plenty—there are several additions I'd like to make to the Bois de Vincennes that will require your specialty, and I'm not satisfied with the set for Loie Fuller's pavilion. She's practically of another world, her dance stage needs something. See? I told you she would come around," Lavallé said to Schwann, just as Nathanael shoved a large empty crate between Clara and the others, knocking Lavallé off balance and toppling two of the automatons. In the confusion, Clara grabbed Nathanael's hand, and they both ran for the door.

Chapter Thirty-Nine

"GOOD THING THAT door actually worked," Nathanael said, once they had slowed their pace and found a tram on the right line to go toward Clara's apartment. "In that garbage dump, I half expected it would be jammed from the outside or rusted shut."

"We'd have thought of something," Clara said. "It took the mice longer than I expected."

"The ropes were old, and they must have been soaked in water at some point—hard for even rodent teeth to work through."

"Are you all right?" Clara said, pausing to grab Nathanael's wrist and pull back his sleeve cuff. Sure enough, rough red abrasions marred his skin.

"It's nothing, really," he said, but he didn't take his hand back right away. His fingers were deft, and his hand felt strong under hers, honed by fine work to the very smallest muscles. She flushed and replaced his cuff.

"Now." Nathanael kept his hand firmly engaged in hers. "Were you bluffing about your key?"

"You mean," she said, "*Thrushman's* key. No, I wasn't. I made sure it went home with my sister. I slipped it into her pocketbook before she left."

"I certainly hope she didn't lose it," Nathanael said.

"Louise? No, she's far more responsible than I am. And besides," she added, "maybe getting lost wouldn't be the worst thing for it."

"Perhaps not."

"Were they lying?" Clara said, unable to avoid thinking about it any longer. "Did Godfather make the key to bring—things back from the anderwelt? On purpose? Did he bring the dancers, do you think?" She allowed herself the cold thought, briefly, that some of the many devices and delights Thrushman had entertained her with as a child might have been stolen from the anderwelt. But no—they could all be replicated in his shop, and she had copied many of the designs. They were simple, compared to the almost biological complexity of the anderwelt's creations. He had only brought inspiration back from the anderwelt.

"Haven't any idea." He slowed his step further as they approached the Seine. "Honestly, Clara, I haven't any idea. The dancers—I had never heard of them until you told me about them, and I have no way of knowing if Uncle Elias had anything to do with bringing them over." He paused. "That kind of thing was never really his interest, though. Marzipan castles, certainly, but not living dolls."

"Did you find anything else in the warehouse? I assume," Clara said, "that you slipped in there without invitation."

"I did indeed," he said, offering his hand as the tram came to a stop. "I sent the mice on a bit of reconnaissance first, and then had to see for myself. I found the—what would you call them?"

"Abominations," Clara muttered. "I suppose I've been thinking of them as automatons, but that seems too generous, somehow."

"I suppose it's the best term we have," Nathanael acknowledged. "What now?"

"I suppose we take what we have to Saint-Luc." She hesitated. "Including that Frau Schwann knows everything."

"I never would have guessed it. But perhaps I should have." He rubbed his temples. "She is of the old, preunification mindset that one's loyalty is first and foremost to one's own guild. She would want to protect her own."

"If it is someone in her guild," she said slowly, "then you may know them, as well."

Nathanael nodded uneasily. "I'd considered that. I haven't any idea who. It's as though, suddenly, everyone I know is no longer above suspicion. I would have trusted Frau Schwann entirely, so to discover she is complicit is…" He exhaled sharply. "It's utterly disorienting."

"She seemed to think that Lavallé is a real threat, too," Clara mused. "I—I don't think we can be too careful about him."

"I agree with that assessment, after having been tied up by the man," Nathanael said. "I will give Frau Schwann one thing—she insisted it was unnecessary and I think she might have cried a little about it."

"Feeling bad about being an accomplice doesn't excuse her," Clara countered.

"We'll let Saint-Luc deal with that." Nathanael sighed. "We still don't have the craftsman, and nothing more can be done tonight. You look, if you don't mind my saying, exhausted. It can wait until the morning to give Saint-Luc the names of the Exposition contacts." He hesitated. "I don't particularly care for the thought of that Lavallé man knowing that you know about his plans, though. Should I—should I drop you off at your door, or—"

"Come in with me," Clara said. She led the way up the stairs to her apartment, and knocked on Annabelle's door. She breathed deep relief when Louise opened it.

"What *was* that?" she said in greeting, almost knocking Clara off balance with her authoritative embrace. "Who was that man? Why did you send me home? Why is there a magnifying glass in my purse? Who is this?"

"She was in a rare pique when she showed up here," Annabelle offered, leaning in the doorway, appraising first Clara and then Nathanael. "Had to open a bottle of good brandy. It's still open, in fact." She beckoned them inside, but Clara shook her head.

"I—we can't. I'm afraid—there's—"

"Poppycock. You're into something dicey, to be sure, but you needn't tell me about it." She waved a hand as though dispersing flies. "What you do need is a drop of brandy and a good sit-down."

Clara hesitated, but Nathanael replied, "We would be glad of a bit of brandy." He met Clara's eyes and nodded lightly. "It will be nice to be with a pleasant, sociable group," he added. Clara understood immediately—he didn't want her to be alone, and he didn't relish the thought for himself, either.

"Well, I've never felt so shaken in all my life," Louise said as they settled on a few cushions pulled off of Annabelle's sofa, the furniture itself having been taken over by a large, old-fashioned cage crinoline. Hector established himself firmly in Louise's lap.

"Let's not talk about it, then," Annabelle said blithely. "Talking about unpleasant things too soon only exaggerates them in the memory. I read that in a magazine last month—at least, I think that's what it meant." She fetched two more glasses from her cabinet and handed Nathanael one of thick red glass and brass filigree like something from a medieval court, and one in delicate pale pink etched with lilies for Clara. "Instead—I haven't told you about the dinner party after you made your exit." She regaled them with stories of stiff-collared Exposition administrators and rumpled engineers until they were all laughing and the ill effects of their misadventure had begun to wear off.

Sometime after midnight Louise announced that they really must all be off to bed.

"Fine, fine," Annabelle agreed, sweeping a tray of mismatched glasses and a half-emptied bottle of brandy away. "Oh! I wanted to invite you ladies, so I may as well invite the gentleman, too— we're having a sort of dress rehearsal for the phosphorescence dance, and it would be just lovely if you could all come." She dug into an overstuffed pocketbook that she fished out from under the crinoline. "I've got four tickets, so you can all come."

"Sunday night?" Louise said, scanning the ticket. "Well, Clara, can you fit it into your busy social calendar?"

"Yes, I think so—Nathanael—Herr Nussbaum"—she blushed— "did you want to come, too?"

"Would be delighted."

"The extra ticket—maybe, just perhaps," Annabelle said with contrived innocence, "you could invite Herr Fritz Krieger?"

"I can make the attempt," Clara replied with a laugh. Annabelle and Fritz—now, that would be a pairing! She wasn't sure if it was the sort of pairing Alma had in mind, but Annabelle was, Clara could attest, a very good friend to have.

As Louise went straight to her bedroom, Clara walked Nathanael out of the building. "I'll go to Saint-Luc with the names," he said. "Just as soon as I've had a chance to change my shirt and comb my hair—*mein Gott*, that man has a way of making one feel like an unkempt sewer rat even when one hasn't been tied up like a criminal in a dusty warehouse."

"Do you think it's safe to go home alone?"

"I'm not terribly worried," Nathanael replied with a stiff smile that told her he was, in fact, nervous. "And if I have any concerns—I do have a key."

"And mice," Clara said with a forced smile. "Be careful."

Chapter Forty

THE PALACE OF Optics still smelled strongly of curing plaster and sawdust, but the stage was complete. The press of the crowd made Clara nervous, even though there were only a few hundred gathered, critics and journalists carefully selected to ensure more excitement about the Exposition, scientists and architects who had worked on the project, and guests of the dancers. Everyone, Clara reasoned, had a ticket and a reason to be present. Still, she had debated long about what to do with her key. Leaving it at home felt entirely unsafe, unguarded in an apartment whose lock was merely adequate. Carrying it with her felt just as risky, except that at least she would know where it was at all times.

So she had looped it through a chain and wore it like a watch, pinned and fastened securely so she was safe from pickpockets, if not outright coercive theft. She felt safer with Nathanael by her side, and strangely comforted, as well, by Fritz. He'd had the graciousness not to mention their meeting on the street, but Clara noticed that he seemed quietly concerned as he'd inquired how her day had been. She'd spent so long ferreting out her apprehension of others, from Nussbaum to Saint-Luc, that she'd forgotten she could easily find herself on the other side of suspicion. But Fritz wasn't suspicious, even when she'd given him every reason to be; he showed only the genuine concern of a friend. Clara found she appreciated that more, even, than the respect he gave her work.

"The telescope is so long," Fritz told Louise, "that it runs underneath this building and all the way—"

"We're here for a dance performance, not a lecture," Clara cautioned with a laugh.

"Now, I was finding it quite fascinating," Louise replied. "The largest telescope in the world—that will be something to see!"

"It doesn't actually work very well—too much light around here, and it isn't calibrated quite properly. You see, the angle is not really correct for accurate scientific observation, but there was nowhere else to situate—"

"Ruining the entire experience, Fritz."

"Now then! Some people appreciate my lectures." Fritz took Clara's arm and pulled her aside as the other two admired the elegant arc of the Palace of Optics entrance. "Are you all right? You have seemed...rather unwell. And distant."

Clara hesitated. She tried to catch Nathanael's eye, but he was busy procuring a pair of programs from a passing usher.

"Ah, I see." Fritz interjected before she could speak. "He is—he seems—a very kind sort of man."

"Oh, Fritz, I—that isn't—" She sighed. "I have not been missing work on account of a gentleman, if that is what concerns you."

"Clara, you could hardly be accused of negligence. That isn't my concern at all. Rather, I was concerned for you. You seemed distracted. If the distraction was of an unpleasant nature, I would have wished to alleviate it, if it was within my power. But if it is not—" He smiled faintly. "Then be distracted."

"No, I—" She was surprised to feel tears pressing the corners of her eyes. "You are so very kind, Fritz. My behavior...I wish I could explain, but I cannot. It is of a personal nature, you are right." She considered her words carefully. "My godfather, the man I apprenticed under, had some very strange connections. Some of them were...of a dubious quality." She reached for the words to explain without the uncanny specifics. Even Fritz, good-hearted Fritz, wouldn't believe the truth from her. "He— he seems to have made a bit of a mess and I am trying to clean it up."

Fritz considered this, and answered carefully. "Are you in some sort of danger, Clara? I was quite serious when I said if there is anything I could do to help, I would—the presence of another friend like your Herr Nussbaum does not change that."

"You are a good man, Fritz Krieger." Clara smiled, clasping his hand in hers. "If you could help me, I would let you. And that's saying something."

"I know it—you are as prickly as the cacti in the horticulture exhibit."

"Now then!" Clara smacked his arm. Fritz feigned surrender and resumed regaling Louise with statistics about the aquarium as yet unpublished in any Exposition visitors' guides.

Nathanael returned and pulled her aside. "I went to Saint-Luc this morning. I just got word from him—"

"How?

"Not everyone who hands out programs is actually an usher," he said. "Saint-Luc sent him to warn us." Clara went cold. "He couldn't find Hilde Schwann, in either the anderwelt or this side.

But there was a woman found—" He caught his breath. "In the Seine. The description matches."

"Nathanael! What are we supposed to do? Should we find Saint-Luc, or hide, or—"

"We ought to go in soon, don't you think?" Louise interrupted. Clara smoothed her face, and Nathanael feigned nonchalance. "Who has the tickets?"

Fritz swiped the tickets from Clara with tactful aplomb and escorted everyone to their row, not quite the farthest back of a sea of chairs set up for the performance.

She found herself between Louise and Nathanael. While Louise deluged Fritz with technical questions about the Palace of Optics that he was only too glad to answer, Nathanael reached surreptitiously for her hand. She let him take it, his agile fingers closing over hers, her heart accelerating in a clandestine clamor in her chest. He didn't let go as the lights dimmed and the blaze of artificial light illuminated the stage.

Lights like hard candies in every hue imaginable surrounded them, summer strawberry and sharp lime and sweet orange glistening with electricity. The dance of the fairy, electricity, in all her beguiling movements, lasted only a moment before the lights winked out and the soft black of the stage shifted into a faded dreamscape.

Dancers emerged, though Clara wouldn't have known they were human; they glowed like strange insects in the gloom, entering slowly into a complex but sedate choreography. They fluttered like great moths in moonlight, then became a river of starlight on the stage, and Clara found herself entirely enchanted.

Suddenly, Nathanael's hand around hers tightened. She started. He laid his other hand across her arm and leaned toward her. Her pulse quickened, fear and his dangerous proximity mingling.

"Something is wrong. Someone is crossing into the anderwelt nearby."

"Is that so very strange?" Clara whispered. Nathanael still held tight to her hand.

"It wouldn't be, except that why would someone be crossing here, now? My key is being pulled toward it." He held the key out in his hand. It thrummed faintly on its ribbon and, as though pulled by a magnet, pulled the ribbon straight out behind it until it was a line parallel with the floor. Clara's eyes widened and she gripped Nathanael's hand.

Without a word, he rose from his seat and pulled Clara behind him. She motioned to Louise to hush, and hoped her sister wouldn't make a fuss. She merely scrunched her forehead in displeasure and turned back to the stage.

Clara let Nathanael choose the path, though she realized once they were in the semi-light outside that he was, in turn, following the button, which lifted and pointed not unlike a hunting dog. "It's backstage," he whispered. "Whoever it is."

Clara pressed her lips together and screwed up her courage. "Then we go backstage."

"Are you sure? It could be dangerous, if someone is trying to... eliminate anyone who knows about how the Exposition has used the anderwelt."

Clara thought of Hilde Schwann, waterlogged in the cold Seine, and threw off a shudder. "I think we have to."

Though the key led them, they had to find their own way through the labyrinth of the palace not meant for the public. Here Clara knew the pathways and Nathanael heeded her directions, letting her course-correct against the key. Clara was surprised that no one stopped them; she prepared a little speech about needing to check the wiring if anyone did.

The key suddenly dropped, hanging like a pendulum again. Nathanael pulled her closer. "We should cross."

"Now? But what if—" She glanced around. No one was there. "All right."

Nathanael held tight to her hand—it was nearly familiar now, though still thrilling in its quiet way. He lifted the key, let it sway, and as it began to thrum the world shifted around them.

Clara caught her breath, the maze of hallways transformed into a true labyrinth, marble and twisting vines precluding their path in all but one direction. "This wasn't here," she whispered. "Last time—this wasn't here."

"Someone probably built this on purpose—maybe to hide their movements more easily. Can you find your way to the backstage area? That is where the key seemed to point, before."

Clara nodded and quickly ascertained the right turns and twists of the labyrinth. She could see where the stage would have been and, surprised, slowed to watch. The dimmed and artificial lights of the stage were gone, but a strange glow remained. Disembodied and eerie, it moved above the ground, coalescing, circling wide, splitting into whorls. She gasped—it was the phosphorescence dance, projected as a cloud of light in the anderwelt.

"Nathanael," she whispered, pointing toward the display. "How…"

"The anderwelt reflects what we do on the other side," he replied, "and if it's strong enough, it does it in real time. And it is beautiful."

"So is this." Clara pointed. In jewel colors and as large as swans, mechanical birds flitted in and out of the glowing reflections of the dance. "Those are my designs, Nathanael. Someone copied my little birds—the ones I made in Godfather's shop."

Nathanael's jaw clenched. "And thought they would add something to the phosphorescence dance." The birds swooped and fell and bore themselves up again, all woven through with shimmering light. "Perhaps they meant to bring them out tonight."

A sharp echo of footsteps retreated from behind the eerie dance. Nathanael pulled her behind him.

"Can you see who—"

"No," Nathanael replied in a terse whisper. "Stay here."

Clara did not like that idea at all, but it hardly seemed like the time for an argument, especially as she couldn't convey quite what she wanted in hand signals and facial expressions. Nathanael slipped away, following the last few yards of the labyrinth. She contented herself with a silence that bristled with static, the strange scent of old smoke still wafting from the space where the labyrinth opened.

Nathanael returned, and Clara wasn't certain that the final turn and curve of the labyrinth didn't lengthen and sharpen as he passed. "No one there. No one there now, at any rate. It seems—"

Footfalls echoed down the labyrinth, which Clara was quite sure had shifted, a curve to the left now veering right and a narrow offshoot growing wider.

Nathanael gripped her hand, pulling her away from the sound, which warped so that they couldn't place its location as echoes bounced from one labyrinth wall to another.

"Wait," Clara whispered, seized by an idea. "I know where no one will find us."

Chapter Forty-One

USING WHAT MEMORY she had of the labyrinth and her instincts to draw her toward the Palace of Illusions, she led them through turns and loops until she found it—the hall of living mirrors. It was unchanged, the mirrors still shimmering with an otherworldly gleam.

Hundreds of Nathanaels and Claras looked back toward them, moving when they moved, yet with slight differences. One Clara quirked her face in a conspiratorial smile, while another bowed her head in chagrined penitence. Another reached a hand toward Nathanael, searching, it seemed, for something it was missing. She flushed and brought her attention back toward Nathanael.

He reflected back at her in his many fragments—curious, awed, anxious, intense—and stood beside her in his complex, layered whole. "You made this," he whispered.

"I didn't realize what I was making until I came here." She smiled softly. "A place where people see themselves, see boundless ways to be themselves."

"It's brilliant. You're brilliant," Nathanael said suddenly, then blushed. "I see it rippling in the reflection of each of those mirrors."

"Thank you," Clara replied, not knowing what else to say. "Now. What do we do?"

"We wait." They retreated into a corner as voices echoed in the distance, growing closer. Clara realized she was holding Nathanael's hand far too tightly, her chest bursting at the suspense of waiting.

A face Clara recognized flooded the mirrors nearest the entrance. She bit her lips together to smother the gasp that rose in her throat, and Nathanael gripped her hand more tightly.

Sandmann.

She had never liked him, always avoided him, but she had never considered before that Godfather's strange friend whose unwelcome presence frequently loitered at the fringes of his workshop and his conversations might be an actual danger. His hair, what remained of it, was grayer than before, but his face was only all the more gaunt and angular, and his eyes all the more globular and greedy. That awful searching gaze he had—it swept the Palace of Illusions as though it could strip the mirrors' fictions from the facts and pluck her and Nathanael out like burrs from a coat.

She glanced at Nathanael, who watched Sandmann, eyes widening first in recognition, then in disgust.

Sandmann's horrid face cracked an equally horrid smile. Clara saw why she had thought him ugly all those years ago—it wasn't his less than comely features but the conniving, grasping way he looked at everyone, at everything. As though all the world were gears and cogs and he was the clockmaker, set to make use of whatever he wished for whatever he willed.

"Miss Ironwood," he said, in a nearly cordial tone, "I do believe you're here. It's been too long, chasing you about the city like a cat running after a ball of yarn."

Clara met Nathanael's eyes. He lifted his key. She shook her head—not yet. They could disappear back into the plain glass and wood of the other palace anytime, and quickly lose themselves in Paris's crowds. But she wanted to see if Sandmann would say anything first.

"You are just like you were as a child. Foolish little chit hiding under the bed. Do you remember that Christmas party when you did that? Hid under the bed just because I had come for a glass of punch with your parents."

She had hidden under the bed, a child of four, not knowing why this man frightened her so, until Godfather coaxed her out with promises that he had left. She remembered—he had brought his nutcracker to her room, cracking walnuts on her braided wool rug until she had ventured out to take one.

"I do hope we can speak as grown adults now, Miss Ironwood. I have a proposition that I am afraid you must be included in, as your godfather has decided to divest himself of the opportunity." He waited a moment. He wasn't as smart as he clearly thought himself to be, Clara surmised, or he would have known she had no intention of popping out for a chat.

Or perhaps not so foolish—she noticed that he had moved while he was speaking, very slowly, very deliberately, canvassing more and more of the room, seeing more and more of the mirrors. And now he had reached a point where he could see one Clara and one Nathanael, reflected in a mirror on the far side of the palace. A reflected Clara and Nathanael stood next to Sandmann in their mirrors, this Clara singularly angry and the Nathanael intently studious. Sandmann leered capriciously at them both in his reflection.

That was the real him, Clara thought, that reflection. As he moved, all of his images held variations on the same greed, avarice, degradation. She took a breath, reminded herself Nathanael still held her hand, and found her key. She considered saying something brash to provoke him, but there was no reason to.

He wanted her key. She had no intention of giving it to him. She nodded to Nathanael, and raised her key to her eyes.

They didn't stop to talk when they reentered the ordinary Palace of Illusions; surely Sandmann would be shortly behind. Instead, they made their way back to the performance, still only just underway, the glow on the stage blurring as Clara tried to bring her breath under control.

"What in the world?" Louise hissed at her. Fritz glanced over, concerned. She must look a fright, Clara thought, white and flushed all at once, breathing heavily. The other patrons probably thought—oh, embarrassing things, she conceded, not caring.

"The same as before," she whispered back. "If we stay together, stay here, we're quite safe." *I think*, she added silently. As much as she wanted to appreciate the verifiable witchcraft Annabelle and other dancers were spinning out onstage, she found she could only think of the awful face of Sandmann.

Godfather must have known, she reasoned. He sent her the nutcracker, the key—

The *stories*.

He had sent her the book of stories, stories in which she had assumed he was merely indulging a child's capricious tastes by naming each of the villains for his colleague. But what if he hadn't? Every story held some small truth, some lesson he ought to have taught her in person but told her in fables instead. What if the greatest lesson of all was simple? Godfather couldn't have penned it any clearer: Don't trust Sandmann. Sandmann is a wicked, horrid man.

As the lights came back on and the audience broke into loud applause, Clara turned to Nathanael. "You know him." She knew this already—she had seen them speaking in Nathanael's hotel. But she waited for his explanation, afraid she had begun to trust Nathanael Nussbaum too soon.

"I know him." His voice trembled faintly, and he looked almost sick.

"You know him *well*," Clara added after waiting produced no further details. "How well?"

"He was a good friend of Uncle Elias, back in Nuremberg. Before—before everything that happened. I'm afraid I've misread things quite terribly."

Chapter Forty-Two

"I'M SORRY." NATHANAEL drummed his fingers against one another, nervous energy pooling with nowhere else to go. "I'm so very sorry—I'm afraid he used me to find you."

Louise and Annabelle had been safely escorted home by Fritz, understanding as ever, and Clara stood outside with Nathanael. Louise had given her a knowing, teasing look that Clara was happy to accept in exchange for being left alone to discuss with Nathanael the very serious business of countering Sandmann. If she was honest, she was also happy simply to be left alone with Nathanael. That was a distraction, she rationalized, and neither of them had attention to waste on distraction, but for perhaps the first time she could remember, she didn't want to be purely rational.

"He came to visit me, several times. Once he inquired after you," Nussbaum said. "I had known him, long ago in Nuremberg, and didn't think much of it. He said that your godfather had contacted him to say that you were in Paris—I realize now that was likely a lie. He'd learned on his own and was after the key from the beginning."

"Oh, then that's what I—" Clara clamped her mouth shut,

flushing. Nathanael waited, eyebrow raised. "I went to your hotel. Once. To see if you were—well…"

"You were right to be suspicious, as it turns out."

"Yes, well, I didn't intend to spy, precisely, only to inquire if you were who you said you were, but then I—I ended up hiding in the cloakroom. And I was a terrible spy because I speak awful German. But you met with someone, and it grew heated—it was Sandmann."

"You saw him then?"

"I did, but he didn't see me. I was hiding in the coats." For some reason this struck her as hilariously absurd, and she burst out laughing, clapping her hand over her mouth. "What a sight I must have been—hiding—" She dissolved again into laughter, and Nathanael's somber expression cracked, too.

"I'm sorry," Clara said, recovering some composure. "I should have admitted earlier what I did."

"And I should have realized that Sandmann's interest in you was more than passing."

"We could go back," Clara offered. "Maybe he left something behind."

"We could. Whatever he was doing, he wasn't successful."

Clara began to ask why, and then realized—that section of the anderwelt Exposition would have been plunged into blight if he had pulled something to the other side, the thought cloying and eerie.

Nothing more needed to be said. They found a lonely alley and crossed to the anderwelt, then made their way toward the Palace of Illusions. Clara was not comforted by the rosewater river or its singing, which sounded more plaintive than it had before. Perhaps it was only her mood.

They saw no one as they entered the fairgrounds, and nothing to suggest anything had happened. Clara led them through the labyrinth to the stage. All was still, no effects of the dance bending the anderwelt's light and colors now.

Clara's gaze was drawn to something that glinted in a beam of sunlight. An arch of metal, some colored glass. Clara gasped. "Nathanael!" She rushed to the contraption on the floor. "It's the lantern I made for Annabelle!" She picked it up, examining it. No—not quite. A very good copy, but the mechanism was less finely tuned and the colors of glass were garish primary colors, no subtle blending of shades possible.

"What is it doing here?" Nathanael asked. "The dance in real Paris—that didn't involve your lamp."

"No, but I wonder—" She pieced it together quickly. "Lavallé must have seen Annabelle's audition. She used the lantern. He must have had the idea to include it here. But a little lantern like the one I made couldn't light up a stage of this size."

"So he got Sandmann to make a replica, and he was going to expand the design with the effects of the anderwelt and then bring it over. How—"

"I don't know. I think he's just getting lazy now. Copying my designs, and doing work here that could be done in our world—at least, I think it could be." She considered. "I don't know."

"There's no reason to keep investigating," Nathanael said quietly. "Given what has happened with Frau Schwann, I think there is more than enough to hand the whole matter over to Saint-Luc." He paused. "In no small part because I am very concerned what Lavallé is willing to do to keep his handwerker working for him."

Clara nodded, though she hated to leave the poor copy of her magic lantern behind. She would have preferred to smash it to bits, but Nathanael suggested they should leave the scene as they found it so that Saint-Luc could see it for himself.

"But how will we find him?" Clara asked. Paris was no smaller in the anderwelt than in their own world.

"Easy. He gave me this." Nathanael produced a bit of folded paper from his pocket. Inside was—

"A match?"

"Just watch," Nathanael said with a grin. He struck it, and it blazed briefly, then winked out of existence. "Now we wait."

"Wait for what?"

"It's a flare. Like ships use, as distress signals. Only it's designed to go right to Saint-Luc and show him where we are."

"But what if he's in the other—the real—you know—"

"He won't be. He's on nearly full-time patrol here now."

"How long—"

A crackle like the brief flame of a match, and Saint-Luc stood beside them. "Well, Nussbaum, this had better be important. I have just informed Frau Schwann's family of the accident she succumbed to here—I would appreciate if you played along with that farce if asked—and now I have to meet with the subcommittee on security."

"I think you'll find it worth your time," Nathanael said, and explained what they had found. Saint-Luc's eyebrows rose, and Clara felt a perverse satisfaction in finally impressing him with something. She would never quite forget the sting of falling for his lie, but proving that she was not just a mark, not just a pawn, counterbalanced it somewhat.

"Very well." Saint-Luc nodded to each of them in brusque thanks. "We will follow the appropriate procedures to apprehend Herr Sandmann and confiscate his key."

"And Lavallé?"

"I'm afraid he is outside any jurisdiction I possess. We can only hope that the investigation into Frau Schwann's death leads to him—though I will confess my doubts. He certainly hired someone, and there will be little evidence to follow. Have you any idea how many victims are dredged from that river every year, and how few of their cases are solved?"

Clara preferred not to know. "And us? How are we supposed to keep ourselves safe from him?"

"The anderwelt will be safe, once Herr Sandmann is dealt with. He's unlikely to trouble you, at any rate. Now—I need to begin proceedings."

Clara blinked, a slow, thin frustration pressing up from deep in her chest. "Begin proceedings? He could be blighting some other part of Paris right now, and—"

"I'm well aware, Miss Ironwood. We will make haste. If you could excuse me?"

"It just—it seems as though—" Clara exhaled. "He's not playing by anyone's rules. He could ruin everything."

Saint-Luc sighed. "I feel as you do, Miss Ironwood. Truly. Perhaps even more so—this is still new to you, but it is ingrained so deep in my bones I couldn't carve it out if I tried. This—" He paused. "I am not a philosopher or a theologian, I don't really care for expressing emotions, but I promise I care for this place. Do you know," he added suddenly, "the biblical story of creation? That man was created in God's image?"

Clara stared at him. "Yes?"

"What does that mean to you?" He let her consider the question only a moment before he held up a hand, one finger pressed against his thumb. "To me, it means *this*. We can change the world. And with just the movements our hands, uniting our ideas to our weak little fingers. This place—it holds that force, that ability for, I believe, the whole world."

Clara nodded. "I understand. I didn't mean—I didn't mean to suggest you didn't care deeply."

"I realize that. Now please—your assistance has been of great benefit, but now let us follow the rules the guilds have given us." He nodded, and then winked away again.

"Now, how did he do that?" Clara demanded, shaken by the earnestness of the conversation and the infuriating feeling that she had been rendered useless again.

"I'll show you someday." Nathanael sighed, then caught her hand. "Someday soon—it seems we're past having to concern ourselves with blights and plots and Sandmen. I want you to know everything about this place. To have a key of your own. You deserve to. I want to see what you would make. You made this place without even realizing you were doing it."

She blushed under his searching, knowing look. "If we are to spend our time in the relative safety of the anderwelt, would you help me change a few things?"

"Here?"

"Well, I'd have to run any plans to change the Palace of Illusions in the other Paris past Fritz, and he'd just say it's too late to order new materials." She smiled. "I wanted to add actualités to the room. You know—films, like the Lumières make. They would look alive, wouldn't they, running across the mirrors?"

"It would. I never even would have thought—and it's brilliant."

"I had to settle for lights instead. But here—oh, it would be easy." She smiled. She half ran to where the back hallways looped through the other palace and found the closet she was looking for tucked into the anderwelt labyrinth, a crevice in the vine-tangled marble. Black paper and scissors, as ordinary as something from the stationer's shop. She brought them back to Nathanael.

"When I was young," she said, folding the paper, "we used to make shadow puppets in the winter. Sometimes one at a time, and sometimes long chains of them." Louise had been more precise than she was in the cutting, never accidentally clipping through the hands that linked her paper dancers. Godfather had been masterful, making whole plays out of paper and fire-light and shadow. Her scissors clipped and curved, and she produced a line of dancers joined by the flower garlands they held.

She handed paper and another pair of scissors to Nathanael. For a moment she watched his deft hands work with the paper, a rush of strange excitement at the confident motions as he folded and pressed. He finished a trio of dancing bears as she made another set of dancers. She set the papers in position and held her breath. Magda had simply wound her carousel to make it come alive; how would shadow puppets dance on their own?

She placed them in a beam of setting sunlight and they leapt to life.

The dance was simple, but the mirrors reflected it in intricate variations. Somehow, a strain of music followed the black shadows as they circled from mirror to mirror, sometimes chasing one another, sometimes joining in a brief embrace before separating again.

Clara laughed out loud.

Nathanael shook his head. "I would never have thought of it," he repeated softly. Then, surprising both of them, his hand rested on her upturned face. As the dancers spun around them, he leaned toward her and kissed her.

"*Mein Gott*, I'm sorry," he said, stepping away.

"No, no," she said. She pulled him toward her. The dance slowed and stopped, the silhouettes flickering like candlelight. She held his hand, the long fingers and strong lines, capable of creating so much, and brought it to her lips. An exquisite longing welled in her, not unlike the feeling she had when she knew what she wanted to make but couldn't quite figure out how yet.

"Even in the anderwelt," he cautioned, "we are not necessarily alone. To be caught by Sandmann would be bad enough, but imagine if it was Magda." Clara laughed. "What do you want, Fräulein Ironwood?" He brushed a lock of wayward hair behind her ear, letting the question hang softly between them.

"I want to be with you." The answer came simply, neatly, unbidden. "I—I want to be quiet and alone and not think of keys or Sandmann or anything else."

For a brief moment, Nathanael gathered her to himself. She pressed her face against his jacket, the faint scent of his soap enveloping her, and closed her eyes. Something shifted; something in her, yes, but around her as well, and when she looked up, they were no longer in the Palace of Illusions but in Nathanael Nussbaum's neat and tidy apartment.

"It's a simple enough trick," he half apologized.

"Afraid I'd change my mind on the long walk?"

"A little." He sat by the fireplace, and with a flick of his hand, a merry orange-and-pink blaze swirled in the hearth. "Can I make you some tea, or there might be a bit of bread still—"

Clara shook her head and sat close beside him. All her usual caution was stripped away. "I've never done anything like this," she admitted. "I—I'm not far off in guessing you haven't, either?"

Nathanael flushed. "It was offering tea, wasn't it."

"I think in most cautionary tales I've heard you're supposed to ply the lady with strong drink."

"Night is falling—the night air would do well enough if you think you need to ply me."

"I don't think either of us really need much plying." Clara paused only a moment before drawing him close, and it was only to take in the entirety of his face, of the play of firelight and shadow across the planes of his cheeks and his earnest eyes. She didn't wait for him. She kissed him, full and confident.

His hands tangled in her hair, the pins loosening and dropping on the carpet. "I have made a study of beauty. The anderwelt expresses beauty at every turn, and yet I've never really known what it meant," Nathanael said, brushing her waves away from her face. "But you are beautiful."

The windows scattered starlight around them as Clara pulled him closer. She should have felt lost, unmoored from practical processes and formulas, but she felt secure, understood. She hadn't properly explained anything, and yet he knew her. Being known—it was strange and sharp and a little frightening, but she wanted it. And, equally fervently, she wanted to know him. Deeper, in a fullness of knowing beyond facts and pragmatic realities.

His favorite book was *Hard Times* and that mattered more than Newton's principles. The middle finger of his right hand had a thick callus on the side, and that mattered more than the whole sum of cosmology. He preferred Earl Grey tea and she couldn't give a fig about the entire periodic table of elements.

She lifted her face toward his, knowing the inevitable result but allowing it to take her by surprise anyway when his mouth finally found hers again. She shivered, falling into the physical sensation of it first, then letting her own desire repeat itself, a current on an exponential chart of increase. He followed her lead, mimicking the curiosity of her hands, the careful study she made of his face, his hands. He never demanded the surrender of what she had not already given. Each inquiry yielded knowledge upon knowledge, depth of perfect impermanence as each moment erased the surety of the one before. They sank into each other, their understanding surpassing all logic and drawing on a deeper, surer magic.

Clara was sure of only one thing—she had never really known anything before. All the trite truths she had balanced herself on were feeble things, brittle imitations of a reality far deeper than she had dared explore. She had been afraid, she understood now, afraid to risk the knowing.

She wasn't afraid any longer. The anderwelt stars played on their faces, pale light casting constellations under Nathanael's fingertips. Heat and cold and a host of impossible contradictions— how could his touch both warm and refresh her? How could she be on the precipice of the loss of all control and yet feel secure? She didn't care. She sighed, contented, curling closer to Nathanael and letting sleep overtake her in slow, gentle waves.

She woke to a muffled scream. Her eyes snapped open. The stars had shifted, new maps of light above them. Another cry. The welcome muddling of sense and tactile reality melted away like a dream and she sat bolt upright.

Nathanael lay next to her, face contorted by pain. He called out again, unintelligible but the language of a familiar origin—pure fear. "Nathanael," she whispered at first, and then grew louder. "Wake up, please!"

She jostled his shoulder and he was on her in a moment, her wrist pinned under his strong hand, his eyes wide and wild. They met hers and for one horrible moment she was sure he couldn't see her, would never see her again. And then recognition softened his face and he crumpled next to her.

"*Mein Gott, mein Gott*—I am so sorry."

"It's—I—are you all right?" Clara checked her wrist quietly—not hurt beyond a bruise.

"Yes." He sat up, running his hands through now-damp hair. "And no. Ever since—ever since I was lost in the dead part of the anderwelt, I—"

"Oh." Clara moved closer to him, and he stiffened and shifted away. "It's all right."

"It isn't." He slumped into himself. She wished he would curl against her instead, aching from his withheld pain. "I have nightmares. I never realized—I didn't think what might happen if someone else was here when I had one."

"I'm not angry," Clara reassured him. "Perhaps—perhaps you can tell me what would be better to do next time."

"Next time?" Nathanael risked a glance. "You're not—I didn't scare you?"

"You frightened the hell out of me. But I'm not leaving." She slid closer to him again and this time he didn't move away. "Would it help to talk about it?"

"I don't know." He swallowed, hard. "In the dreams, I'm back there. And it's never the same twice, because it was never the same there, either. Darkness, all darkness—"

"You don't have to say anything," she said, laying her arm around him. "But I'll always listen. If you do."

It was a long moment before she realized he was crying, inaudibly but heavily, grief thick in the silent starlight. She wouldn't have been anywhere else for the world.

Chapter Forty-Three

FOR ONCE, MAGDA was dumbfounded. "Sandmann? That cowardly little weasel? You are quite sure?"

"For the last time, Magda, yes, I'm quite sure." Nathanael ran a hand through disheveled hair, fingers catching on tangled waves. He winced. "I would know him anywhere."

"Who wouldn't? He's got a *schnauze* like a *gurke*." She threw her hands in the air. "I suppose it makes a bit of sense, now that I consider it. He was always a bit obsessive over the idea of automatons—lifelike dolls, he always called them. Wanted to make all sorts—well, you met Olympia."

"She's so lovely, I couldn't ever believe that she was created by that awful man."

"He perhaps wasn't always so awful—when he was young, he was almost tolerable." This was high praise, Clara considered, coming from Magda. "But I never thought, never, that he'd stoop so low." She trailed off into a muttered tirade of German obscenities. "And I never much enjoyed Hilde Schwann's company, and she should have had the book thrown at her for collaborating with Sandmann, but she didn't deserve to be drowned like a rat in a cage."

"It's all over," Clara reiterated. "Saint-Luc seems like a very efficient man when he wants to be."

"I had the same impression," Magda said dryly. "Somewhere about the time he held my key hostage and interrogated me."

"I still want to know why Sandmann did it," Nathanael said. "I never would have believed it of him."

"And what does Godfather know about it?" Clara mused. "Clearly enough."

"There is one thing we haven't tried," Nathanael said, turning his key over in his hand. "The anderwelt has many tricks. One of them—one of them would let us ask Elias ourselves."

"We have that trick here, too," Clara replied. "It's called a telegram."

"Yes, of course, but—we both know that Elias may not want to put anything in writing." Nathanael sighed. "And for once, he might not be entirely incorrect in his paranoia."

"How do you propose we ask him? Magic telephone that can cross the ocean?"

"Nothing so grand as all that! Far simpler, in fact. Even simpler than the guilds' door. The anderwelt can fold itself, under the direction of someone with a key. That's what I did last night—" He paused under Magda's slowly rising eyebrow. "After we met with Saint-Luc," he said.

"Wait." Clara's breath hitched. Folding space and time seemed less complicated than what Nathanael was asking her to do—see Godfather again. "What could Godfather tell us that we can't figure out ourselves?"

Nathanael half laughed. "I haven't any doubt we would eventually uncover everything. But until Sandmann is safely in guild custody, I'd rather stay one step ahead of him. If you're willing."

"Me? I haven't the slightest idea how to go about it."

"It isn't hard, really. You can imagine a map—find Paris on it, find Milwaukee, and fold the two to meet. The anderwelt will work that way, if you ask it."

"Yes, that explains everything," Clara retorted, more sharply than she intended. She didn't want to see Godfather, not after how they'd left things, and certainly not after he'd dragged her into this. "Why can't you just do it?"

"Because it's not like an ordinary map. It's a map based on—well, to simplify it, your memories. Your own ties to both places. You will locate Elias's house, his hearthside, his favorite chair, exactly where it exists in the anderwelt because it's *real* to you." He folded Clara's hand inside his. "You've surely noticed, how things become more real in the anderwelt? It's the only anchor, the only guide."

"And if you tried—"

"If I tried I'd land—oh, I don't know. Kansas somewhere, I suppose." He smiled. "Or I wouldn't go anywhere at all. But it wouldn't be wise to try, I don't think. Unless I fancy a detour through Wichita. Or losing myself in a vast Nowhere."

Clara's hand found the key, safe in her pocket. *What a terrible amount of trouble you've caused*, she thought, *just a bit of metal and glass*. She sighed. "I suppose that does make the most sense."

"Good! Now, if you want to drag us along with you—"

"Oh, no," Magda interjected. "I have no interest in seeing Elias again after all these years, and I don't care for folding myself up in the space and time of the anderwelt to do it, either. You hardly need me to answer the question."

"I don't fancy the idea of any one of us being alone," Clara said, the timid suggestion almost farcical given Magda's arsenal of crossbows and sharp instruments on her tool bench.

"I don't much, either," Magda surprised her by replying. "But I'll manage. Hell, if I'm desperate enough, I'll give the neighbors a shock by popping in for a cup of tea."

Clara laughed. "All right, then. Nathanael, I—if you would come, I would—"

"Of course! It's been quite a while since I had the pleasure of seeing Uncle Elias." A strained smile drew pitiable lines into his face. The Uncle Elias who had dragged him into the anderwelt and left him stranded in a perpetual nightmare; it was all but certain he was content never seeing the man again. Clara knew the feeling. Her parting with Godfather had been strained enough, but she had long years of fond memories instead of long years trapped in a toxic cloud of chaos.

"All right." Clara cleared her mind and squared her shoulders. "How does this trick work?"

"In your mind, you have a map of where things are, yes?" Clara raised an eyebrow. "I don't mean only, you know, the capital of Austria or the Canadian border. I mean where you keep your hairbrush and the route you take to work and where your pictures were hung in your bedroom when you were a child."

"That's quite a few maps," she suggested.

"It is. But if you think about it, it's all layered in your mind, somehow."

"A sort of spatial memory."

"But colored with emotion. When you're in the anderwelt, those ties between memory and space are more potent. You can see, if you try, the distance between your memories of places. And you can just—fold that distance away."

"You know, that's the part that's still a bit confusing," Clara replied, cracking a smile despite the seriousness of the whole matter.

"I promise, it will fall into place like coins in the fountain."

"You do realize someone *throws* the coins, in a particular direction, usually at a low velocity—"

"Fine, fine. But trust me." He caught her hand. "You can do this. And I think we have to, sooner rather than later."

"All right." Clara turned to Magda. "Be safe, please. Don't stay alone if—"

"If I think something is off, yes, yes, I know. For pity's sake, the child is stubborn." She waved an impatient hand. "Be off with you!"

Before Clara could reply, Nathanael deployed his key, and in a topsy-turvy moment they were in the anderwelt. Clara blinked at the proliferation of projects on Magda's anderwelt workbench, but didn't linger over them. She stepped outside, orienting herself to what precious little was familiar to her in Paris.

"Don't get flustered," Nathanael cautioned.

"Easier said than done."

Nathanael smiled. "Hold the key, let it center you a bit. Try to quiet your mind and think of home. Of your walk from your own front door to Uncle Elias's house. Of what you would expect to find in Elias's living room. In his study." He kept his hand wrapped around hers.

Clara closed her eyes and pictured it—the stone stairs leading from the front door of her parents' house down the long drive to the sidewalk, their sandpaper texture and gray and pink and purple tones. Snow settled on the pillars, and the dogwood bloomed pink in the front yard, and autumn leaves scurried into the crevices of the iron fence. The lake sparkled in the distance. Godfather's house—down the street, turn left, across the lane— and there it was, an eclectic cottage painted deep moss and thick raisin. His brass knocker shaped like a snail. The scent of tobacco and oil and metal shavings.

She felt a sharp tug, almost physical, the space reaching out to hold on to her. "Oh," she whispered.

"There it is. Imagine the space between there and here just—"

He didn't finish before they had both landed in Godfather's little parlor.

Chapter Forty-Four

CLARA WAS NOT surprised to find it a brighter reflection of his real house, stuffed with just as many oddities and lined with bric-a-brac, except that in the anderwelt each little statuette seemed quite alive, and each miniature was perfectly rendered in impossible materials, crystal and gingerbread and silk ribbons all mingling together. A mechanical parrot, as real as life but made of stained glass, chattered at them and swooped down from his perch. The fire in his fireplace actually laughed merrily.

"Well, that's a bit disturbing," Nathanael said, nodding at the fireplace, which darkened slightly and glowered at him.

The parrot tapped his claw on a table topped with what Clara was quite sure was marzipan. "State your names and business, names and business."

"We are looking for Christian Elias Thrushman, but I imagine he's not here?" Clara inquired politely.

"Names and business!" the parrot squawked in defiant reply.

"No need for that, Whittington." Godfather stood in the doorway, wearing his Chinese silk dressing gown and cap. "I know both of them quite well."

"Names and business," the parrot repeated in a sulk as he flapped away.

"Whittington takes his duties quite seriously," Godfather said. "I do hope he didn't strike you as rude. It's a failing in his mechanics that I have tried to remedy, but there's only so much one can do to alter the nature of a thing, you know."

"Not at all," Clara stammered. "I—I—how are you here? I have your key."

"Yes, indeed you do." He nodded toward a crystalline mirror mounted on his wall—right where a mirror hung in the ordinary house. "A craftsman may only make one key. But a gate? A craftsman can make as many gates as he likes."

"I thought that required—well, I thought the guilds held that secret," Nathanael said, stepping closer to examine the mirror.

"Of course they would let you think that," Godfather said brusquely. "I created the method and have refined it since letting them use the idea. Don't touch it, you might tumble out into the other Milwaukee. And it's too cold there to be without a scarf and coat."

"Remarkable," Nathanael whispered, looking at the mirror from all sides. Clara realized that it held in its shimmering reflection not the anderwelt, but the image of Godfather's parlor she remembered, unchanged from her childhood.

"Aren't you surprised to see us?" Clara asked abruptly, insisting that the discussion move back to the necessities and away from Godfather's apparent genius.

"Not entirely, no." Godfather swept his hand toward a trio of chairs clustered by the fire. "Please, sit. I can send for refreshments, if you're so inclined?" He didn't wait for an answer, ringing one of a trio of little bells hanging from the belt of his dressing gown. The marzipan-topped table unfolded itself and spread out a full tea set, the pot already steaming. "I recall you prefer Earl Grey," he added, turning to Nathanael.

"Yes, thank you." Nathanael finally let go of Clara's hand and sat down next to her in an overstuffed chair of brilliant peacock blue. Clara sat in its twin, leaving Godfather with a cane chair intricately carved of peppermint sticks. *Won't it gum up his dressing gown?* she wondered absurdly.

"All right. You have some reason for being here, I am sure." Godfather poured them each a cup of tea. "I presume you figured out how to use the key," he added, glancing at Clara.

Quite abruptly, anger welled over. How dare he sit there, calmly sipping his tea from his stupid magic table in his ugly yellow dressing gown, behaving as though he'd done nothing wrong? As though she were the little fool who needed to catch up—*just catch* up, *Clara*, he used to say—to his ridiculous methods. He had sent her a veritable target drawing all sorts of unsavory attention and had never even bothered to school her in the entire world it could unlock.

She stared at him over her untouched cup of tea. "You knew very well what you were sending me. A clever trick, wasn't it?"

"I did think so."

"And you didn't think to consider what would happen to me next?"

"Yes, but you had Nathanael. I told him to take care of you." Nathanael raised an eyebrow but didn't speak. Godfather sipped his tea slowly. "Rather a good blend."

"Damn it, Godfather! Don't you care what happens to anyone else?"

"Of course I do." He sighed. "I don't know how to tell you half of what I should."

"Perhaps you ought to try." Clara clamped her hands in her lap, willing them to stop trembling. "Perhaps you have a lot to explain to me. A lot to apologize for."

"Oh, must we apologize? I do so dislike that particular dance—the you're sorry, I'm sorry, we're all dreadfully sorry—yes, yes, let's get back to the real problem, though!" He smacked the marzipan table, making its legs wobble. "By now you have perhaps realized that my key is unique. Special. The only one of its kind ever made."

"It can bring things back from the anderwelt," Nathanael said quietly. "In almost perfect condition. Almost."

"Quite correct. And if there is one thing I should, in all justice, apologize for, it is that. When I created my key, I was bound and determined it should be a magnificent key. The best ever made, a unique experiment that could do something nothing else could—actually bring the spark of the anderwelt into the world of mortal humans with no detriment to either side."

"Wasn't that against the rules?" Nathanael asked.

"Rules? No one had ever thought it could be done. There were no rules against an impossibility."

"Wasn't it terribly stupid?" Clara interjected.

"As it turns out, yes, it was. Because no matter what I tried, I couldn't actually do it. The things brought back could only be facsimiles. The spark of the anderwelt must, it turned out, remain across the veil. Even though I didn't blight anything, I didn't accomplish what I'd tried to do."

Clara thought of Olympia, rendered lifeless in the real Paris, and felt her hands fold into fists. "How many times did you try?"

"Don't get yourself worked up over it—only enough to learn it couldn't be done, and I restored them all to their proper places in the anderwelt. Including Whittington." At the sound of his name, the parrot chirped in the other room. "I realized the trouble quite rapidly and resolved never to use my key to that purpose again."

Clara forced her hands to relax. "Then why wasn't that the end of it?"

"I had a friend. You know him."

"Sandmann."

"He was obsessed with the idea of automatons—it's all he made in the anderwelt." Thrushman shrugged, the tassels of his garish dressing gown bobbing along with him. "To be honest, that ought to have suggested something was a bit off about the man."

"We are both acquainted with Olympia," Nathanael said. Clara almost laughed—as though this was a regular teatime visit and they were comparing people they had met during the social season.

"Ah, Olympia! A lovely creation. Too bad, really, that a proper choreographer didn't assist in making her. Sandmann gave up halfway."

"Why are we talking in niceties when your old friend has been stalking me with a shadow creature?" Clara demanded.

"Yes, yes, we should stay to the point. Who knows how long we have?" Godfather poured more tea in obstinate counter-argument to his point. "Sandmann first tried to copy the properties of my key, though of course that failed—dear girl, when you make a key, remember this—once it's made, you can't change it," he said, paused, then resumed his story. "After that he tried to convince me to use the key to bring his automatons back into the other world. He thought they could still be quite useful—or, at least, fetch a good price. Sandmann always had finer tastes than his means allotted. Before I had realized that my goals in the experiment could never be achieved—true life spark, that is—I had moved three of his creations, all dancers, over to the other side. He hid them from me and I was never able to recover them."

"The dancers at the party!" Clara cried. "I've seen them. They were wonderfully made, truly, and I felt just terrible about disabling them."

"Disabling them! Oh, I'm sure that made him quite irate. Ha! Old fool. To let you see them and think nothing would happen— that's my girl." Clara felt an odd surge of pride, but quashed it back.

"At any rate, I wouldn't permit any further experimentation with my key. And I never told anyone else about the particular merits of my key, either, much as it pained me not to be able to discuss the theoretical underpinnings of my discovery with my fellow craftsmen. As long as Sandmann thought he might persuade me to his thinking, he had no interest in allowing the secret out, either— and share the profits? Hardly. Ah, but when it became clear to him I was not to be bought, he orchestrated my humiliation."

Clara crossed her arms. "From what Nathanael and Magda have said, you did that all on your own."

"Dear girl, use your head. You're such a very clever young lady when you've a mind to be. Would I truly fail so spectacularly at such a simple trick? Hiding something in my void, blessed heaven, like suggesting you'd fail a third-grade spelling test."

"To be fair, Uncle, none of us have ever seen you do it." A smile twitched at Nathanael's lips, and he tried valiantly to curb it.

"Because seeing it defeats the point of *hiding*—oh, never mind. The point is, I did hide those troops—for a short time—and the battle would have been averted if it hadn't been for Sandmann.

If I hadn't been interrupted, we all would have been quite happy about the whole affair."

"I'm afraid that after spending decades trapped in the wasteland you created, I can't quite believe that." How could Nathanael speak so calmly, so steadily? Clara's hands trembled just thinking of what had happened to him.

"Think!" Godfather smacked the table so hard Clara worried the marzipan would crack. "That annihilation of the anderwelt is the side effect of trying to transfer anything made with its essence across the veil using a conventional key like Sandmann's. My key prevented the destruction even if it didn't carry the spark of life along with it. But his? His just tears the anderwelt to smithereens in the process."

"That's true," Clara interjected. "The ruined places in Paris—that certainly wasn't Godfather."

"So Sandmann set you up."

"Indeed. He transferred perhaps a dozen of his living dolls at once, and then pinned the blame on me. He knew he'd only have one chance to transfer so many at once, so he made sure it was quite worth it, for the both of us." Godfather snorted. "As far as I know, he sold them to various circuses and boardwalks as sideshow acts. He had only shown me one—an awful monstrosity that laughed like a maniac. I thought it was useless and told him so. I felt poorly about it afterward, but then he sabotaged me, so I decided I was glad to have been honest. He thought people would pay to see his wretched automatons. Idiot."

"Perhaps not—I imagine people did pay. And they still are, unfortunately." Nathanael explained the automatons they'd found in the Paris warehouse, to a chorus of cursing from Godfather. "But if you didn't cause the ruin, why didn't you ever tell anyone? Even me, for pity's sake."

"Well, I was quite sure you didn't want to hear from me. You blamed me for what had happened, and who could fault you? I hated it, hated that I couldn't tell you. But I had resolved, you see, never to tell anyone. And I didn't. I came here—well, the other here—and made a new life. Clara, you will never know how grateful I was that your parents befriended me, an eccentric immigrant with no family, and made me a part of yours."

Clara caught her breath. Godfather had never spoken like this before. "I—I think we would always have said the same," she finally stammered.

"I thought I'd hidden everything. I'd committed the perfect murder, you know, of any knowledge of the key. Of the memory of myself, even, among the guilds. And then Sandmann found me. When you were but a child, Clara, and oh, but if you haven't the knackiest instincts for sniffing out a fraud."

"You know, for years I blamed myself for judging him too harshly on his appearance and manners."

"Those are both sorely lacking. Then again, so are mine." Clara couldn't help breaking into a smile—that was true. She had often defended her beloved godfather against teasing from other children mocking his shock of white hair and his odd mannerisms. "But no, he had a scheme thought up to use the key and figured he'd try his luck. Oh ho, but he thought he'd find me starving and desperate in America! And he was quite wrong, and you will remember, Clara, eventually he had to go back to Nuremberg with his tail betwixt his legs."

"Except now he's back." Clara shook her head. "I presume he came to you first, to harass you for the key, and that's when you sent it to me." Godfather nodded. "But why?"

"He'd become more...persuasive. I have determined that he's

awfully in debt to the sort of people who take that very seriously. He's learned from his creditors not only a newfound motivation, but new tactics for getting what he wants."

Clara winced. "The man he's working for has that reputation, too."

Nathanael paused, drawing in one more piece of the puzzle for Thrushman. "You remember Hilde Schwann? Of the Nämberch?"

"Frau Schwann, of course, yes, a brilliant metallurgist if I recall—"

"She's dead." Nathanael explained what they knew, and Godfather shook his head, increasingly agitated by the news.

"Hilde, always thinking of the guild first. Old-fashioned fool." He coughed, covering, Clara thought, coming a bit too close to tears for his comfort. "I should have known Sandmann and the sort of people he was involved with were capable of violence, but I never... I never..."

"Yes, you should have. And," Nathanael said, voice tersely controlled, "you sent the thing Sandmann wanted to your goddaughter, like baiting him to her." Clara flushed—Nathanael's protective assertion drew out a strange vulnerability that went straight to her cheeks.

"I never, ever intended for him to know Clara had the key."

"How did you intend to *prevent* him from knowing?"

"I don't know!" Finally Godfather threw his hands up in frustration. "I don't know. I only knew that he could not, whatever occurred, find the key." He softened, the crags in his face deepening as his expression sagged. "And I knew I had done horribly by not training you properly." Clara's breath caught in her throat. "I was so worried about attracting Sandmann's attention that I quite wasted years of time that we ought to have had.

"In that last year, when you formally apprenticed, I knew it quite well, too. It's why I was such an awful bear. Part of me was simply furious with myself for withholding your true rights as an apprentice. And another part of me hoped you'd get so fed up with me that you'd leave."

"And I did." Clara ached at the memory of their last day, a picture that turned itself inside out even as she considered it. The lines of chronology were all the same as before, but the colors had changed, shifting to paint the events in entirely new shades.

"You did. I knew I'd driven you to it." He sighed deeply. From the other room, Whittington chirruped in concern, and then came sailing in to perch protectively on Godfather's shoulder.

Clara waited for him to ask forgiveness for at least one of his sins—which was the worst? she wondered. Creating the key, trying to push the boundaries of the anderwelt outward to suit himself? Applying the discretion of an addled goldfish when he let Sandmann in on the secret? Keeping the secret all these years?

Wasting their time together, he had said. That was his greatest regret. The words didn't come, but she reached for his hand, an impulsive gesture alien to both of them. "That's over now."

"And so are Sandmann's escapades," Nathanael added, quickly sketching out the involvement of the guild of the Sacré-Coeur and Saint-Luc.

"Stuff and nonsense!" Godfather stood up. "Do you think Sandmann will comply with guild orders? Even if his key is taken—hasn't he shown he's quite willing to go after another?"

"I—I suppose, but—"

"I doubt very much, dear girl, that he ever truly cared about the blights. He knew if he used my key, he could slip on unnoticed by the guilds a little longer. Schwann, bless her silly head, never did think poorly enough of him. Oh, damn his eyes. I'd very much like to have more time to talk to hear all about your work, Clara. But now we have to figure out how to stop Sandmann from ruining the entire anderwelt."

Chapter Forty-Five

"ONE THING BEFORE we go," Godfather said, tending to a curio cabinet of tiny dragons made of jade and copper. He was feeding them, Clara realized—little droplets of honey. "This will keep my menagerie for now, won't it? Won't it, pets?"

"Godfather!"

"Yes, yes, I need to set out tea and biscuits for Whittington, too." The parrot sulked in the other room, having been informed that his master was leaving for an unspecified amount of time. "Do not eat it all at once, Whittington!" He was answered by a shrill obscenity.

"I really ought to have given him better manners." He doffed his dressing gown and put on his jacket. "I must step out for a moment. Very important errand."

Nathanael's ability to curtail his frustration was, Clara thought, truly a work of art. "May I inquire as to what is so important as to delay stopping your horrid friend from destroying all of the Parisian anderwelt?"

"Louise."

"Louise!" Clara laughed. "Louise is in Paris, and she certainly isn't in the anderwelt, and—"

"And if I show up quite unexpected in Paris, she is bound to have questions. So. I will take proper precaution to allay her suspicions. Now, children, do be good—"

"We are not children," Clara interjected without quite meaning to. Her voice was sharper than she would have intended, but once she had said it, she was glad she had. "I'm not a child, and you have no right to treat me as one. You haven't had any right for years."

Godfather began to argue, but stopped. "There is some truth in that," he finally said. "If I had accepted earlier that you had grown up, this all would have unfolded quite differently."

"I would have learned to make my own key." For some reason, that was the thing that stuck out, sharp and jagged, among all the other grievances. "You kept all of this from me. This place, this beauty. Why?"

"I was afraid—"

"No, you've said that already, and it's not enough. You were afraid of Sandmann, fine—but that shouldn't have stopped you from training me." She bit her lip, then forced herself to continue. "Why wasn't I good enough?"

"Oh, Clara." Godfather's head sank into his hands. "No, you were the best I ever encountered. Better even than he was," he added, nodding toward Nathanael. "No offense, dear boy. Clara, you were exceptionally, prodigiously good. But you must understand. So was I."

"I don't understand. You were good, yes, among the best— Magda told me so."

"If even Magda admits it, you know it must be true." He smiled softly. "Yes, I will abandon all affectations of modesty and tell you—there was none better than I. And now you tell me. What did I do?"

"You—oh."

"I made a key that only engendered greed. I had to be sure—I had to be sure you were not only skilled but wiser than I was." He tried and failed to meet her eyes. "And even when I knew, I found I was still afraid. I told you stories of the anderwelt and hoped you would believe in it, in some way, without seeing it, because I was too afraid to show it to you. But, Clara, it was in your blood and your bones, even before you saw it."

"I think I understand that now."

"I—I'm only going to say it this once, perhaps." Godfather pressed his mouth into a taut line, and then, slowly, "I am sorry."

Everything softened. Her godfather, her awkward, stumbling, brilliant godfather—how long they had misunderstood each other. "I—I want to make up for lost time, I think," she said.

"I do, too. I do. But for now—plans must be made." He stepped up to the mirror. The image of his other parlor wavered briefly as he set his hand on the glass, and then melted around him, absorbing him completely. For a moment she saw him through the mirror, fetching coat and hat, and then the mirror went still but for the shadow of a cloud moving across the sunlit floor.

"Very well, fine, be mysterious," Clara grumbled as Godfather swept into the real Milwaukee and left them quite alone in his parlor, save for Whittington, still complaining vividly.

"I want to learn how he made that thing," Nathanael breathed, "but for now, I want to see the popcorn tree."

"What?" Clara laughed. "Of all the things to worry about right now, the popcorn tree?"

"You said he told you a story about a popcorn tree, and I think it only fair that I should get to see it after all this trouble we've been through."

"I'm afraid that, if the popcorn tree is in the park, it's going to be too far a walk." The popcorn for the princess to feed the swans—that was certainly the anderwelt mirror of Clara feeding ducks at the park. "But who knows what he has outside?"

Clara knew how to make her way through his house—it was the same footprint as his house in the real Wisconsin, with fewer clockwork oddities than she would have expected. The reason why was clear as soon as she opened the kitchen door. His back garden, which she remembered as a tangle of half-feral rosebushes and a few spindly trees, was astonishing here in the anderwelt. He had spent his time and attention here, tending a garden of wonders.

The trees were living stalks of cinnamon, lemon peel bloomed as flowers, mint grew from glassy rods into transparent, fragrant leaves. The bushes flowered into impeccable sugar rosebuds. And yet nothing was merely confectionary; it was all alive. The roots ran deep into the ground. The foliage reached for the sun. Dew trembled on flower petals.

"I've never seen the like," Nathanael said.

"Do you think…do you think you can actually eat it?"

"You certainly can." The voice made Clara jump, in the direction, it did not escape her, of Nathanael, whose hand she reached for. "They were made for precisely that purpose. However, I don't find candy all that agreeable."

Sandmann stood in the gate, which was fashioned of filigree marzipan. For an absurd moment Clara thought he might be like the pastrycook in the story and unable to pass the marzipan walls, but to her dismay he strode toward them. Her second thought was frustration with Saint-Luc, that he hadn't managed to stop Sandmann, that his protocols had been useless, that his promises had been empty.

"I'll ask you to keep your distance," Nathanael said, voice low.

"For the moment, but I must be clear—there will be no niceties about what has to be done. The key must come with me."

"Why did you take up with Lavallé?" Clara demanded.

"I'm surprised your godfather didn't explain. Debts," he said simply. "I owed him quite a bit of money. I preferred my life and limbs intact, so I proposed a form of repayment."

"That hardly explains it. You'd sell the anderwelt to pay off your debts?" Clara said, horrified.

"I'd sell just about anything to pay off my debts to the sort of man I'm indebted to," Sandmann retorted. "And so would you."

Clara looked around them, seeking any means of escape, but though they could certainly outrun Sandmann if it came to a footrace, it was clear it was merely evasion—if he could fold the anderwelt, he could catch them anywhere they ran. *Damn his eyes*, Clara thought. Where did she know that Sandmann didn't, that he couldn't follow quickly? Perhaps the park with the swans could provide temporary escape.

Before she could summon a memory of the real park, of its fat ducks paddling on a milfoil-encrusted pond, Sandmann had a mirror in his hand and was directing the anderwelt sunlight into their eyes. Clara blinked, and realized that was all she could do— her hands were locked at her sides. Her feet were rooted to the ground.

"What did you do?" she managed to gasp through stiffening lips.

"My own invention—it bends light into a sort of net, flexible and yet very strong." Despite herself, Clara's curiosity flared. "Won't last forever, don't fret."

"This is utterly outside the guilds' rules." Nathanael's words

371

were thin, forced through the same constraint Clara felt sinking into every muscle of her body.

To her surprise, Sandmann actually looked chagrined. "I fully expect, my boy, to be the first handwerker stripped of his key since the rogue artillerist of 1798."

"Then why—" Nathanael strained next to her.

"I've told you why!" Sandmann said. "I have debts. I made mistakes, I did. I've been so very careful," he almost pleaded.

"You've been very careful while blighting the anderwelt?" Clara choked out.

"I've been very careful to do it sparingly, to avoid being caught! And to keep the balance from tipping. I simply cannot go on without Thrushman's key, or all of Paris will be sucked into blight. And then it's only a matter of time…" He looked genuinely pained. "You have no idea how delicate it all is—"

"So you paid your debts with the life of the anderwelt itself, even if it means you'll eventually be caught and your key taken." Nathanael shook his head.

Sandmann's voice pitched to a near whine. "If I don't pay my debts, I'll be far worse off than I would be without a key. I can live without going into the anderwelt." Clara wondered if, having seen the anderwelt, she could. "I'll throw myself at the judgment of the guilds before I rely on the mercy of my type of creditors."

"Are you merely working for Lavallé," Clara asked, "or is he your creditor?"

"What does it matter?" Sandmann seemed more agitated by this than any accusation about the anderwelt. "Yes. He—he traced an automaton in Brussels back to me and he offered me a bargain. My debts were paid if I took a very particular job for him. The Exposition, of course."

"You could have just made him automatons," Nathanael said. "But you told him, didn't you?"

"I can't just make automatons! I required the anderwelt. If someone asked you to replicate that silly spun-sugar spiderweb, could you? Of course not. You'd need the anderwelt to do it." He shook his head. "Enough. I'm not on trial, not yet. There's only one thing to discuss, and that's Thrushman's key."

"Would that really be the end of it?" Nathanael asked. Clara started. "You take the key, you finish out your debt to Lavallé, and then you turn yourself—and the key—over to the guilds? You would leave Clara alone?"

"The end of it. Even if you never saw Thrushman's key again, you'd have a bargain. You know as well as I do that the key only lives as long as its creator. The key itself is of very limited value."

"Absolutely not," Clara retorted. "You've seen what the key does to the living things of the anderwelt. It's like—it's like murder to take them away from where they were made, what that does to them."

"Strong words for a neophyte. The created things of the anderwelt aren't truly alive. They're imbued with the anderwelt's creative potential, but they're not really living. Surely you don't think dismantling a clock counts as murder? That taking the gears out of a music box would send you to the gallows?"

"It's not the same," Clara protested.

"Your argument certainly wouldn't stand up in court," Sandmann replied, almost chuckling. "Imagine! 'The defendant is charged with intentional removal of clockwork! Murder in the first!' Hardly. Our ability to use the anderwelt gives us a certain range that is impossible in the real world, but it doesn't change the fact that created things are simply that—things."

Clara saw him again as she had as a child. Grasping, conniving, seeing the whole world as his to use. To him, the anderwelt was only another commodity to trade. "I can't accept that."

"This doesn't have to be nasty or complicated. It's not even *your* key. You could still make your own. Just give me Thrushman's and I'll never bother you again."

"I won't. I can't."

"I'll ask one more time." Clara gasped as Sandmann pulled a revolver from his pocket. The metal seemed to suck in the light of the anderwelt, appearing dull and dark in Sandmann's hand. Clara's heart raced even as the net tightened around her body. "Or I'm afraid I'll have to use more persuasive methods than philosophical argument."

Nathanael found the strength to shout. "If you do that here, if you spill blood on the anderwelt, you'll ruin it—"

"I think I've made it clear I cannot consider that a deterrent." He stared at Clara. "Now. Tell me where you've got the key."

"You can kill me first." She found she really meant it. This place had infiltrated her bones, made a home in her soul—she would protect it.

"Oh, there's no purpose killing you. You know where the key is." He pointed the gun at Nathanael. "But I have no such uses for him." His hand trembled slightly, Clara noticed. He was a coward, at the end of it—not a bold man but a frightened one, using any means necessary to avoid pain for himself.

Clara's heart sank. She managed to meet Nathanael's eyes. Their depth, their gentleness—no, she couldn't let Sandmann harm him. Even if it meant selling the anderwelt. They could get the key back, perhaps. No, certainly—with the guilds involved, it wouldn't be difficult. Of course, she thought rapidly—the guilds, they would stop Lavallé, they would—

The report of the gun cracked the anderwelt wide open.

Three things happened very quickly. First, the net of light binding them dissolved. Clara felt as though her limbs, after straining against their bonds for so long, flew wide. Second, the garden around them darkened. The gingerbread tree trunks crumbled, the glassy sugar leaves shattered, the roses and lilies seemed to fester and collapse. A web of decay spread over the entire garden.

Third, Nathanael fell to the ground beside her.

She felt a thin scream rise in her throat as she dropped beside him, but it strangled itself before she could give it voice. Nathanael grimaced, clutching his arm. A bloom of blood spread outward, lapping up his sleeve and pooling on the darkening ground beneath him.

"The key, Miss Ironwood." Sandmann stood over her, the gun in his wavering hand pointed at Nathanael.

She had no choice. She pulled the key from her pocket and threw it as hard as she could, hoping it would shatter against the moldering rock candy sculpture nearest her.

It merely pinged off the surface and fell into some gray moss.

"Can't—be destroyed—except—" Nathanael gasped.

"Your key," Clara replied while Sandmann dove for Godfather's glass. "Can you use it?"

"You do it. Fold the anderwelt, bring us back to Magda." His face drew tight under the pressure of pain. "Left coat pocket."

She reached into the pocket and held the key suspended between her fingers, trying to set it into its pendulum swing while keeping Magda's workshop firmly in her mind. Her memories of Magda's shop were not nearly as strong as those of Godfather's house. The images in her memory were smudged like faded pages of an old book, and slipped out of her mind when she tried to hold on to them.

Somewhere else stood more starkly. Nathanael's room. His Earl Grey tea. His neatly stacked books. The golden wood of his bed. His fingers in her hair. The scent of his soap. She closed her eyes, folded the space, and quick as breathing, there they were.

Chapter Forty-Six

CLARA AND NATHANAEL tumbled through the anderwelt into his apartment, clinging together, her hands slick with his blood. "I'm sorry, I'm sorry, I couldn't find Magda's in my memory."

"It's all right. This is—this is—" Nathanael gasped. Clara helped him sit down on his bed and then propped a pile of pillows behind him. He leaned back. Her own head swam, a thick headache tightening around her temples.

"I'll take us back to the other side and find a doctor," Clara thought out loud. "But first." She pulled the sheet from the bed and struggled to tear it, finally ripping it against a fire iron. She peeled back the sleeve of Nathanael's coat and nearly choked at the tangle of flesh that lay underneath.

"Don't look," she begged him.

"I don't have to. I know it's bad." He winced as she wound the strip of cloth snugly, willing the bleeding to stop. "It's all right, do what you have to do."

"Let me hold it—here—" Her hands felt useless, shaking as she tried to put pressure on the wound. "I'm so sorry. I didn't—I didn't know—"

"That Sandmann was willing to do that?" Nathanael shook his head, his face almost gray. "I should have known. But I didn't, either. I didn't believe it."

"Now what?"

"I don't know." He blinked. "No, I know one thing. Take the box above the mantel down." He nodded toward something the size of a shoebox but made of a tight lattice of wood. "There are butterflies in it."

Usually Clara would have been inclined to make inquiries after being told there were butterflies kept in a box, but not now. She made her way shakily across the room and fetched the box for Nathanael. She opened it tentatively. Sure enough, there were jewel-colored butterflies slowly testing their wings inside. He took one out and whispered to it. It sprang to life and flew out the window. "I've sent for Magda."

Clara was too exhausted and terrified to be amazed or even very curious. She drew Nathanael close to her, leaning his weight against her, feeling the tremor of his heartbeat between their bodies. Blood already stained the bandage. "Should I take us to the other side?" she asked quietly. "I don't care what people might think."

"No. There will be questions, inquiries—it's better to get Magda. If I—I don't think I will, mind—but if I do lose consciousness, I think sending for Saint-Luc would be wise." Nathanael spoke softly but rapidly, as though trying to put as many words in as few breaths as possible. "He needs to know about Sandmann."

"What if we can't wait? What if—"

"This isn't going to kill me. Not quickly, anyway." Nathanael swallowed hard. "We'll wait for Magda."

Clara's father was a doctor. He mostly dealt in the ordinary

afflictions of ordinary families—whooping cough and rheuma-
tism and heart trouble and strokes and the occasional broken
bone. But he had books in his study, books Clara had plucked
from the shelves to learn about traumatic wounds, and the effects
of bullets and shrapnel, and gangrene and amputation. She was
no doctor. But she knew, now that the immediate danger had
faded, what Nathanael had surely known for some time now.

He might lose the arm.

She squeezed her eyes shut, fighting tears of anger at the injus-
tice of it. Sandmann got what he wanted, even now was probably
brokering his deal. Godfather—how could he help, all the way
from Milwaukee?

"All will be well," Nathanael whispered. "I hope he didn't ruin
the popcorn trees."

Despite herself, Clara laughed. "There was a glass castle, too.
All made of spun glass as a roost for the swans. They were ducks,
really, in our world. Just ducks." She reached into memory for the
rest of the story. "And there was a princess who fed the swans.
Popcorn from the trees, of course."

"Swans love popcorn."

"I'm sure they do. It melts in the water, though, so they have
to eat it quickly. Sometimes they would swim so quickly around
their little pond to get to the popcorn that it made a whirlpool."
She invented things to add to the story, anything to keep talking.
To give them something to pretend instead of thinking about reality. "One day they made an entire waterspout, and it swept them
up into it. The whole pool was carried away. The princess chased
after it"—Clara laughed even though laughter hurt the hollow in
her chest—"chased after it with a net. The net was made of... was
made of..."

"Spider silk and fish scales," Nathanael whispered.

"Of course it was. The net was made of spider silk and fish scales. And she threw the net at the whole waterspout just before it fell into the ocean and caught it. A good thing, too, because it would have been lost forever."

"How did she carry it home?"

"She didn't!" Clara stroked his hair, tucking the loose waves, damp with sweat, behind his ear. "She plucked the swans out and they carried it back to the pond, which of course wasn't a pond at that moment. But soon was again."

"What in the actual absolute hell?" Magda stood in the doorway.

Clara found she didn't know where to start and burst into tears. She managed to stammer out a decent enough explanation that Magda understood to call for Saint-Luc. "I can't stand that little upstart, but I suppose you're right."

"You suppose!" Clara cried.

"And I know a decent enough leech. Should take less time than waiting on the guilds if I send for her. We'll get you patched up right quickly."

Nathanael nodded, forcing a thin smile, but Clara knew what he was afraid of.

"I'll be back." She disappeared, and Clara busied herself making Nathanael some weak tea that he attempted to sip. Her own head throbbed, and her stomach clenched in nauseous cramps.

Magda appeared again, forgoing the niceties of using the door. "She'll be along shortly. And while we wait, you're getting a cup of tea and probably a nap." Magda took Clara firmly by the arm and ushered her from Nathanael's bedside. "You look like death. You sure he didn't hurt you?"

"He didn't hurt me. You don't need to coddle me, I should be taking care of Nathanael—"

"He can have a little rest without your interruption. You were there when the spark of the anderwelt was drained from it. It saps the life out of a person, too, you know. You need to rest. Have some tea. Eat something if you can."

"I don't think I could eat."

"You need to, at some point, but I can't make you." Magda sighed. "I didn't realize—I would never have let you go if I realized how desperate Sandmann was."

"I keep underestimating him," Clara said.

"It will come out all right." Clara didn't believe her, and Magda didn't seem like she believed herself. "Just drink your tea."

The tea steamed and warmed her hands, but Clara didn't taste anything. She drained most of the cup, staring at the fire Magda had kindled, the sparks growing to tongues of flame that encroached further and further, consuming. Was this what Sandmann would do to the anderwelt if he was allowed? Snatch more and more of it up and leave it gray as ash?

The firelight began to swim in her vision. She was so tired—no wonder. The weight of the day settled thick behind her eyes. She heard a sharp rap on the door and roused herself long enough to watch Magda bustle to let the doctor in—a tall woman with wiry blond hair, dressed in a sharp black dress.

"He's been sedated?" The doctor set her bag on the table. Leather, like Clara's father's, she noted. Her father—she wished he were here. He would know what to do. Surely, even though he mostly just set broken bones and told people how to bring down a fever. Surely. She shook her head, trying to clear a cloud that muffled her thoughts.

Magda answered in a hush. "Yes, I've given them both a draught. Distillation of night air, it's what I had handy. I thought it best—"

"Yes, certainly. The poor girl. As much of a patient as he is in some ways." Her motherly cluck was unexpected.

Clara's thoughts coalesced briefly—the tea. *Damn it, Magda,* she cursed half-heartedly. Her head drifted toward the uphol-stered side of the wingback chair. *Damn it, Magda.* She wished she could hide. What was Godfather's story? "The Giant's Pocket." She wished she could hide them all, she thought as a gray cloud descended, in a giant's pocket.

Chapter Forty-Seven

CLARA AWOKE WITH a splitting headache and a stomach churning on empty nausea. She couldn't tell for a moment where she was, and any movement stirred the headache into bright torment. Before she could make up her mind if it was worth attempting to sit up, Magda was by her side.

"I'd stay still if I were you. You're in a bad way."

Everything from the past day came rushing back to her. She was still in the anderwelt, tucked into bed on Nathanael's sofa, cocooned in a nest of pillows. Someone had taken her shoes off, but her clothes had grown almost stiff around her. "Nathanael. I want to see—"

"He's resting," Magda said gently. "And Dr. MacCallan is still here."

"Is he all right?"

Magda hesitated. "He will be, girl. If there is no infection—that's what MacCallan is keeping a watchful eye over right now. But he's rather weak and lost a lot of blood and of course the shock."

"Magda."

"I don't know yet. The doctor says he could lose the arm."

"But…but no," Clara protested. "We're in the anderwelt. Wasn't there some other way?" She pressed her lips together against the words, but they spilled out anyway. "It's not fair. It's not fair, Magda!"

"No, it certainly isn't. Usually isn't, you know. The anderwelt gives us some gifts—night air, for one, it's kept both of you out long enough to prevent either of you from feeling the worst of it. But it's got its limits. Everything does."

Clara could only respond by beginning to cry. She hadn't considered until now that perhaps they would fail—that Sandmann would continue his wretched operations, that he would crush them under the weight of his plans.

Magda flushed. "I'm not going to tell you to be grateful he's alive or any of that bullshit. This is far from easy and far from over. But I will tell you that he's going to need you. So take advantage of the time you have to heal what you've got broken."

"I'm not broken, I'm just—"

Magda rolled her eyes. "A piece of the anderwelt died around you. You're at least stained, poisoned. And until you get that purged from your system, you're going to feel like a pile of shit."

"Fine, Magda." Clara leaned into the pillows. "What now? Anderwelt leeches? Purgatives like the doctors of yore?"

"Hardly." Dr. MacCallan came around the corner. "Rest and bland foods. Quiet. Sunlight. A bit of exercise when you feel ready for it." As if to prove her point, she gathered a cup of tea and a plate of toast and brought them to Clara. "It turns out that allowing yourself the space to heal is sometimes the best medicine of all."

"I don't have space," Clara retorted. "Or time. If you know what's happened, that Sandmann—"

"I'm well aware. But tell me, how likely do you think it is that you can get up without fainting or retching all over this fine carpet?"

Clara refused to admit out loud that she was not entirely sure she would be able to sit up.

"So, we see, you'll have to submit to the demands of your own body. It will not take as long as you fear if you are compliant to what you yourself need."

"You sound like a mystic."

"I'm just a doctor." She set a tray next to Clara. The tea was lukewarm. Somehow that seemed less intimidating to attempt to keep down. "And I prescribe tea and toast. And then if you'd like, Magda could read to you. Or you could sleep. I've other things to attend to, but I'll come back when I'm needed." She nodded briskly to Magda, and Clara didn't bother asking what kind of magicked telegram they planned to use to summon the doctor back.

Clara agreed silently to the prescribed regimen, nibbling on toast and sipping tea, surprised that the nausea subsided rather than grew and that, after finishing, she actually felt hungry. Magda fixed her another round of tea and toast, finding a bit of applesauce as well.

"What about my sister? At some point, time will catch up with the other side and she'll notice I'm gone."

"I thought about that. We'll figure out something—might be you'll be well enough in quick pace and it's no trouble. If not, I'll lie to her somehow. I'm decent at that. By my reckoning you've got another day or so."

Clara consented to being coddled by Magda, at least as far as Magda could coddle anyone, which consisted largely of ferrying tea and toast and applesauce to her and leaving various books lying around. Clara only read from *Hard Times*, feeling very far away from Nathanael, though he was only in the other room.

But as Clara improved, Nathanael deteriorated. Within a day, she felt well enough to get up and dress, and wouldn't be kept apart from him any longer. Clara curled next to him in bed, straightening the blankets that he twisted as he dreamed. He burned with a stubborn fever, and the wound, though bandaged and clean, felt cold under her hand. She coaxed him into drinking lukewarm tea when he was awake and wiped his clammy forehead while he slept and murmured stories of swans and glass palaces while he slipped between the two.

"We'll have to call for the doctor," Magda said, finding Clara nestled protectively into Nathanael's side for the third time that day and choosing to say nothing about it.

She buried her face into Nathanael's pillow and willed herself to catch the scent of his soap, long overlaid with his sweat and a vague sallowness Clara could only describe as smelling like sickness. "Please. Can't anyone do anything else? Some poultice or tincture or..."

"There's nothing." Magda checked his bandage again. "But we've got to do something or—" She shook her head, refusing to say it. "Maybe you should go, get back to your sister. There's nothing more you can do here, and God knows Sandmann—"

Clara interrupted. "I'm not leaving. I'm not leaving Nathanael until—until—" Magda began to argue, but she held firm. "I know you want to protect me, but I'm not a child."

"No one doubts that, but you care for him and—well." Magda paused. "This could be a grisly business."

"Nathanael can't avoid it. I won't run away, either."

"Very well," she said. "You give him the dose of night air I've got ready in that vial. The whole thing."

The night air smelled of vanilla and jasmine and something deeper and headier that made her eyes swim just uncorking the bottle. She lifted Nathanael's head gently and he stirred.

"Has he come here?" he asked. "Or is he busy making the other place into his land of dolls? He will, you know, his own land of dolls..."

"It's all right," she whispered. "You can sleep, it's all right."

"It isn't all right and you didn't answer my question."

"No sign of Sandmann, or of anyone from the guilds, either." They should have come by now, shouldn't they? "We need the doctor, Nathanael, for your arm."

"I know." He lifted it slightly and grimaced. "It's all right, you know. Whatever happens. It isn't as though I'd be losing my key. That would be something to fret over."

"Oh, shut up, you silly fool," Clara said, voice catching. "I've half a mind—"

The door slammed—Magda was wasting no time in fetching MacCallan. That alone shook her. She pressed the fears back. Nathanael didn't need her fear, he needed what little strength she could scrape together.

"What do you need? Tea? Some broth? Magda left some. I could probably make soup, even, except that I don't know how your cookstove works or if you've anything to make soup out of, or—"

"I don't want anything."

"Magda said—she said I should give you some more of the distilled night air. Before—before—"

"Yes, I know. Soon." His eyes gazed, clear and sad, at the light dancing on the far wall. "You won't believe me, but there are times I hate this place."

"The anderwelt?"

"It's given me as much pain as it has joy. I suppose I'm unusual in that regard." He pulled on her hand, the slight tension begging her to come close. The distance between them closed as she lay next to him. "But it brought me to you, so I won't begrudge it. Even if—well. I think we know what must happen."

"Please don't."

"Then tell me something else. Tell me something that makes me believe in the anderwelt."

All Clara could think of were Godfather's stories, and perversely, most of them featured Sandmann in various hideous permutations. One, however, did not. One that didn't tell her anything she didn't now know about the anderwelt, but that seemed to express its innate joys.

She told it quietly, twin tears rolling down her cheeks that she didn't bother to brush away.

The Sugarplum,
by Christian Elias Thrushman,
dated 6 January 1882

Once upon a time there was a very clever baker. He was a very orderly man. There was never a missed streak of flour on his counters or dab of chocolate on his apron. The great marble slab at the center of his kitchen was always spotless. His rolling pins knew not to tumble out of place. His spoons were ordered by height. His shelves were neat and tidy with rows of spices labeled and arranged by type. Some might have expected them to fall in line alphabetically, but that was too simple a system for this baker, who set their marching orders by a complex taxonomy of sweetness, strength, depth, and heat of flavor.

He was known for his gingerbread and for his confections, marzipan and sugarplums chief among them. Astute listener Clara or Louise, you might find yourself confused as I have described this man as a baker rather than a confectioner, but you must remember that this was a very long time ago and the schism between the Bakers' and Confectioners' Guilds had not yet happened and therefore there were many clever and talented artists who did not discriminate in the art of sugar. Because every town needs a baker but a confectioner is quite superfluous, most attempted to corner the baking market first, and then began to dabble in confections.

This baker went well beyond dabbling.

He sculpted marzipan like granite into statues of anything you could imagine. Entire pastoral scenes of sheep and shepherds, opera companies performing silent Mozart, royal courts of sugared kings and queens. His chocolates were formed into tiny animals and birds. Even his peppermints were delicate snowflakes, not the simple drops and canes of most candy shops. And every Christmas he built a castle of gingerbread to decorate his front window.

He would populate the castle with people of pure sugar, painted with dyes he made himself that scented and flavored the sugar as well as colored it. This was rather a waste in the end, as no one ever ate the brilliant little people who lived in his gingerbread palace. But they delighted the townspeople who came each year to see what new creations the baker had imagined. One year he created the castle of a Russian tsar; another, the palace of a Spanish queen. Everyone agreed that the gingerbread armada engaged in a battle with a hard sugar sea serpent was probably his best work. The year in question, he had built a fairy-tale palace complete with a stained-glass tower of hard candy and a moat of spun sugar.

One day a woman was ordering her confections to hang on her Christmas tree when she mentioned, offhand as one is wont to do in light conversation with a shopkeeper, that even a master of baking as talented as he could not make her favorite confection look lovely. Slightly affronted, he asked which confection this might be. She answered him—and his face and spirits fell, for he knew she had cornered him.

The sugarplum.

Esteemed reader or listener, though you no doubt love sugarplums, their sweet, dense heart and the crunch of bright sugar coating them like frost on the skin of a real plum fresh from the orchard, you must agree with the lady. They are odd little globules that do not hold even a round shape well. The sparkling sugar is enticing, but it is in the end a mask for the ugly blob beneath. The baker was crestfallen. If he could not create a sugarplum as beautiful as his marzipan and hard candy and gingerbread, he was a failure in his endeavors.

He began that very day. Hours of frustration he undertook, attempting to mold the recalcitrant mixture of fruit and nuts. He adjusted the ratio of plum to walnut. He minced the fruit finer. He chopped the nuts more coarsely. Nothing seemed to work until finally, as the clock began to chime midnight, his first success came together. A delicate body formed of the soft—but not too soft—filling, dusted with the finest glittering sugar, and the final touch, a pair of wings formed of the most delicate clear candy.

A fairy, made, quite impossibly, of sugarplum.

He hung her in the window above his gingerbread castle and went to bed exhausted. He rose late the next day and his ovens were too cold to bake bread before the morning rush of customers, but he did not care, for two things happened before he awoke.

First, word had spread of his achievement, and people

thronged by the window to see the impossible—a fairy made of sugarplum. His reputation was confirmed, and the newspaper had already printed a story of the impossible sugarplum fairy that was destined to be reprinted in at least three dozen other newspapers before the month was out. Second, his kitchen, his orderly, perfect kitchen, was a mess.

Flour streaked the counters and the walls. A smear of chocolate marred the great marble slab. The spoons were entirely out of place. Worse, and horror of horrors, the spices had been rearranged in a nonsensical order.

Beside himself, the baker began to clean immediately. Sweat beaded and knuckles cracked as he scrubbed as he had never scrubbed before. Then, thin and wisp-like on the air, he heard a faint laugh.

You see, in the intensity of creating his sugarplum fairy, a strange and entirely unexpected thing had occurred—the fairy was imbued with the spark of life. This has happened on rare occasions with other art forms, but never before or, as far as I know, since in the realm of confections. Unfortunately for the baker, the sugarplum fairy was a bit of an imp.

She flitted about the kitchen while he worked, asking questions in a nonsensical language he could not understand and sampling each of the spices in turn. She sneezed quite vexingly at most of them, toppling jars and making an even larger mess. As the baker turned to the only task he could be expected to complete that day—a batch of spice cookies for his holiday stock—she refused to leave him alone, hovering at his shoulder and offering bits and bobs that were entirely unsuitable to cooking, such as down from his pillow or a few glass beads.

He managed to put the cookies into the oven without contaminating them with the fairy's unhelpful additions—or so he thought, until he tasted one and realized that he had swapped the nutmeg for pepper in his confusion. At first he was nearly inconsolable, but a second and third bite of the cookie suggested to him that this was perhaps serendipity. The balance of sweet and spice, the bite of the black pepper—it was, perhaps, his most ingenious creation to date.

And so pfefferneusse were born. For all I know, the baker and the sugarplum fairy lived a very happy if often confusing life ever after.

Chapter Forty-Eight

AFTERWARD, ALL CLARA could think of was the blood and the confusion of it, the way a human body is nothing at all like clockwork. In repairing a clock or even Olympia, it was no hard thing to take one gear at a time, to unpick a cog from another. But a human body—it was tangled and messy and even the precise ministrations of Dr. MacCallan did not make it any less so.

"Won't spilling blood—won't it harm the anderwelt?" Clara had asked cautiously as the doctor had set up an array of cruel bladed instruments.

"It's all in intention," she'd replied crisply. "It isn't as though blood is some sort of tainted magic liquid. The anderwelt, she knows if we are trying to repair something that is broken. She understands that."

It had not looked at all like repairing something broken. It had looked, to Clara's untrained eye, like a butcher shop.

They had left her with Nathanael, still deep under the spell of the night air. She wondered at his dreams and hoped for the only thing she could hope for—that they were not the nightmares of the blighted anderwelt or even the nightmare of their current reality. She sat beside him, gingerly at first, afraid of the clean white bandage, of the empty place below it where his hand should have rested on the blankets.

Slowly she eased his good hand into hers, slowly she moved closer to him. When he woke, something new would begin; she knew it by a kind of intuition she'd never felt before.

The tincture kept him asleep for the rest of the day, and Clara barely left his side, letting Magda and MacCallan bustle about her, changing dressings and making tea and toast. As evening rolled across the anderwelt in shades of purple and the scent of lilacs, Saint-Luc appeared at their door.

"Appear" was certainly the right word, Clara thought as she answered the knock, as no one had heard or seen him coming.

"Good evening, Miss Ironwood," he said.

She scoffed—the formality was absurd, especially now. "What happened with Sandmann?" she demanded.

"I filed the appropriate warrants with the committee the day you came to me about him. I've given—"

"You've filed paperwork? That's it?" She felt her voice go shrill. "We could have been killed. Nathanael nearly was."

"You could have stayed out of it entirely," Saint-Luc snapped. "I understand he found you at your godfather's."

Days of anger, frustration, helplessness all combined to produce a nearly uncontrollable rage, deep and guttural. "He could have found us anywhere. I can't stay out of it, because I am part of it."

Saint-Luc faltered. "We have never encountered anything of this nature before. You must understand that—we have had rogue craftsmen, and we've dealt with them. Some have tried to use their keys for gain in the ordinary world, it's true. But they've never had opportunity quite like this. The Exposition, yes, but the whole world is changing. Cinema, telegraphs, automobiles— the line between the impossible and the real is always thinning, always blurring. What would have been rejected as witchcraft in an old age is mere technical progress today."

"And when you write a history book, you can include all these platitudes." Clara's hands were in fists by her side. She heard Magda and MacCallan behind her, but neither ventured to inter- rupt. "For now, do you think a warrant will stop Sandmann? We have to find him, and we have to stop him."

"I'm beginning to think you are correct, Miss Ironwood. Which is why I'm here."

Clara stopped, almost speechless. "You do?"

"Yes. I had hoped you could be kept out of harm's way, I admit. Don't mistake me, Miss Ironwood, but I am not—I am not with- out feeling. The time we spent together, it was a charade, but it revealed to me a very intelligent, remarkable young woman. I am fond of you." He flushed. "Not in any particular way, of course. But the way one appreciates a fellow craftsman."

"Thank you," Clara replied stiffly. "Don't think me unfeeling, either, but I couldn't give a cracked nutshell for your opinions of me right now."

"I understand." His moustache twitched in a rueful smile. "The threat has never been so great. One more blight, and—Mr. Song's calculations frighten me, if I am quite honest."

"Then what do you propose we do?"

"I suggest we find Sandmann, recover your godfather's key, and bind Sandmann's key."

Magda snorted. "And that's simple enough, isn't it? Find him, sure. And how do you suggest we do that?"

"I hate to say it, but I wonder if he would come to you."

"No," Clara said. "No, Nathanael is ill, and we are not prepared for another fight with that man. I have the feeling, Monsieur Saint-Luc, that you keep forgetting that he is not interested in playing by any rule but his own self-interest."

"I'm quite aware, Miss Ironwood. That's precisely it—if he believes that you are all still a threat to him, he will not hesitate to strike you while you are, well, in a weakened state. We can put out the necessary rumors—that we've determined the allegations against him are baseless, providing that there are no eyewitnesses." He paused. "You are, of course, eyewitnesses."

Clara's eyes widened. "You want us as bait."

"I would hesitate to put so crude a point on it, but yes." He raised a brow. "Magda, do you still make your famous compasses?"

Magda snorted. "Spit it out, Andrès. You want one?"

Saint-Luc straightened. "It would be most helpful, and given that you have never shared the secret of how they're made with anyone else, it seems we're at your mercy."

"Fine. I've got a couple I keep in reserve." She pulled out her key before Clara could ask why they would need a compass. "Just wait a second."

"Magda!" Clara cried. "Don't go"—Magda winked out of existence—"alone."

Saint-Luc smiled a lopsided grin that reminded Clara why it had been so easy to fall for his charms. "She will be fine, I am sure."

"Everyone has been far too sure about everything," Clara said, more angrily than she had intended. "What is this compass?"

"Do you know how pigeons find their way home?"

"Do I—what?"

"Neither do I. It's a great mystery. But they do—a pigeon will find its way to the roost. And so will the kind of compass Magda makes. It's in two parts—the north, and the compass."

"There's only one north," Clara retorted, annoyed at these riddles.

"Be that as it may, a compass always points north, and Magda's compass always points at the north she makes."

"That makes no—" Clara was interrupted by Magda's return, flashing into existence. "Sense. It makes no sense." ·

"What, Saint-Luc's suit? I agree, it had to have cost too damn much." Magda sighed. "What's your plan? You want to lead him here, only to track him somewhere else? Why not just take him here?"

"Because of what the astute Miss Ironwood pointed out. He's all too willing to resort to violence. So we need to find him in the ordinary world, if we're going to apprehend him, where any damage he does is only to life and limb, not to the anderwelt itself. We can track him through the anderwelt and meet him on the other side." Saint-Luc paused and turned to Clara. "Ah, I forget, you are not familiar. Frau Metzger's ingenious compass can only be used in the anderwelt, but it will track on both sides."

"Doesn't taking the . . . the north back to the other side cause a blight?"

"It's not part of the anderwelt," Magda replied. "It's ordinary glass, actually." She produced a bead, jet black and the size of a pea. "The compass is attuned to it, but it's not of the anderwelt."

"Brilliant theoretical treatise on that subject, by the way," Saint-Luc said. Magda started, surprised by the compliment. "I read it years ago. *D'accord.* We plant the north on Sandmann, track him, and cross over to the other side with, hopefully, a decent-sized contingent to arrest him. That part," he added, "I will handle."

"One problem." Magda folded her fingers around the jet-black bead. "How do I get the *nord* on him so we can track him?"

"I've got that part well in hand," Nathanael called shakily through the doorway.

"Back to bed, young man," Magda said. "Have you been listening this whole time?"

"Of course I have," he replied. "And I'm in bed, so there. But when the time comes—my mice. I'll get the north planted."

"And I will collect the compass from your workshop," Saint-Luc said.

"No," Magda said. Clara stiffened. "It's in a warded box, you can't just 'collect' it."

Saint-Luc reddened. "Am I to gather you don't trust me, even now? Give me the wardbreak."

"I don't trust much of anyone. What does it matter to you?" She squared off against him. "We'll plant the *nord*, and then I'll give you the compass. We can meet in the ordinary lobby of this ordinary hotel."

"Isn't this all a bit silly?" Clara interjected. "We're all on the same side."

"Alliances of necessity don't mean I'm on his side," Magda retorted.

Saint-Luc sighed, exasperated. "God, spare me from stubborn old Germans. Fine. I will see you on the other side," he said. "And we will finish this."

Chapter Forty-Nine

THEY WAITED ANOTHER full day for Saint-Luc's rumors to infiltrate the Parisian anderwelt. Magda assured her that she wouldn't be missed returning to ordinary Paris in the meantime, and though she didn't want to leave Nathanael, she knew she had to. The passage of time might have been slower in the anderwelt, but it never stopped entirely, and at some point Louise would miss her.

She emerged from an ordinary Paris alley at the height of midday, the streets busy under a mild spring sun. She caught a glance at a newspaper, relieved that the date meant she had left the apartment the night before. Less than one day lost to the anderwelt. One day—it felt like a month. More, even.

And Louise would certainly ask why she hadn't come home. The thought of her sister's admonitions, her disapproval—it was almost enough to send Clara right back into the anderwelt. But if she was missing too long, Louise would create other sorts of trouble—the kind with missing persons reports and police investigations.

Besides, Clara found that she felt guilty leaving Louise shut out of this deep, vital part of her life. This was what Magda had said was the hardest part—keeping the anderwelt a secret from those a craftsman cared the most about. She did care about Louise, and the rapport they had rebuilt was threatened by the distance Clara was forced to wedge between them.

Still, she braced herself for the scene she knew would unfold once she was back in her own apartment. She turned the key with trepidation, rehearsing patent lies to throw her sister off the scent of the anderwelt even if it threw Louise into a lecture scolding Clara.

And Louise was waiting. "Where have you been?" The rage on her sister's face, born, Clara was sure, of anxious worry, was unrivaled in all their long history. It was worse than when Clara broke her favorite doll when she was eight, worse than when Clara threw away her diary when she was eleven, even worse than when Clara told Edgar Hopkins that Louise thought he had a dog face when she was fifteen.

Louise had never been this angry with her before. And she'd never had less right to be.

"When I left last night, I . . ."

"About last night! Last night you left with some man you barely know!" Louise stood and began to pace. "And this was after you both disappeared during a public—a very public!—performance, insinuating God only knows what!"

"I apologize," Clara said through gritted teeth, "if I embarrassed you."

"Me! You didn't embarrass me! You—you risked ruining your own reputation, and in front of your employer! What were you thinking, Clara?" Louise shook her head and dropped onto the sofa again. "This isn't like you, it's not like you at all. That's what worries me most."

That Clara hadn't expected. She had expected Louise to be

fretful, yes, angry, yes, concerned over propriety, most certainly, yes. But her sister was worried, primarily, it seemed, simply about her. "I didn't think it through, I suppose, Louise." She paused. That was true—she hadn't been considering her reputation. What else was true? "Herr Nussbaum is a craftsman, like me." That was true, too—Louise didn't need to know that the connotations of the word involved a magical otherworld. "We went to look at the mechanics behind the stage."

"What an utterly foolish thing to do!" Louise said, still angry, but now bewildered, as well. "I'll never understand you, Clara. Never." And then, to Clara's astonished horror, she burst into tears.

"Louise! What in the world—why are you crying? I didn't mean anything by it, I didn't mean—"

"I was so worried! You—you went off with some man, and I—you would never have done that before. But you're so strange lately. Like you've been lying to me."

Damn it. Clara wanted nothing more than to admit everything, to tell Louise that she wasn't trying to shut her out. That this was nothing like when they were younger and Clara had tried to keep her sister at arm's length, because—

Why had she done it, exactly? She'd always blamed Louise for not understanding her, but there was more to it. She'd been envious of Louise, how easily she moved through the world, how easily the world accepted her. It didn't help that Louise always tried to be kind to her, to reach out to her—no, it made it worse.

And none of that had been Louise's fault.

"Louise, I'm sorry." Clara sat gingerly on the sofa next to her sister. "I really am. I've been—I've been awful, haven't I? You only ever wanted to be my friend, to really be sisters—and I was too bullheaded to see it."

Louise hiccuped lightly. "But last night—I—it's not like you, not what I would ever have dreamed you would do. Where were you?"

Clara steeled herself. There were some truths she could share freely, without implicating the anderwelt. "I was with Herr Nussbaum last night," she said softly. "We went back to the fairgrounds and then…" Clara paused. "I know it was unbecoming to spend all night out with a man. I'm sorry, as I wasn't considering how it might…it might make you feel."

"Oh, hang my feelings for a moment—Clara, you really like this Nathanael Nussbaum, don't you? You—you've never—" Louise cracked a small smile. "I never would have guessed that even Paris could contrive to make Clara Ironwood fall in love."

Clara's heart twisted painfully. Yes, she was, she acknowledged, fully and completely in love, and Paris had nothing to do with it. And Clara couldn't tell her sister that Nathanael was hurt, in danger, that her mind was half in another world, with him.

"Well." Louise straightened. "Well, I'll be damned."

Despite herself, Clara laughed. "You aren't going to write to Mother?"

"No, I'm not going to write to Mother! Promise me the same dignity if I'm ever indiscreet," Louise replied. "But please—please do be a bit more careful?"

"I will, Louise." She couldn't help adding, "But not too careful." She sobered. "I have to go. Louise, I—I may have to stay away tonight."

Louise raised an eyebrow. "I said I wouldn't write to Mother, but don't get too overconfident."

"It's not like that. I—" She bit her lip. "Do you remember Godfather's awful friend, Sandmann?"

"How could I forget?" Louise pursed her lips. "He was a phony—always playing up nice to Father, but did you ever see how he growled at the servants?" Trust Louise to have read Sandmann—if only Clara had asked her opinion months ago. "He was an awful man."

"He was," Clara said. "He's here, in Paris, and he's—he's causing problems with the Exposition. If he ever…" She swallowed hard, realizing she had perhaps endangered Louise as well as herself getting caught up in Sandmann's game. "If he ever shows up here, don't let him in. Don't speak with him."

"All right." Louise's eyes widened. "Is he—he wouldn't hurt one of us, would he?"

"I certainly hope not," Clara said. "I shouldn't have made you worry, but—"

"No," Louise said firmly. "Tell me things. Make me worry. I prefer it that way." She smiled softly.

"I'll see you soon," Clara promised, keenly aware of how many things she had withheld from her sister, who certainly thought she was returning to her office, not to Paris turned inside out.

As she walked back across ordinary Paris, she began to doubt the plan—perhaps Sandmann would ignore the bait they'd set. Perhaps he had some other plan in place. Perhaps, even now, he was wending his way toward her apartment, ready to pounce on Louise—what that would accomplish, she had no idea, but she couldn't avoid the nagging suspicion she'd failed to account for all of his possible moves and motives.

She crossed to the anderwelt in the cloakroom of Nathanael's hotel, preferring to navigate the ordinary door and lobby instead of the portcullis of the fortress Nathanael had built around the entrance in the anderwelt. In his apartment, Magda waited by the window like a sentry. While Nathanael slept, Clara waited with her. "Sure wish I'd learned that trick Elias had, of hiding things in a void. Could be useful right about now," Magda said.

"Better than going back to the other side?" Clara asked. As soon as Magda's north was safely planted on Sandmann, they intended to move to the other side quickly to avoid whatever Sandmann had planned for them.

"I wish there was some way to avoid drawing Nathanael through the veil right now." Dr. MacCallan shook her head. "For one, the nightdraught will wear off instantly, and he'll be in rather ungodly agony. But it's also a strain on the body, to some degree, crossing over. We don't notice it normally, but in his state—"

"I know," Magda said. She glanced at Clara. "But there's really no avoiding it."

"You should go," Clara said. "This isn't your fight."

"I think it's already become all of our fight," MacCallan answered. "But I'll go keep watch on the other side, in case you need help when you cross over." She pulled a bronze coin from her pocket, flipped it, and disappeared. Clara took a cup of tea to Nathanael, dosed with enough nightdraught to counter pain while leaving him, they hoped, conscious enough to control a few mice when the time came.

Clara had begun to wonder how long she could stomach the strange limbo of waiting when, at sunset, a roll like thunder made the floorboards tremble and glass in the cabinets shake.

"What in the hell?" Magda yanked the curtain away from the window. The old woman was rendered speechless for, perhaps, the first time in her life.

She eased Nathanael's hand from hers and joined Magda by the window. Outside, Sandmann stood at the head of a small army.

Chapter Fifty

CLARA TRIED TO quell the shaking in her hands as she gripped the window frame, speechless at the sight of Sandmann and a company of eight-foot-tall tin soldiers. They were identical to the ones Clara had found in the Exposition grounds and were no less horrifying within the bounds of the anderwelt than they had been outside of it.

"Couldn't he have at least given them noses?" Magda finally muttered. "They're ugly as sin."

"Almost as ugly as Sandmann," Clara said, trying and failing at gallows humor. Another peal of thunder—Clara realized it was the rolling tattoo of a drum. "All right. Your north—is it ready?"

Magda nodded. "I hadn't expected quite that level of resistance, but I suppose mice don't care about armies of tin soldiers."

"Yes, but we might need to care." Clara hesitated. "We'll have to move quickly. Who knows what those things are capable of."

"We can hold out awhile," Magda said. "Nussbaum didn't know who or what to expect, but turning this hotel into a fortress was a very good idea." Clara recalled watching him rearrange the facade of the building, back when, perhaps, he feared she was an adversary. "Get Nathanael up."

Clara ran to the bedroom, but Nathanael was already awake, propped on his pillow and concentrating. Within the walls, a light skitter of feet cascaded from ceiling to floor, and four gray mice tumbled out of a hole in the corner of the room.

They ran to Magda, who entrusted one with the glass bead. What if the mouse dropped the bead? Clara thought. Their whole plan, resting on a mouse. It was foolhardy, impossible—but Nathanael whispered something she couldn't understand, and the mice slipped into a crack by the window. Outdoors, Sandmann barked some order—what it was, Clara couldn't hear, but she ran to the window as the soldiers relayed the message through the ranks. They marched forward, rocky movements nothing like a regiment on parade, and reached the walls. They began to pull them apart, stone by stone.

"Impossible," Clara breathed.

"Hardly—see how their hands wedge right through the mortar?" Magda peered keenly at them.

For the first time, Clara felt the cold creep of fear. "It won't take them long to break past the defenses. Will we finish in time, do you think?"

"Of course we will. But…" Magda hesitated. "Perhaps you should go early, Clara. I could give you my key, and you could get somewhere safe." Below them, Sandmann directed his soldiers. He held something in his hand, but Clara couldn't quite make it out.

"That's—that's just the trouble, though, isn't it? There's no reason that we couldn't just go to the other side. What does he think he can accomplish?"

"Saint-Luc expected him to come alone, to try to sneak in

somehow. I had the whole place guarded with extra eyes—not now, I'll explain my mechanical eyes another time." Magda sucked her lips tight against her teeth. "But to come like this—he has to know we can just use our keys to escape him."

Below them, Clara saw a quartet of mice balancing on the high stone wall, impossibly small and far away. Sandmann turned, and she saw the glint of a mirror in his hand. "Magda," Clara said urgently. "Try using your key."

"Why? There's no—"

"Just do it. There and back again, quick." Clara watched Sandmann, too far away for her to hear him, but she could have sworn a cruel smile twisted on his face as he held the mirror aloft.

Magda pulled out her silver needle and—

"Nothing." Her eyes widened. "It's not working."

"It's his damn net," Clara said. "He can bind people with it. I guess we're too far away. But it looks like it binds keys, too."

"Scheisse." Magda pursed her lips. Below them, giant hands ripped away another layer of stone, close to reaching the entrance. "They haven't gotten through the portcullis yet," Magda said, "but I'll be damned if those things can't get through it without much trouble."

Clara's eyes widened. And yet, there was one part of the plan that hadn't gone awry—the mice continued on, undeterred. Clara glimpsed them as they scurried under Sandmann's feet, but he was oblivious to the tiny creatures, his eyes trained on his giant soldiers. One managed to climb, undetected, to Sandmann's pocket. With the bead secured inside, it leapt away and, with the other three mice, ran for safety.

"Well, now I wish I'd just given Saint-Luc the damned instructions to get at the compass," Magda said.

"Magda!" Clara gasped. "You're not giving up?"

"I don't know what else to do! Key's bound, we've got no weapons, and damn it, I'm not sure I'm willing to harm even that rat of a man if it means another blight." She sighed. "If for some reason I don't get out of here but you do—the compass is in the red silk box under my workbench."

"All right, but you—"

"No, you listen. You'll need to untie all the ribbons, starting with the blue one, in clockwise order, then retie the blue one. That's how the box opens. Precisely that order. Otherwise you'll never get the compass out."

"How would I make it out of this?" Clara winced as another shower of mortar fell on the street outside.

"You've got two feet. You could make a run for it. If it comes to it, the compass will work like a key to go between worlds, but only while it's tracking, and it won't track for more than a day or so at a time." Magda paused, ready to argue further, but both stopped, listening to a sound even stranger than the enormous soldiers below. Behind them, in the walls, a rustling as though a forest of trees lifted their limbs into a brazen wind. Clara turned. Dozens of mice, hundreds, scurried over the floor, spilling out the broken window and to the street below. From other buildings, from alleys and garden walls, from every possible direction, swarms of mice convened on the company of soldiers below.

Clara looked behind her, into Nathanael's room. He stood against the doorframe, pale as snow and with intense concentration beading sweat across his brow. She flew to his side just as he faltered and helped him to sit. The mice hesitated in unison, and then resumed their forward march.

Their nimble feet found purchase in the crude rivets and pins of the soldiers, covering them in squirming bodies and a tangle of tails. Sandmann himself, Clara saw, was encircled by mice and held at bay. Clara watched, breathless. Surely an eight-foot tin monster wouldn't yield to even a legion of mice. Yet, under the swarming rodents, the soldiers teetered and shuddered. One by one, the soldiers fell. As she watched, they were swiftly rent full of holes, warped, and mangled.

Nathanael, meanwhile, laid his head against the back of the chair, mouthing words through dry lips. "Hold," he murmured. Below, the mice surged and then faltered again. Nathanael squeezed his eyes shut, but the mice wavered, indecisive. Some broke away and scurried back to the alleys and walls they had come from. The sea of rodents began to tremble and dissipate, only those closest to Sandmann holding firm.

They tightened their circle around him. Clara bit her lip. Any retreat on his part was good enough, even escaping back to the ordinary side of Paris.

"I wish I—" Nathanael whispered. "I wish I could hold him— could capture him here—" His face was like wax, and Clara could tell it was impossible for him to hold on much longer.

"Let him go," Clara said. "We'll follow him on the other side."

Nathanael sighed and mouthed silent orders. The mice ebbed back, still arrayed in threatening numbers, but falling back just enough that Sandmann could move. He had his hand in his pocket and produced his own key in an instant, and winked out of sight. Nathanael grimaced and gasped, his will finally giving out. The mice scattered as though they'd seen a legion of cats.

"Tell me," Clara said, trying to cover the tremble in her voice, "is going away like that without so much as a goodbye considered rude among handwerkers? Like slamming a door? Or leaving the table right after dinner is finished?"

"Terribly rude, but so is Sandmann. Did you see his key? The damned thing is an actual key—no imagination. Whoever took him on as apprentice has a lot to answer for," Magda shouted out the window to no one in particular.

Clara let Magda rail; she was more concerned over Nathanael, who leaned his head against the wingback of the chair, panting lightly. "*Scheisse. Scheisse.* Fucking hell," he muttered.

"Are you all right?"

"Hurts like hell and I couldn't hold him. It's my fault."

"You idiot, you saved us." She tried to smile playfully, but she found she couldn't quite manage it. "We should go."

"And quickly," Magda said. "Saint-Luc will be waiting to use the compass. It will only work as long as Sandmann's got my *nord* on him—so we'd best hope he doesn't change his jacket first thing."

Chapter Fifty-One

DR. MACCALLAN WAITED on Nathanael's ordinary wing-back chair in his ordinary room when all three came tumbling through using Magda's key.

"Where's Saint-Luc?" Magda demanded immediately. "He's supposed to be here."

MacCallan rose. "I don't know. He never came." Her voice was tense with the unspoken significance of this. Something—someone—had prevented his coming.

"There's no time to lose waiting," Clara said. "I'll go. Like you said, Magda, if he takes the coat off—"

"What are you going to do when you find him?"

"I don't know!" Clara was surprised to feel tears biting the corners of her eyes—they'd come so far, and now Sandmann might slip through their fingers. "Well, I could see where he goes, map his movements, you could say. Then when we find Saint-Luc, or—or whoever we need to find—we can at least tell them where we've seen him, how to look for him among a city of millions."

"It's not a terrible idea," MacCallan said. "At least your trick with the compass won't go to waste. And given that—"

"Absolutely not," Magda said. "If anyone is going to serve as a bloodhound, it will be me."

"No, both of you," Nathanael said. "It's too dangerous. He—" Entirely undone, Nathanael's face went white and he collapsed.

Clara looped an arm under him and hoisted him to his feet, Magda joining her as she propelled him toward his bed with sheer willpower. She settled the pillows and tucked the blankets as he stifled his pain, and MacCallan hurried in with something not quite like nightdraught but the best that ordinary medicine could offer—opium, Clara assumed.

Neither woman noticed that she had plucked Nathanael's key from the pocket of his housecoat. When she slipped out the door without a word, she wondered how long it would take Magda to realize she was gone.

As she hurried down the stairs and into the street, the full weight of what she'd committed to bore down on her. After all, what would she do when she found Sandmann? Confronting him seemed a spectacularly stupid plan, but that meant avoiding his notice. What if he caught her tracking him?

Well, that part would have to come later, she reasoned. She found a tram heading in the right direction, reorienting herself to the strangeness of the ordinary Paris, the mundane feeling almost alien as she remembered how to count out francs for the fare and map out stops. As soon as she arrived at Magda's shop, she crossed in to the anderwelt feeling almost relieved, like coming home.

Clara wasted no time in ransacking the shelves under Magda's workbench for the red silk box. As promised, it was tied at all four corners, one ribbon blue. As quickly as she dared, lest she fumble and leave the box warded for good, she untied and retied the ribbons in the right order. The lid lifted easily.

Inside was a disk of burnished silver, inlaid with mother-of-pearl to imitate a compass rose. The points were unmarked, however, and the slim mother-of-pearl needle at the center quivered. Clara wondered how it worked as she gently lifted the compass from the box. Did she have to hold it a certain way, or say something, or point it? She laid the compass on her open palm and the needle whirred as though stirring from sleep, spun three times, and then settled into a direction.

She began to follow it, but then remembered Nathanael's key in her pocket. The compass would work as a key, Magda had said— and she didn't want to risk losing Nathanael's. She set it in the nest of red silk inside the box and tied the box shut again, warding the key inside.

Then, she followed the compass needle out of the workshop and into Paris. She plotted her course by its slight movements, sometimes tracing her path along the anderwelt streets and some-times crossing green space at a brisk diagonal until she came to a nondescript corner not far from the Grand Palais, hemmed in by wiry metallic trees on a side street. The needle spun meticu-lously, circling the points of the compass. She shouldn't have been surprised to find Sandmann in one of the blank, plain places—at least, Clara allowed, it wasn't blighted. It looked like a hotel, or perhaps a restaurant. The facade was so scrubbed of detail it was hard to tell.

She guessed that Sandmann was more likely to be on the ordi-nary side of Paris than the otherworld, but she still entered the building cautiously. A hotel, certainly—perhaps it was where Sandmann was lodging. The lobby was empty, except for echoes and pale dust and a pair of wan palm trees growing from the stone floor. Clara found the cloakroom—she was good at hiding in cloakrooms, she thought with a wry smile—and slipped back to the other side. She could inquire as to the guests at that hotel, claim she was a friend—no, a relative, a niece—and see if Sandmann was staying there. That would be enough for Saint-Luc, when she found him.

The pallid lobby of the hotel was almost as empty as its anderwelt counterpart, except for a couple of anemic potted palms and a collection of newspapers on the table by the fire. There was no one at the desk, so Clara circled the lobby and peered down the hallways. As she turned back to the lobby, a strong hand clamped her wrist and dragged her into an unused parlor.

Sandmann. He glowered at her, and she yanked her hand away, the marks of his grip still stinging and red.

"Would you care to explain what you're doing here, Miss Ironwood?"

He looked so ordinary, she thought, dressed in an ordinary suit and ordinary shoes and carrying an ordinary umbrella. "You— you know perfectly well! You—" It felt stupid, childish even, to say aloud that he had been abusing the powers of the anderwelt, had risked blighting all of Paris or more, had attacked her and her friends with gigantic tin soldiers, standing here in an ordinary lobby of an ordinary hotel.

"I did nothing that you can even discuss, let alone prove, here." A bellhop passed by them with a polite smile, as though reinforcing Sandmann's point.

"Why not just give it up? Whatever arrangement you have with the Exposition, surely your debts have been adequately paid. So end it, end the blighting, and make an honest living. Your work is certainly good enough on its own merits."

"Any living is an honest one, so long as you stay alive." He was a foolish, selfish man, and he was afraid. Clara saw that instantly. Very afraid, and willing to do whatever he could rather than face up to what he'd done.

"That's hardly true," she argued. "This business with the Exposition was not honest at all."

She was surprised when Sandmann cracked a smile and laughed. "You must see, dear girl, you can't get in the way of progress. What I did—it's messy, but it's progress. All part of the indominable march forward and all that."

"Change isn't necessarily progress," she answered. "You've got it all wrong—that progress is what is good for *you*. It isn't, Mr. Sandmann. Progress is what is for the greater good. The anderwelt can never be a tool for a single individual, or for business, or even governments. Not even the Exposition. True progress is another thing far finer than that, Mr. Sandmann—"

She didn't realize that Sandmann's hand was on her wrist and he had dragged them into the anderwelt until it was too late. The bland lobby was even plainer and had a damp, clammy smell she hadn't noticed before. She pulled away from him, retreating toward the frail palm trees and pulling the compass from her pocket at the same time.

Sandmann advanced on her, his awful grip on her wrist forcing her to drop the compass. He caught it and laughed. "One of Magda's! I haven't seen one in years. It seems a shame to destroy it, but since I can't have you tracking me and leading the guilds my way—" He dropped it on the blank stone floor and crushed it with his heel. Clara winced, but Sandmann wasn't finished. He had a slim silver knife in his hand, with a fine bone handle. An ordinary pocket knife.

Clara started back. "What do you mean to do, you old fool—"

Sandmann lashed out and sliced her arm, deep enough to be painful but far from severe enough to stop her. "I'm sorry. But I can't let you run straight to Magda and Nussbaum—if he's even still alive—"

She smacked him hard across the face without thinking. She stood back, stunned, clutching her bleeding arm as Sandmann staggered back, just as surprised. His mouth worked once or twice before he spat out, "Sit here and rot, then." He pulled his key from his pocket and disappeared.

For a moment, Clara didn't understand. Then she saw the anemic palm trees begin to disintegrate. They faded into gray ash and crumbled, the fronds falling like crumpled newsprint on a carpet of moldering moss. The pale aura shifted and grew dim. A gray pallor settled over the room.

And then it began to roll.

He'd blighted a little patch of the anderwelt and left her in it. The horror of what had happened to Nathanael was now hers, too. She was trapped here, she realized with ratcheting fear, trapped in a hostile little corner of a magic world that wouldn't let her leave. The gray had already spread as far as she could see.

If only she had a key. Sandmann must have counted on her not having one—that he had Godfather's, and that she was using the compass, which, unlike a key, could be destroyed with a well-placed kick. It still laid on the floor, broken. She picked it up, scrambling, praying it might work just once more, but the snapped needle didn't budge, and she stayed frustratingly put. That wretched pustule of a man!

Focus, she told herself. But it was almost impossible, as the gray landscape around her shifted. Shadows grew out of nothing and lapped one over the other, a pile of ever-deepening darkness, confusing her perception of depth and size. Worse, a thin, high buzzing permeated the room. She wondered if she could get outside if it would be better, if perhaps she could even escape the blight itself.

She reached the door and it threw her back.

The anderwelt folded back on itself, dropping her where she had been. Or was it? The shadows swam under her feet and over the walls, except now there were no walls. It was all vague confusion painted in grayscale. Vertigo assaulted her as the buzzing grew louder. She sat down on the ground, hard—at least that was still solid.

For now—she had no idea what other ways the diseased anderwelt could unspool itself. Oh, Nathanael, her heart seized—how many years? She was almost mad after a few minutes. How could she survive here until the borders of the blight softened and let her leave? How long would that be, she wondered—days, months, years? Was the depth of the blight proportional to the depth of the wound?

No way of knowing. Desperate, she scrambled toward the door—where the door had been, at least. Now it was only a smudge in the shadow. She felt herself tumble back. Her head swam.

If only she had a key, she thought again. Nathanael hadn't had a key, either—but he had made one. Eventually, he had made a key.

And it had taken him years. She wondered, in abstract horror, how long it had been since Sandmann had left her here. Already time folded in on itself and it felt like she had been curled in gray shadow for eternity.

She closed her eyes and willed the buzzing to stop.

Chapter Fifty-Two

EVENTUALLY, CLARA THOUGHT to herself as a colorless sun shifted the light around her, they would know she was missing. Either Louise, or Fritz, or Magda, or Nathanael. Someone would notice the new blight in Paris. Someone would find her. She had to believe that.

No, she told herself. They would surely look for her, but how long until they found her? Paris was large enough in the ordinary sense, but the otherworld Paris was even more complex and full of places to hide—or be hidden. She had no idea, either, if one could even find something in a blight, or if its shadows obscured any search.

She sat up, even though it was like pushing aside pounding ocean waves. She had to find a way out on her own. There was only one way she knew of to accomplish that.

She would make a key. What did she have? She dug through her pockets. Several francs, a business card with the name mostly rubbed away, a scrap of paper from work. Two hairpins. A swatch of fabric and a mother-of-pearl collar pin.

She spread the items in her lap—she didn't trust them to the undulating ground beneath her—and thought. What did it take to make a key? There was a secret, she knew that much, but what was it? Godfather's was clearly a work of art, but Nathanael's was simple—just a button on string. So intricacy didn't appear to matter. Material didn't seem to make a difference, for though Godfather did like working in glass, Nathanael's key was crafted out of scrap materials, like hers. What did they have in common? She considered every key she had seen so far, and realized that in all their diversity, each one had some kind of dynamic element—Nathanael's swung like a pendulum, MacCallan flipped a coin, Magda's was a needle, she'd had to look through Godfather's. That was a place to start.

She began to fiddle with the bits and bobs in her lap, wondering how they might go together. A hairpin woven through paper—but no, that was static. She could suspend the pin from the shoelace, but she had a feeling simply copying the mechanics of Nathanael's key wouldn't work. She had to make something she could act with, effect some small change with, and it had to be her own idea.

There it was. The buzzing around her seemed to fade slightly as she focused on the task. She used the pin to carefully pick a rent into the fabric, then tore three thin strips from them and braided them with a strip of the paper. The plait was just long enough, and a bent hairpin provided the structure and closed the circle she made out of the braid. And for the centerpiece, the collar pin was a bit large but served as the requisite decoration.

A ring. An awkward, almost ugly, ring, but a ring—one she could take on and off. She lamented briefly that, had she more time, she would have made a beautiful piece of silver and silk and glass, even gemstones, and that this was her only chance. Only one key, that rule was clear.

She slid the ring on her finger.

Nothing happened.

She sighed, disappointment biting even though she chided herself for expecting anything to happen at all. She shouldn't have thought it would be that easy; after all, Nathanael had spent years at it. Most craftsmen did. To think she could have figured it out in—was it hours, days? Maybe weeks, she didn't know. It was arrogant at best, foolish at worst. Probably both, she scolded herself. But she had to find the answer, and quickly. How else would they find Sandmann, how else would they stop all of Paris from descending into the black mire she found herself wallowing in now?

It wasn't only the anderwelt, either. She had grown to love the bright bustle of ordinary Paris, recognizing it was far from ordinary—no place, she appreciated more fully, was truly ordinary. Even the plainest corner of the world hid imagination and creation and art. Ruining the anderwelt would ruin that, would strip the originality from the streets and cafés and galleries of Paris as surely as it would condemn the Exposition to be a tawdry wasteland.

She bit back tears as she slipped the ring off. She'd find a way, somehow. She just needed to think about it more, dissect what she knew of the keys and their functions. Silently, she lamented Godfather's negligence again, sure that more education from him years ago might help her now.

The collar pin was loose and sprang open, piercing her finger as she slid the ring off. She cursed, then closed the pin into place as a drop of blood welled and fell on the tightly braided strips. The red stain seeped into the fabric and shone on the metal. It didn't hurt, not really, but the frustration, the indignity—they pressed in an angry knot at the back of her throat.

Then her hands froze. The ring began to glow faintly, and then, stronger, exuded a golden light that made Clara blink before it faded away again. The ring was the same, but changed, somehow—it seemed more solid. The braided strips didn't wobble any longer, and the pin held firm. A key, Clara thought. A key couldn't be broken. Her ring—it had become a key.

She almost laughed. All the careful planning, all the meticulous calculations, the fine workmanship—it couldn't make a key. It required something more, something mere cognition and craft could never yield. It needed blind serendipity, and it needed a part of her.

Breathless, she lifted the ring again and slipped it onto her finger.

The anderwelt very gently fell away from her as the other world settled around her.

She was horrified to remember where she was, in the public lobby of a public hotel with, possibly, plenty of people around. She scrambled to her feet to meet the astonished face of the same bellhop as before.

No time to fuss over details like traumatized bellhops. "What day is it?" she demanded.

"*Jeudi*. Thu…Thursday?"

Three days lost. Only three—that was a small miracle. She turned toward the door and promptly hit a wall of nausea. The aftereffects of time in the blighted anderwelt—damn it. She'd have to push through it, force herself onward until she had time to rest.

The floor hurtling toward her convinced her otherwise.

The bellhop, bless him, caught her despite her surprise. She pressed her hands against her head. "Can you please send for the woman who lives at this address?" she asked, rattling off Louise's name and the apartment's street and number. The young man dutifully wrote them down. "If she isn't there, the landlady, Madame Boule. Or my neighbor Annabelle Forsythe. Please, it's very—"

"Mademoiselle, je ne veux pas savoir." She pawed her way onto a sofa and curled herself into a ball against the churning in her stomach until she fell into a fitful sleep.

"Clara!" Louise woke her with a start. "Clara, you look like death! Are you all right? Where have you been? Is it Sandmann, is he the problem? Where is he?"

Who knew, now, where Sandmann was? She sank back into the sofa, retreating from Louise's questions. "Everything is awful and I don't know what to do," she finally said.

"I have no idea what that means," Louise replied. "But how can I help—oh, God, your arm is bleeding!"

Clara had forgotten about her arm. In the strange timeline of the broken anderwelt, it was still a fresh wound, seeping into her sleeve. "I'd almost forgotten," she muttered. It hurt more when she looked at it. Why had Louise mentioned it? Inconsiderate, Clara thought to herself with a hiccup of a laugh. The movement sliced through her head like a knife and she winced.

"You are not well."

"Just take me home," Clara begged. Somehow she managed to wrestle through a tram ride, other passengers edging away from her pallid face, but the short walk to her apartment nearly undid her.

Louise eyed her warily. "I'll call for a doctor—"

"No," Clara said. "They can't do anything. Not for this—this is—" The room spun. She needed Magda's nightdraught, her expertise. She needed to know that Nathanael was all right, that Sandmann had left them alone, that maybe something could still be done.

Damn it all to hell, she needed Louise to leave the room.

"I'm calling for a doctor," Louise said. Yes, that would do it, Clara thought. *Go fetch the doctor and when you get back*—"I'll talk to Madame Boule, is what I'll do. I'll have her run and get a doctor."

"No, please, Louise, I—" She could have cried, if crying wouldn't have rent her head so badly. "Please don't ask any questions. Don't tell anyone."

"Then I'll stay right here with you. I don't think you should be left alone. You look like death, Clara."

"Fine." Clara bit her lip. "Fine. Just—just leave me alone for a moment."

Louise agreed uncertainly and turned for the kitchen. Clara drew her key from her finger and then slipped it back on, back and forth, the anderwelt settling over her.

Chapter Fifty-Three

CLARA DIDN'T REALIZE until they landed in the anderwelt that Louise had clutched her sleeve as she'd used the key. Her sister blanched white. "What have you done? Is this some kind of trick? Am I being hypnotized?"

Clara, almost undone by the effects of crossing on her nausea, agreed readily to this explanation. "I'll bring you out of it if you hold my hand."

Louise consented to producing a shaking hand, and Clara snatched it in one hand and gripped her key in the other, willing herself to remember Nathanael's sitting room filled with light, his stacks of books, the scent of his soap and tea brewing in the teapot. The memories reached out to her and held her, and in a moment she was there.

"It didn't work!" Louise cried. "I'm still hypnotized!" Despite herself, Clara laughed at the absurdity of it, at Magda's shocked face, at Louise's flushed cheeks, at the way she blinked stupidly in the anderwelt light. Then the laughter lanced through her head like a spike and she nearly threw up.

"What in God's name?" Magda stood, arms crossed, in front of the window. "What happened to you? Why is she here?"

Nathanael appeared next, moving slowly but on his own from the bedroom, his bandaged arm hidden under his housecoat. "You disappeared," he said. "I've never been so worried, I didn't know where you'd gone."

Louise edged away. "Clara, I'm seeing other people now."

"Louise, you are not hypnotized. This is real. You're in—it's too hard to explain." She couldn't hold out any longer against the poison of the blight and fumbled for the nearest receptacle, which happened to be a teapot, and retched into it.

"I knew it was too soon," Magda muttered. "Nathanael, can you help me with your *liebste*?"

Clara let Nathanael loop an arm under hers and guide her to the bed, even allowing him to help heave her into it.

"No, I was fine, except Sandmann did it again, it was three days here, I don't know how long—"

"What do you mean, 'did it again'? Did you find him? Is he—"

"Nathanael, put a cork in it." Magda sighed. "You can tell us about it after you drink your tea, Clara." Clara knew this trick and she didn't care.

"I suppose now isn't a good time to scold you about stealing my key," Nathanael said softly. "A most criminal act, you know, to steal a handwerker's key."

"Does Sandmann know that?" Clara muttered. She sipped the tea Magda brought her slowly, sensing the dolorous thickness of nightdraught underpinning the ordinary bergamot and black tea.

"It seems the lesson didn't stick in his case." Nathanael knelt close to her. "What did you mean, that Sandmann did it again?"

"His favorite trick—trapping people in blighted anderwelt." She lifted her arm, the slash still angry and red. Nathanael went white. "No, it's—it's not—"

"I know what it is," Nathanael whispered. "At least you had my key, I suppose. I forgive your stealing it."

The nightdraught was beginning to have an effect. The walls shimmered and the ceiling felt very close and sleep called to Clara. "No, I didn't. It's in Magda's workshop. I left it in her warded box."

Louise interjected before he could ask any more questions. "Is—is Clara all right? Will she be all right? What key are you talking about? What can I do—was I supposed to bring our apartment key with me?" She asserted herself next to Clara, who found she didn't mind in the least when Louise caught her hand up in hers.

"I'll explain everything," Nathanael promised. He shrugged as Magda protested from the other room. "It's too late to hide anything from her. She's not the first person to get just a little too close to the anderwelt. Who knows, perhaps she's a handwerker in her own right."

"I don't know what any of those words mean, but thank you, I think?" Louise gripped Clara's hand more tightly. The room felt dim and close, but Louise stood out to Clara in a haze of warm light. Her sister. Her sister, whom she loved, who loved her back. Clara smiled, and Louise leaned closer. "I have no idea what's happened to you, but I'll stay right here with you until you're well. Just like when I had the measles and you told me stories about your dolls." Clara felt the nightdraught pulling her deeper, warmer, but the soft comfort of her sister's hand was, she was sure, real, not an effect of the laced tea.

"She'll sleep for quite a while," Nathanael warned. Then, curiosity insistent in his voice, he added, "Clara, if you didn't have my key, how did you get out?"

Clara lifted her right hand, showing him the ring on her finger. "I figured it out. The secret. I understand now."

Nathanael's eyes widened. "You made your key. Incredible," she heard him whisper as her eyes closed, the nightdraught pulling her away. Sandmann, Godfather's key, the Exposition, the Palace of Illusions, everything that had absorbed her for months now faded. There were only two anchors—her sister's hand, firmly in hers, and Nathanael's weight settling on the foot of the bed. What a curious feeling, she thought as sleep ebbed closer and closer, a rising tide against the shores of her consciousness. It was like being a child again, but knowing so much more. Like Christmas Eve parties, Mother's hands still scented with vanilla and sugar from her pure white cake and Father's expansive laugh filling the parlor, full of shining holly and mistletoe and candles. Like falling asleep watching the candles flicker amid the pine-dark boughs of the Christmas tree, like waking up in her own bed next to Louise's in the nursery and knowing it was Christmas morning, deep-seated joy filling her down to her very marrow as first winter's sunlight filtered through the frosted windows.

It was so simple, and yet more complex than any mechanics she had ever designed. She found the word for it floating in the nightdraught—she felt loved.

Chapter Fifty-Four

SHE DREAMED IN broad swaths of the anderwelt, colors and light blending together like watercolors. She dreamed of glass palaces and lakes of swans, of gingerbread trees and snow that fell into drifts of sugar icing across her mother's cakes. She dreamed of her childhood dolls, acting out the stories she and Louise had pulled out of the magic of rainy afternoons. Her unsteady rag doll Miss Trudie came into her bed and tugged on her sleeve, whispering about mice under the floorboards, mice behind the stove.

When she woke up to a bright anderwelt morning, she had no idea if it had been a single night or a week of Sundays. Louise sat nearby, reading one of Nathanael's books.

"Well!" She marked her place carefully and set the book down. "What a set of stories your friends have told me. I never would have believed that Godfather's popcorn trees were real, but that's the least surprising thing I've learned, I'd say."

"How long has it been?" Clara asked, blinking against the unfiltered sunlight streaming through the windows.

"You slept all yesterday and last night. Good thing, too—I had no idea what was wrong with you until Frau Metzger explained it. It does make sense, doesn't it, that exposure like that could cause systemic distress? I'd love to discuss it with Father, but of course—" She shrugged. "How did you manage to keep this a secret?"

"I don't talk as much as you do," Clara replied. "Is there tea?"

"Yes, and you've no idea how glad I am to hear that you want some." Her brow creased. "I was so worried, Clara. So very worried."

"Nathanael," Clara said, sitting bolt upright and regretting it immediately. "Is he all right? Where is—"

"I'm here," Nathanael said, sliding quietly into the room. "Louise, would you get the tea and toast from Magda?"

Louise acquiesced pleasantly and Clara wondered what had transpired in the day and a half since they had tumbled through the anderwelt together to produce such a tranquil domestic dynamic. She glanced down, suddenly well aware that she was only wearing a worn white flannel nightdress—probably Magda's. Blushing, Nathanael handed her his housecoat, a plain dove-gray silk that she accepted gratefully.

"Magda took the liberty of sending Uncle Elias a telegram, simply telling him we are...well, alive." He smiled a thin, bitter line. "Who knows what he thought when he saw we'd disappeared and found his house and garden in ruins."

"What now?"

"Well, to hear your sister tell it, you will rest so you can attend the opening of the Exposition."

Clara groaned. "Oh no—and Fritz must be ready to have my head."

"I sent Louise to deal with Fritz. He believes you have had an attack of migraine."

"But Sandmann?"

"I don't want to say he has us beat," Nathanael said. "But no one has heard from Saint-Luc, and the guilds are recovering their bearings the only way they know how—slowly. At least with your godfather's key he isn't creating any more blights, at least not in that fashion." He glanced at his bandages and then pretended he hadn't.

Anger flared, deep and crimson-tinged. This—this was the best they could do? Accept defeat and hope someone else would deal with Sandmann? "No," Clara said, softly at first and then gathering strength from her resolved anger. "No. I won't accept that. He could get away if we don't act quickly."

"Well," Louise said, setting down a tray laden with tea and generously buttered toast, "you're not doing any acting yet—at least not until I'm quite sure you're not about to keel over again. I've never seen someone actually look gray before, but you managed it."

"Thank you," Clara said, accepting a cup of fragrant tea. "You don't need to fret, I'm already feeling quite well." This was not exactly true, as her head was haunted by the ghost of a migraine and her legs felt like bags of oatmeal when she moved. "So you know everything there is to know about the anderwelt now?"

Louise laughed. "There wasn't much else to do, you know, except to talk. Frau Metzger was staunchly against telling me a word until I'd helped her in the kitchen and let her lecture me on how to make schnitzel—she is very knacky at it, I'll give her that—and once I'd proven myself an attentive pupil, she couldn't be stopped." Louise paused. "I think I may have irritated her into it. You see, I can't stop asking questions, it's all so fascinating. So beautiful."

Louise's gaze drifted toward the open window, where a pair of pure white moths the size of small ducks hovered near a rooftop garden of glass flowers. "I wonder," Clara whispered. "Louise, if you could, would you—would you want to make things here, too?"

Her sister breathed a low sigh. "Oh, yes. It's just like pulling swatches for a dress, or reading the seed catalogs and planning a garden, or mapping out a quilt, except it's not at all like any of those things." She watched the moths wistfully. Their wings reflected all the colors of the glass flowers. "I know Godfather already chose you to be his apprentice, Clara. It's all right. I— he—well. You took to mechanics and clockmaking, and I suppose I can't fault him not seeing that I can make things, too."

"No, Louise, but I should have seen." Clara shoved herself forward on her elbows, nearly upsetting the tea tray. "While I was taking apart clocks, you were making dresses for our dolls. While I was making wind-up toys, you were turning weeds into flower crowns. And when all I could see were gears and cogs, you saw stories and connections and beauty everywhere." She reached for her sister's hand. "Louise, Godfather picked his apprentice already. But I still get to choose one for myself. If you'll accept the apprenticeship, I'm choosing you."

Her sister's eyes widened. "Oh, Clara, I—I feel I shouldn't—"

"Why? Because it's not what Mother would have chosen for us, or it doesn't seem ladylike, or—"

"None of that, no, no—I admit I've worried too much about all of that, growing up." Louise looked away. "I have probably even made you feel that I thought you were foolish or untoward. If I ever did, I'm sorry."

"I think we've both grown quite a bit," Clara said softly. "But if it isn't that, why do you feel you shouldn't?"

"Because what if you want someone else, someday? What if—what if you regret making this decision now, feeling that you must because of all that's happened?" She hesitated. "What if you have…a child? Or run across someone else, I don't know," she hastened to add.

"Oh, for the love of—" Magda's exasperated voice preceded her as she flew into the room, a silver-haired tempest. "Why don't I take Louise as my apprentice? I've never had one, and the chances of finding another suitable pupil at my age are getting slim."

"Magda! Have you been listening this whole time?"

"I certainly have," she replied. "It's about time you two dunderheads said the things you needed to say to each other."

They were interrupted by a businesslike knock at the door. Clara straightened, heart accelerating. She wasn't even dressed, let alone ready to tangle with Sandmann again.

"Stay here," Nathanael warned.

"Don't fret," Magda said, a nervous edge to her voice. "If Sandmann wanted to show up, he wouldn't go through the niceties of knocking on the door."

"That, Frau Metzger, is very true." Andrès Saint-Luc strode into the apartment. "I am sorry to intrude—"

"Oh, thank God!" Clara almost jumped out of bed before remembering she was still wearing Magda's frowsy nightdress and a man's housecoat. "We were very concerned when you didn't meet us."

A wry smile played on Saint-Luc's face. "I was delayed, you see. By a Monsieur Lavallé, who it appears is high enough in the pecking order of the Exposition that he has the police in his pocket."

"He didn't!" Clara exclaimed.

"He most certainly did. I was accused of trespassing in—you

will enjoy this, mademoiselle—the Palace of Illusions. He claimed I must have been trying to steal proprietary secrets of its design."

Despite herself, Clara laughed, then groaned. "He didn't actually manage to get you thrown in jail?"

"Again, Miss Ironwood, he most certainly did. I have never wished more that I didn't care about discretion, or I would have used my key quite quickly. If you think Paris a modern city, don't disabuse yourself of the notion by visiting her jails." He sniffed. "They finally decided they had nothing to hold me on, but of course I had already missed our appointment."

"How did Sandmann know?"

"I am sure he did not know about our plans, precisely, but he is quite aware of who I am and that I pose some threat." He paused. "None of that particularly matters now. I want to stop him."

"And how are you planning that?" Magda crossed her arms.

"I have the full support of the guilds to use whatever means necessary," Saint-Luc replied firmly. "And I will, short of damaging the anderwelt."

"I have an idea," Clara said, surveying the map of the Exposition in her mind, seeing all the puzzle pieces coming together. All of Sandmann's anderwelt additions, all of the marvelous promises of the Exposition, all of the millions of hours worked and millions of visitors expected—everything hinged on an opening only a week away. "Fritz is not going to like it."

Chapter Fifty-Five

"I WISH YOU could stay with me the whole time," Clara said. She was dressed for the Exposition opening, in the deep indigo evening gown that Louise had insisted on—Louise, who was right about everything when it came to fabrics and colors. Her sister had also fixed her hair, so the woman staring back in reflection was more sophisticated than Clara felt. She looked so mature, so worldly—though Clara had argued to Godfather that she was no longer a child, she didn't feel she was the urbane woman looking back at her, either.

Nathanael pulled her onto the settee next to him. He looked better than he had even a few days ago, the color coming back to his cheeks. "I do, as well. To be seen in the company of the toast of Paris, if nothing else."

Clara flushed. "Hardly—Louise and Annabelle look far better than I do." They had better hair, she appraised. And knew how to get away with a little bit of carmine.

"They didn't design the Palace of Illusions." Nathanael smoothed the deep blue skirt of her gown spilling over his knees. "But I have to stay back and direct my little part of this endeavor, which is all the better because I don't much want to retailor my suit jacket sleeve yet." Clara winced—she wasn't yet ready for jokes at Nathanael's hand's expense, but he seemed to cope by cracking them.

"Between the two of us," she suggested, "we could design a prosthetic so realistic no one would notice. Or a clockwork one that—"

Nathanael grew quiet. "I don't think I'm ready for that quite yet. I have to—well, I have to get to know myself, I suppose, having changed. Having lost something." He paused. "Before, when I was trapped in the blighted anderwelt, I changed, I lost something. There are no outward signs of it, but I did. It's almost, well, a comfort, in a way, to match on the outside how I feel."

"I didn't realize," Clara whispered. "I supposed I have a mind to fix things—"

"That can't be fixed the way Olympia could be," Nathanael said with a smile. "There are other ways of healing, you know, that don't involve your pliers and tweezers and wrenches." Clara couldn't have put it to words, but she understood. She leaned toward him and kissed him on the corner of his mouth.

"You should get up before you wrinkle your gown," Nathanael teased.

"I don't much care if I wrinkle my gown," she replied.

"I do," Louise called from the bedroom. "Don't make me come out there and play gooseberry."

"We should leave soon anyway." Clara fussed with the ring on her finger. While she had rested, she had refined it a bit, but found it stubbornly clung to the shape she had fashioned originally. The key couldn't be broken, but it also couldn't be altered. Too bad, Clara thought—she had a thousand better ideas now that she knew how it worked.

But that was the magic of the anderwelt, she reasoned—it would hold enshrined forever one of her ugliest efforts as her crowning achievement.

"You called for a hansom?" Louise said, emerging from the bedroom, a vision of pink moiré silk. "I know this is all quite serious, Clara, but am I allowed to be a little bit excited, too? Your dress! My dress!"

Despite herself, Clara laughed. "Yes, I think it's impossible not to be a little bit excited about the opening of the grandest fair the world has ever seen."

The opening of the Exposition was attracting all Paris society, and the streets were thick with coaches and hansoms, the trams packed with everyone who had not been invited but wanted to be near the grand opening and glimpse what they could of the fairy electricity gracing the city.

As arranged, Fritz met them where the carriages dropped their silk- and velvet-clad cargo. The main entrance gate loomed over them, a transplant from a fairyland of arches and domes and dazzling with lights. Clara couldn't help but take in the entire fairgrounds, alight and buzzing with life for the first time.

"Are you quite sure about this?" Fritz whispered as he took her arm. "I have no idea how you cleared the idea, but—"

"I told you, I can't tell you *all* my secrets." Clara smiled coyly, her best effort at lighthearted teasing dropping flat and empty into the weight of what she had to do. "Louise, how in the world are you going to keep that gown from getting absolutely filthy?"

"Magic, I suppose," Louise answered, scowling at the dust already accumulating on the sidewalks. Fritz led them toward the Palace of Illusions—a strange place for the debut Clara had proposed, of course, but she had her reasons.

Louise gave Clara's hand a final squeeze as they passed the Palace of Optics entrance and moved toward the Palace of Illusions. "I'll be waiting," Louise whispered. Clara forced a smile as her sister peeled away. The crowd had already gathered in the palace, the few dozen allowed in at once multiplied into a legion in the mirrors' reflection. Clara allowed herself to take in the scene, the wonder—she had spent months creating this place and now it was unveiled. A woman pointed and gasped at the infinite repetitions of herself in the mirrors. This was what she had wanted to make, a spark of magic in the ordinary world. Whatever else happened tonight, she had succeeded in that.

"Just look at it," Fritz said. "We've really done it, haven't we?"

"We?" Clara retorted.

Fritz laughed and clapped her on the shoulder. "Mostly you, I'll confess. All right, it's time. I'll make the announcements." His deft French pierced the swelling noise in the palace and the crowd quieted. Clara slipped unnoticed toward the makeshift stage at the center of the hall.

Olympia stood in a delicate pose at the center of the palace, reflected into a corps de ballet made of one dancer. Of course, it wasn't really Olympia—Annabelle had procured a dark wig and managed to apply her stage makeup to mimic the doll-like red and white of Olympia's face under Clara's direction, and Louise had managed a near-perfect copy of the shepherdess costume. But Olympia was what they had advertised—a mechanical ballerina, fulfilling rumors from weeks ago that one had been seen by schoolchildren in the Jardin des Tuileries. Exactly the sort of thing the spectators of the Exposition expected.

And precisely the kind of temptation she hoped would draw Sandmann to them.

"You look brilliant," Clara whispered to her false Olympia. Annabelle, committed to the part she'd been hired to play, didn't move a muscle. The costume included a false key, the final touch in turning a flesh-and-blood dancer into an automaton ballerina. Clara turned the key with an exaggerated flourish. At the same time, Fritz tuned the Graphophone specially purchased for the exhibit, letting the tinny reproduction stand in for an orchestra just as a mechanical doll stood in for a dancer. Louise had identified Olympia's variation from *Coppélia*, and a recording had been found at the last minute by Saint-Luc, who surprised no one in being an astute music aficionado.

The novelty of an automaton's perfect articulation, maneuvering through precise motions, lines executed with more technical mastery than artistic expression, the lightness of her steps and the blankness of her expression—they watched, mesmerized. Olympia as soloist was reflected in the mirrors by Olympia the corps de ballet, all in perfect synchronicity.

Annabelle was a perfect foil, Clara thought with a tentative smile. She played the part of automaton perfectly, yet never losing the artistry of the dance that would convince even Sandmann, at a distance, that his creation had been somehow transported without his knowledge or consent to Clara's Palace of Illusions. The gambit had to work—that Sandmann would, enraged by lack of either accolades or compensation for his creation, show himself. In addition, Clara had let a tempting rumor slip that several firms wished to hire the man who had created such a masterful example of machinery. With the Exposition open, his arrangement with Lavallé had to end, and Clara gambled on his avarice driving him toward new schemes.

Praise, money, offers of employment—all the kinds of things

Sandmann seemed loath to resist—were dangled like a lure. Any uncertainty Clara had about Annabelle's ability to reproduce the dance faded as she watched her friend's precise movements.

The audience watched in mesmerized silence. From the edges of the palace, dozens of pairs of black eyes winked in the lights—mice, Nathanael's eyes and ears.

Annabelle finished her dance in Olympia's abrupt manner, having been convinced that this breach of artistry would complete the ruse, but the audience barely took note that the variation was abbreviated. They burst into applause. And then, the coup de grâce. Clara took a deep breath. This was the greatest risk in her plan, the part that bordered the closest to breaking the rules of the craftsmen.

Clara stepped next to Annabelle, who took her bow, concluding her performance as Olympia. Underneath the stage was a trapdoor, and she found the foot lever that she and Annabelle had practiced using a dozen times. When pressed, the lever opened the trapdoor but also pivoted a pair of mirrors to perfectly hide the dancer's drop. As Annabelle raised her hand in graceful salute to her audience, Clara tripped the lever, and the mechanical ballerina, to the amazement of the audience, disappeared.

At the same moment, Clara slipped her ring on her finger and winked out of sight.

She reemerged in the anderwelt Palace of Illusions, the mirrors shimmering with variant light and the real Olympia waiting for her. On the other side, the audience was surely erupting into speculation on how the trick had been effected. Was it the mirrors, they would be debating, or a trapdoor? A manipulation of the light? Some clever ones might guess at a new application of actualités—that they had been watching a film all along.

No one, she was quite sure, would assume that they had witnessed an actual display of not only mechanical skill but real magic.

Olympia broke into a bright smile when Clara appeared. "How was it? Did your dancer friend do well? I so would have liked to see it—it's a strange thing, to be a dancer who has never seen anyone else dance!"

"She was marvelous," Clara said. "But please—you're supposed to pretend to be a dead thing, remember?"

Olympia nodded sagely and folded her prim hands over her pert white apron.

They didn't have long to wait. Sandmann appeared in the maze of mirrors, his key in his hand. She maintained her poise. Olympia stood mute and motionless, her waxen expression frozen in place.

"Very unusual." Sandmann stood in the maze of mirrors. "I'm surprised at you, really. I thought your ethics barred you from such use of anderwelt creations. Especially given you must have created a blight in order to move Olympia over."

"My employer required an automaton after the debut of your other pieces at the dinner, and I wanted to keep my job. Did you enjoy the performance?"

"I've seen it many times," he replied dryly. "The addition of the mirrors was a pleasant alteration. However, I'm a bit confused. I had expected tricks, of course, but a disappearing act seems out of character."

"You're the one who didn't finish Olympia's choreography."

He waved her away with a disgusted hand. "I got bored of the whole thing. She was the last one, you know, before Elias put an end to the experiments. What was the point in continuing with her?"

Behind Sandmann, vines had begun to creep along the floor. They slid from the corners, spreading and reaching farther with every moment, a summer's worth of growth spurred on all at once. Leaves unfurled, buds swelled. Sandmann hadn't noticed.

"All right," Clara said. "I suppose you want to discuss business."

"I would. I confess, if you're going to make such a simple gambit as trading Olympia for the key, it was a foolish play. I don't particularly care about the dancer." Clara winced—Olympia might have been pretending to be a lifeless mannequin, but she could certainly hear. Not only had Sandmann abandoned her, he was uninterested in her now. Still, a consummate professional, Olympia didn't even twitch.

What an ugly, ugly louse of a human, Clara thought to herself. No matter—the vines were growing closer. Let him keep talking if it kept him distracted. Let him, even, believe he had won.

Clara heaved a sigh. "Then why did you come?"

"Curiosity." He laughed—a terribly unpleasant sound. "It did kill the cat, didn't it? And I confess, I didn't like the idea of anyone else getting credit for Olympia."

The vines stretched and unfurled new tendrils; Clara saw them twining and blooming in reflection. Midsummer orange and velvety purple blossoms scattered petals on the floor, and a strange perfume began to waft through the space. Surely, Clara thought, Sandmann couldn't fail to notice them forever.

She amplified her performance, crossing her arms in a huff. "Well, I'm afraid we're at an impasse, then."

"Why?" Sandmann laughed again. "Nothing is stopping me from going to the Exposition Board myself. I have my own connections, much higher up the chain than yours. I can easily prove I created Olympia. I don't have to go through you."

Clara feigned shock. "But I'm the one who made this possible."

"You've been nothing but a bother," Sandmann said, tone turning sour. "But this?" He produced Thrushman's key. Clara tried not to hold her breath. "This is mine now, and so is Olympia."

"Why would you do this to your own friend?" Clara said. Sandmann started. He hadn't expected this turn of questioning, Clara guessed. "He was your friend, wasn't he? My godfather. And yet you stole his key and blighted his home in the anderwelt."

Sandmann paused. "He was, yes. I do feel bad about how it all ended, you know, but he didn't want to continue our work. I couldn't convince him of the necessity and—"

The vines leapt into movement. Thick ropes of trumpet vine and clematis threw themselves around Sandmann and tightened their loops, trapping him. Brilliant orange and purple flowers covered the botanical prison Sandmann found himself bound in. Beside her, Olympia's poise broke, and she clasped her hands to her face and gasped.

They weren't finished yet. A squadron of mice swarmed Sandmann, plucking the key from his startled fingers and scurrying away to the spaces under the baseboards, within the walls, where they traveled past the veil.

"Well done, Louise!" Clara called.

"That clematis and trumpet vine deserve most of the credit—now let me pull him back."

The vines, still enveloping Sandmann, retreated out of the Palace of Illusions into the labyrinth that, on the other side, was a vacant back hallway. Louise panted with the effort of controlling the vines, which now wanted to grow wilder and larger.

"Truly well done," Clara said again. "Can you manage the next bit?"

"Yes, certainly." Louise took a steadying breath while Clara kept her eyes firmly on Sandmann. The vines retreated in one swift motion, tangling themselves on the floor. Clara didn't wait to see what Louise did with her botanical creation, trusting her sister's knack with gardening and Magda's assiduous training over the past week to keep the vines well in hand. Instead, she grabbed Sandmann by the collar and slipped on her ring.

The anderwelt turned inside out and she emerged to the riotous noise of the Palace of Illusions on the other side of a thin wall, surrounded by Magda, Saint-Luc, and several others she didn't know. She let go of Sandmann as though dropping a venomous snake, leaving him to scramble to his feet, his face reddening with embarrassment.

Louise popped into the hall a moment later. "Thank you for letting me use your key," she said, handing Magda the slim silver needle.

"You'll have to work on your own soon enough," Magda said, gruff but smiling. "She's as knacky as Elias with botanicals, don't you think? She's gotten better with plants in less than a week than I am. Awfully talented, the little minx."

"She is indeed," Clara replied. "Now what do we do with him?"

Saint-Luc laid a hand on her shoulder. "You'll do nothing at all," he said. "The guild leadership will handle everything from here. You've done quite enough," he added, not entirely unkindly but with a stern shake of his head.

"Are you really going to criticize the method, if it delivered the result?" Magda snorted.

"Yes, I am." Saint-Luc fixed his eyes on Clara. "An entire room full of people were just given a glimpse of the anderwelt. That's entirely unprecedented and a forbidden action."

"They didn't know what they were seeing," protested Magda.

"The only reason I am not pursuing censure is the fact that it was carefully orchestrated to avoid anyone knowing what they were seeing," Saint-Luc replied. "I recognize the unusual circumstances, and that you were not properly trained in our rules, but you can see, Miss Ironwood, the precarious nature of the anderwelt. Treading heavily upon it bruises it, you understand?"

Magda began to argue on her behalf, but Clara stopped her. "I understand. Godfather trained me my whole life to understand the anderwelt, even if I am only realizing it now."

"Good." Saint-Luc turned his eyes toward Sandmann, who had been placed in very pedestrian handcuffs and had his key confiscated by nameless members of Saint-Luc's Sacré-Coeur guild. "Now, this fellow has no such excuses," Saint-Luc said crisply. *"Au revoir, mesdames et messieurs.* Enjoy the Exposition."

With that, the guild officials left Clara, Louise, and Magda alone in a back hallway of the Palace of Illusions on opening night of the Exposition Universelle.

Chapter Fifty-Six

WHILE LOUISE AND Magda waited, Clara found Fritz and Annabelle in the pandemonium of the Palace of Illusions. Annabelle had scrubbed the stage makeup from her cheeks and changed into a gown of purple silk that shimmered under the electric lights. "You'll have to answer to someone for this," Fritz whispered. "I'm afraid I can't cover any longer—first there are rumors of automatons, then there are none, then we have them, then we don't—"

"Give me a month and I'll make you automatons that dance, sing, or spin plates, for whatever display you want them," Clara replied. "They won't be quite as good as Olympia, though." Clara winked at Annabelle, who curtsied genteelly.

Fritz suppressed a laugh. "I don't suppose you want to explain."

"I'm afraid I can't," Clara said, sobering. "Please don't ask, Fritz—you're closer than anyone has any right to be already. But consider it this way—this was a bit of family business that I have now cleared up, and I will not be dragging it into my work any longer."

"Work—who wants to think of work on a night like this?" Fritz offered his arm to Annabelle. "We have a reception to attend, and there will be champagne and cheese that smells awful and cake. At least, I hope there will be cake."

"I was given to understand that there would be cake," Annabelle agreed.

"Can I impose on you to wait for me for one more moment? I'll be quick." Clara excused herself to the back hallway, finding a secluded corner and slipping back to the quiet of the anderwelt.

Nathanael waited in the silent labyrinth with Olympia. The vines still lay in a tangle on the floor, purple and orange blossoms scattered where Sandmann had thrashed in his struggle.

Olympia wrung her hands. "I do feel awful, you know. He was my maker, you see. I had no idea, no idea at all."

"You couldn't have known," Nathanael said, reassuring.

"And we're not the people who make us," Clara added. "You're not him or his mistakes—you are yourself."

Olympia smiled. "Thank you for that. I am glad I could help, even if all I had to do was stand there. How funny! Sandmann made me to dance, but to be of any use tonight, I had to be perfectly still." She smoothed her skirts and adjusted her hat. "Now then. It's a nice long way to the Christmas Wood, and the perfect evening for a walk."

"I'll take you, if you like," Nathanael offered, but Olympia waved him off.

"No, no, you have more important things to attend to, and besides, I shall enjoy exploring at my leisure. Do come visit soon!"

"We will," Clara promised. "And thank you again—you were brilliant." Olympia curtsied one more time and skipped away.

"And now. You have a bevy of admirers to appear before, I'm sure." Nathanael brushed an errant strand of hair out of Clara's face. "Receptions and a grand ball, if I understand correctly?"

"I am, I'm afraid, required to attend all sorts of silly functions." She caught his hand. "You're coming with me, yes?"

Nathanael laughed. "I look like a clockmaker, grease stains and all," he replied, gesturing to a pair of stained trousers.

"Your excuses can't stand up to my sister's forethought," Clara said. She pulled a black tailcoat ensemble from behind a mirror. "Very sorry, but you're not exempt. Fritz is quite sure it's the right size—or close enough."

"You're not sorry at all!" He began unbuttoning his creased shirt. "Are you going to watch?"

Clara flushed and retreated. "We can return Godfather's key to him soon," she said. "I've half a mind to ship it back in that ugly little nutcracker."

"You don't want to keep the nutcracker as a souvenir?"

"I considered it. But I'll be moving soon enough anyway—I don't need a lot of bric-a-brac that I'll only have to pack up."

"You won't be staying in Paris?" Nathanael's reflection emerged before he did, looking shy and uncertain in his formal wear. "I had—well, I'd had a few stray hopes, I suppose…"

"I'm accepting a job with the Lumière brothers, working under Fritz." She turned her face toward the nearest mirror, fussing with her hair and her necklace. "Louise is staying, too, to keep up with her apprenticeship under Magda, and I cannot keep sharing a bedroom with her, so we're on the hunt for a larger place. But you—you're staying in Paris?"

"I hadn't entirely decided," he admitted. "I could return to Nuremberg, or I could find work here…"

"How do you feel about cameras?" Clara suggested.

"I know very little about them, but the concept is quite fascinating."

Clara smiled. "Fritz wants to find at least one more mechanically minded person to bring onto the Lumières' project. Do you have any recommendations?"

"I do, indeed. He's handy with a wrench, knows the inner workings of a clock fairly well. Imperfect work with timing mechanisms, but he does all right." Nathanael caught her around the waist. "And he works very well with others."

"He works well enough with me, at any rate." Clara leaned toward him and let him find her in a kiss.

They returned to the Paris Exposition hand in hand, emerging in the nondescript back hallway where Louise and Magda still waited.

"Took you long enough." Magda sighed.

"They've barely been gone," Louise countered.

"I know how long things should take in the anderwelt and how long those two tarried." Magda grinned.

"Magda!" Louise covered her laugh with a gloved hand. "You're incorrigible."

"Another new word from this one! I learn something from her every day, you know. As much as she learns from me."

"Annabelle and Fritz are waiting," Clara reminded them.

Magda shrugged. "Not for me. I've no interest in parties or dances or whatever nonsense you've got cooked up here."

"Now, Magda, just for a moment—you really ought to see the fairy." Louise caught the old woman's hand, who relented with little resistance.

"Fairy?"

Louise laughed. *"La fée électrique!"* Magda raised her eyebrow but followed dutifully, just in time to see the lights as they came to life all across the Exposition grounds.

"It's beautiful," Louise said with a sigh. "And I finally have something I can write to Mother about!"

"And a lovely letter I'm sure it will be." They all knew the voice, familiar but entirely out of place. Louise halted mid-step, Magda blanched, and Nathanael caught Clara's hand, all of them registering, as Clara did, who had spoken. Silhouetted in the dancing lights of the Palace of Illusions was none other than Godfather. "It is good to see you," he said. Falteringly, with an almost boyish flush at seeing Magda, he added, "All of you."

Louise was the first to regain her composure. "Godfather! I had no idea you were coming! How long have you been in Paris?"

"Only just arrived today. You will forgive that I've barely had a moment to freshen up."

Louise kissed him on the cheek in a solemn culmination of her absurdly ordinary greeting, given the circumstances. Then she whispered in his ear, so low Clara could hardly hear. "By the way, I know everything, and I've been to the anderwelt, and I'm Frau Metzger's apprentice now."

Godfather blinked twice, slowly, and Clara nearly laughed aloud seeing his confusion slowly build. "You are—have been to the—and you mean to say—Magda Metzger took an apprentice?"

"Now then, Elias, keep your opinions to yourself!" Magda crossed her arms. "The girl's got real talent. Shame's on you for not noticing, you old duffer. She's brilliant with plants, like nothing I've seen before."

Godfather blinked again. "What a fool I've been, my dear Louise. Of course—you bring such beauty into the ordinary world, I should have seen that the anderwelt called you, too."

Louise blushed. "Thank you, Godfather. But you ought to see what Clara can do!"

"I'm sure I shall. But first—" He turned to Nathanael. "Thank you, for looking out for her. For both of them, as it turns out. I—I see I have missed quite a lot." He glanced at the empty sleeve and winced.

"You ought to thank Clara. I did very little, in comparison, in catching Sandmann."

Godfather's enigmatic smile suggested he was not entirely surprised by this. "And I am sure I shall hear all of the curious story soon enough. But for now—the fair is open and the lights are shining. What a waste to spend time discussing unpleasant things!"

"And we mustn't forget Annabelle and Fritz!" Louise added.

"Or certain receptions that certain very important Exposition employees must make appearances at," Nathanael reminded Clara.

"Of course, of course—Godfather, I—" She smiled. "I wanted to show you one thing, first." She produced the ring from her pocket and offered it to him. Everything she had ever made had been dissected under his scrutinizing eye, and yet she didn't feel shy or nervous any longer. No, she was proud of the twisted bit of metal and paper and thread bound up into a key.

"Why, you did it already," Godfather said quietly. "It's lovely, Clara. Truly lovely."

"About time you said something like that," Magda muttered.

"Ah, Frau Metzger. As the others are all otherwise engaged this evening, may I make so bold as to offer you a stroll around the Exposition? We've a great deal to catch up on. A very great deal indeed."

Magda sputtered, then flushed, then cursed in German, and Clara knew that she had already forgiven Elias almost everything.

"It's beautiful," Clara said as Fritz and Annabelle joined them, picking their way across the crowded Champ-de-Mars to where all of them gathered under the lights of the Tour d'Eiffel. "It's all more magnificent than I could have imagined."

"I'm not entirely sure that's true," Nathanael said, "having gotten a glimpse of your imagination."

"If you've the right sort of eyes for it, this place seems as full of magic as any otherworld," Godfather said, offering his arm to Magda, who didn't even bother with the pretense of refusing.

Clara caught Nathanael's hand in hers, leaning into his shoulder as the fairgrounds bloomed, teeming with a thousand colors and echoing with voices in a dozen languages. Music drifted on currents of conversation. The Seine threw back the lights of each of the palaces in a rippling dance. In one brilliant, breathless moment, Clara saw the otherworld mingled with her own, boundless potential and fathomless imagination brought to glittering life from the dust and trammel of the ordinary. And though she had helped to make it, one puzzle after another solved, one knot after another untangled, those successes quickly paled as she heard her sister laugh, saw Annabelle's eyes widen with wonder, and felt Nathanael's hand press tightly into hers. Her Palace of Illusions—all the grand rolling expanse of the Exposition—found meaning at last, here, surrounded by those she loved.

Paris was beautiful, Clara decided as she entered the human current flowing into the fair arm in arm with her friends. It was all beautiful.

Acknowledgments

I suppose I should thank, first, E. T. A. Hoffmann and Pyotr Ilyich Tchaikovsky (even though neither is likely to read this), whose visions of the nutcracker tale sparked my imagination and shaped what this book became. I have always loved the story of the nutcracker, both Hoffmann's eccentric novella and Tchaikovsky's iconic ballet—and a good thing, too: as the parent of young dancers, I see and hear it quite frequently. In fact, in addition to being inspired by the lush, imaginative ballet and the stranger, darker, ultimately profoundly beautiful short story, much of this book was written while strains of "Dance of the Sugar Plum Fairy" and "Waltz of the Flowers" wafted through the dance studio lobby where I had camped out with my laptop.

After inspiration, of course, comes work. And books are the work of many talented people, and I appreciate all of them.

First, my agent, Jessica Sinsheimer—your enthusiasm and support are deeply appreciated! Nivia Evans, thank you for your vision for this story, and Alyea Canada, you have been an incredible and insightful editor—thank you! Thank you to managing editor Bryn A. McDonald and your staff—I don't see most of your work, but I know it's there! Thank you to my copy editor, Kelly Frodel, your attention to detail was utterly brilliant! Lauren Panepinto and Lisa Marie Pompilio, the cover is beautiful! Everyone at Orbit has always been a delight to work with—thank you all!

All my writer friends—you are too many to list, but whether I find you in the coffee shop, my email, or the bunker, thanks for a never-failing supply of encouragement, advice, extra eyes on tricky pages, and reality checks.

Thank you to my husband, for planning a trip to Paris with no idea it was research (to be fair, I didn't know then, either), and for all your support, patience, and love. Thank you to my parents for letting me be a weird little kid who made up stories. And thank you to my own daughters, who have given and continue to give me the opportunity to look at the nutcracker story, Paris, and a host of other things with their own particular wise wonder. In other words, the right sort of eyes to see the right sort of things.

Meet the Author

Emily R. Allison

ROWENNA MILLER lives in the Midwest with her husband and daughters, as well as several cats, two goats, and an ever-growing flock of chickens. When she isn't inventing fantasy worlds, she teaches writing, trespasses while hiking, and gets into trouble with her sewing machine.

if you enjoyed
THE PALACE OF ILLUSIONS
look out for

THE FAIRY BARGAINS OF PROSPECT HILL

by

Rowenna Miller

In the early 1900s, two sisters must navigate the magic and the dangers of the Fae in this enchanting and cozy historical fantasy about sisterhood and self-discovery.

There is no magic on Prospect Hill—or anywhere else, for that matter. But just on the other side of the veil is the world of the Fae. Generations ago, the first farmers learned to bargain small trades to make their lives a little easier—a bit of glass to find something lost, a cup of milk for better layers in the chicken coop.

Much of that old wisdom was lost as the riverboats gave way to the rail lines and the farmers took work at mills and factories. Alaine Fairborn's family, however, was always superstitious, and she still hums the rhymes to ensure dry weather on her sister's wedding day.

When Delphine confides that her new husband is not the man she thought he was, Alaine will stop at nothing to help her sister escape him. Small bargains buy them time, but the price for true freedom may be more than they're willing to pay.

1

Where flowers bloom unfading
And leaves are ever green
Fortune's winds are shifting
By fairy touch unseen

—Folk song

WHEN THE MADISON Railroad laid the tracks at the base of Prospect Hill, there were no roads cleaving the thickly forested slopes and no houses overlooking the distant river. A few farmsteads were nestled into the beech woods on the other side of the crest, out of view of the rail workers driving spikes through oak ties into untouched clay. Horatio Canner was one of those rail workers, and when he looked up into the tapestry of boughs, he thought it was the most beautiful place he'd ever seen.

He took his lunch breaks at the edge of the clearing for the railway, shorn saplings and ragged trunks of great oaks and walnuts crowding the space where sunlight ended and the shade of the forest began. Horatio sat on a walnut stump, feeling a bit like a trespasser. And then he heard a soft rustle and saw a shimmer of light in the shadows of the branches.

A girl. Not a girl, exactly, he amended, as he stood hastily and swept his hat off his close-cropped hair. A young woman, hovering on the edge of adolescence, eyes wide and thin lips parted to speak. Instead she turned and slipped between the trunks. After a moment's hesitation, he followed. It seemed almost as though she led him on purpose, slowing when he lost the pale form of her white dress through the trees, hastening again when he came too close, until she stopped beneath a linden tree in full blossom.

Horatio Canner was not a country boy, or he might have paused to wonder why a linden tree was blooming in the first fits of spring warmth. He had been born out east, and had never pressed into the thick forests and still-wild places beyond the mountain ranges until he took work with the railroads. He could be forgiven, then, too, for assuming that the plain white dress the girl had on was what country folk wore, so unlike any fashion he'd seen back home or in the outlying towns along the river as the steamboat chugged past. Horatio Canner didn't consider any of these things as the girl met his eyes, held out her hand, and finally spoke.

"What do you offer, and what do you ask?"

Horatio blinked. "I reckon I—that is, I don't quite know what you mean," he said.

She cocked her head. Her neck was as slender as a swan's, Horatio thought, and the plain dress skimmed a figure that could have been one of the saplings circling the tree. "You followed me to the gate, but you don't mean to ask for anything? Well." Her smile was sharp and tight. "Perhaps, still, you've something to offer, and I could tell you what it's worth."

Horatio still didn't understand, but he dug into his pockets anyway. "I've got a bag of tobacco, and the pipe for it," he began, and she winced and pulled away. It stood to figure a young lady wouldn't be interested in smoking, he chided himself. "And this kerchief." He dug out the red printed cotton and held it out.

Her eyes shone. "You'd part with it, then?"

"I suppose." He took a step closer, but she held up a hand.

"It's dear enough," she murmured, eyes still on it. "A true red." She scanned him up and down, and he felt read for the simple man he was. "If you could ask for anything, what would you want?"

"A parcel of Prospect Hill, I suppose," he said with a laugh. "Fifty acres. I've the will to tend it."

She plucked the kerchief from his hand. In her pale fingers it looked somehow more real, more solid. "A most unorthodox transaction," she said, amused. "But as you will."

The girl stepped into the tree and disappeared, leaving Horatio Canner gaping at nothing.

"And that is how Orchard Crest came into our family," Papa Horatio finished with a flourish, tipping back his coupe of sparkling wine made with the grapes from the north slope.

"I didn't realize I was marrying into a fairy-favored family until we'd said the vows," Jack Fairborn said with a wink at his wife.

"You ought to have guessed," Alaine replied, playfully swatting his arm. "After all, how do you think you managed to end up on my dance card for the waltz every ball of the season the year we got engaged?"

Alaine Fairborn had heard the story of her grandfather's encounter with the Fae a hundred times if she'd heard it once. He'd never seen the pale woman again, and no one else in the family had ever seen one of the Fae. Still, the fairy-woman kept her end of the bargain. Within two months, he bought a farmstead at the crest of Prospect Hill for a song, the seller shaving fifty acres off a sprawling tract of land to pay off a gambling debt. It was a stroke of luck of a magnitude Horatio had never had before and hadn't had since.

The other story she'd heard a hundred times if once was how a disoriented Horatio, wandering away from the blooming linden tree between the Fae and human worlds, had stumbled upon the Riley family farmstead and met a plump, tanned, very human girl feeding a flock of ruddy chickens. Gran had always laughed at this when she told her side of the story, that she knew that her husband had perfection on his mind from that Fae woman and she could never live up to it. And then Papa Horatio would flush red and protest that Lilabeth was the loveliest woman in the world, in any world, and that he'd never been happier than their wedding day.

"That's enough, Papa," Alaine's mother said with a sigh, swiping his glass before he could refill it. "You have to leave us a few bottles for the wedding. I've been wearing my fingers to the bone for two weeks, getting the garden ready. I won't have a last-minute wine shortage to account for, too."

"Having it in the garden—I never heard of such a thing. Me and Lilabeth got married in the church, proper," Papa Horatio said with a sly twinkle in his eyes. "And so did you and my son, Iris. And now my granddaughter gets married in the garden?"

"It's fashionable to be married at home!" Delphine protested. "Besides, is there anyplace in the world I love better than Orchard Crest?"

"Hardly," Papa Horatio said. "But it doesn't rain inside the church."

"It won't rain," Del replied. "Alaine will see to that."

"She paid the best attention to Lilabeth," he agreed. "Still, no guarantee like a roof over your head."

"When will the Graftons be here on Saturday?" Mother asked for the fifteenth time.

"At eight o'clock in the morning," Delphine replied. "And the ladies in the wedding party can get ready in my room, and the fellows in the study."

"Is Emily allowed in with you?" Alaine asked. "She's talked of nothing but her flower girl dress since last week."

"Of course!" Delphine said, a genuine smile breaking the tension in her jaw. "She's my best niece."

"Only niece," Mother corrected.

"So she's clearly the best." Delphine grinned. "The judge will be here at ten so we can begin by eleven. And then luncheon at noon."

"Judge!" Papa Horatio shook his head. "The Graftons have some pull, getting the damn judge to officiate."

"You might forget that we have some pull now, too, Papa." Mother stood, her silk taffeta skirt rustling as though punctuating her point.

"*Some* pull," he said. "Hardly Grafton pull. Oh, Alaine, I keep getting mail delivered up here for the farm—something came from the bank." He rifled in his jacket pocket and produced a rumpled envelope.

"The bank!" Mother chided. "That's hardly after-dinner talk."

"Is this the Waldorf-Astoria? Are we at a formal dinner party? Have we had the sorbet course already? Here I thought I was in my own dining room, Iris." Papa Horatio laughed. "I'm sure it's nothing to worry over, but—"

"But I'll worry about it if it is," Alaine said, taking the papers. She traced the sealed envelope fretfully. Probably another notice. "We should go soon." Alaine laid a hand on Jack's in a silent signal. No letting Papa Horatio draw them into one more story, no letting Mother finagle Jack into looking at a leaky pipe in the kitchen. His glance went from her hand to the envelope in her lap. He gave her a barely perceptible nod, understanding. "It's almost past Em's bedtime as it is."

"Is she still out in the garden?" Delphine turned to look out the bay window, lithe neck encased in a high collar of lace. Alaine could have been jealous of her sister's fashionable gown and the filmy white lace if it hadn't looked so mercilessly scratchy at the seams. She smoothed her own practical wool skirt, the plum color hiding several jam stains.

"She would spend the night there if we let her," Alaine said. "But not tonight."

"Not any night!" Mother said, appalled until she realized that Alaine was joking—at least, mostly. Mother had always reined in Alaine's penchant for the woods and wilds, trying to teach her flower arranging and piano and, one disastrous summer, water-colors. Alaine took the opposite tack with Em, indulging her pref-erence for an open afternoon of exploring the forest, tattered hems and muddy shoes notwithstanding.

Alaine followed Delphine's gaze out the window. Emily was hanging upside down from the low-hanging branches of a crab apple. Delphine fought back a grin. "I'll call her in."

Alaine watched her sister go with an odd tightness in her throat—even crossing the family dining room of Orchard Crest, where they'd eaten thousands of breakfasts and dinners, played thousands of games of checkers in the hollow of the bay window, spent thousands of afternoons reading in its long swaths of sun-light, Del was graceful. Alaine's little sister wasn't just grown up— she was an accomplished lady who had mastered all the genteel arts their mother had tried to impart on them. Flower arranging, piano, and especially watercolors. Alaine had long ago stopped begrudging her that.

Delphine brought Emily in by the hand, the six-year-old's face beaming with admiration for her aunt. She had once told Alaine that Aunt Del must be a princess. Alaine had very little argument to the contrary.

"Time to go, love. Say good night to Grandmother and Papa Horatio."

Jack and Alaine let Em skip in front of them on the dirt road that wound through the orchard on one side and the woods on the other, linking Orchard Crest to their cottage, tucked away near the back ridge of the hill. Papa Horatio and Grandma Lilabeth had built a small cabin on their fifty acres when they were first married, a rustic square of hewn logs and mortar. It still stood where the trees thinned near the ridge, but even Alaine, with her staunch loyalty to every piece of the family farm's history and especially anything Papa Horatio had made, had to admit it was cramped and dark. When the orchard had made its first profits, Papa Horatio built the house facing Prospect Hill and named it Orchard Crest. He raised a family there, and Alaine and Del had grown up there, too.

When Papa Horatio had offered the strip of land along the ridge to her and Jack, she knew she could never tear down the cabin, but they had built nearby, a lavender Queen Anne with white gingerbread trim and windows tucked into sloping eaves that, as they approached from the lane, even now gleamed with the lamps inside.

If she was honest with herself, Alaine had always assumed that Delphine would do the same when she was married—take the offer of a parcel of land, build a cottage as fashionable and pretty as she was, and keep the little world that was Orchard Crest spinning along as it always had. Then Pierce Grafton had come along and knocked the perfect balance off-kilter. Alaine wasn't sure how to right it again, how to imagine the family farm without part of her family.

"You're thinking deep thoughts," Jack teased softly as they rounded the curve in the road and Emily ran ahead to catch up with the chickens foraging in a tangle of blooming multiflora rose.

She snorted. "Hardly." She held back a sigh, and it stuck in her throat, tight and painful. "No, the opposite. I was thinking about the wedding and—well, I suppose anything I could say sounds petty or childish."

"What? Don't you like Pierce Grafton?" Jack's blue eyes pinched at the corners, half laughing but not entirely.

"Oh, it's not that." Alaine caught herself. "Not that I *don't* like him, of course." It was an open secret between her and Jack that she didn't care for the Perrysburg glass magnate, with his impeccable manners and his thin moustache and his bellowing laugh, but she still never said it out loud. "It's that she's going away. Doesn't that sound silly? Like something Em would say."

She pushed back a sudden urge to cry, the feeling gumming up the back of her throat.

"I don't think it's silly at all." Jack caught Alaine's hand and slowed their pace, turning to face her as they stopped. "You've both lived at Orchard Crest your whole lives. I thought you must have some sort of secret sisterhood blood pact to never leave," he teased lightly, but the furrow between his eyes deepened. He sensed her fears, her griefs, even if she hadn't articulated them.

"Maybe we should have." Not, Alaine thought with a flash of

anger, that Delphine wouldn't have broken it anyway. For Pierce Grafton, for the new house in Perrysburg's best neighborhood, for the chance to be the wife of the sort of person who had season tickets to the opera and invited the mayor for dinner parties. Alaine felt her ears getting hot, and she clamped down on her runaway thoughts, shamed by her selfishness. There was nothing wrong with Delphine wanting any of that, she reminded herself, even if Alaine couldn't see why. But she couldn't shake a feeling that, somehow, Delphine was turning her back on something more important than both of them. Especially now, with the bank sending notices every other week.

Jack squeezed her hand. "It's only Perrysburg. Hardly anything on the train. Maybe we'll get you one of those electric motorcars that so many ladies seem to favor."

"I don't want an electric motorcar, thank you very much." Alaine sighed. "Del's really leaving the farm," she added in a whisper.

Alaine stopped herself, but she knew what she meant, at its core—that she had thought the farm was as important to Delphine as it was to her. That, just like her, Delphine felt the rhythm of the orchard pulsing in her blood, that she would do anything for the fifty acres on the slopes of Prospect Hill. And now Delphine was leaving, without a glance behind her. Alaine felt the sting of deep betrayal.

Jack settled an arm around her shoulders and pulled her closer. "It's a hard change for us. We're used to Delphine at dinner and Delphine helping in the orchard on harvest days and Delphine's jam thumbprint cookies for teatime."

"And now someone else gets to have Delphine at dinner, and Delphine's tea cookies," Alaine said, fully aware that she sounded petulant, but unable to tell even Jack what she really thought. "But one thing is sure—Delphine is still going to help at harvest."

"Was that the blood pact?"

"No, but try keeping her away." Alaine smiled, pretending for the moment that she believed Delphine would come back for the autumn harvest. "Listen," she said, reining in the tremor in her voice, "I've got one more thing to do before we turn in. There's the election tomorrow for the Agricultural Society to think of."

Jack grinned. "First woman to run in the county."

"In the lower half of the whole state," Alaine retorted. "Howard Olson is running the organization into the ground, and Acton Willis right along with him. The two of them are businessmen, not farmers—preying on farmers, more like."

Though Olson managed a granary and Willis owned a transport company that catered to farmers, they weren't truly integrated into the community. And, after last year's dismal harvests and Olson's lukewarm response, it was clear that the Agricultural Society needed better leadership. When Alaine looked around the stuffy fellowship hall of the Free Methodist Church and didn't see anyone else raising their hand, she couldn't stop herself. Someone had to push the Society out of the slump Olson had driven it into, and if no one else would volunteer, she'd be damned if she'd sit idly by.

"It did have to come right at the same time as the wedding," Jack joked. "I'm sure Olson is running the old campaign wagon around town, and you're tied to the house, making macaroons for the reception."

Alaine laughed, but she tasted bitterness in the joke. Her sister's wedding was a trump card over her plans. The oncoming cherry harvest, the bank's demands on the mortgage, the health of the Agricultural Society—these were more important than the cake or the flowers or the dress for the wedding, but Alaine found her attention dragged time and again back to this one day, this pretty picture Delphine was painting. She didn't want to resent Delphine, but there were other things in her life to tend to.

"I think I still have a good shot at it. Olson sunk himself raising prices at the granary in the middle of the worst harvest we've had in a decade." She raised a conspiratorial eyebrow. "Besides, I've got another plan."

"A bargain." Jack's mouth pursed, the way it always did when he was thinking. Usually when it pinched shut, it was over a legal contract or a political editorial in the paper, and Alaine knew he had a thesis-length torrent of thoughts percolating on the subject. "I don't recall one for local elections."

"It's not for elections, specifically. Lands, imagine if it worked that way, picking a side to win!" Terrifying, actually—thank goodness bargains didn't work like that, or the political parties would have commandeered them long ago. "It's just an extra pinch of good luck. It may or may not work—I haven't tried it before." Her hand hesitated over her pocket, grazing the black soutache trim along the opening. "I'll only be a moment."

Jack gave her a curious look, but didn't press. Unlike most Prospect Hill newcomers, he didn't tease her about bargains or question their efficacy—he'd seen enough for himself. But he considered them her domain, just as much as she considered the law firm where he was primed to make junior partner his territory. Respected, but foreign.

She fished out a length of scarlet ribbon and another of white weighty silk pooling like liquid in her palm. She threaded both through a pair of silver rings so that when she spun the rings the ribbon alternated white and red, red and white. A bargain for change, for switches, for reshuffling the cards. As Gran had said, it would take the first and make him last, and the last, first—and more efficiently than the preacher at their white clapboard church ever had.

Alaine stopped at the garden gate, hanging the ribbon and rings in a loop over the latch. Then she slipped a paper copy of the ballot into the latch, too, the Agricultural Society seal partially hidden by the silk ribbons.

"Silk and silver," she whispered, remembering the words Gran had taught her, though she'd never used them, "chance and curse, favored and spurned, now reverse."

Alaine left the bargain wedged in the creaky latch of the garden gate. It was a less clear-cut bargain than she'd employed before—it didn't ask specifically for no rain or an averted snowstorm or more eggs in the chicken coop, but something intangible, applying a bit of reversed luck to her particular circumstance. She hoped her meaning was clear enough. Gran had instilled in her a healthy distrust of Fae logic, warning her that they'd use a bargain to their own ends whenever they could. Still, this was one of Gran's bargains, tested and safe. She let the gate swing closed behind her.